Before She Knew

FALLING LEAVES, BOOK 1

KATIE BINGHAM-SMITH

To the women at my local McDonald's
who kept me fueled with Coke Zero
and asked me, almost every day,
when this damn book was going to be published.

Emily

Emily and her older sister had been told to go to their room and stay there until their grandmother left. But Emily watched out the living room window for the shiny maroon Buick anyway, squinting through the fogged up glass and chilly rain that wanted to be snow. Gray puddles were beginning to pool in the driveway. What was so terrible about their maternal grandmother that she and Rachel weren't even allowed to say hello?

Maybe her grandmother would want to hear about the fashion show? Emily and a few other girls in her third-grade class were going to put one on next week, and she couldn't wait. When they'd asked their teacher, Miss Jones, about it today at recess, and she'd said yes, the girls were giddy for the rest of the day. It had been so hard to settle down, and they'd been warned the privilege would be taken away if they couldn't stop passing notes back and forth during class.

As soon as Grandmother's car pulled into the driveway, Rachel wrapped her arm around Emily's shoulders and pointed her toward the stairs. "Let's have our Barbies get caught up in a tornado!"

Whenever Grandmother came over, Rachel always came up with strange things to do in their room; things she never suggested otherwise. But the louder the fighting between Grandmother and Mother got, the less Emily wanted to play.

Emily enjoyed listening. It gave her such satisfaction to hear Grandmother yelling at Mother. Maybe it would make Mother realize she loved Emily as much as she loved Rachel, and she needed to do a better job of showing it.

Rachel would try to talk over their raised voices, but it was never long before her voice couldn't mask Grandmother's yelling.

"Your brother would've taken care of me, but now he's gone, and I'm stuck with you. He would've helped me. You have plenty to share, but you keep it all to yourself. Maybe it should have been you!"

Emily narrowed her eyes at the memory of that stormy January night when Mother fell to her knees while talking on the phone. Emily missed her Uncle Todd. He was funny and always brought them gifts.

The two girls sat cross-legged across from each other on the blue shag carpet of their shared room, their Barbies in a forgotten pile between them.

"She'll leave soon," Rachel said, faking a smile even as her brown eyes filled with tears.

Rachel was Mother's princess. She'd never understand the gratification Emily felt to hear Mother get yelled at like that.

Rachel paced the room before picking at the blue floral wallpaper that had just been installed. "Dad's going to be home soon. I'm scared, Emily."

Emily wasn't scared, though. If Father found out Grandmother had come over, she wouldn't have to remember to keep the secret.

The sky had turned purple, and Emily was clipping feathers in her long blond hair when the girls heard their grandmother's car rumbling away. They both ran to the window to watch her leave.

Thirty minutes later, Father's tires turned into the driveway. Emily jumped up, her insides warm with anticipation. She couldn't wait to talk about the fashion show. They were all going to wear neon socks, jelly shoes, and acid wash jeans. Jen's mom was a hairdresser, and Jen said she could feather their hair and curl their bangs high, just like the older girls at school. Emily was going to suggest they all wear the feathers, too. She had enough for everyone.

The sisters ran downstairs and sat at the dining room table. Emily hated eating in that room. It always made her feel sad. There were no windows, and the walls were painted a dark red. Even though Mother always lit the large brass candle centerpiece for dinner, Emily would much rather eat in the bright white kitchen.

The girls folded their hands in their laps—the rule was no elbows on the table—as Mother stood next to the table, straightening a large white platter that held a roast surrounded by carrots and potatoes.

Her brown hair was pulled back in a tight knot, and her eyes were red and swollen. Pearl earrings hung from her droopy earlobes. Her lips were shiny and red and she pursed them when Father's briefcase hit the kitchen floor with a thunk.

Mother's eyes were closed when he stormed into the dining room behind her. "Lynn? I thought this rug was getting cleaned today."

"It got cleaned! They did a great job. It smells—"

"This was my grandfather's oriental rug! It's an antique and should've been taken to their facility to get properly cleaned!" Father kneeled to inspect the burgundy and blue design, his face twisted in a grimace.

"I'm sorry. You're right." Mother pulled out Father's chair. A few lines had appeared on her smooth brow. "I'll call them in the morning and have them come pick it up, Dear."

He sat down and placed his napkin on his lap, barely sparing a glance at the roast. Father's hair was completely gray, and he had tufts of hair growing out his ears. Most of Emily's friends thought he was her grandfather when they first met him.

"So, girls! How was your day? Do anything fun after school?" he asked, looking at them over his glasses. He clutched his fork in one hand, his knife in the other.

Mother remained standing, her smile tight as she spooned meat and potatoes onto his plate.

This was Emily's moment. If she didn't say something soon, Rachel would hog the spotlight and talk about how she got an A on a math test or had been asked to submit another poem to the school newspaper. "Mom, Dad! My friends and I are going to put on a—"

Mother froze, clutching the large silver serving fork. "It's *Mother*, Emily. When will you learn?" She looked at Father. "And after school was fine. Just the usual snacks and home-work, right girls?" Mother looked back and forth between her daughters, her eyes cold with expectation, until the girls nodded in agreement. Emily felt her shoulders fall.

Mother rounded the table to Emily's seat and spooned a sliver of meat and extra carrots onto her plate. Emily's stomach growled, and she placed a hand over it, pressing hard at the tiny bulge. Mother ran her hands down Emily's long blond hair, giving it a painful tug where it lay between her shoulders.

"Elbows off the table, Emily." With the platter still balanced, she lowered her head to Emily's ear. "You've got to lose that extra layer," she whispered, pinching her daughter on the back of her arm.

Emily blinked hard, preparing for the delayed stab of pain that ran through her arm all the way down her toes.

"What were you saying, Emily? Go on," Father said, glaring at Mother as he mashed his potatoes with the back of his fork.

Emily sat up straight, immediately forgetting the sting, and seized the invitation to talk. "Miss Jones said we could put on a fashion show. Jen's mom is going to do our hair, and I have feathers we can all wear. Missy had the idea of turning off the lights in the classroom and having a few people in the front row shine flashlights on us. I'm bringing in my Madonna tape!"

Just when Emily was getting to the best part, about how Miss Jones said she'd take pictures and they could hang them up on the bulletin board, Mother interrupted, "That's nice, Emily," before forcing a tight smile.

Mother had clapped for Rachel when she'd shared she was running for Class President a few weeks ago. "Of course you are! You're a leader, just like your father!" she'd said.

Mother always let Rachel finish *her* stories.

"That sounds fun." Father stuck a sizable piece of meat into his mouth and reached for the newspaper Mother always placed next to his plate.

Emily shifted her food back and forth on her plate, watching the meat juice smear over the delicate blue floral design. Everyone ate in silence, and each swallow and scratch of the silverware hurt Emily's ears.

Father stood up, taking the newspaper and his plate in one hand. "Emily, the fashion show sounds great. I have to finish up some work in my office," he said, squeezing Emily's shoulder.

He owned some big company that Emily could never

remember the name of. His job was very important, and he usually finished his dinner upstairs in his office. Sometimes Emily would sneak up there and sit in his big brown chair and look through his boring papers.

Father stopped by Mother's seat, bending to whisper something in her ear. Mother flinched, then closed her eyes as Father turned to walk upstairs. He was still wearing his dress shoes from work, even though he constantly complained to Mother about all the scuff marks in the house.

Mother took a deep breath, and Emily's shoulders tensed. Whatever Father had said, she knew it would be taken out on her later.

Mother's gaze was on the platter of food in the middle of the table, though she seemed not to see it. "I had art club today," Rachel said, her voice pitched higher than normal.

Emily rolled her eyes. *Why do you have to steal every speck of Mother's attention?*

Emily had eaten every morsel of food on her plate, but a juicy slab of meat sat on the platter in a sea of juice, one end plump with fat—her favorite part. She slowly reached for the serving spoon, glancing up to see Rachel watching her. When their eyes met, Rachel twisted her attention back to Mother. "Are those new earrings?"

Mother cleared her throat. "I don't think so. Emily. You've had enough to eat tonight." Her lips pressed tightly together as she leaned slightly toward Emily. "Little girls who want to be in fashion shows should watch their figure."

Rachel's eyes darted from Emily to Mother. "Mother, you look so nice in that sweater. The blue really brings out your eyes. Didn't you say you needed a new dress to wear to Father's Christmas party? I could go with you and help you pick something out if you'd like."

Mother's expression softened, and she leaned back in her chair, pausing as if to consider which daughter would continue to get her attention. "I'd love that, Honey. Thank you." She let out a long sigh and gave Rachel a faint smile. Mother's plate was still full, and she moved her meat around with her fork.

"I need to bring in a cereal box and some pictures of things I love for a school project tomorrow. Will you help me pick out some good magazines?" Rachel stood up, pushed in her chair, and stacked Mother's plate on top of hers. When she reached for Emily's, they made eye contact, and although Emily was thankful Rachel had distracted Mother, she cringed back from her arm. Rachel lowered her eyes and carried the dirty dishes to the kitchen.

"Not tonight." Mother slowly pushed herself away from the table and followed Rachel. "I'm going to take a shower and get some rest."

After dinner, once everyone had drifted to their rooms, Emily crept into the kitchen to see if she could sneak some more food. The low moans of Mother's familiar sobs seeped through the walls from where she showered.

Emily swung open the refrigerator door, her eyes immediately going to the bottle that was always lying on its side in the back of the fridge, hidden behind perfect rows of club soda and Tab. Mother's rule was to always have all the labels and logos facing forward, even in the refrigerator.

Sometimes the bottle was light yellow, and sometimes it was pink. Emily wondered if it tasted like lemonade. She slowly lifted the bottle, careful not to upset the rows of Tab and club soda as her heartbeat thumped through her ears.

Anger burned in her gut as she thought about Mother's reaction to the fashion show. She couldn't seem to please Mother the way Rachel, or whatever was in the bottle, could. After a few glasses, her eyes would get shiny, and then she'd fall asleep. Surely it tasted better than it smelled since she drank so much of it. *She must hide it and tell us not to tell Father so he won't hog it all.*

Emily held the cold bottle in her hands, then set it on the counter. She grabbed a container of whipped chocolate frosting and a spoon, dug out a heaping spoonful, and shoved it all in her mouth. She sucked on the spoon until it was gone, then dipped it in again and took another large bite, letting it sit in her mouth—she might need it to buffer the taste of the wine. Many times, she'd caught whiffs of it on Mother's breath, and it certainly wasn't a pleasant smell.

She tried smoothing out the remaining frosting with the back of the spoon to hide the evidence of what Mother called her "gluttony."

A ball of disgust grew in her belly as she pictured the back of Mother standing at the fridge. She'd always make sure the bottle was hidden, then take a step back and stare a little longer, making sure no one could see it in its hiding place.

Condensation had formed on the bottle. Emily drew a heart on the neck with her chubby finger for Mother to find when she reached for it after her shower. But after drawing one half, she scribbled it out.

Mother would be too busy filling her wineglass, then quickly hiding the bottle behind the cans of club soda and Tab, to notice.

Mother thought no one knew she did this. But Emily knew.

She'd stood in the dark dining room many times watching Mother race to hide the bottle, sometimes taking a large drink before putting it back, she'd memorized her movements.

She rocked the cork back and forth until it came loose, the smell immediately burned her nose. She lifted the bottle to her lips, then tipped it back and shut her eyes. When nothing reached her mouth, she tipped it back more, and a slug of wine poured into her mouth.

Emily grabbed the counter, trying to steady herself as she coughed into her elbow and gasped for air. The bitterness stung all the way down to her belly. She swallowed it back with the rest of the frosting, then tried to rinse away the ball of fire inside of her with a long drink from the faucet.

She pushed the cork back into the bottle and stood on her tiptoes, making sure she placed it to the back of the fridge. Holding the door open, Emily took a step back. She couldn't see the bottle. She closed the fridge, then opened it again to be absolutely sure everything was in its place.

"Did you get enough to eat, Em? I'm sorry Mom always gives you a hard ti—"

Emily jumped, her heart suddenly pounding through her chest. "I was just looking for some carrot sticks." Emily said, opening the crisper drawer.

"Do you want to come into my room and listen to my new Prince tape?" Rachel asked. Emily stared into the fridge, willing her sister to leave. She didn't.

A deep burn stirred in Emily's stomach, and she whipped her head around to face her sister. "Why are you always so nice to me when Mom is a jerk?" She closed the fridge and crossed her arms. "And why are you always so nice to Mom? You make her stop paying attention to me. It's annoying."

"I'm only trying to help, Em.

"Well, don't! You make it worse!" She sucked in her cheeks, hoping it would trap her tears.

Rachel's eyes held hers for a few seconds before she stalked away, leaving Emily alone in the dark kitchen, the faint taste of wine still souring her mouth.

Rachel

"Honey, take these things out of your ears and focus." Rachel reached across the kitchen island and tugged the earbuds out of her son's ears. "Listening to music will not help you get your math done any faster."

"Mom! Be careful with those! Aunt Emily just gave them to me. Besides, I work better when I listen to music." Benjamin raked his hands through his blond hair that stood up on the top of his head. The sides were shaved into a fade, and he preferred the top to be a spiky mess. His freckles were dwindling, along with the bit of padding he had left in his cheeks.

"Not according to your grades, Benny. Come on. I know you can do this." Rachel rested her elbows on the pile of towels she'd thrown on the island to fold, studying her son. Now that he was thirteen, it seemed like everything was too much work for him.

Trying to get him to do homework was becoming a daily chore, and Rachel wanted to lie in the warm pile of towels and say, "Okay, fine. Don't do it. I give up." Her throat was scratchy, and her shoulders ached. Was she coming down with something? She put the back of her hand against her forehead to see if she had a fever.

Elsa walked into the kitchen, opened the fridge, and filled her arms with a package of sliced turkey, mustard, and a bottle of water as their Golden Retriever, Cora, panted at her feet, hoping a scrap would fall. "I can help you, Ben." She turned and nudged the fridge door shut with her heel. "I had Mr. Chase in 8th grade for math too."

"Cool," Benjamin said, reaching for his earbuds, which were sitting next to the pile of laundry.

"Not with these, Mister!" Rachel said, grabbing them from his hands. She took a step over to her daughter and hugged her from behind.

Elsa was taller than Rachel and built exactly like her father; long and lean. "Thank you, Sweetie. I appreciate you helping your brother with math. You have a lot of patience." She smoothed the back of her daughter's long brown hair. "Lord knows I have little of it."

Elsa may have gotten Adam's long and lean body type, but she'd gotten Rachel's brown hair, olive skin, and brown eyes. It was a total mystery where she got her patience from.

"Mom, stop," Elsa said, half laughing as she shimmied from Rachel's embrace.

Elsa sat next to Benjamin, scooting her brown leather barstool closer to him before she plopped down her water and snack. Benny shoved his paper toward her, and Elsa studied the sheet.

Rachel felt a wash of relief as she grabbed a towel and folded it. Elsa was mostly out of her moody teen years and didn't hide in her room as much. Now it was Benjamin's turn. Lately, Elsa had been an enormous help with him, and Rachel was so happy the two weren't going through that difficult stage at the same time.

Elsa took the pencil from her brother's hand. "You're on the right track—you just keep forgetting to simplify the result to get the variable value. Then you can check your answer by plugging it back in to see if it works." She slid the paper back to her brother and picked up her phone.

Rachel didn't understand a word her daughter had just said. "You two sure didn't get your math skills from me," Rachel said, mating a pair of socks and rolling them into a ball. "Thank your father for that one."

"What are you talking about, Mom? I suck at math," Benjamin said, grabbing a piece of turkey and dangling it over his mouth before dropping it on his tongue. He grabbed the mustard from his sister's hand and squirted it into his mouth.

"Hey! Easy on the mustard." Rachel threw the ball of socks on the island. "And don't do that. Get some bread and make a sandwich."

"Too much work," Benjamin said, his mouth full of turkey. "I didn't touch it with my mouth."

Rachel opened her mouth to protest, but stopped herself when Benjamin picked up his pencil and got to work. Elsa smiled beside him as she tapped away on her phone.

They're fine. He's getting his work done without a meltdown. Leave it alone.

Rachel crossed "deep clean kitchen" off her to-do list. Yesterday, she'd scrubbed the subway tile backsplash that reached the ceiling. Then, she'd taken all the dishes off the open shelving and wiped the shelves down with her home-made potion of water, organic dish soap, and a few drops of lavender oil before mopping the floors. A clean kitchen made her ridiculously happy, and there was no way she had the energy to tackle it today.

She stared at the rest of the list, hoping another Diet Coke would get her through the rest of the evening. There was a painting to finish, dinner to make, and one more load of laundry to catch up on. She grabbed a can from the fridge and popped it open, feeling the fizz tickle her fingers. The carbonation felt wonderful on her raw throat.

"*Moommm*, easy on the Diet Cokes," Benjamin said in his best Mom voice without looking up from his work.

Rachel bent over to pick up the laundry basket, then got tunnel vision when she stood up too fast. Her clogged ears thumped behind her eyes, and she leaned against the island until everything came into focus. She took another swig of soda before heading to the laundry room to throw in one last load.

Get through tonight and go to bed early. As she shoved the whites into the dryer, she felt the dreaded nasal drip creeping down the back of her throat. Elsa used to call it "hot slime" when she was little and was coming down with a cold.

Rachel headed upstairs to get the Neti pot from the hall closet and as she opened it, the once neatly folded towels spilled out. She caught them just in time and shoved them back in place, then sorted through the bottles of medicine and extra shampoo and conditioner.

"Kids, do you know where my Neti pot is?" Yelling burned her throat, and she clutched her neck and leaned against the shelves.

All she got in response was laughter. "Hello?!"

"Benny and Hank used it to do the Diet Coke and Mentos explosion!" Elsa yelled. "Diet Coke and Mentos explosion" was muffled, and Rachel knew Benjamin was trying to cover her mouth with his hand.

"Stop, you idiot." A slapping sound made Rachel shake her head.

"I told you to put it back when you were done," Elsa said.

Rachel shook her head and popped a few Advil before walking back downstairs.

"Sorry, I don't remember where we put it." Benjamin

smiled widely, keeping his teeth together. "Maybe in my room?"

"Well, I'm not going in there to look for *anything*." Rachel sighed and put her hands on her hips. "Okay, are you good here? I'm going to finish that painting for Joanna's mom." She took Benjamin's earbuds and tucked them into her pocket, and grabbed her can of soda. "You can have these back when you're done. And feed Cora please." She tousled his hair as she passed him, and he ducked away from her touch.

Rachel's "studio" was a corner in their finished walkout basement, where the kids always headed as soon as they had a friend over. The white leather sleeper-sofa they'd gotten from Ikea was perfect for when they had sleepovers, and Rachel always smiled when she saw the tiny bite marks Cora had taken out of a brown and ivory cowhide rug she'd tucked under the sofa.

She'd never put curtains or shades on the two small windows and glass door that led outside. She wanted as much light down there as possible. Something about dark rooms made her toes curl.

Each time Rachel went down there, she'd retrieve her painting supplies from the closet, set everything up, then put it all away when she was done. She dreamed of having a real painting studio with large windows, easels set up everywhere, and shelves that held every color of paint. In rainbow order, of course.

Her new neighbor, Joanna, had gone crazy over the navy blue and orange abstract painting Rachel had done for Benjamin's room. Rachel had given her a tour of their home after she'd come over to meet the family, and Joanna had stopped in her tracks as soon as she saw it. "Oh, can I commission you to make one just like that for me? I *have* to have it." Now Joanna's mother wanted a painting the same size, but requested neutrals—Rachel's favorite color palette—and "some kind of nature scene."

Before starting, Rachel sat down with the half-finished canvas in front of her and closed her eyes. *You should be in bed, but you promised you'd do this.* Joanna had reminded her this morning that her mother was hoping to have the painting done for her annual fall harvest party, which was this weekend.

Yesterday, she'd swirled browns and tans together across the entire canvas to create a moody sunset, and let it dry overnight.

It needs trees. She squirted tiny dots of black paint along the bottom of the canvas, then took a ruler to spread the paint about three quarters of the way to the top.

After taking a few steps back, she smiled—the black lines resembled tree shadows stretching up to the sky.

The hum of Benjamin and Elsa talking made its way downstairs. She stopped painting and tried to listen in. They could be a handful, but mostly, her kids were great friends. There was nothing that made her feel more at peace than witnessing their friendship.

As Rachel continued painting, the Advil kicked in and took the edge off her cold. She made the trees a bit taller and painted in some clouds by adding a few white paint blobs to the sky, then blotted them with a sponge.

Joanna had said her mom loved fireflies, which inspired Rachel to take a small brush, dip it in gold paint, and flick it gently over the entire canvas.

She nodded her head after a few shakes of her brush, then reached for her Diet Coke. It was warm and had lost its fizz. A few hours to herself where she could get lost in her creativity always gave her new life.

Slowly standing up to admire her work, she let out a sigh and gathered her paints. She put them back in the closet, in rainbow order, and brought her brushes, sponges, and ruler up to be washed.

Until your next session.

Adam was standing at the kitchen island when she came upstairs. "Hi, Honey. I didn't even hear you drive in. How was your day?"

She dropped her supplies in the farmhouse sink and turned on the water. Adam had set his Yeti cup on the counter next to her. *Why can't he put this in the dishwasher?* She loaded it into the dishwasher with the other dirty dishes. He'd want his favorite mug ready for tomorrow. Every morning she handed him his coffee before he left, making it exactly how he liked it for his drive to one of his three real estate offices.

"It was fine." He stood in the middle of the kitchen, flipping through the mail, ignoring Cora, who sat at his feet, waiting for some attention. "I'm beat. Everyone wants a home that's move-in ready." His thick, dark hair was longer than usual, and he hadn't shaved for a few days.

He set the mail down on the island and let out a sigh. "This new office in New Hampshire is gonna be the death of me." He rubbed his eyes with the heel of his hands, then peeled off his jacket and dropped it on the island.

Rachel had warned him of this when he'd told her he wanted to tap into the Southern Maine and New Hampshire market, but he'd told her she didn't know what she was talking about, and she needed to let him handle it.

He slowly headed to the living room and plopped down in the black leather Eames chair and stared at the blank sixty inch television that hung over the fireplace.

Rachel had loved the completely open first floor when the kids were younger. She'd painted the trim a light gray and the walls a creamy shade of white. It was bright and tranquil, and she'd loved watching them play with their toys on the plush throw rug on the livingroom floor as she baked in the kitchen.

But now, a few walls wouldn't be so bad.

"I'm beat too," Rachel said, squeezing water from her brushes and sponge. "My sore throat is getting worse. Maybe you can help make dinner?"

He'd been busy and stressed out with the opening of the New Hampshire office, and she hadn't been asking much of him lately. But she was exhausted too and genuinely felt like shit.

"You're sick?" Adam asked, clicking on the television, turning the volume up to sixty.

Rachel closed her eyes as hot resentment rose in her chest. "I told you this morning before you left, I felt like I was coming down with something." She picked up his jacket, about to go through the motions of hanging it in the closet like she always did, then thought better of it and threw it back down on the island.

She already had two children. Should she have to pick up after a man-child too?

"Oh, right." He nodded his head, eyes locked on the basketball game. "I'll help as soon as this quarter ends." He moved to the edge of the chair. "Jesus! It's like they don't even know what defense is!" He glanced at Rachel distractedly. "Have a Diet Coke, hon, that always makes you feel better."

Rachel slammed the packet of chicken on the counter. She could ask the kids. *No. They've been in school all day and just finished their homework. Just do it yourself.*

Once the chicken was popping and sizzling in the oven, Rachel started a pot of rice, then got out all the fixings for a salad and started chopping.

Adam was still laser-focused on the game, now leaned back in the Eames chair, one khaki-clad leg crossed over the other. Rachel narrowed her eyes at him. *You shouldn't have to ask him again. You shouldn't have to ask in the first place.*

She pushed the thought away and set her knife aside

before digging her phone out of her purse to text Joanna and let her know her mother's painting was ready to be picked up.

While her phone was in her hand, *another* email from Benjamin's science teacher came through. Apparently, he'd been late three times this quarter and was often "disruptive in class." *Not again.* A knot of worry clung to her chest.

Have Adam talk to him after dinner. You aren't getting through to him.

She returned to cutting up the tomatoes, peppers, and carrots, throwing everything over the bed of lettuce and then getting out all their salad dressings.

She took a deep breath before entering the living room to interrupt Adam's game. "Dinner is ready. Can you call the kids?"

"Sure," he said, his eyes not leaving the television. "Benny, Elsa, dinner!" he yelled.

Rachel returned to the kitchen, got out the black cloth napkins, and folded them in half before tucking them under the new black silverware she'd just bought. There was something about setting a nice table that relaxed her.

Adam shuffled to the kitchen. "I'm sorry, I said I'd help. You should have said something!"

"I did say something. I shouldn't have to beg for help from my husband," she whispered between clenched teeth, worried the kids would hear. "I'm sick of asking you the same thing over and over. Not to mention I'm *literally sick*."

She rolled her eyes as he observed the set table.

"Can you please turn off the television?" she asked, spooning the rice from its pot into a bowl, setting it next to the platter of chicken on the table.

The kids came down, and everyone took their seats.

"Finish your math?" she asked Benjamin as he piled chicken onto his plate.

"Yup!"

"Good job. And you need to get it together for science class. I just heard from your teacher. *Again.*"

"K," Benjamin said, stabbing an uncut piece of chicken with his fork before taking a bite.

Rachel watched him and sighed. "We have knives, you know."

"Too much work," Benjamin said, bringing the chicken to his mouth again.

Adam raised his eyebrows.

Rachel leaned closer to Adam. "I heard from Mr. Miller again. He's still coming to class late and messing around." They both looked over at Benjamin, who was still gnawing at the colossal piece of chicken hanging from his fork. "Can you *please* have a talk with him after dinner? I'm tired of these emails, and my words don't seem to sink in."

"Sure," Adam said. He turned to Elsa. "How was your day, beautiful girl?" He took her phone and put it down on the other side of his plate, where she couldn't reach it.

"It was good." She rolled her eyes and let out a sigh, glancing longingly at her phone.

"You know the rules. You can have it back after dinner." Adam bit into his chicken, then looked down at his plate. "Didn't you put the usual seasoning on this tonight?" He grabbed the salt and shook it over his plate. "It's much better like that."

His dark hair was graying at the temples, and his blue eyes were bloodshot. The scowl on his face made him look like an overgrown, bratty teenager who wasn't getting his way.

"No, we were out of teriyaki marinade and I forgot to get more while I was at the grocery store yesterday. It's fine like this."

Rachel pressed her thumb into the edge of their dark antique dining table as she watched her husband wrinkle his nose and chew on his chicken. He swallowed hard, and her toes curled as she listened to him dig food out of his teeth with his tongue.

He'd unbuttoned his dress shirt, and his salt-and-pepper chest hair was peeking out, reminding her of an old rug. The lines between his eyes were deep, and he scrunched his face up the same way it always was when they'd argue about the lack of sex in their marriage. Which was often.

Rachel felt Elsa watching her and straightened herself up in her chair.

"What are you guys going to do for Halloween this year? Want to have a party with your friends like last year?"

Both kids lit up at the suggestion. "I think this year we should put a bunch of different slimy, nasty things in buckets with lids. Make people put their hands in them and guess what they are," Elsa suggested.

"Yeah, like slime, worms, and cold oatmeal!" Benjamin chimed in, his mouth full of meat.

As the kids hatched their plans, Rachel concentrated on *not* shooting disapproving looks at her husband. When Benjamin and Elsa picked up on the tension in their marriage, which was pretty thick lately, it killed Rachel.

After dinner, Rachel hugged both kids, turning her face away so she wouldn't breathe on them and get them sick. "I'm headed up to bed. I'm exhausted."

Upstairs, she washed her face and brushed her teeth, but skipped applying her retinol and didn't do her nightly Gua Sha ritual.

She sank into their king-sized bed, pulled the plump down comforter up to her chin, and stuffed two tissues in her nostrils. After a few minutes of watching HGTV, she fell into a deep sleep.

. . .

Hours later, the sound of Adam's electric toothbrush woke her up. One tissue had fallen out of her nose onto the bed, and she picked it up and put it on her nightstand. "Did you talk to Benny?" she whispered, as Adam crawled into bed.

"Yeah. He'll be fine. Just a stage." Adam rolled toward her, slowly rubbing her arm. His breathing hitched, and Rachel's shoulders stiffened to her ears.

"I hope so. I just don't want it to get worse. He's too old to act like this," she said through a yawn. *He must know you're too worn out for sex right now.*

"Don't stress, Rachel. It'll be fine." His hand made its way up to her jawline, and he traced his thumb down her neck, the pressure hurting her swollen throat.

Did he touch that other woman this way?

Nausea swam in her gut. "Adam, please. You know I'm not feeling well. Maybe tomorrow." Rachel rolled onto her other side. It *had* been a *really* long time. But even if she wasn't feeling shitty, the fact that he hadn't helped her with dinner, and his display about the chicken, was enough to turn her off for a while. They'd had so many talks like this since Elsa had been born, and it seemed to be white noise to Adam.

He let out a long sigh and slapped his hands down on the bed. "Rachel. It's been like five months." Cora's head popped up from the foot of the bed, and she scooted closer to Rachel, as if choosing sides. *Good girl.*

Rachel clenched her eyes shut and took in a long breath. "Okay, it's been a while. But I am feeling awful tonight. I'm sure tomorrow night I'll feel better and we can—"

"You're always happy once we do it, Honey." His tone was gentler now. "You need to ... try. It's like you don't even try anymore." He propped his head up with his elbow, his silhouette backlit by the plug-in nightlight on the wall behind him. She'd been so attracted to him once, and could tell when they were in public that other women found him attractive. *You can get it back.*

Adam kissed her mouth and then her neck. She held in her squirms and the urge to shout, "Stop touching me!" Instead, she took in a sharp breath and whispered, "Not tonight, Adam. Tomorrow. I promise."

Adam rolled over on his side so his back was to her. "You always have some freaking excuse, Rachel. Whatever."

During sex and fights about their lack of intimacy, she wondered if he had continued cheating on her since the affair ten years ago. *If you hadn't caught him, would he have told you? If you had a higher sex drive, would your life be different? Was his affair your fault? How would you feel if he never wanted to have sex with you?*

He'd said it was just the one time, a horrible slipup. And she'd believed him. But she also never would have believed he'd hurt her the way he did. She'd married Adam because he'd made her feel safe. But then, his affair took that safety away.

Rachel stared at the back of his head, half relieved and half filled with dread, knowing she'd have to make good on her promise tomorrow night. But was that really so terrible?

He still wants to have sex with you, even though you have snot and tissues coming out of your nose. It could be so much worse.

She thought about the look Elsa had given her at dinner. It made her want to try harder for them. "Tomorrow night," she whispered. "I promise."

Brad

⚮

B rad woke before his alarm and rolled out of bed as softly as he could, careful not to wake his wife. He paused on the white oak floors to look out the floor-to-ceiling windows that stretched across the south side of their bedroom. The sleepy Autumn sun was rising, and Brad watched a few squirrels scurry along the dewy backyard. The foliage would be at its peak this weekend—perfect for taking out the canoe. Beth wasn't exactly *into* canoeing, but maybe she'd be up for a pleasant ride to look at the leaves.

Her breath was heavy, and she had one leg hanging out the side of the bed. Half of her face was smashed in the plush pillow, and something rattled in her nose. Her pink silk sleep mask was too big for her face, reminding him of his second graders playing virtual reality games.

His lips curled up. This was a stark contrast to the daytime put-together version of his wife.

Careful to slide the heavy barn door quietly behind him, he turned on the water and waited for the steam cloud to float out of the marble shower before getting in. The hot water felt wonderful on his scalp, and he ran his hands through his thick brown hair, thankful he still had all of it.

The door slid open. "Brad, why do you always stand there and look out the window after you get out of bed? You're always rocking back and forth, and it makes the floorboards creak."

Brad startled and opened his eyes. A blurred version of Beth's petite frame stood behind the steamy shower door. A tuft of hair had come loose from her long braid and was sticking out of the top of her head, and her hands were at her sides. She looked like a stick of dynamite ready to explode.

Were you rocking back and forth? "Sorry, babe. Just waking up to greet the morning!" Brad was absolutely certain the floorboards hadn't creaked. Or had they, and he'd been enjoying the view too much to notice?

He hurried to finish his shower and dried off as Beth brushed her teeth. Her silk sleep mask dangled around her neck.

Angst bubbled in Brad's chest as he watched his wife. Foam oozed out of the left side of her mouth as she scrubbed with the same vigor she'd used when she'd scrub the baseboards after the maid had come and gone, back when they could afford a maid.

"She never gets in the little cracks where the dust collects," Beth would say, crouched on her hands and knees with her face about an inch away from the baseboards. "I've told her so many damn times that you have to fold the cloth and slide it in this ridge."

Does anyone ever really notice the damn baseboards? Did she have any enamel left?

"Hey, I'm sorry," he said louder than before, so she could hear him over the running sink, wishing he could lean over and kiss her on the cheek instead of walking on eggshells first thing in the morning. "I was trying to be quiet." He patted her on the butt. "You can always go back to sleep."

Beth sighed and reached for a towel. "No, it's fine. I'm just a grouch when I get woken up. I have to help my mom get ready for the party this weekend, so I needed to get up, anyway."

"Oh. Um, that's ... *this* weekend?" Brad held his towel at his waist with one hand and tilted his head to the side, dread filling his stomach.

"Brad. I've told you *so* many times." Beth rolled her eyes. "It's Friday evening! So I guess you haven't planned what you're going to wear?" She was feverishly making sure every speck of toothpaste went down the drain.

"Hmm, maybe I'll—"

"You should wear your gray suit. And the red tie." She spun toward him. "I'm wearing the red dress that goes with my Manolo Blahnik heels. You know, the ones I got before you quit working for Dad?"

Brad clutched his towel tighter in his fist. "Oh yes, I know the *shoes,* Beth. From when I made sooo much more money. Maybe we could go a day without the passive-aggressive comments?" He gently tugged on her braid. "We've been through this, Babe. My compensation doesn't come in the form of a paycheck." He stood on the plush bath mat with their initials embroidered in scrolly letters across the center, another remnant from richer days, and ran the towel over his back faster and harder than usual. "And I guess it's decided what *I'm* going to wear. My gray suit it is."

He looked in the mirror, brushing his hand over his new scruff. *Leave it. It's kind of a good look on you.*

"Okay, it's just ... everyone's going to be there." Beth stood on her toes and purred in his ear, "I have the most handsome husband, and I want to show you off." She squeezed his arm before walking out of the bathroom, and Brad rubbed his arm where her hand had been, knowing she was being affectionate because she wanted something.

Fancy parties and perfect suits did nothing for him anymore. He'd had a taste of that life early in his marriage to Beth, and it got stale, boring. He'd tried to keep it up, hoping he'd somehow catch the same high from living a fancy lifestyle he'd once had, but it wasn't who he was.

Beth stopped and turned around in the doorway. "Aren't you going to shave?"

Brad rubbed his chin again, now feeling a little self-conscious. "I kind of like this scruffy look. I feel like a mountain man."

Beth watched him, blinked twice, and left the bathroom without a response.

After a moment, he followed her. "I was hoping ... maybe we could go canoeing on Saturday?" Beth was opening dresser drawers, pulling out stacks of leggings.

How many black leggings can one person have?

"The foliage will be beautiful," he offered.

"Oh, *God,* no. I'm not getting into that thing with you again! You almost tipped us over last time." Beth stepped into a pair of black leggings that looked like all her other black leggings. They had that symbol on the back, which meant they were expensive. *Loo-Loo Limes?*

"They don't really make leggings for women shorter than 5'2". Even when they're cropped, they're still too long." She yanked on a pair of ankle socks so hard, Brad half expected her toes to poke through. The pile of leggings toppled onto the floor, and Beth didn't seem to notice.

"Come on! That was years ago, and it happened once!" Brad stood in the middle of their bedroom, naked, cleaning out his ears with his towel-covered finger. He tried to remember the last time they'd done something fun together that didn't involve sex. "I'm going to your fancy party. You can go canoeing with me. What happened to us doing things together?"

"It's not *my* fancy party," Beth said, turning to face him. "It's Dad's—Brad! Get a Q-Tip or something! Those towels are new!" She cleared her throat and lowered her voice. "It's *Dad's* fancy party, and these are people you used to work with before you left to go teach second graders how to finger paint and blow things up." Beth laughed and put her hand up before Brad could protest. "I'm kidding, Honey. That was the last one, promise. Okay, I'll *think* about going. And hey, we did something together last night you seemed to enjoy. My mouth is still tired."

Her back was to him, and she pulled on a black fitted long-sleeve top, poking her thumbs through the thumbholes.

"So is mine, but it was worth it. It had been a while." He walked over to her and ran his hand over her butt. The leggings really did a great job of showing off his wife's perfectly perky backside.

Beth moved away from his touch, and he felt a jolt of annoyance. "I'm off to help Mom, then getting my hair done. Look at these roots. I miss when my hair was the perfect shade of blond on its own." She separated her part with her fingers, showing him a shade of hair that was only slightly darker than all the rest of her hair, before giving him a kiss on the cheek. "Sushi tonight?"

"We always go for sushi when we eat out. I was hoping we could cook. Saw a new recipe on—"

Beth shrugged her shoulders. "Um ... we'll see. Love you!" The door slammed behind her, and Brad blew out a breath and finished getting dressed.

Beth grew up with a certain lifestyle, and she wanted to maintain it. Brad couldn't fault her for it—the old money had been exciting to him, too. But it came at a cost—squeezing into stiff clothes, pretending to be interested in people he didn't actually like, keeping up with what everyone else had.

He craved the simpler life and wanted to show Beth they could be happy without him working his life away to afford overpriced cars and second homes.

It was how he grew up, and his parents had always been peaceful and content. They had real friends, and expensive things didn't impress them.

During all the years he'd work for Beth's dad, he'd never met anyone like his parents. Everyone had cared too much about what others had and worked nonstop to keep up. He'd spent the past two years trying to show Beth a different way of life *was* possible, but he was giving up hope.

After getting dressed in his favorite brown sweater and jeans, he noticed Beth had left her pile of leggings on the floor. It wasn't like her. Beth was always super particular about everything being in its place. *She must've been in a hurry.*

Brad bent over to pick up the pile of toppled over leggings, and put them back in her bottom drawer. When he opened it, he saw Beth's prized, oversized Gucci bag stuffed at the bottom, which was odd because she usually displayed it on the shelf in her closet.

He pulled it out and looked inside. It was lined with foil. Beth had once told him a story about how she and her friends had stolen a dress in college. "You line a bag with foil, and the store alarm won't go off. Oh please, I only did it once! Stop looking at me like that!"

A sinking feeling stirred in his stomach. He blew out a sharp breath and looked up at the ceiling before putting the bag back where he found it and stuffing the leggings back into the drawer.

· · ·

The clock in his car read seven-twenty five a.m.—enough time to take the scenic route up Pine Hill road.

You'll get an iced coffee and figure out how to approach Beth. He'd had a feeling something was off with her when she came home the other night. She'd slipped by him too fast, too eager to get to their room.

Autumn leaves twirled and swirled on the road in front of his car. Normally they would have calmed him, offered a meditation before starting his teaching day, but the bag lined with foil chewed away at his brain. Could his wife really have stolen something? Or ... many somethings?

The more he thought about how disconnected they'd been, the more unsettled he felt. He knew she'd never wanted him to be a teacher, but had he driven her to shoplift to keep up with her friends?

The distance between the two of them had been growing over the years. They enjoyed different things, and both were trying to cope, find themselves in their own ways.

He'd stopped playing basketball with the men's league on Sundays so he could spend time with Beth since he'd worked so much. Beth had seemed happy when he'd told her he wanted to spend Sundays with her, but she was more interested in going out to brunch with her friends or hanging out with her parents at the country club. It was clear she didn't care if he was there or not.

He rarely went canoeing because she never wanted to go. His old job at Beth's family firm left him too exhausted to cook, something he loved to do, and now when he made dinner, Beth complained that they never went out to eat.

As he drove up a hill toward the elementary school, a runner appeared in the distance, running in the same direction he was driving. Her head was down, her wavy brown hair flowing in a ponytail from the back of her hot pink hat. Her calf muscles were visible through her white leggings, and her arms pumped effortlessly in a matching long-sleeve top as she crested the hill.

Inspiring. *You need to start running again.* He hadn't run regularly since he and his college girlfriend, Rachel, used to go together. It was how he'd kept in shape for basketball during the off season.

He slowly nodded when he thought about getting back into it. He'd never necessarily loved running like Rachel did, but he couldn't ignore the post-run high that left him feeling like he'd been scrubbed from the inside out. Nothing had pulled him out of a bad mood, or helped him solve a problem, like a run had. He wasn't sure why he'd ever let his lifestyle impede something so therapeutic.

It was time to do more of the things he enjoyed.

Taking the canoe out this weekend was a must. He'd been an avid runner once. It would come back to him like riding a bike. His mother, who now lived alone since his dad died a few years ago, was always cooking and loved to have company. Maybe if he joined the basketball league again, Beth would come watch him play every once in a while and skip some country club time.

When Brad pulled into the elementary school parking lot, new anticipation running through him, he'd almost forgotten about the foil-lined bag stuffed in his wife's legging drawer.

Rachel

The local indoor Farmers' market was something Rachel looked forward to visiting every week. She was finally over her cold, and after checking off the bread, eggs, fresh herbs, and tomatoes from her list, she perused the new shop that had opened up in the building's corner.

As soon as she opened the door, the smell of coffee and pine made her stop, close her eyes, and take in a deep breath. A basket full of pine-cone embroidered pillows sat at the entrance.

She picked one up, squeezing it in her hands until she felt the crunch of the pine needles in her palm, sending an extra rush of pine scent to her nose. It would fit perfectly in the car door compartment, and her car would always smell amazing. She slid her fingers along the whitewashed brick wall as she strolled, admiring the handmade bowls and coffee mugs that adorned the tables in the middle of the space.

"Hello, thank you for coming in," said a woman behind a glass case. Her short, gray hair had a blue streak in the front, matching her pointy-framed glasses that sat on the tip of her nose. "I just opened this week!" She said over the loud jazz music coming from the ceiling. The glass case was filled with delicious-looking croissants, muffins, and loaves of bread.

"Ahh, it's lovely here." Rachel picked up a pair of earrings and held them up to her ears in front of the mirror sitting on the table. They were brown leaves made of leather and dangled just above her shoulders.

"Genuine leather. The artist makes all kinds of leather jewelry," the woman said, wiping down the pristine counter.

"They're beautiful." Rachel put them down and picked up a slightly shorter pair when a woman and little girl entered the shop. They both had fiery red hair and red eyebrows. The little girl was wearing a turquoise coat and had a pink stuffed kitten shoved in her pocket.

"Now, be careful and don't touch anything," the woman said, patting the top of her daughter's head. "We'll get you that raspberry muffin when I'm done, okay?"

Rachel turned and smiled. Her days of rushing through a shop like this, or skipping it all together when the kids were younger, were over. But she missed that time in her life now that Elsa and Benjamin were so busy with school, friends, and sports.

"Hello, Lily! I'm so glad you came in!" The shop owner grabbed an oversized muffin and put it in a bag, then leaned over the counter. "That's three times this week! I need to make more muffins!"

Rachel wandered to the back of the store. It was covered with paintings, and she recognized the artist's name, Kathleen Douglas, right away. Her paintings had hung in her ex-therapist's office.

She'd only gone to therapy for a few sessions after Adam's affair. She'd tried to get him to join her, but he kept telling her he didn't have time to go. "I know I want to be with you, and it will never happen again," he'd told her. "Can't we work this out on our own?"

Rachel had stuck with it for a month, then decided she wasn't getting anything out of it. She didn't like the way her therapist pressed her about why she didn't want to know more about his infidelity. Adam had told her it was a client. Her name was Jen, and she'd been thinking of relocating to Maine from New York, but had changed her mind. It was completely over—just a onetime occurrence.

Rachel hadn't asked anymore questions. She'd wanted to focus on moving on and keeping her family together at any cost. The less she knew, and the less she talked about it, the easier it was to push it to the deepest corners of her brain and move on.

The one good thing she'd gotten out of therapy was the urge to start painting. She'd always been creative, and after seeing how Kathleen made beautiful pieces of art with simple shapes or by swirling a few different colors together, Rachel had decided she wanted to try it.

The first time she'd sat down to paint, she'd felt a sense of contentment she never had before.

Aimee, her best friend from college, was constantly pushing her to take her talents seriously. "Everyone wants to know where I got the painting you made for me for my birthday. I could literally get you like five orders right now!" She'd pester Rachel about setting up a website or Etsy shop, and she was her biggest supporter when Rachel told her she was finally going to turn her hobby into a business.

Nerves still pulled at her stomach every time she thought about selling her paintings to actual clients, and even more when she thought about marketing herself. *You're not an actual artist,* she always convinced herself. She was an English major and knew nothing about advertising her work.

But last week, while she was getting highlights, her hairdresser had told her she'd seen her Instagram page and loved her art. When she'd requested six for her salon, Rachel had been more excited than when she'd been promoted to Editor In Chief at *Maine Women Magazine* before Elsa and Benny were born.

Looking at Kathleen's paintings now—some were dark and moody, others were vibrant with shades of red and hot pink—gave her a jolt of inspiration.

She got out her phone and started jotting down notes: *black, white, silver, gold. White oak frames. Two large paintings for the lobby area.* The wood frames would bring in some warmth to contrast with the cement floors, stark white walls, and modern furniture.

You'll get started on these tonight. Maybe a pop of color in there somewhere? Green? Pink and orange?

Gathering her goods, she headed for the counter to pay and checked the time. There was still an hour before she had to get Benjamin from school, so she could go to the art supply store and pick out paint colors. Adam was supposed to pick up Elsa from soccer practice on his way home from work, which meant she'd have most of the evening free to work on her biggest commission yet. Except she hadn't thought about dinner.

"Actually," she said, placing her earrings and pine pillow on the counter. "I'll take a half dozen croissants too. Breakfast for dinner tonight!" About a dozen rows of twinkle lights hung vertically behind the woman, and Rachel made a mental note to mention it to Elsa. Something like that would look cute in her room.

"Wonderful. Can I also recommend some of this cheddar?" The owner lifted the top off of a huge cake stand that held a white wheel of cheese. "This is the absolute best cheese you will ever taste. I get it from a local farm in Freeport." She cut off a tiny piece and handed it to Rachel.

Rachel let the cheese melt in her mouth and felt her eyes close. "I'll take a half pound."

As opened the shop door, Rachel smiled at the crisp yellow and orange leaves skittering across the sidewalk. Autumn was her favorite time of year, and she couldn't wait to get home, light a candle, and get to work.

Before putting the car in drive, she heard her phone ding three times. It was Elsa.

Mom, I forgot my soccer clothes!

Can you drop them off?

I need my blue running pants too if you can find them. Thanks! Love you.

Then, a few more dings, this time from Adam.

I have to work late tonight, so I can't get Elsa. Have you seen this? It was a link to a story about the dangers of drinking Diet Soda.

Rachel leaned her head back on her seat and closed her eyes, gripping the steering wheel as if it were a lifeline that could reel her back to the pleasant reality of five minutes ago. She'd get it all done. It was just a few hiccups.

She opened her eyes, put the car in drive, and headed home to gather Elsa's soccer stuff. She could get paint supplies later.

Brad

Beth was already late. It was Saturday afternoon and Brad sat outside Wild Oats, one of his favorite lunch spots. He'd put off the conversation about the foil-lined bag for a few days already, and the plan was to bring it up, gently, over lunch.

Beth was out with her friend, Julie, who was going through a nasty breakup, and apparently they needed more time to talk than she originally thought. Beth also still hadn't given him an answer about canoeing.

Late afternoons on the lake, in the fall, were so good for the soul. If she'd just *try*, just go with him one time, maybe she'd see that.

Her father's work event had exhausted him the previous night, and he yawned, checking the time on his phone—she was a half hour late now. His hips and back were getting tight, and he stood up to stretch. The days of eating outside were numbered, and he wanted to soak in the fall air.

"I said no cilantro, and I want two limes!" Brad turned to see a man in a button-down with thick, slicked-back hair. His blue shirt was buttoned all the way up, creating a neck roll above his collar. The way he treated the server, then went right back to his phone call, reminded Brad of his father-in-law, Charlie, and many other men at the party last night.

Thank God I got away from all that.

"Sir, that's shredded lettuce," the server replied. "And your limes are right here in this ramekin." She pushed the bowl closer to his plate.

"Oh," Top Button replied without looking at her. He lifted one taco, dipped it in sour cream, and chomped on it. A piece of lettuce fell on his phone, but he was too busy talking with his mouth full to notice.

Brad took a deep breath and sat back down in the wooden chair.

"Have you decided on what you want yet?" The server had already been to his table twice to check on him, but he was trying to be polite and wait for Beth.

A line was forming outside, and the café had little seating. "I'll go ahead and order." Brad scanned the menu. "She always gets the chopped Kale salad with lemons on the side, so that's safe to order. And I should get the same, but I can't resist your loaded bacon cheeseburger with everything." He handed her the menus. "Oh, and sweet potato fries on the side, please."

"Perfect, I'll put this right in." Brad made a mental note to leave her a big tip to make up for Top Button's shitty behavior and reached for his vibrating phone. *Sorry, Honey. I was on my way, but Julie is having a really hard time, and I feel bad leaving her.*

He blew out a hard breath and closed his eyes. His cheeks flushed with anger. *How many times have you been stood up by your own wife for some hair appointment or one of her girl-friends?*

He also wanted to get this talk about the bag out of the way and was frustrated with himself because he hadn't mentioned it yet.

His stomach rumbled as he thought about his meal. It had been a while since he'd had a burger, and now he couldn't wait to devour it. He half smiled when he thought about enjoying every bite, without Beth's comments about how he should eat more greens.

Julie must really need her. It's fine. We can talk later.

Brad's thoughts about Beth were interrupted when he saw a woman in a knee-length floral dress carrying a green canvas tote, filled with bread and vegetables, walking toward the café.

He didn't notice the two teenagers behind her until she stopped to turn around and talk to one of them. When she turned back around, she hooked a piece of hair with her pinky that was stuck to her clear, shiny lips.

Rach? He'd kissed that sharp jawline, and those toned legs had been wrapped around him many times. He suddenly felt his heart banging in his chest, felt his neck and ears go hot. He stood up, then sat back down.

Rachel's hair pooled around her shoulders, still the same shades of caramel brown as it had been in high school and college. It'd been over twenty years since Brad had seen his first love, but he was positive that was her walking toward him.

His entire body buzzed as he stood again, this time heading for her. His belly swam with nerves as he pictured Rachel's face when he'd told her he'd wanted to experience other people. Their last encounter had been awful—he'd ended their four-year relationship after he'd fallen for Beth. So many times over the years, he'd thought about how Rachel had deserved better, and seeing her made all his guilt resurface.

Talk to her.

As soon as she saw him, Rachel stopped fast, and the two teens trailing behind almost crashed into her back.

"Mom, what are you doing?" A mini version of Rachel looked up from her phone, a vaguely annoyed expression on her face.

"Rachel!" Brad lengthened his stride to get to her faster. Without seeing her reaction, he wrapped her in a hug and lifted her a few inches off the sidewalk.

She smells the same.

Mini Rachel's eyes widened, her phone still clutched in both hands in front of her. Brad put Rachel down instantly.

"Well, hello! Brad! How are you?" Gently pushing away from him, she smoothed her dress and turned around. "These are my kids, Elsa and Benjamin. We're doing some shopping and thought we'd stop for lunch." She bit her lower lip and looked at her nude, strappy sandals. "Are you eating here or ... I mean, obviously you are eating here, you were just sitting right there."

Rachel pointed to his seat, and Elsa rolled her eyes. "Oh my God, Mom."

Brad scanned her left hand, clocked the platinum wedding band and large solitaire diamond, and cleared his throat. "Oh. Yes. I was waiting for ... Beth, but she couldn't make it. Hello Elsa, Benjamin." Brad nodded his head toward the kids. "I'm a friend of your mom's. We went to high school and college together. You're both tall, just like her!" He studied them for hints to see if they knew who he was, but they couldn't be more disinterested.

"Hi," they said in a bored unison. Benjamin leaned against the café wall, appearing to be very annoyed, and Elsa's eyes relaxed as she went back to her phone and stayed standing by Rachel.

"So, you recognized me?" Brad smiled and shoved his hands in his pockets.

"You really haven't changed," Rachel said, switching the tote bag to her other shoulder. "Your hair is darker brown, and you have red in your beard." She leaned in a little closer and squinted to inspect. "I like it."

She looked down and fiddled with the back of her earring,

then cleared her throat and took a step back. "How is Beth? Do you have any kids? I ... I thought ... Do you still live in Massachusetts? It's been so long since I've seen you." She laughed and fiddled with her earring again.

"I'm fine." He nodded. "I can't complain. I'm ... it's just so good to see you." Brad could feel warmth spread to his cheeks. "We moved back to Freeport a few years ago. I wondered if you still lived in Brunswick. I can't believe we haven't run into each other before now."

Rachel's face flushed.

Are old memories creeping into her head too?

They'd both grown up in Freeport, the town next to Brunswick where they'd attended college. When they'd both been accepted to Bowdoin, they'd ignored everyone's comments about how they should explore other places, other people.

His mom had told him years ago that Rachel was living in Brunswick, which made sense. She'd always talked about moving to this small town when they'd roam the sidewalks, strolling by little capes and brick homes.

Instead of answering her questions, he wanted to tell her how sorry he was, how he thought about her. Clearly, this wasn't the time or place.

"And Beth is fine. We've ... decided to not have kids." Brad shrugged and jammed his hands deeper into his pockets, and glanced at Elsa and Benjamin. "But *I* have kids."

Rachel raised her eyebrows.

"Nineteen second graders. I'm a teacher." Brad took his hands from his pockets and crossed his arms across his chest. "What have *you* been up to, though?" He reached out and gently tapped on her arm. Her skin was soft, and he yanked his arm back.

Rachel rubbed the spot where he'd touched her. "You are a teacher! That's all you wanted to do in college." Rachel put her arm around Elsa, who didn't take her eyes off her phone. "These two keep me busy. I've started selling abstract paintings, too. I have a few special orders I'm working on. So, things are good."

Brad clapped his hands together. "That's great! You were always so creative. All that pottery you made. Oh, and that time you and Aimee painted a mural on your wall in college? Didn't you get a fine for that?"

Rachel laughed and nodded. "Yes, we did. I washed it off, though!" Brad couldn't take his eyes off hers. He'd almost forgotten how well you could see little specks of green in them when she was in the sun.

"I'd ... I'd love to see your work, Rachel."

"Sure." Rachel cleared her throat again and readjusted the bag over her shoulder. "Well ... I'll let you get back to your lunch." Turning toward Elsa, she said, "I think this place is too crowded, Honey. Let's go grab some pizza."

"Thank God!" Benjamin said, pushing himself off the wall. "I'm literally dying of hunger."

Rachel laughed, her eyes not leaving Brad's, as she shook her head at her son. "Oh you poor thing, maybe we need to call ahead; tell them it's an emergency."

Brad remembered how she'd always had a way of being sarcastic and nurturing at the same time.

"Okay. Yes." Brad's heart sank. "So good to see you, Rach. And nice to meet you, Elsa and Benjamin."

"Good to see you, too. Take care, Brad." Rachel turned back to the parking lot, and Benjamin and Elsa gave him polite smiles before turning to follow their mom.

"Enjoy your pizza!" he yelled, watching them walk away for a moment before heading back to his table to sit down.

. . .

His burger waited for him. The lettuce and bacon hung out the sides across from Beth's kale salad.

Before seeing Rachel, he'd been ravenous. But now, he couldn't think about eating.

She'd entered his mind many times throughout the years, but he'd always tried not to wonder what his life would look like if he hadn't fallen for Beth.

Back then, Beth's boldness and high standards had felt exciting and refreshing compared to Rachel's easy-going nature. Now, more often than not, Beth came across as controlling and entitled.

Beth had wanted him in a way no other woman had. He often wondered if she'd made him feel so irresistible in college because she hated being told no, which is what he'd said to her the first time she'd approached him.

Every time he let himself think that was the reason Beth had pursued him so hard, he'd ignored it. It made his stomach turn to think he'd thrown away something so wonderful for a fleeting feeling.

He lifted the collar of his polo shirt and sniffed it. He could still smell Rachel.

"How's everything over here?" the server asked, eyeing his uneaten burger and bird-bath-sized salad. "Is the burger okay?"

"It's great, thanks. I'll take two to-go boxes when you get a chance." He handed her his credit card.

"Hey! Another seltzer with lime over here!" Top Button yelled to the server, raising his half-empty glass and snapping.

At the party last night, one of his father's colleagues, Mike, had asked him what his biggest regret in life was. It was clear Mike was prying, trying to see if Brad would admit that he regretted giving up his job at the firm to teach.

Brad had thought about Rachel for a split second before saying, "I do wish I had started teaching sooner."

It was just for a half second. He really didn't think of Rachel *all* that often anymore. Early on, he'd had to work to keep his memories of her at a distance—the way she'd made him feel at ease, the way she'd wrapped her legs around his hips when they had sex, the way she'd always had to have the windows cracked on a chilly fall day so she could take in the crisp air. It was a weird coincidence that she'd popped into his head like that at the party, and then he'd run into her.

It would be even harder now to keep her out of his head. She still smelled the same. Still had that bright, serene smile that always seemed to warm him from the inside. And those legs.

Brad got his to-go boxes and dropped a fifty percent tip, hoping it would make up for Top Button's behavior. He pulled his phone from his pocket and responded to Beth. *Won't be home tonight after all. Going to my mom's to help her get her fall decorations out of the basement. Enjoy your time with Julie.*

He hit his mother's number, and she picked up on the second ring.

"Hi, Brad. How are you, Dear?"

"I'm good, Mom. Hey, you up for a visit later? I thought I could come over and help you get the fall decorations out of the basement. Maybe we could make dinner together?"

"Oh, I'd love that. How about we make the beef stroganoff? I've got all the stuff. Beth is coming, I assume?"

"That's perfect, Mom. I'll be over in a few hours. Going to get the canoe out before the sun goes down. And no, just me tonight. Beth has plans with Julie." He could talk to Beth about the bag later.

"That sounds wonderful. I'm so glad you are getting out on the river again! Be careful though. Oh, and I made you something to hang in your classroom. It's an apple garland. I saw it on The Pinterest."

"Oh, yeah? The kids'll love that." He held in a laugh. "And Mom, it's just Pinterest. Not *The* Pinterest."

"Whatever. Judy and I made so many of these garlands. We stayed up late last night. She brought over the Schnapps, but I told her I couldn't drink that anymore."

"Sounds like a wild time." Brad loved hearing about his mother's adventures. After his dad died, his mom's friends had kept her busy with seemingly endless crafting.

"Son, is everything okay?" The last few times he'd been to see her, Beth hadn't come. She'd either been at pilates class or too tired to go.

"Yeah ... why?" Brad wandered to his car, scanning the streets for Rachel.

"You sound ... a little down, is all."

Mom was a worrier, and he didn't want to set her off. Besides, he always kept his relationship with Beth between the two of them. He didn't want to be like a few of his friends who constantly complained about their wives.

"I'm as good as can be, Mom. See you soon. Love you." Brad opened his door and relaxed in his seat. The sun had warmed up his car, and he tilted his back head to catch some sunlight on his face.

Before pulling out, he looked Rachel up on Instagram. He'd purposefully avoided searching for her on social media all these years. But now, he couldn't help himself.

You'll just look for a second to see if she posts any pictures of her paintings. Then you won't give her one more thought.

Rachel

R achel sat cross-legged on the floor and set down the large fountain soda she'd gotten on the way home from lunch. Cora settled down next to her, and her eyes drifted closed as Rachel petted her smooth, red head and stared at a blank canvas.

She wondered if Brad and Beth had a dog. Back when they'd dated, Brad always stopped to pet every dog they saw out in public. His childhood dog, Lady, had died the year they got together, and he'd always gotten misty eyes when he'd talked about her.

Rachel shook her head. *Okay, you need to get to work.*

This painting for the salon needed to be fun and whimsical, since everything in the space was already so square and symmetrical.

She gently pencil-sketched large intersecting ovals, a vision appearing in her mind of each oval being a different color. Lining up her bottles of paint, she arranged them until she liked the sequence, settling on white, ivory, tan, gray, silver, and black. She set a shade of emerald green next to the row, then removed it. *No, that doesn't feel right.*

She squeezed a generous glob of paint in each oval and began blending the last quarter of each color into the next one, creating an ombre effect.

Rachel had only taken one ceramics class in college with her best friend, Aimee, and she hadn't attended any of the painting classes the local high school offered for adult education. What she'd learned through experience is that you could *always* paint over something you didn't like. Besides, her work came out a lot better if she didn't overthink the design, and she let her brush surprise her.

Cora sighed, and Rachel relaxed into a familiar rhythm as she swirled ivory paint into the white before dragging it into the next oval.

Does Brad have any art in his house?

Adam always chuckled at her paintings, telling her it was a hobby she'd probably be over soon. He'd warned her not to waste too much money on supplies.

She stopped painting and leaned back to study her work so far, thinking about how Brad had thought everything she'd made in that ceramics class was amazing.

Does he still have those little bowls you made for him?

Her cheeks grew hot when she thought about how vulnerable she'd felt around him today. Even in front of her kids, the old feelings had come flooding back, and guilt brewed in her belly.

Brad's skin was still golden from summer, and he still had the same broad shoulders she remembered, though his arms were thicker. And the way he'd studied her so intently, as if she was the only person in the world, made her stomach contract.

She was afraid Brad had seen right through her—and worse, that her kids had seen through her, too.

Grabbing her phone, she opened her chat with Aimee. *Guess who I saw today?* She set her phone down, then picked it back up, this time to call her sister.

She had to talk to *someone*. She'd been so in love with Brad, so sure of him, and she wanted to defuse the reawakened sting of what had happened between them.

"I'm on the Peloton. What's up?" Emily blurted out before Rachel could say hello.

"I was going to text you, but this was too big, so I had to call. And you're a machine, Emily. I hope you didn't work your entire Saturday away." Rachel took a sip of her watery fountain soda. "I was hoping you'd be able to meet me and the kids for lunch—did you see my text?"

Emily was a successful life and business coach and spent the temporary work breaks she gave herself pedaling furiously on her Peloton, which Rachel could hear whirring in the background.

"Shit. I saw it. I was on my way to a meeting with a new client and completely forgot to respond. I'm sorry. How do the kids like their AirPods?"

Emily wasn't one for spending a lot of time with her niece and nephew, claiming she wasn't good with kids, and tried to make up for her absence with material gifts instead.

"Oh, they love them. Especially Benny, he won't go anywhere without them. I know they were hoping to see you today."

"I'll make it up to them. I know Elsa has her heart set on a pair of boots, but I need an idea for Benny. Work is just ... insane right now. Not a good body image day so, I had to get a ride in. Things would be different if I was the one with the handsome husband who paid all the bills so *I* could stay home and paint." Emily laughed.

Rachel's stomach dropped.

Are you lazy? Does she really wish she had your life, or is that a jab at your lifestyle?

"You know I'm kidding, right, Rachel?"

47

Rachel forced a laugh. "That's the nicest thing I've heard you say about Adam in years."

In between hard breaths, Emily said, "Oh, I still think you should leave him. Why you've stayed with his cheating ass is beyond me."

"Clearly," Rachel said, trying to keep her tone light. They'd talked about this for ten years, and she knew how her sister felt about Adam, but she'd called to talk about Brad, hoping to ease some of this angst.

Her sister could be distant—she was married to her job—but Emily had been there for her when Brad had broken her heart, and when Adam had cheated. She would understand. *You just need to get this off your chest so you can stop thinking about him.*

"How much longer are you going to keep me in suspense? You said you had something big to tell me." Emily's voice was laced with annoyance.

Rachel hesitated before divulging, "I ran into Brad Turner. Today. I went to Wild Oats to have lunch with the kids and there he was, just ... sitting outside." She peeled the lid off of her plastic cup with one hand and shook ice into her mouth.

"You saw fucking Brad Turner?" The sound of Emily's Peloton pedals stopped. "I hope you gave him a knee in the sack. What's it been, like, twenty years? Is he still with Beth?"

"Oh, stop. We were just kids when that happened. You wouldn't want to be held accountable for everything you did when you were twenty, would you?"

Rachel looked out the window. Her old pain felt new again.

We're so young, Rach. Don't you think we should experience other people before we make all these plans to get married?

She couldn't remember exactly when her memories of Brad

grew further apart, when other things and people started to take up more real estate in her mind than he did. *Did the memories fade naturally, or was your mind protecting your heart back then?*

She swallowed hard. "Anyway, yes, he's still with Beth."

"So you talked then? He went from planning a life with you to getting so infatuated with Beth practically overnight. That must have been so ... awkward."

Rachel winced and pressed her paintbrush into the canvas. "Awkward" was leaving a bathroom with toilet paper stuck to your shoe. What Brad had done to her was infinitely worse than "awkward."

"Hello ... Rachel, are you there?"

"I'm here. I just ... it still bothers me. Seeing him brought it all back up. I know what he did. But it was so out of character for him. I remember I used to think he was going to realize leaving me for Beth was a huge mistake and come back. I loved him so much."

Visions of Brad rushed through her—holding his hand as they strolled along the campus sidewalks, his head between her legs as she exploded, the way he used to run his fingers down her back every night until she fell asleep.

"Of course it still bothers you. I was there, wiping your tears while Mother poured wine and told you to forget about him. Remember? So what else did he say? What did he look like? Are you going to tell Adam?"

"He looked ... good." She let out a sigh and closed her eyes. "*So* good. He smelled the same. Elsa and Benny were there. I felt so ... exposed."

Rachel ran her hand over her leg, watching her wedding ring diamond glint and sparkle in the overhead lights of the basement. "I felt like I was doing something wrong." She hadn't even considered telling Adam. *Should you tell him?*

She uncrossed her legs, knocking over her plastic cup, and

the straw fell onto the painting, spilling the water from the melted ice.

"Shit!" she said, picking up the cup. "I just spilled water on my painting." The water was spreading across the canvas, threads of paint lifting and swirling with the water, the colors muting. Rachel got up to get a paper towel from her supply closet, trying to think of a way to salvage her work.

"Geez, you weren't doing anything wrong. The world isn't going to freaking crumble if you talk to your ex-boyfriend." Rachel heard the velcro on Emily's bike shoes unstick, then the clunk of the shoes on the tile floor.

Rachel lowered her voice to a whisper even though she knew Elsa and Benjamin were probably in their rooms two floors away with headphones on, gaming or TikToking.

"He hugged me and picked me up. It felt ... I can't stop thinking about the way it made me feel." She leaned against the doorway of the closet and crossed her legs, as if that could stop the sudden rush of blood she was feeling there. Even her nipples tingled.

It all felt so foreign. All these years, she'd thought her sex drive had just dried up and blown away. But thinking about Brad relit something in her.

"Hmm. I'd say seeing Brad shook you up a bit. It's not that big of a deal, though. *Is* it?"

Rachel hesitated for a beat longer than she should have— long enough that Emily wouldn't miss it. "No. Definitely not a big deal. I just wanted to talk it through, you know?. It was strange seeing him again. Anyway, how are you?"

"Oh yes, *I know,*" Emily answered.

Rachel could practically hear the smirk on her sister's lips. She pinched the bridge of her nose and closed her eyes. "I really want to get together soon." She took long strides back to her painting to check it, mad at herself for letting thoughts of Brad distract her from work.

"I'm slammed with work. But, yes, soon. I want to catch up. Got my hair dyed red. I love it!"

"Oh, send me a picture. I want to see."

Rachel leaned over her painting to inspect the damage and was surprised to see ... there was no damage.

The white and tan ovals had marbled together, and in some places the paint resembled water colors instead of acrylics. The effect was flowy and feminine, nothing like what she'd envisioned, but perfect nonetheless. She grabbed a tube of tan paint and squirted it in one oval, then lifted the canvas onto its side, now deliberately allowing the water to mingle with the paint.

"I ran into Mom at the grocery store and she told me it washed me out, and I should try a shade of brown like yours." Rachel recognized Emily's "I don't care" tone. It always appeared when their mother compared the two of them.

"I hate how she always compares us, sorry, Em. You're so beaut—"

"I don't need you to protect me. Or try to make me feel better. I really don't care what she thinks anymore." Rachel thought the pinched tone of her voice said otherwise, but didn't say so.

"By the way," Emily continued, her voice brighter, "I just pulled up Brad's Instagram page. Have you looked at it? His bio says he's a teacher. And you're right. He looks *gooood*. Like Matthew McConaughey, but like, pre-woo-woo Matthew McConaughey."

"Oh, I don't need to go down the social media rabbit hole," Rachel said, filling in the third oval with paint, and reaching into her cup for the last few ice cubes. She held them in her hand for a second to melt, then dropped them onto the tan paint.

"Of course, *you'd never* do that. I'll do it enough for both of us. How's that?"

Rachel rolled her eyes at her sister's sarcasm. The paint began to lift and curl as it reacted to the water.

"Well, if you decide to do something *crazy* like look at his page, or *God forbid*, meet up with the love of your life behind your husband's back, make sure you tell me first," she laughed.

"Oh please, that's never going to happen." Rachel glided her brush up and down the water, then used the wet brush to pull each color into the edge of the next. "We ran into each other. End of story." Though she realized, a beat too late, that she hadn't corrected her sister's "love of your life" comment.

"Ha! Okay, whatever you say, Rach."

"Oh, shut up. And thanks for listening to me vent. I've got to start dinner."

Adam would be home soon. She'd reheat the leftover pizza from lunch, throw together a salad, and put some frozen wings in the air fryer.

"Yes, go back to being a dutiful housewife who sends her husband off to work with a perfectly made cup of coffee every morning, and stop lusting over your ex-boyfriend." Emily snickered as she crunched on something, which was most likely dried seaweed or Kale chips.

She used to call herself fat when they were young, but now she was a self-proclaimed health nut who never missed a workout or touched alcohol.

Rachel hung up the phone, feeling better. She was so excited about the accidental water spill; she got lost painting for another hour.

When Adam sent her a text letting her know he was on his way, breaking her painting trace, she sprinted upstairs to start dinner. He drove in as Rachel pulled the wings from the air fryer. Benjamin and Elsa floated down the stairs as the smell of pizza warmed in the oven. "Do we still have some of your homemade blue cheese dressing, Mom?"

"Yes, it should be on the top shelf." Rachel arranged the saucy wings on a platter.

That's Brad's mom's blue cheese dressing recipe. She still had the recipe card Corinne had given her, shoved in the back of her *Joy Of Cooking* cookbook. After he'd broken up with her, seeing Brad's mom's handwriting had pulled at her heart too much. She'd memorized the recipe, though, and couldn't help but use it anytime there was a need for blue cheese dressing.

"Oh, and grab some Frank's buffalo sauce, too. I like extra on my wings."

Adam opened the side door that led out to the garage, peeled off his blazer, hung it on the doorknob to the coat closet, and set his empty Yeti mug on the counter. "Smells good. Wings?"

"Hi! Yes, wings, salad, and leftover pizza from Portland Pie. Your favorite. The kids and I went there for lunch today." Rachel pursed her lips as he meandered toward the island, leaving his blazer dangling from the door and his empty coffee mug right next to the empty dishwasher.

Adam rolled up the cuffs of his sleeves as he bent to check out the food options. That cuff-rolling move used to get her hot. He *was* handsome.

The first time she'd seen him, she was serving at the Miss Brunswick Diner. It was the summer after she'd graduated college, and she hadn't quite decided what she was going to do with her English degree yet. He'd worn a backward baseball cap. His short black hair poked through the strapback, and he'd had the thickest eyelashes she'd ever seen on a man. When he'd ducked his head, so he wouldn't hit it on the door frame, it was the first time a man had given Rachel butterflies since Brad.

"Before we eat, I want to show you something!" She

grabbed his hand and led him down to the basement, her pulse quickening, thinking of her happy accident. This was her favorite painting yet, it will impress him.

"I was talking to Emily and painting and my cup spilled water onto the canvas. I was going to clean it up, but I love what it did. It's all marbled and looks like a watercolor painting."

Adam stood next to her, narrowing his eyes at the painting. "Oh. Why were you talking to Emily?"

Rachel's body tensed at the question and his lack of excitement over her hard work.

"What is it?" he asked, turning toward her.

"Well ... it's an abstract painting. I still want to fill in that black oval and do some more experimenting with water. What do you see when you look at it?"

"I'm not sure I see anything besides blobs of color?"

Rachel locked her back teeth together before saying, "Well ... someone's paying me for it, so I guess *someone* finds it interesting."

"It looks like a second-grade painting to me."

Rachel pressed the heel of her hand between her eyes and instantly pictured Brad in his classroom, helping his students create mini-masterpieces. She knew her hurt was written all over her face.

"It's because of the shapes—it's not bad, Honey," Adam said, backpedaling as it apparently finally registered that he was being mean. "It's nice. Great job!"

"Thanks," Rachel muttered, wondering why she even bothered.

Adam rubbed his hands together and turned to go back upstairs. "I'm starving! Can't wait to have some of that pizza and wings!"

She hoped he hit his head on the door frame.

"You know," she said suddenly, just as he mounted the

first step. "Those are the comments that keep you from getting laid." She surprised herself by snapping at him, but once the words were out, and as he turned to gape at her, she felt a rush of relief.

"Geez, I told you I liked it. Are you seriously mad? Aren't we supposed to be honest with each other?"

Rachel pointed at him. "And why did you ask me why I was talking to Emily? Why do you always ask me that? She's my sister."

"Oh, come on!" Adam gently slapped the top of his head with both hands and took slow strides toward her. "Let's not fight. The painting is great. I'm no art critic anyway, so don't listen to me. And ... I don't know, Rachel. Emily's not the best sister in the world, you have to admit." He laid a hand between her shoulder blades and guided her toward the stairs. "Let's just have an enjoyable night."

"Sure," Rachel said, hurrying up the stairs to get his hand off her back.

Rachel

Adam twirled his wedding ring with his thumb as they waited for their coffee order, an impatient habit he'd developed the moment he slid the ring on. She had no idea how they were going to celebrate their seventeenth anniversary, since Adam had said it was a surprise. When she'd woken up this morning, he'd told her to go for her run, that he'd get the kids to school. It was a lovely, and very surprising, start.

As they sauntered back to the car, clutching their hot coffee cups, Adam put his arm around her shoulders. "Okay, I can't keep it in anymore. We're going to Boothbay Harbor for the day. My mom's getting the kids from school, so we can take our time, have lunch, and look around the shops."

This was one of Rachel's favorite ways to spend the day with her husband, something he knew but rarely wanted to do. She lifted her eyes in surprise. "Oh! That sounds perfect." She hooked her arm into his. Boothbay Harbor was where they'd gotten married, and they hadn't taken a day trip there since the kids were little.

She pressed her cheek on his brown wool jacket and was

glad she'd grabbed her beanie and fingerless gloves since they'd be walking around outside near the ocean. "Thank you, Honey. It seems like you put a lot of thought into today." She opened her door, smiling at him over the roof of the car. A twinge of guilt landed in her gut. She'd been thinking of Brad a lot since she'd run into him.

Rachel was a planner and felt a little uneasy about not being there to get the kids after school, but Mary could handle everything. When she got in the car, she sent a quick text to Elsa, reminding her to walk Cora when they got home.

"Well, you've planned the last sixteen. I figured it was *my* turn." Adam flashed her a smile.

Maybe the fact you snapped at him the other night made him think about putting in more effort. On the way, Adam suggested they stop by the tiny stone church where they'd been married.

It started to rain, and Rachel got out and ran up the stone steps as soon as Adam put the car in park. The handle only clicked when she tried to pull open the door. "Aww, I had a feeling it would be locked." She cupped her hands over her eyes and leaned over the sea rose bushes to peer into the window. Adam was beside her now, and they were both getting wet.

"Can you see anything?" Adam asked, holding his coat open over the two of them to block the rain.

"It's pretty dark. I forgot how small it was in here. How'd we fit everyone?" Rachel closed her eyes and pictured that chilly September day. It had been sunny and cool, but they'd kept the church doors open so the autumn air could waft in as they exchanged vows.

The rain turned into a downpour, pulling her from her memories, and they ran back to the car.

Rachel straightened her beanie and wiped off her face with a napkin. "Let's go to that seafood place for lunch. Do you remember the name?" She sat back in her seat and pulled her seatbelt in place. "It has a screen porch, so we can still have a magnificent view of the water while we eat." She reached in her purse for her clear lip gloss.

"Do we really have to eat outside? It's pretty cold." Adam glanced over his shoulder before pulling out of the parking lot.

Rachel pressed her lips together. "It's almost sixty degrees! And look," she said, tugging at his jacket, "you're wearing a wool jacket."

"Okay—lobster and french fries it is."

The tiny streets in the Harbor were narrow and windy, the stone walls of the buildings curling with the shapes of the roads. Rachel loved looking at all the old, quaint houses. There was something so peaceful about taking a slow drive on a dark rainy day and seeing someone's chandelier or lamp glowing from inside their home.

The restaurant was empty given the busy season had ended, and they were seated right away.

"She'll have a Diet Coke and we'll both get the steamed lobster and a side of french fries," Adam said before the server set down menus.

"Ah, you know me well," Rachel said, winking at her husband. Normally, Adam would lecture her about her soda drinking after she'd order one.

He must be really sorry for what he said about her painting the other night and trying to make up for it. Of course, it would be better if he simply stopped saying stupid things. Then he'd have nothing to make up for.

When the server was out of earshot, Adam reached across the red and white checkered tablecloth and took her hands in his.

"I'm excited about *my* anniversary present later." He winked back. "You know I always want the same thing." He laughed, and Rachel felt her stomach churn.

She tried to manage a smile. She should *want* to have sex with her husband on their anniversary. A twinge of jealousy always twisted in her gut when Aimee talked about how she'd crave a night of intimacy with her husband.

But she hated the pressure he put on her. Did he really think it was sexy?

"It's like you're always trying to take something from me," she had told him once during an argument. He'd been infuriated and had gone on a long rant about the importance of intimacy in a marriage and how it was about "mutual giving." He'd intimated that he might not have felt compelled to have an affair if he hadn't felt so "starved for sex."

Was he right? Their marriage *had* been sex-starved before his affair. He'd always slip his hand into Rachel's robe while she was folding underwear or packing lunches and ask her if they were ever going to have sex again, offering no help. Rachel tried to mask her resentment about it. How could he proposition her like that and not understand what she meant when she said it felt like he was taking something from her?

"What?" Adam's voice broke through her thoughts. He clearly recognized the tightness in her smile. "Is it *so bad* that I want to have sex with you?"

"No, it's not. I'm sorry. I've told you when you expect it and approach me like that, it's ... overwhelming."

Like you're taking something from me, she wanted to tell him, but then he would go off, and it was their anniversary.

Adam freed one of his hands to rub his eyebrows, then took a deep breath.

"Sitting here next to the ocean reminds me of our honeymoon. Remember how much it rained? I bet the kids would love Hilton Head Island. We should take a family trip." Rachel squeezed his hand, grateful for the change of subject, and Adam's shoulders relaxed.

By the time they'd finished their steamed lobster and fries, the rain had stopped. They walked hand in hand through the narrow stone streets, browsing the museums and shops and exchanging small talk about the kids. When they approached The Ritz, a jewelry store full of estate diamonds and emeralds, Adam led Rachel in.

Rachel had always wanted to stop in to browse the heirloom jewelry, but she'd never mentioned it when they'd passed by before. The kids had always been too young to go in, and they'd most definitely run their sticky fingers all over the glass cases and it wouldn't be enjoyable for anyone. There were times she'd daydreamed about taking the hour-long drive herself to enjoy a quiet lunch and shop alone, but she never did.

The wide plank floors creaked under Rachel's feet as she took slow steps along the antique curved glass case, admiring the neat rows of antique gold charm bracelets. Vintage diamond rings snuggled into open cushioned boxes, and long necklaces dangled from jewelry stands sitting on top of the cabinets. Rachel reached for a crystal bowl filled with tiny green mint chocolates and put two in her purse; one for each kid.

The owner of the jewelry store stood behind one of the glass cases, gently polishing a plain gold band. The rain started up again outside, and yellow leaves blew around the wet stone sidewalk.

Hunched over the counter at the front of the store, Adam gazed at something inside. The store owner laid down his work and turned his attention to Adam, whispering to him. Rachel couldn't hear over the roar of the rain.

Adam responded to the man, who pulled something out and placed it on a piece of black velvet. Adam picked it up as Rachel made her way toward the two men and stood beside Adam, grazing his arm. "What are you looking at?" She saw a beautiful three-stone diamond ring.

"This is white gold," the jeweler said, finger-combing his long gray mustache as he watched Adam check out the ring. "An estate piece brought in by a woman after her mother died."

Adam reached for Rachel's right hand. "Try this on."

"Why?" she asked, laughing. "What are you doing, Adam?"

"Nothing!" he said with a wink. "I just want to see something. Try it on."

Rachel picked up the ring and slid it onto her slender finger.

"Ah, this is a small ring. Size four and a half," the jeweler said. "It was meant to be."

Rachel took it off and put it back on the velvet. "I'm sure it's too much. I don't need—"

"I want to get it for you." Adam picked up the ring and stared at Rachel, his eyes stern and pleading at the same time. "Okay? We're getting it."

"I ... I love it, Honey. Are you sure? This is such a surprise."

And so unlike you.

Adam nodded at the jeweler and reached for his wallet. "You've put up with me for seventeen years. It's the least I can do."

A few drops fell on them as they left the store. Rachel clenched the new ring on her finger with her opposite hand as the wave of guilt came over her again.

"You *never* surprise me like that. Did you plan this? Adam ... I love it." A vision of Brad's face flashed in her mind, and she had to shove it roughly away.

Yes, definitely guilt.

"The mood just struck me, I guess. It looks great on your hand, Sweetie." Adam took her hand in his and kissed the top of it. "Are you in the mood for some apple pie?"

"Always," Rachel said as they approached the car. They headed toward home, knowing they'd find a place on Route One to stop. As they drove over the wet pavement, leaves whirled up around the car in that magical way that Rachel loved so much. She felt so relaxed sitting in her heated seat, she almost drifted off to sleep.

When Adam hit the brakes, she opened her eyes. "Let's stop here!" He slowed the car, pulling into the parking lot of a chippy white building.

The small entrance door was red, and two brass chandeliers hung from the ceiling through the large side windows. The beat up sandwich sign on the ground read: *Come in for our famous apple pie before we close Sunday for the season!*

They waited for the pie in a relaxed, companionable silence. Adam checked his phone and responded to some work emails, and Rachel watched cars driving by the window.

You're not thinking about Brad that much. Look how hard Adam is trying. You can put in the effort too and have sex with him tonight.

When the server dropped off their pieces of pie, Rachel mashed her vanilla ice cream into the thick cinnamon-y crust. The apples were warm and gooey and she rolled them around in her mouth; she'd taken too big of a bite, and the ice cream didn't cool the hot pie filling enough.

"How is it?" Adam held up his fork, watching her mash vanilla ice cream into her last few bites of pie.

She nodded her head, then reached for her glass of ice water. "Definitely homemade."

"I should have gotten ice cream like you did." Adam slid a gooey chunk of apple from beneath the crust. The steam wafted in the air as Rachel spooned half of her ice cream up and plopped it on his plate.

"Thank you, Honey." He lifted a forkful of pie and ice cream to his mouth.

Rachel took her next bite of pie with less ice cream, so she'd have enough for each bite, making her think of something that had happened when she and Bard first started dating.

She'd gotten apple crisp from the snack shack during a soccer game. Brad had told her he wished he'd gotten some too, and she'd given him a bite from her plastic fork. He took that one bite and refused to take any more, though she offered. Instead, he took the container from her and fed her the rest, telling her she deserved to have it all, that he'd rather watch her enjoy it.

After the game, they took a drive in his dad's navy blue Volvo station wagon down Lovers' Lane and had sex for the first time.

Adam's phone pinged, shaking her out of the memory. "Your phone is blowing up. Lots of work emails today?"

"It's nothing important." Adam glanced at the screen before slipping the phone into his pocket.

Rachel felt the familiar pull of dread as she took the cream throw pillows off the bed before pulling down the covers. *It's our anniversary. He got you this ring. You should have sex with him. What's wrong with you?*

The sweater and the gift certificate to the golf course she'd given him when they got home was fine, and he thanked her over and over.

But Rachel knew her husband, and what he really wanted was a blow job. More than that, he felt he *needed* it; was *owed* it. Not doing it would lead to resentment and anger that would only fester.

If they didn't have sex tonight, she wouldn't be the only one to feel the tension, either. She knew Elsa and Benjamin could sense their father's moods.

After she went into the kids' rooms to kiss them good-night, she softly closed the bedroom door behind her.

Adam grabbed her from behind. "Adam! You scared me. I didn't know you were up here." He pressed himself firmly against her back and slid a hand down her arm, encircling her wrist and holding up her hand.

"Look at that beautiful ring. How about a little lovin' to end this perfect day?" He lifted the hem of her nightgown and glided his other hand up her hip.

Rachel couldn't stop her body from wiggling away. "I might need a minute. I think I ate too much today. My stomach is upset."

Adam's body went limp behind her. "Really, Rach? I got you that ring, spent the whole day doing something I knew you'd love, and you're going to give me an excuse? On our anniversary?"

"I just said I needed a minute, Adam," she whispered. "I need time to—"

"I know! I know! You need time to decompress. You need a back rub first. You need to be relaxed. Well, by the time you're relaxed, you're practically asleep and I've wasted a half hour rubbing your back for nothing!" Adam raked his hands through his hair. "I'm so frustrated. Are we ever going to have a normal sex life, or am I going to be married to someone who always has to be primed first?"

Rachel flinched and looked down at her ring. Her heart sped up, and she sat down on the bed.

Is he right? Are you just a frigid prude? Is it going to be like this forever?

She should have known he'd only put this kind of effort into the day to get himself laid. She tried to hold in tears as she crawled into bed.

Adam went into the bathroom to brush his teeth, and Rachel laid on her back, taking deep breaths.

If he tries again when he gets back in bed, you'll try too. It's not like it lasts very long, anyway.

After an hour of lying together in the same bed, listening to the same silence, Adam grabbed his phone from his nightstand and went downstairs in a huff.

Immediately, Rachel could breathe easier, and she wondered when *not* being around her husband had become more comfortable than being around him as she drifted into a deep sleep.

Rachel

Rachel woke up to rain pounding on the roof, and a sinking feeling came over her as she thought about how last night ended. Adam's breathing rattled next to her, and she checked the time—it was five-thirty in the morning.

She rolled slowly out of bed and tiptoed downstairs to the laundry room. Her fluorescent yellow running jacket and black leggings were in the dryer, and she waded through the clean clothes to dig them out.

As she pulled on her leggings, she thought about what she could do to semi-make up for last night.

He put so much effort into our anniversary. Don't you owe it to him to give him something he wants? Why does it always have to be sex, though?

Things were different after they'd had Elsa, but they'd really drifted apart after Benny was born. She'd tried explaining to Adam she wasn't in the mood to be intimate, and needed a little more time, when her doctor had cleared her to have sex again. Adam didn't understand. At all. Instead of being supportive, he'd remind her every night how hot the sex between them used to be and how she'd seemingly changed overnight.

Rachel wondered every day what was wrong with her, and Adam always made her feel worse. He'd stopped wanting to do things with her like make dinner together and dig in the flower garden on Saturdays. He'd stopped seeing her, noticing how she always made his favorite cookies, and stopped commenting on what a good mother she was. Yes, she'd changed. But *he'd* changed too.

If he'd have given you space then, maybe things would be different.

She pulled her hair into a messy bun on top of her head.

You should just go up there and wake him up with your mouth like you used to.

As she wiped the sleep from the corners of her eyes, every muscle in her body tensed.

She couldn't do it. Instead, she'd go to his favorite bagel place and surprise everyone with bagels, and tonight would be the night.

Even she was sick of listening to her excuses.

After zipping up, she sent Adam a quick text, letting him know where she was going.

A vibration came from the kitchen. Adam's phone was sitting on the butcher block counter near the large gas stove. As she picked it up, she looked at her text on the screen. His background photo was a picture of Benjamin and Elsa, taken at the beach about ten years ago.

She remembered the day clearly. They'd taken a trip to Camden on Labor Day weekend, a few days before she'd heard her husband fucking another woman.

Staring at her kids' sweet, tanned faces, she blew out a sigh. Since Adam's affair, Aimee had asked her several times why she didn't press him about any of the details.

Everyone seemed to think that getting a play-by-play of her

husband with another woman would somehow help, but Rachel always knew it wouldn't.

"I just don't see the point. He told me it was a client, and she moved away. What else do I need to know?"

The day she found out, she'd been running errands and stopped at a red light in front of a small insurance office. Adam's white Suburban was parked outside, and she'd figured he must be doing a showing, though there wasn't a For Sale sign outside.

Rachel had always wanted to see the inside of the old building though, and she thought it would be fun to surprise Adam and say hi. She'd parked behind him and skipped up the building's steps, so blissfully trusting, so foolishly unaware of how quickly her world could be smashed.

Knocking on the locked door.

Adam's voice coming through the cracked window. "God, yes, I'm going to come."

Knocking again, this time so hard the skin on her knuckle split and bled.

The silence that emulated from the building because they were too ashamed to answer the door.

When Rachel had tried yelling his name, nothing came out. She'd felt like she was in the middle of one of her dreams where someone was chasing her, and she'd try to yell for help, unable to make a sound. She wasn't even sure how she'd driven home.

Rachel put his phone back down on the counter. The strange thing was, she hadn't been jealous. Devastated, yes. But not jealous. She'd only admitted that to Aimee. Saying it out loud made her feel abnormal. She wished she *could* muster up some jealousy over the situation.

She'd thought about leaving him, but even after he'd betrayed her, she still loved him. Every time she really dug into the logistics of what divorcing him would look like, she'd get so overwhelmed by the thought of custody schedules, lawyers, and wondering what she would do for work and where they would live. So, she justified her misery. Staying wasn't only the right thing to do, it was the easy thing to do.

It's not that bad. It's not like he hits you.

She grabbed her purse and headed for the car.

She shivered and tried to focus on the day ahead. *You'll put the seat warmer on and grab a Diet Coke on the way home. It will be a good start to the day.*

When she arrived at Mr. Bagel, the smell of fresh bread, garlic, and bacon hit her.

She and Brad used to get bagels on Sunday morning, and Brad always got bacon and scallion cream cheese and joked about how she took tiny bites.

Those mornings felt suspended in time, like she and Brad would have forever together, stay just as they were in those youthful bodies. The slant of the sun would come pouring in as she'd straddle him. He'd always cupped her breasts, told her she was perfect.

Her cheeks flushed as she stood in line.

Get ahold of yourself.

"Can I help you?" the woman behind the counter asked, smiling at Rachel. Rachel spun her new ring on her finger, reminding her of how Adam always fiddled with his wedding ring.

"I'll take a half dozen salt bagels, and a small container of bacon and scallion cream cheese, please." Rachel's eyes wandered over the tubs of bagels behind the counter. There were some topped with melted cheese, blueberry, cinnamon raisin, whole grain, but salt was everyone's favorite, and she hadn't had one in a long time.

Maybe you'll clean out the closets after your run. Get some painting in and bake some zucchini bread. You've got to shake Brad out of your head.

When she got home, the kids were still upstairs, and Adam was getting his Yeti out of the dishwasher. Rachel handed him a hot cup of coffee. "Here, I got you one from McDonald's instead. I know you like their coffee, and I had to stop and get a soda, of course."

"Thanks," he said, reaching for the cup, giving her a tight-lipped smile.

Rachel heard Elsa and Benjamin clomping downstairs, and she met them at the bottom. "You two must have smelled the bagels." Rachel leaned in to kiss their warm cheeks.

Benjamin hurried to the kitchen, tore open the paper bag, and opened the tub of cream cheese. Rachel slapped his hand before he could dip his bagel directly into the container. "Get a knife and spread it on your bagel like a human."

"Didn't you get anything else, Mom? I can't go to school with scallion breath!" Elsa said as she grabbed a bagel.

"There's butter, Elsa. Just use that and stop complaining," Adam huffed.

Rachel narrowed her eyes at him.

Don't take your frustration with me out on them.

"We've got twenty minutes until we need to leave school, so let's eat!" she said, turning her attention from Adam and heading toward the breakfast nook in the kitchen.

"Aren't you going to eat, Mom?" Benjamin tore off a piece of his bagel and dipped it into a lump of cream cheese he'd spooned onto a napkin.

"I'm saving mine for after my run. I can't exercise on a full stomach," she said, reaching out to straighten his bangs.

Elsa grabbed the butter from the fridge and sliced her bagel. "I've got ceramics today. I'm making *someone* a Christmas gift!" She smiled at Rachel.

"How cheap. You can't even buy your own mom an actual gift." Benjamin ripped off a piece of his salty bagel and shoved it into his mouth.

"It *is* an actual gift, you jerk." Elsa flicked the back of his head.

"*Better* than an actual gift." Rachel winked at her daughter and squeezed her shoulder.

"Okay, I'll see everyone tonight." Adam kissed the top of Benjamin's and Elsa's head.

Elsa stopped buttering her bagel and looked at her dad. "What about my soccer game tonight? Will you be there?"

"Oh, yes ... I'm planning on it! But, I bet it will be canceled. It's supposed to rain all day, Sweetie." Adam pulled on his black coat and stole a look at Rachel.

"Aren't you going to have a bagel?" Rachel stood up and straightened her running jacket.

"My stomach isn't feeling well." Adam grabbed his coffee and plodded out the front door.

Rachel sat back down and examined the kids' faces for any sign they'd noticed the tension between her and Adam. Thankfully, they seemed to be in their own self- absorbed world, as teenagers deserved to be.

Their innocence will be shattered if we can't get our shit together.

Brad

B rad drew a crooked row of circles, hoping his students would know they were supposed to be apples on the whiteboard, as he waited for his second graders to file in. It was apple week, and his class was going to dissect apples and make applesauce.

Last night, he'd brought up the foil-lined bag to Beth as he'd made dinner. Their talk had been short. It hadn't led to an argument, but that was only because he hadn't pushed her. When he'd asked her about the bag, and why it was lined with foil and stuffed in her drawer, Beth's cheeks had flushed. "Oh, I'm taking it to get repaired," she'd said.

"Why was there foil in it?" he'd asked her.

"Oh ... um ... well, I bought a bunch of face oils and serums for that ladies' night makeover party I went to last week. I didn't want any oils to get on the bag," she'd said before walking over to him and pressing her breasts against his arm. "I got the recipe for those appetizers you liked at Dad's party. The ones with the jalapeno peppers, cream cheese, and bacon." She was a master of distraction.

"Beth. Talk to me." He'd reached an arm around her and pressed her closer.

When she'd pushed away from him and said, "There's nothing to talk about. I told you what happened." Brad knew this would not be a one and done conversation and shelved it for another time. Beth had been fidgety and overly cheery for the rest of the night.

The third grade teacher, Nancy, ducked her head in his room. She'd been at the school longer than any other teacher, and her gray and brown curly hair was pulled into two short ponytails. Apple earrings dangled from her ears, and she set a steaming cup of coffee on Brad's tidy desk. "Oh, you're here early again. I brought you coffee. The bakery does a two-for-one special before nine in the morning." She set the coffee on his desk. "You're such an artist. You can come do my drawings if you're bored," she giggled.

"Hilarious. And thank you for the coffee. Nice treat this morning." Brad lifted the cup to his lips, taking a small sip.

"And look at you, showing off with that apple garland!" She pointed to the garland hanging across the top of the blackboard.

"Ah, my mom made that for me. I can't take credit."

"Well, that's not fair. Your mom is making the rest of us look bad."

Brad laughed. "I have complete faith in your apple-drawing skills and your garland-making skills."

Nancy sliced the air with her hand. "I don't have the time with my new grandbaby and all." She turned toward the door. "I guess I better get to it. We have about ten minutes before the munchkins get here. And you're welcome for the coffee! It's my pleasure."

Ten minutes.

Brad marched to his desk and opened the top drawer. He'd found one of the little white bowls in his mother's basement.

He flipped it over and ran his finger over the initials Rachel had engraved on the back. He held the little piece of pottery to his chest as his thumb tapped across his phone, going right to Rachel's Instagram page, as if it had a mind of its own.

A rush of warmth filled his chest.

He scrolled through pictures of Rachel on the beach with her kids and standing next to them on a large porch on the first day of school. When he spotted a picture of a bunch of people standing in front of a Christmas tree, dated about two years ago, he clicked on it and zoomed in.

There was a tall man next to Rachel with his arm around her. *The husband.* Brad recognized Rachel's mom standing on her other side with a glass of wine in her hand, of course. Emily, Rachel's sister, was standing on the other side of their mother. Her mouth was in a straight line, and she looked uncomfortable.

Brad held his phone closer to his face, remembering the night in high school when Emily'd had too much to drink at a party and called Rachel to come get her. Rachel had been asleep, so Brad had picked Emily up instead. On the way home, Emily had tried to kiss his neck and unzip his pants.

When he'd told her to stop and pushed her away, Emily had said, "Why does everyone think Rachel is so much better than me?" Her head bobbed to the side and hit the window. He'd practically had to carry her in the house.

It had been so unsettling. Brad had struggled with what to do and ultimately had decided not to mention it to Rachel. Emily had been so drunk she probably wouldn't remember, and it only would have upset Rachel. She'd always talked about how she wished she and Emily were closer, and she was weirdly protective of her sister. Brad couldn't understand it— he didn't think Emily deserved the unwavering loyalty she got from Rachel.

Rachel had posted a few pictures of her paintings a few

weeks back, with the caption: *I'm now selling my paintings after getting so many requests. Let me know if you'd like something special!*

Brad's eyes caught on one in particular: it looked like white waves on a sandy beach. The black frame she'd put it in offered a stunning contrast against the pale tones of the work. Rachel's talent did not surprise him. She'd always had an eye for decorating and an amazing sense of style. When they were together, strangers always stopped her on the street, asking her where she'd gotten her earrings or scarf.

His thoughts were interrupted when his students stumbled into the classroom. He slipped his phone into his desk, stood up, and clapped his hands together. "Good morning! Who's ready for apple week?"

The kids were pulling off their jackets and hanging them up. Some of them jumped up and down and yelled, "Me!" while others seemed less than enthused.

Randy, a boy with curly brown hair, shouted, "We should have a Roblox week instead!" and the class cheered.

Brad laughed. "That's probably *not* going to happen, but guess what? You all get to make applesauce with Mrs. Miles today!"

Brad strode over to Grayson, who sat quietly in his seat, to let him know they had selected him to go into Mrs. Miles' class early to help her wash the apples. Grayson was painfully shy, but Brad had noticed that whenever he had a special job to do, he inched a little farther out of his shell.

Maybe we could do a painting project, and Rachel could come in and help...

Brad shook his head and forced himself to refocus. He was thinking about Rachel a lot more than he should be.

Rachel

"To what do I owe the pleasure?" Rachel laughed, answering Emily's call.

"Well, I wanted to hear the latest in Rachel land," Emily said. "I'm in between clients. How was your anniversary? Still have Brad Turner-brain?"

Rachel had pulled everything out of the hall closet and was sitting on the floor, refolding towels.

"It was good, thanks. And I'm doing everything in my power to stop thinking about Brad. Lots of cleaning out closets and scrubbing bathtubs for me today." Rachel put Emily on speaker and stood up to wedge the thick stack of towels onto the shelf.

"That's normal. I think? Are you ... sexually frustrated? It sounds like it." Emily's voice was cheery, and Rachel could hear her fingers pecking away on her computer.

"I am *not* sexually frustrated. Just nostalgic." Rachel reached for the paper towels and toilet paper and began lining them up in perfect rows.

"Oh, so I assume your sex life with your husband is better? When was the last time you two did it?"

"God ... Emily ... I don't know." *Six months ago, after two glasses of wine. Geez, you can't even say it out loud.* She crossed her arms, admiring the neat closet. "And when have I ever told *you* about my sex life?"

"You've told me a few times you two aren't as *active* as you once were."

The typing stopped. Rachel furrowed her brows, trying to remember when she'd shared that with Emily.

"You told me it had been a while right before he cheated, though a lot of it was your fault. I guess I assumed things had stayed the same." The keyboard pecking began again, faster this time.

Rachel remembered admitting that to Aimee, but it was hard for her to talk about it, so she'd mostly kept it to herself. Whenever she thought about how she didn't want to have sex with her own husband anymore, the shame practically swallowed her whole. But she supposed she must have mentioned it to Emily at some point.

"My sex life is just fine." She opened a bottle of lavender essential oil and brought it to her nose. "We're getting busy tonight, *actually.*"

Emily laughed through her nose. "Hmm. Scheduled sex. How organized of you."

Rachel's stomach twisted. Her sister was right.

Why can't you just be attracted to your husband again? Maybe you're just incredibly boring.

She didn't feel boring when she thought of Brad. When he'd picked her up in a bear hug that day on the sidewalk, his scruff had brushed her cheek, and she'd breathed in that same woody scent she used to find so sexy and comforting. Now, every time she'd looked at his pictures on Instagram, she swore she got a whiff of his soap, and her hand went directly to the spot where he'd rubbed her cheek.

"I'm a busy mom. Everything is scheduled."

"So, not much time to think about ex-boyfriends?"

"Well, Brad followed me on Instagram and I followed him back. Which hasn't helped matters at all."

"Oh! The ol' social media-follow from the ex-boyfriend. Bad news. *Or* good news. Does he look at your stories?"

"Oh Lord, Emily I don't know!"

Yes. Yes, he does.

"None of this matters. We're both married."

"That didn't stop Adam," Emily fired back.

Rachel leaned against the wall and stared at the black and white photos of Benjamin and Elsa that hung in the hallway. She zeroed in on a large photo of them holding carved pumpkins as Cora sat in-between them. Benjamin was missing his two front teeth, and it was the year Elsa insisted on wearing her pink cowboy hat every day.

She ran her fingers down the picture.

They were completely filled with joy, and Rachel could never imagine hurting them.

"It was all so long ago. I'm just having all these feelings because I saw him for the first time in forever."

She pictured Beth sauntering out of Brad's dorm room, just weeks after they'd broken up. One of Beth's eyes had mascara under it, and her hair looked like a lion's mane. Aimee had told her she'd seen them leaving the bar together the night before, but Rachel couldn't believe Brad would move on so fast. All these years later, it still sent a shot of pain through her stomach to remember it.

"And," she said now, "because he broke my heart."

"Yeah, just a minor detail."

A shiver ran through Rachel as she tried to shake off the memory. "Hey, let's do dinner this week? You've been working too much. Tuscan Bistro in Freeport?" Emily was picky about where she ate. She'd struggled with binge eating and was careful not to go anywhere she'd get triggered. "They have great salads—super filling, too."

"Sure. Thursday work for you? Looks like my day ends around six."

"That's perfect. I'll let you get back to work."

"Yeah, I've got a bunch of coaches coming in for a meeting in a minute." Emily lowered her voice. "Oh, and don't be afraid to let Adam suffer a little longer."

Man, if she only knew how long it had been, and how much he actually was suffering.

Rachel lined up all the medicines from shortest to tallest, then stood back to admire her organized closet.

Emily didn't need to know she'd seen a few pictures on Brad's Instagram of him at Tuscan Bistro. He *did* live in Freeport, but there were plenty of other restaurants there. Besides, this was nothing. Just a little nostalgia, like she'd told her sister.

Rachel opened her underwear drawer, pulled everything out, and started neatly refolding her underwear. When she found a pair of white lace panties she hadn't worn in years, she held onto them for an extra moment, rubbing her thumb over the lace.

Before she and Brad had gone to the winter formal during their senior year of high school, she'd gotten new lace underwear to wear under her dress. After the dance, they'd gone to his house and while his parents were asleep, they'd lain on the sofa and Brad had lifted her dress and kissed her over her underwear.

It was the most erotic thing she'd ever experienced up to that point. He'd teased her over those underwear until she thought she'd explode before finally sliding them to the side, giving her what she'd wanted. It had been almost impossible to hold in her moans so as not to wake up his parents.

Crumpling up her underwear, her nipples tingled. She

stuffed them all back into her drawer and slammed it shut. She stared at the drawer as if it were haunted, as if it might pop back open on its own, breathing as if she'd just come back from a run.

You can't even organize your damn underwear drawer.

She let out a deep sigh and headed downstairs to paint.

Rachel

Rachel slid on red flats and critiqued herself in the mirror. Her jeans were loose in the butt, and her sweater felt too tight around her neck.

Two weeks ago, she wouldn't have cared about what she was wearing. She would have changed out of her painting clothes and been happy with a fresh pair of leggings, leather converse, and an oversized flannel.

But two weeks ago, she wasn't constantly thinking about Brad, wondering if she was going to run into him every time she left the house.

Two weeks ago, her mind was full of things like the kids' schedules, when to call about having the gutters cleaned, expanding her painting business, and trying to hold her marriage together.

Two weeks ago, she was a different person. She wasn't daydreaming about the intimacy and all the memories she'd shared with Brad. But now, those thoughts were devouring her.

She peeled off the sweater and returned to her closet to

grab a fitted button down black shirt, which she tucked into her jeans.

Better.

Reaching in her shirt, she tightened up her bra straps and stood sideways, appraising her reflection.

She popped open another button and stepped out of the red flats, exchanging them for a pair of black peep-toe heels she'd gotten for one of Elsa's dance recitals a few years ago. A smile played at her lips as she admired the contrast of the baggy jeans paired with the heels and fitted shirt.

Perfume.

A few dabs of her favorite vanilla scent on her wrists and behind her ears, and she felt more together than she had in a long time.

Her hands were shaky, and her cheeks were hot. She felt exposed, like somehow everyone would know she'd dressed that way for someone other than her husband.

You're just having dinner with your sister. Besides, there's nothing wrong with someone inspiring you to put effort into your appearance.

Only the person inspiring her wasn't just someone. It was *Brad.*

She kissed the kids, then touched Adam on the arm to let him know she was leaving.

"We won't be late," she said, kissing the top of Adam's head.

"Where are you guys going again?" he asked, turning to look at her. He sounded annoyed as his eyes drifted up and down over her body. "Whoa. Heels, huh? What's the occasion?"

Cora nudged Rachel's leg with her wet nose and gazed up at her imploringly. Rachel bent to kiss her head and received a tail-wag of gratitude in return.

It had taken two years of begging Adam before he'd finally agreed to get a family dog. Rachel had been sure that when she and the kids had carried Cora's chunky, furry body through the door, Adam would fall for her immediately. That didn't happen, and now, years later, he still hadn't warmed up to the sweet pup.

"'You look great,' would be nice to hear," she told Adam, nudging his arm again. "And I told you, we're going to Tuscan. That place on Main Street in Freeport?"

"Right," he said, turning back to The Discovery Channel.

"Are you in a bad mood because I'm going out?" she whispered, bending close enough to ensure the kids wouldn't hear. "I literally *never* do anything like this." She peeked in the kitchen at Elsa and Benjamin. Elsa was setting up the blender to make a smoothie, and Benjamin was sitting at the island with a stack of cheese slices and a bag of pepperoni. They both had their AirPods in.

"I'm not in a bad mood." Adam replied, without looking at her.

Rachel straightened and scratched Cora's head before heading for the door. She stood in the middle of the living room, looking at everyone as she pet Cora.

"Listen, you two, try to get a balanced meal for dinner. There's leftover lasagna in the fridge, and try to have a vegetable."

"Okay," they mumbled in unison, not looking up at her.

Looks like the only one who needs you here is Cora.

The smell of pizza and a wood fire hit Rachel as soon as she opened the door to Tuscan Bistro, making her feel instantly hungry.

She was a bit wobbly in her heels, but she maintained her

posture and channeled her younger, high-heel-competent self as she clicked across the old wooden floor planks toward her sister. Emily was sitting at the bar drinking a seltzer with lime —her signature since she'd quit drinking.

The place was packed and buzzing. Rachel was glad she'd called to reserve a table. Glasses clinked and meat sizzled behind a long, black stone bar that led to a fully open kitchen. A man with a dark beard and glasses slung pizza dough at the end of the bar, as a fire blazed behind him.

Rachel took a deep breath.

You feel better already.

The restaurant was warm and welcoming, with tall black ceilings and oversized rattan chandeliers hanging low over tables, some of which had cozy olive green loveseats for seating instead of chairs.

Rachel was already envisioning a painting in tan, black, and olive green to complement the decor even before she let the hostess know she was there.

Emily looked stunning in a fuzzy mohair sweater that revealed just a touch of cleavage. Her leg muscles were showing through her leather leggings as she sat cross-legged, typing feverishly on her laptop. Reading glasses were propped on her forehead, and her diamond earrings sparkled.

Rachel strode toward her and reached out for a hug and saw a look of disappointment flash across her sister's face. Her heart sank.

"You look great as always, Rach. But, I was hoping to get a client call in before you got here," Emily said, slamming her laptop shut. She tucked it into her oversized gold tote without hugging her sister back and grabbed her drink. "Let's see if we can get a table with a sofa."

"Our table is ready," Rachel said, pointing to a table near the back of the restaurant where the hostess was waiting. "And I requested one with the sofas, of course!"

Emily was already weaving her way among the other diners, and Rachel practically had to run to catch up with her. "Of course you did," Emily sang, circling a finger in the air without turning around. "Rachel always thinks of everything."

Rachel slowed her pace and pressed her lips together. She could tell Emily wasn't as excited about their dinner as she was, which was the norm, but she'd hoped tonight would be different.

The hostess asked for their drink order as they sat down, and Rachel smiled. "I'll have a Diet Coke, please."

"Just get your Moscato or whatever sickly sweet wine you get," Emily said, looking at the menu. "Don't not drink just because of me. I can handle it."

"I'm not," Rachel said. "You know me, Diet Coke is my drink of choice." Ten years ago, Emily had fallen and was knocked unconscious after hitting the back of her head. She had been rushed to the hospital and needed twenty stitches.

When Rachel had gotten to the hospital early the next morning, the doctor explained they'd wanted to keep her overnight to monitor her for any other head injuries. "Her blood alcohol content was extremely high, and she was asking for you all night," he'd said.

Emily had grabbed her hand and whispered through gritted teeth, "I don't want to be like Mother. Please, don't let me be anything like her, and please don't leave," before falling back asleep. Rachel had seen signs of irresponsible drinking, but Emily would assure her she had it under control when Rachel would ask her about it. Emily hadn't touched alcohol since that night.

The truth was, Rachel really wanted wine, but she wasn't about to sip on alcohol in front of her sister.

"I'll have another seltzer with lime," Emily said, holding up her glass. "And *please,* don't bring *any* of that bread to the table." She pointed to a server who carried a cutting board topped with a crusty loaf to the table next to them.

Rachel loved how they served fresh-baked bread to everyone before dinner with whipped garlic and herb butter.

Emily paused, studying Rachel. "Unless you want some?"

"No, I'm all set," Rachel said, folding her hands on the table, spinning her new ring on her finger. She was the only one that knew Emily struggled with disordered-eating. Not having a few pieces of bread was a small sacrifice.

"I'm sorry, Emily. Was this place a terrible suggestion? With the bread and all."

"Nah." Emily batted the air with her hand. "I'm used to going to all different places since I meet some of my clients for coffee or lunch. It's just better if I don't have certain foods in front of me. Some days I can handle it, others, like today, not so much."

Emily's eyes flicked to the ring, and she arched an eyebrow.

"Oh. Adam got me this new ring for our anniversary."

"Yes, I see that. I'd have to be blind not to miss it. Pretty sure it's visible from space."

"Yeah, it's extravagant. He really surprised me." Rachel stretched out her hand, admiring how the diamond sparkled under the chandeliers.

Emily leaned toward her sister, her arms tucked under the table. "How is it that everything just works out for you?"

Emily shook her head, and Rachel recognized the biting tone in her sister's voice. Every once in a while, Emily would lash out at her and accuse her of having a perfect, peaceful life, as if it was her fault.

A few years ago, Elsa had overheard them arguing on the phone and had said afterward, "Mom, you know how sometimes I'm upset about something from school or a friend, and I take it out on you but I don't mean to?"

"Yeah," Rachel had said, blotting her eyes and blowing her nose.

"I think that's what Aunt Emily does to you sometimes. She's probably just upset about something else."

Rachel stared at Emily. "What's up? Why are you so short with me tonight?"

Emily's eyes didn't leave her menu. "Nothing is up. Work has been so busy. I'm having my kitchen redone and there's dust everywhere." She took the glasses off her head and folded them next to her. "I'm always rushing to meet a deadline. *I* don't have a partner to talk things out with."

"You have a pretty amazing life, Em. Being single isn't a flaw, you know." Rachel took a long sip of Diet Coke to keep from rolling her eyes. "I mean, you could probably buy several of these rings yourself, and you're in better shape than any twenty-year-old around."

Emily shook her head, and a laugh erupted from her mouth. "Ha! Here you are with two rocks in your hands. Two beautiful kids. You get to choose how you spend every day. You have a charmed life." She squeezed her lime into her seltzer water, then plopped the curled peel in her glass. "You were the favorite kid, and got handed everything. And you're *still* getting everything handed to you. So, don't sit here and tell me *I* have a charmed life."

Rachel took a deep breath. "I don't get *everything* handed to me. I work hard too. Emily. Adam is so busy with all his real estate offices, I can barely keep things straight at home." Rachel poked her own chest. "And don't forget, he cheated on me. And this anniversary was the *first* time he's ever planned anything." She pressed her thumb over her diamond and bit her bottom lip. "I deserve this ring."

"Well, it looks like you two have sorted things out." Emily slid her menu to her side, then looked at Rachel and crossed her arms. Her mouth had turned down at the corners, and her chest heaved.

"Emily, I was looking forward to this. If you don't want to have dinner with me, then you don't have to, but I want to see you more. You're my *only* sister."

Emily's eyes watered, but no tears fell.

"I rarely talk to Mom these days because of the way she treats you. What else do you want from me?" Rachel leaned forward, forcing Emily to make eye contact.

"Nothing. I didn't ask you to do any of those things. In fact, I've been asking you for *years* to stop trying to protect me. Decades." Emily picked up her seltzer and pulled a long sip.

"Then stop with the bitchy attitude," Rachel half joked, trying to lighten the mood.

Emily set her glass back down and poked at the lime peel with her straw.

Rachel watched Emily fiddle with her drink for a few moments before saying, "Your hair looks great, by the way. Even better than the picture you sent me." Rachel twirled her own straw around, watching the ice cubes tumble in her glass.

Be the bigger person here. She's right—you were always the favorite, for no good reason at all, and you have no idea what that must feel like to her.

Rachel had read somewhere that some kids of alcoholics were the peacemakers of the family. They usually were too afraid to express their feelings if it meant disrupting other people. *Is that what you do? Is that who you are?*

"I'm sorry, Rachel," Emily said at last, exhaling. "Just ... between work being so busy, and the holidays coming up ... *Not* my favorite time of year. I still struggle with binging sometimes...." She closed her eyes. "I've been off lately. I'm sorry."

Rachel caught Emily watching a server bring a tray of over-sized brownie sundaes to the table next to them.

"I'm sorry you're struggling, Emily. You know I'm alway—"

"It's fine," she said, shaking her head. "I don't want to talk about it. Let's just have a nice evening. Let's talk about you." She tilted her head to the side. "How are the Bradley thoughts going? Or is that all forgotten?"

Rachel sucked in her cheeks, trying to hold in a smile at the mention of his name. Her new ring was heavy on her finger, and the way she defended herself about deserving the ring, a ring she wasn't sure she wanted and was obviously a way for Adam to buy sex from her, made her heart sink.

"Adam and I are ... we're trying, but things are a little rough between us. Then seeing him ..." She raised her eyebrows. "Not the best combination. But I'll get on with my life, and he'll fade. Again."

"Are you sure you *want* him to fade?" Emily winked.

"Yes. I mean, we are both married." Rachel shook her head. "And I'm sure he's happily married to Beth. This is so juvenile. Silly, really, when I think about it."

Rachel realized Emily wasn't listening at all. Her chin pointed up, and she was looking over Rachel's head at something behind her.

Rachel recognized the expression: it was the same one she'd get before she'd sneak a sip of mother's wine or check Father's pockets for his package of cigarettes.

"What are you looking at?" Rachel turned her head to see, just as her sister yelped. Rachel's head whipped back around to see Emily's cup was on its side, seltzer and the lime peel spilling onto her lap.

Emily jolted out of her seat. "Hold that thought." She grabbed a napkin and wiped at her wet lap. "I really want to hear about this, but ... after I clean up. And I really should make that call. I don't want to lose her to a competitor. I'll be back in just a minute."

Emily was gone before Rachel could respond, and she turned to watch her march to the "restrooms" sign.

Rachel picked up Emily's glass and took a whiff, making sure there wasn't any alcohol in it. Whatever was going on with her sister, Rachel knew it was more than just being overwhelmed with work, she was going to remind her she was there for her. Emily could be as annoyed at her as she wanted.

Brad

"Let's go out for dinner tonight," Beth said as soon as Brad entered the front door. Her voice came from the living room, and he walked through the foyer to see her curled up on their oversized camel sofa.

It was already past six—he'd been staying after school on Thursdays to run the lower grades' math club. Jane, the fourth grade teacher who normally ran it, was out on maternity leave.

"That sounds like a great idea. I'm starving." Brad headed for the kitchen to wash his hands in the large copper sink. "You should see those kids whipping through those multiplication facts. One of the first graders knows his facts better than—"

"Why did you come through the front door? I heard you park your car in the garage."

"I wanted to check on the apple trees out front. We have quite a few apples this year." He threw his thumb toward the window.

"Hurry and get ready and tell me about your apples on the way." Beth stood in the doorway, holding her purse. "I'm starving too, and I've been *waiting* for you."

Brad shook his hands out and grabbed the black-and-white striped towel that hung over the sink. He was pretty sure it was new, and was positive it felt very expensive.

"Um ... give me a second to decompress, would you?" He looked over at his wife as she entered the kitchen and shook his head. "You must be hangry."

"I hate when you say that. And I hate when you work this late. I miss eating at a decent hour with my husband." Her words weren't unreasonable, but her snotty tone reminded Brad of a spoiled rich girl from a '90s movie.

Beth examined herself in the round, gold-framed mirror that hung on the wall next to the garage entrance door. She smoothed out her blond hair, which was parted down the middle with perfect, symmetric precision and curled neatly at the ends.

"You could have a snack, you know." Brad opened the sliding barn closet door and replaced the brown Chelsea boots he'd been wearing all day with a pair of black Nikes.

Beth rolled her eyes. "You should wear the boots! And you know I hate to cook. Plus, I'd rather go out." She was wearing a slim black turtleneck, tucked into fitted black jeans and black booties. It was the first time he'd seen her use the black shiny purse he'd gotten her last year for Christmas.

"Don't you miss those big fancy dinners we used to go to when you worked for Dad?" She pouted as she moved closer to him, sliding her hands underneath his jacket and around his waist.

"Well, the club is important to those kids, so it's important to me." He kissed the top of her head and hugged her back. "Not going out for nice dinners whenever we want to shouldn't change our relationship."

"When is the science club going to be done? How long is Jane going to be out?" Beth pulled away and started fiddling with the collar of his green button down.

"It's a math club. And I'm not sure. She might give it up to spend time with her baby."

"What? Uggh. You aren't going to step in for her, are you?"

He shrugged. "Honestly ... maybe? They are so into it, and it's fun to work with kids who are so stoked to learn."

"Well, I'm not pressuring you or anything, but you should know, Dad's offer from the other night still stands. If you were to go back, you'd more than triple your income." She batted her eyelashes at him.

Was she serious? "I'm not even going to dignify that with a response, Beth. We've discussed this." Brad rubbed at the back of his neck where a knot had suddenly formed. "I'm not quitting this job. I'm happy. I earn enough money."

She shook her head. "Aren't you worried about our future? I don't understand how you can turn down such a generous offer. I thought we wanted to travel, maybe buy a second home on the lake. My inheritance isn't coming for a long time and—"

"You know," Brad said, putting a thumb under her chin and gently tilting her head up, "*you* could start working again. When you quit your job, you said it was to find a new career. That was like five years ago. And besides, I was away from home a lot more when I worked for your father. If you want me around more, working for him isn't the answer." He let go of her chin, and his stomach grumbled.

Beth resumed her pout. "Well, at least then I knew all the hours you were putting in were going to lead to a better life. And I didn't need to work when you worked for Dad. None of my friends work, my mom's friends don't work. It's just ... what I'm used to."

He glowered at her, noticing she had said nothing about wanting him home more. Now he was the one feeling hangry.

"Okay, *okay*. I'm sorry, Brad. I won't bring it up again."

If you had a dime for every time she said that, we'd really be financially set.

Beth gave him a bright smile and said, "Let's go eat!" Then, she pushed past him and opened the side door to the garage.

He retrieved his keys from the table by the front door, then paused to look at the wallet-sized wedding picture that hung on the side of the fridge with a magnet as he passed through the kitchen. It was faded and bent on one side.

It had been a beautiful day. He'd just started working for Beth's father, and they were about to spend their honeymoon in the Maldives, daydreaming about their future. He'd been on board with the white collar corporate job that paid big bonuses. But the things he'd wanted then, or thought he wanted, just didn't hold the same appeal for him now.

Brad climbed in the car and combed his new scruff. "Where do you want to go?"

"Tuscan Bistro! It's close and always good."

"It is. And we haven't been there for a while."

"Round Here" by The Counting Crows hummed through the speakers when Brad started the car. He and Rachel had gone to see them in concert the summer after they graduated high school. They'd stood in the open field, listening to this song, and she'd slid her fingers in his. Brad ran his thumb along the underside of his fingers at the memory.

Since he'd run into her last weekend, there were signs of her everywhere: a new student in his class named Rachel. The scent of vanilla in the coffee shop this morning before work. The woman in front of him at the grocery store who'd reached into the cooler at the checkout to grab a Diet Coke and said, "My afternoon pick-me-up."

He blinked hard, trying to snap out of his daydreams and focus on his wife and the bag he'd found. "So, I've been thinking ..." Brad reached over and put his hand on Beth's wrist. "Are you ready to talk about it now? "

"About what?" Beth freed her wrist to smooth out her hair.

He waited a beat to see if she'd come around on her own. When she gave him a blank look, he said, "About the bag I saw. I don't think you're being honest with me." He tapped her arm with his hand. "Talk to me."

Beth moved closer to her door, so she was out of his hand's reach. "I don't know what you're talking about. I told you the truth. My friend Jen wanted to borrow it, and I didn't want her to ruin it. She's so—"

"Whoa." Brad gripped the steering wheel tighter. "You told me it was to keep your face oils from ruining it or something. Now, you are saying someone wanted to borrow it?" He took a deep breath. "Beth."

She sliced her hand through the air. "Same thing. I mean ... that's what I meant."

"You told me once that foil would block theft detectors, remember? That time you said you stole something in college. I found a foil lined bag stuffed in the bottom of your drawer. I'm not an idiot, Beth. What's going on?" He shot her a quick look as he drove down the road.

When she didn't respond and turned her entire body to look out the window, he said, "We're going to talk about this. If not now, later."

Beth slid even closer to her door, gripping the armrest.

When they got to Tuscan Bistro, the hostess told them it would be a forty-five minute wait. "You're welcome to eat at the bar, though," she said.

Beth groaned. "I *hate* sitting at the bar. It's uncomfortable and reeks of stale beer. If I'd known you were going to be so late, I would have made reservations so we could have a table with the sofas," she said behind clenched teeth. She tapped her clutch impatiently against her hip, scanning the dining room as if she'd find an available table the hostess had missed.

"Well, we can wait for a table, or we can eat now," Brad whispered. "I think we should take the seats at the bar."

Two other couples filed in, and the hostess gave Brad and Beth an impatient look. "Bar seats are great," Brad told her. "Thank you." He put his hand on the small of Beth's back, leading her to walk in front of him. "It'll be fine. The food here makes up for it."

Beth climbed onto one of the bar stools, rested her head in her hand, and stared at the television.

The aroma from the brick oven made Brad's mouth water, and he suddenly craved pizza with goat cheese—something he'd always avoided when he was with Beth because she didn't like the smell. The menu had a pizza with shaved beets, caramelized onions, and goat cheese, which sounded amazing.

Brad took a sip of the Allagash White beer the bartender placed in front of him—his regular treat every time he ate here.

Letting out a big, "Ahh," he leaned back in his seat to enjoy the football game on the television that was mounted on the shiplap wall in front of him. He was determined to enjoy his dinner regardless of where they sat.

Beth let out a deep sigh. "So, how was the rest of your day?"

Brad turned to look at his wife, wanting to say it was great until he came home. As soon as he'd walked in the door, she'd wanted to leave. She'd brought up her dad's offer, didn't want to talk about the foil-lined bag, and was being picky about where they sat for a dinner she *had* to have.

Brad shrugged his shoulders. "School was excellent. I'm doing a lesson on abscission, which the kids love. I just want to enjoy our dinner, Beth."

"Listen, I'm sorry." Beth reached out, putting her hand on

his knee. "Let's start the night over. I'm in the mood to splurge since I've been living on greens lately. We are getting carbonara and mussels, right?"

"Sounds great." He could get the pizza another time. Brad leaned closer to his wife. "I accept your apology, Beth, but I'm frustrated. You've been making digs about my job and our life way too much. At first I understood. Figured you were letting off steam. But not a day goes by that you don't say *something*."

Beth lowered her gaze and fiddled with a coaster on the bar.

"I need you to be supportive of me. And we hardly spend any time together unless it's on your terms. It doesn't feel like a partnership." He took another sip of his beer. Cheers erupted from the television as the Patriots got into position to score, and Brad resisted turning to look. He could practically predict what Beth was going to say, and he didn't know if he could stomach it.

"I guess I'm just frustrated, too. It feels like you're drifting away from me. You've just ... changed so much." Her elbows were on the bar, and she rested her head in her hands.

They'd started having this conversation a year into his teaching career. Beth had admitted she'd thought he'd teach for a while, get bored, then go back to work for her father. After he'd confided that working for her dad made him more miserable than he ever thought possible, she'd been better about it. But lately she'd become more persistent.

He wondered if Rachel was status-obsessed. She certainly wasn't when they were together.

Is this what marriage is supposed to be like?

"I *have* changed, Beth. I want a simpler life, and I'm tired of repeating myself. And I don't want to drift apart. But blowing me off when we have plans, like you did the other day, isn't helping." He half smiled and lowered his voice. "I know the bag I found is a sensitive subject. And when you quit working, yes, I was making more than enough money for the both of us. You were very clear from the beginning that you didn't want kids. And I'm fine with that. Teaching is so fulfilling to me. And I want you to experience a career like that too. Especially if you want more material things." He leaned back, sliding his napkin back and forth on the bar. "I think working might make you happier."

Brad put his hand on hers. "We're supposed to be a team and cheer each other on." His other hand went to his heart. "I want you to be happy, Beth. It doesn't seem like you are."

Beth nodded, her parted lips closing into a straight line. "You're right. I'll get a job." She gazed down at his thumb moving over her fingers.

Brad smiled and squeezed her hand. "I really think it will make a difference. And I know your dad offered you a job in the accounting department at the firm, but it doesn't have to be there. What's something you'd really love to do?"

Beth shrugged and picked at the label on his beer bottle.

"You'd make a great personal shopper, I think."

After a few silent moments, Brad stood up. "I'm going to use the bathroom. That beer went right through me."

When he reached the bathroom, he let out a long sigh. He felt like a heavy blanket of exhaustion was weighing him down. He was glad Beth had agreed to look for a job, but she still refused to address the bag he found.

He stood at the sink, washing his hands, wondering if he was accusing Beth of something she didn't do. *Was there some other legitimate reason to line a designer bag with aluminum foil?*

As he pulled a paper towel from the machine to dry his hands, Brad saw a figure standing behind him in the mirror and nearly jumped out of his skin. Emily, Rachel's sister, was standing in the doorway, staring at him.

Her hair was now a shade of red, though even if he'd

hadn't recently seen her on Rachel's Instagram page, he still would have recognized her instantly. Emily had striking almond-shaped, green eyes and wore the same raspberry shade of lipstick she'd worn when they were younger.

"Emily! You scared the shit out of me." He placed a damp hand on his chest and felt his heart thumping through his shirt. "What are you doing?"

Emily smiled. "I *thought* that was you walking to the bathroom." She pushed herself off of the door frame. "I'm having dinner with Rachel. As you probably know." Emily took a step toward him, looking him up and down.

Is she drunk?

"Huh? I ... Rachel is here? If she is, I had no idea. Why would I know that? And what's this all about? Do you always follow men into bathrooms?"

Emily glided toward him, and Brad squinted his eyes at her. "What are you doing?"

"Don't worry, Brad." Emily laughed as she took another step closer and ran her hand down his chest.

Brad slid across the counter so he wasn't directly across from her.

"Oh, *relax.* I won't try to shove my hand down your pants again." She glanced down at his crotch, then back up at his face. "Unless you want me to."

Brad shook his head. "Go enjoy your dinner with Rachel."

He turned to leave the bathroom, and Emily stepped in front of him. She was blocking the door, her hands on her hips, clearly intending not to let him pass.

"Hey, you still have all your hair. Good for you." Emily tried to run a hand over his head, but he flinched out of her reach.

She laughed. "Heard you and Rachel ran into each other the other day. I remember how in love you were with my sister."

Brad prayed someone would walk in on them and break up whatever stunt Emily was trying to pull. Didn't any man out there need to use the restroom? "Emily, I don't know what you think you're—"

"How did it feel to see her again?" Tilting her head to the side, she continued, "Any regrets?" Emily reached out, hooked her finger in his belt loop and tugged on it, trying to pull him closer. Brad intended to step backward, but there was a slick spot on the floor and he stumbled forward instead, into Emily.

He'd had enough. Brad pushed himself off of her, ignoring that she was pawing awkwardly at him even as he moved past her.

He straightened his pants as he left the bathroom. Had Emily really not changed in the last twenty years?

You need to get out of here and away from Emily before she causes a scene.

Brad took long strides to get to Beth while quickly scanning the restaurant for Rachel. He spotted her golden-brown waves toward the back of the restaurant, wishing he could see her face.

When he reached Beth, he took her hand. "I'm sorry. I'm not feeling well. Can we get out of here? *Now.*"

Rachel

Rachel wondered if the couple at the table in front of her were celebrating some kind of anniversary.

The man stood, holding out a long black tweed coat, his eyes crinkling with evidence of decades of joy as he smiled at the woman easing her arms into it.

She moved slower than she probably had in her youth, but she was sure to turn up the big fur collar so it fluffed up luxuriously around her neck. Her posture was impeccable as she reached over to straighten the man's blue and cream pocket square poking out of his navy blue blazer. Rachel guessed they were probably in their seventies.

Red shiny shoes with about a half inch heel tapped on the floor as she hooked her arm in his, and they strolled toward the door without a break in their conversation.

You and Adam haven't looked at each other like that since ... you can't even remember the last time.

How long had this couple been together? Had they had their difficulties, too? Had he ever pressured her to be intimate when she didn't want to? Had he stopped seeing her around their ten-year anniversary?

It certainly didn't seem like it.

Out of her peripheral vision, Rachel caught two people practically running out of the restaurant. She turned to get a better look and felt a sudden tinge of nervousness. Then it hit her: she was looking at Brad's sandy, tousled hair.

He was wearing the same jacket from the other day, when she'd seen him at the café, and her palms started to sweat.

When she recognized Beth trailing behind him, her mouth dropped open, and she pressed her back against her seat. Brad was tugging her along by the hand as she half-jogged to keep up. His head was down, and he was saying something to Beth. Her sleek blond hair whipped back and forth as she turned her head from side to side as if looking for something.

Rachel felt a breeze, followed by Emily dropping into the seat across from her, which made her jump. Emily's cheeks flushed, and her eyes looked like they were about to spill over with tears. Beth and Brad disappeared around the corner.

"What? Why is your mouth hanging open like that, Rachel? You looked like a guppy." Emily straightened her sweater.

Rachel blinked. "I just ... I'm pretty sure I just saw Brad and Beth run out of here like someone was chasing them."

Rachel studied the restaurant to see if there was any other commotion—a fire? A roach?—but everyone seemed to enjoy their dinner and drinks. The bartenders and servers were calm, going about their business as usual.

When Emily didn't respond, Rachel stared hard at her sister, who was fidgeting with her hair.

"Did you hear what I just said? Brad and Beth were here."

Emily looked around the restaurant.

"No, I mean, they just left. They were basically running out the door."

Emily shrugged. "Strange."

"I don't think he saw me." She took a long sip of soda,

then reached for the straw wrapper and tied it in a knot. "Maybe he did. I don't know. Did you see him?"

"Nope." Emily was balling and unballing her cloth napkin. "Are you ready to order?"

"Seriously, what's wrong with you? Why are you so distracted?"

"I'm not distracted." The server approached their table. "You order first," Emily said.

Rachel looked from Emily to the server and smiled. "Okay ... I'll have ... I'll have the giant meatball and a side of roasted root vegetables, please." She handed her menu to the server as Emily scanned hers. "Emily," she whispered after a few beats.

"Oh, sorry. I'll get the ... I'll have the Autumn Harvest Salad. Dressing on the side." A tight smile crossed her lips, and the server picked up her menu from the table.

"Can I start you off with an appetizer? Maybe our famous truffle fries?"

Rachel cringed. Emily told her once that sometimes she went to McDonald's and would order three large orders of fries and eat them all. Another trigger for her sister, for sure.

"No! We are good, thanks. Just our meals and no dessert, either." Rachel smiled, hoping she didn't sound rude.

"Great. I'll put this in and get you another Diet Coke." She tucked the menus into her apron and grabbed Rachel's empty glass.

"Thank you so much. We really appreciate it."

Emily pulled out her raspberry colored lipstick from her purse and blotted her lips. "What, are you the food police now?"

"I just know that stuff is a trigger for you."

"Even though I still have the occasional slip up, I don't need you to protect me from food, too. I can speak up for myself." She rubbed the back of her arm where Mother used to pinch her.

"I only want to help, Emily."

Emily tilted her head to the side. "So ... you saw Brad?"

"Yes, I did." Rachel touched her cheeks and took in a breath. "At least I think I did? It was so strange—he and Beth ran out of here. Are you sure you didn't see him? He still has the same—"

" Rachel! Yes, I'm sure. I didn't see him or Beth." She leaned in toward Rachel. "And I *lost* that client. I was ten minutes too late. She'd signed with someone else."

Rachel studied her sister's feverish face. Had she been drinking in the bathroom? Had she just lost the client who was supposed to cover her kitchen renovation?

"I'm sorry, Em. Do you want to talk abou—"

"Stop projecting, Rachel. You're the one who has stuff to talk about." Emily raised an eyebrow at her sister. "Maybe Brad ran out of here because they saw you?"

"I hope not. It's not like I approached them or anything. He didn't even see me." Rachel inspected her nails. *Or maybe he did. Maybe that's why they left.*

"Yeah, if they saw you, I'm sure that would have been really awkward. Especially for Beth. You remember how she was." Emily's neck was still blotchy and red. "I wonder if he told Beth you saw each other last week."

Rachel raised her eyebrows. *Would that be enough of a reason to leave?*

"Tell me again why you still haven't gotten revenge? It would be so ... *easy* for you. Haven't you even thought about it? Pictured yourself with anyone else? With Brad?"

"It wouldn't solve anything if I fucked someone else. Besides, if I did, it'd be just as bad as what Adam, and whoever he was fucking, did to me." Rachel eyed the door, lifting her head up when a couple walked in. *Not them.* Not that she expected them to come back.

Emily cupped her hands over her mouth in a pretend gasp. "Oh my God, Rachel said, 'fucked.'"

"Hilarious. You know, I do swear." Rachel held her hands up in surrender. "And, fine, I *occasionally* think about my ex-boyfriend. I may have pictured ... a few things." Her cheeks flooded with heat.

Emily smirked, a hardness in her expression. "Oh please. We both know you're going to go home to your husband, have missionary-style sex once every other Tuesday, and make scratch-dinners for your family, and cookies for the bake sale."

"Oh, you're funny, Emily."

Once, every other Tuesday is a lot.

"Maybe if you're feeling extra spicy, you'll start running a different route or you'll buy new sheets that aren't organic cotton." Emily's tone had taken on a nasty edge.

Rachel was trying to play along with this banter match, but she'd had enough.

"You know, Emily, I was looking forward to tonight. I thought I could confide in you. One minute you're encouraging me to cheat on my husband, and the next you're mocking me. I just don't get why."

Emily knit her eyebrows together. "Why? Because it seems like you're only telling me all this because I'm the fuck-up sister who won't judge you because I've done worse. We both know whatever happens, you'll be fine whether or not you confide in me."

Rachel crossed her arms. "Um, who's projecting now? And what is that supposed to mean? I've *never* said that, Emily. And I want to talk to you about it because you're my *sister*. And I thought you'd understand since you seem to hate Adam so much and were there for me when Brad broke up with me."

Emily rolled her eyes. "Oh please, you'll live if we aren't besties. You always get what you want. Mom and Dad paid your way through college. Meanwhile, I went to community college and paid for it myself. You're Mom's prized possession."

Anger bubbled in Rachel's chest. "Why are you bringing up Mom and Dad? What does this have to do with me seeing Brad run out of here with his wife?"

It's like you aren't even the same person you were on the phone the other day.

Emily lifted her hands, then slapped them back on her lap. "Because. I'm reminding you everything works out for you. It always has. Seeing Brad isn't the problem you are making it out to be. And you certainly don't need to act like you *need* me in this situation. Adam cheated, big deal. He came running back, and now you're dripping with diamonds, living in your perfect house with your perfect family."

Rachel forced down a dry swallow. "Are you kidding me? I'm not exempt from having problems in my life, Emily."

The server approached the table with their meals. "I'm so sorry to do this," Rachel said, putting her hand on the server's arm. "Something came up, and we need to get this to go as soon as you get a chance. I'm so sorry for the hassle." She slid over her credit card.

"Oh. Um, sure, no problem," the young woman answered, taking the card and giving Emily a nervous glance before hurrying away.

Emily got up and clutched her purse with both hands. "I'm just going to go. Give my meal to Adam or something. I have those boots for Elsa and a pair of Nikes for Benny in the car, but I'll get them to you later."

"Yes, why don't you go home and get some rest. You obviously don't want to be here, and I will not force you to spend time with me." Her voice sounded much calmer than she felt inside.

Emily's eyes were wet, and a tear spilled down her cheek as she turned and stomped out of the restaurant.

Rachel's temples pulsed as she wondered what the hell had just happened.

As she waited for the bill and food to come, she rested her head in her hands, hoping her sister wasn't headed to a fast-food restaurant or gas station to binge.

When you bite your tongue, she walks all over you. When you speak up, you're afraid she's going to do something destructive and it will be your fault.

Rachel's pen ripped through the paper and she signed the receipt, wondering how this night had turned into such a shitshow.

Brad

"What the fuck was that all about? Why are you acting like a lunatic?" Beth belted out as soon as they got in the car. Brad sat looking straight ahead, his hands gripping the steering wheel as he tried to get control of his breathing.

Getting assaulted by Emily while he was in the bathroom was disturbing, and he wondered if he should tell Beth.

But then he'd have to explain their history and the incident that happened when they were younger and he was dating Rachel.

Not tonight.

He'd only seen Rachel for a second. At least he was pretty sure that was her. All he could make out was her hair as she sat at the table alone, but that tiny glimpse made his heart swell as he started the car. "I'm sorry, Beth. My stomach turned. I had to get out of there."

It was dark now, and most of the shops were closed. He pulled out of the parking lot, then slammed on his brakes when a couple stepped in front of the car to cross the road.

"Do you mean you're going to get sick or something?" She

pressed herself against her door, getting as far away from him as possible.

After what happened with Emily in the bathroom, he'd gotten so worked up thinking she was going to burst out from behind him and make more of a scene in the restaurant, he'd felt the only thing he could do was get out of there.

And now Beth was screaming at him, and he didn't have an explanation for her. It's not like he could tell her that his ex-girlfriend's bat-shit sister had accosted him in the men's room. "I'll be fine. It just hit me suddenly. Thanks for the concern."

He felt Beth's eyes studying him, but she said nothing else for the rest of the ride home. He did his best to look as queasy as possible, which wasn't hard.

As they pulled into the driveway, Beth said, "We need to get this damn driveway sealed before winter. Have you called the guy yet?"

Shit, he'd meant to do that last week. He'd also forgotten to call to have their oil tank filled up too, like he said he would.

"Yeah, they're booked out for a while," he lied.

Beth got out of the car, slammed her door, and stormed inside, leaving the side door open. Brad sank further into his seat as the night's tension drained from his body.

He knew Beth was caught off guard, but he'd told her he didn't feel well, which ... wasn't a lie after seeing Emily. *Couldn't she at least try to act concerned instead of always thinking of herself?*

When he'd gotten sick in college with bronchitis, Rachel hadn't left his side. She didn't even care about missing the sorority formal that she'd put so much work into planning. He'd begged her to go, but she said there was no way she was leaving him when he was sick.

Later, when he'd told Rachel he wanted to see other people, the look on her face had knocked the wind out of him. He'd denied Beth once, but she persisted, and it wasn't long before his curiosity about her turned into something more. It was only fair to end things with Rachel. He'd thought settling down with his high school sweetheart at such a young age would be a mistake. His friends had all confirmed it was completely normal to want to experience other people. They'd even ragged on him about how he'd only been with Rachel, how he was "whipped."

It was *still* hard for him to think about the hurt in Rachel's eyes and how her chin had quivered when she'd told him she'd always love him.

How could you have treated her that way? She deserved an apology twenty years ago.

He'd expected her to bang on his chest or yell at him. Maybe he'd even wanted her to fight a little harder. But she was classic Rachel; completely selfless. Even though it was clear she was crushed, she wanted him to be happy. She had just ... let him go.

She still showed up in his dreams occasionally, but seeing her, not once but twice, in a matter of weeks, and not getting a chance to apologize for his behavior all those years ago, chewed away at him.

He sat in the garage with the car running and stared into his dark house, his legs heavy. Beth appeared in the doorway and watched him for a few seconds before throwing up her hands. "Hello! What are you doing?"

"I'm going to get some antacids for my stomach. I'll be right back."

"Why are you acting like this? Come in and eat. I'm starving and I'm not waiting for you!" She peeled off her coat and dropped her purse on the floor as she stood in the doorway.

Brad started backing out of the driveway, then stopped the car. "You know, Beth, *you* could call about the driveway."

He watched his wife's eyes grow big as she took a step

back, looking at him like he'd slapped her across the face before slamming the door.

Sitting in his car in the Tuscan Bistro parking lot, Brad realized he didn't have a plan. *What the hell are you going to do? Go in there and join Emily and Rachel for dinner?*

He took a deep breath. The beer he'd drunk hours before felt sour in his empty stomach. The thought of leaving again without getting to talk to Rachel made him feel even worse. He just wanted to apologize to her.

What if you never run into her again? What if you never get another chance?

Even if Emily had said something to Rachel about their interaction in the bathroom, Brad hadn't been the one acting crazy in the men's room. He never called women crazy out loud, but damn, Emily seemed to be actually *crazy*. He picked up the pace, his need to get to Rachel building.

As he crossed the parking lot toward the front door, Rachel exited the restaurant, two to-go boxes in her hands, and turned to walk in the opposite direction.

"Rachel! Rach." She didn't seem to hear him, and he jogged to catch up, calling her name again.

Rachel turned. Her mouth was half open, and she started laughing. "You scared me!" She clutched a few to-go boxes to her chest.

Brad caught up to her, then took a step back, trying to hide that he was gasping for air.

"I thought that was you." He took in a breath. "I just wanted to say hi. Again."

"Hi Brad. It's nice to see you. Again. I thought I saw you earlier ..." Rachel pointed at the restaurant door. "Running out of here with Beth?" Her eyebrows knit together, and she let out an incredulous laugh, as if her night had been as weird as his had.

Brad's hand went to his stomach. "Um, yeah. That was us. We left. I wasn't feeling well. I came back out to run to the pharmacy to get some antacids," he said, pointing at the Walgreens across the street.

"But you aren't getting antacids. You're here."

The tips of his ears burned. "I am. Yes. I saw you ... I wanted to ..." He opened his mouth to ask if he could hug her, then stopped himself.

"What is it? You were going to say something else." Rachel crossed one leg in front of the other and slipped a hand into her back pocket, almost fumbling the boxes. He'd obviously caught her off guard, and her awkward anxiety was not only incredibly sexy to him, it also put him at ease.

She was wearing the same style Levis she had worn in high school, only she looked even better in them now. Brad noticed red toenails peeking out of her heels.

"I just ..." He'd imagined this conversation a thousand times, but right now, he had no idea what was going to come out of his mouth. "Rachel ..." He put a hand over his lips, then dropped it to his side. "I wanted to tell you ... I'm sorry about what happened in college. That day I left you standing in front of the dining hall, I never should have—"

"Oh, that," Rachel said, waving her hand as if to shoo away their entire history. "That was silly, silly young love. We were kids, Brad. I don't even think about it anymore," she said, making his heart sink.

Rachel cleared her throat, and Brad saw the color rise in her cheeks, even under the dim glow of the parking lot lights, wondering if she was being completely honest.

"You deserved better than the way I treated you. You were nothing but wonderful."

"That's nice to hear." They locked eyes for a few seconds

before she added, "But I've been married for sixteen … no, seventeen years. It all worked out." Rachel turned slowly and started back down the sidewalk, holding Brad's gaze, so he followed. She slid her hair back over her shoulder as she walked. "I take it you're well?"

"Yes, things are … things are good."

"I'm so happy you're a teacher. I know I said this last week, but you were so passionate about it when we were together. Nice to see you followed your dream."

A whiff of vanilla floated up Brad's nose, and he wanted to stop her right in the middle of the sidewalk and tell her how much he'd been thinking of her since last weekend. She had a magical way of relaxing him. It was familiar and novel, all at once.

Rachel smiled and stopped walking. "Well, here's my car. I should get home." The apprehension he'd felt the other day while saying goodbye to her took him down again.

"Oh. Okay … Um, yeah. It's chilly tonight. Fall is here! Your favorite. Will you drive with the windows cracked?"

Rachel stood by her car, clutching the handle without opening it, the to-go boxes still pressed awkwardly against her chest. "You remember that?"

"Well, how could I forget? You were always so … happy. Cracking the windows … lighting your fall candles. Your joy was so cute and contagious." Brad smiled. The urge to touch her, smell her hair, was overwhelming.

Rachel shook her head. "And all that stuff never bothered you." It was a statement, not a question.

"No. It was one of the things I loved about you. You noticed, and took pleasure in, the little things. You always had such a positive, optimist way of seeing things. I've never forgotten you, Rachel."

Rachel's cheeks flushed as she sat in her car. She set the to-go boxes and her purse down in the passenger seat and gripped the steering wheel. A large diamond on her right hand caught the light of a street lamp.

From her husband?

"Sorry. I ... Actually, I'm not sorry. It's true. But I *am* sorry about what happened between us. About how I handled things. I was young—"

"I already told you, no apologies. Things have a way of working out." Rachel's mouth was in a straight line, and her eyes looked sad.

"I'm really glad I saw you again, Rachel." His heart was thumping, and his mouth was suddenly too dry.

"Me too," she said, looking up at him.

"Could I ... is a hug okay?" Brad shrugged his shoulders and held out his arms.

"Sure," she said casually, but when she stood up and embraced him, he felt her clutch the sides of his jacket and then wrap her arms around him tighter.

He wanted to nuzzle into her neck, smell her hair, ask her if she was really happy, if she ever thought about him.

When he stepped in a little closer, he felt Rachel's body lean into his. She felt the same, yet so new.

Okay, you've said your piece. Now you can stop thinking about this; about her.

"I have to go," Rachel said, pulling away.

It took him a moment to realize he was hanging onto her arms as she turned to get back into her car.

He watched her drive away, knowing there was no way he was going to stop thinking about her. That apology wasn't going to be enough.

Rachel

R achel rubbed the outside of her cheek, trying to unclench her jaw. The street lights stung her eyes, and she squinted, causing everything to blur. The more she tried to control her breathing, the harder it was to catch her breath.

Why haven't the last two decades been enough for you to move on from this? How can seeing him do this to you? You've had an entire life without him.

As soon as she'd put her arms around Brad, her knees had gone wobbly, and she'd had to grab handfuls of his jacket to steady herself. All the feelings for him she'd thought had faded resurfaced in an instant, and it was hard to let go of him. Her body reacted the same way it used to—Brad always made her feel secure and beautiful, and she couldn't deny how badly she'd wanted to kiss him.

But he'd shocked and hurt her deeply. Every time she drove past Bowdoin College, she still felt a slight stab, remembering how he'd ended their relationship—their four year long love affair—in front of the dining hall on campus. She'd hibernated for two weeks after that, in disbelief that he'd left her so suddenly, so callously.

And yet, if he'd tried to kiss her, she wasn't sure she would have stopped him. *And if you didn't stop him, you'd be doing exactly what Adam did.*

There was no way she'd call Emily after their shitty dinner.

You need to talk to Aimee. She's rational, and she won't judge you.

Rachel tapped on her touch screen, hitting Aimee's name. They'd been through so much together, and talking things out with her always made Rachel look at things with a fresh perspective. Even though her best friend lived in Massachusetts, their bond was as close as it was when they lived together in college.

"Hello there." Aimee answered on the first ring, and Rachel heard her husband, Matt, yelling in the background, "Rach! What up?"

Rachel laughed, picturing Matt yelling into the phone. "Hey! Tell him I said hello." Rachel drew in a breath. "Do you have the emotional capacity to listen to some major verbal diarrhea?" Her voice cracked, and she reached for a tissue in the glove box.

"Oh Rach, of course. Hang on. Matt is watching the game, and I can't hear myself think." Matt's yelling faded, and a door closed.

"Yes, I'm sure Adam is watching the game too, and we all know it's exciting!" Rachel said, rolling her eyes.

"That man. He's in rare form tonight. The Celtics are on a roll, and he's possessed," Aimee snorted. "Okay, I'm in the bathroom. What's up?"

"Well, first, how are you two?"

"Rachel. Don't deflect. I know that tone. Talk to me?"

Rachel was steering her car aimlessly through downtown Brunswick. She pulled into a parking space so she could talk.

"Promise you won't judge me," Rachel said, putting the car in park and then cracking her window. The leaves rustled in the wind outside and a few spun and landed on her windshield.

"Please. You know who you're talking to. Out with it already, Rachel."

"I saw Brad Turner. *Twice.* We ran into each other at lunch that day I texted you, and I just saw him again. I haven't been able to stop thinking about him. Adam and I are struggling. I went out to dinner tonight with Emily, and when I was leaving Brad was there, outside the restaurant. He came running toward me on the sidewalk. He was there earlier with Beth—I saw him leave, like saw him run out in a hurry. But then, as I was leaving, he was there again. Without her." Rachel gasped for a breath, feeling like she'd run a sprint.

"Okay ... so, you're thinking about him. I think that's normal. You two were together for four years, and you thought you were going to marry him." Aimee's voice was steady. "You haven't seen him since college, right?"

"Right. I feel like it's more than just thinking about him, though. Like tonight, seeing him made me feel ..." Rachel put her hand over her heart. "I've just never loved someone the way I loved him. If he'd kissed me tonight, I don't think I could have stopped him." Picturing herself kissing Brad made her feel teenage-butterflies dance in her belly, and filled her with guilt.

"Did you *feel* like he was going to kiss you?" Aimee asked.

"No. I don't think so. He's still married to Beth. Happily, I think ... I don't know." Rachel stared at her dashboard, unseeing. "He apologized for what happened between us in college, seemed like he felt so guilty about it. He said he thought about it—thought about *me*—a lot."

Rachel paused and Aimee, ever the wise friend, gave her space to sort out her thoughts.

Why would he come back to the restaurant? Was it just to see you? Just to apologize? Why didn't you ask him?

"I feel like a horrible person."

"Well, we both know you aren't, so stop that. And you did nothing wrong. You *deserved* that apology." Aimee snickered. "Unless there's a juicy tid-bit you're leaving out?"

"No ... I hate the angst ... the longing. I'm *not* supposed to feel this way." She hit the steering wheel with her palm. "It's been twenty years!"

"You know I was kidding, Rachel." Aimee sighed. "You're the most loyal person I know." Aimee had told her a few times she wouldn't be able to stay with someone who'd cheated.

"Adam and I barely have sex. And we're fighting more than ever. I just can't get there with him anymore—there's a part of me that doesn't even feel like trying." A tear slid down her cheek, and she dabbed under her eyes with a tissue. "Sometimes ... I feel trapped." She blew her nose and dropped the tissue in the passenger seat, then reached for another one. Her admission hung in the air. She felt better. And worse.

"This is tough, Rachel. Adam cheated, and I know you've been unhappy for a while. Things don't seem to be getting better like you'd hoped."

Rachel let out a loud sob. "It's so stupid. I've only run into him a couple of times. It's not as if I'm being forced to make a lifelong decision or anything." Rachel balled the tissue in her fist and tilted her head back, staring at the car ceiling. "I could handle the fact that my marriage wasn't great before. But now ... I'm so torn up. Is this what marriage is supposed to be like?"

"Listen, I'm sure Brad is shining a brighter light on your troubled marriage. I still haven't quite forgiven him for what he did. But he was a great guy, and you two were madly in love. I think everything you're feeling is ... normal."

Aimee once told Rachel that she and Matt never went

more than a week without having sex. "I'm still so hot for him," she'd said. "Even after fifteen years of marriage!"

They hadn't been able to have children, and Rachel's kids called them Aunt Aimee and Uncle Matt. Maybe being childless had something to do with their steamy sex life, but Rachel thought about it a lot and wondered what life would be like if she were still hot for Adam.

"As far as what marriage is *supposed* to be like, I'm not an expert. But, even when Matt and I fight, there's no doubt in my mind about us. No question."

"What you and Matt have is rare," she said. "And he's amazing. I'll never forget how he booked us that weekend away at the Equinox Spa after I found out about Adam's affair." Adam had blown out her candles the morning she'd told him she was going away with Aimee for the weekend, complaining that he didn't want to smell like an apple cobbler when he got to work.

"Yeah, there's not a day that goes by that I don't think about that." Aimee's voice lowered. "So, what can I do? How can I support you through this?"

"Just listen I guess. This is so … juvenile." Rachel twirled a strand of hair around her finger. "I got dressed for dinner tonight hoping I'd see him … it's so … dumb."

Her heart sped up, thinking about the possibility of running into Brad again. "My emotions are all over the place. I mean, how did my marriage come to this? I think I still love Adam, but if I'm being totally honest with myself, it's really the kids that are keeping us together."

Rachel closed her eyes and thought about Elsa coming home in her soccer uniform, and Benny drinking from the faucet earlier this afternoon before he stopped and told her that her hair looked pretty.

How can you live your life without these moments every single day?

"You're answering your own questions, Rachel. Sometimes it takes time for our hearts to catch up to our heads, but what do you mean, *you* let this happen? There are two of you in that marriage, and he fucking cheated." Aimee paused. "And just to be clear, I've watched you try with that man ever since, and he's *still* an entitled dick. Has he changed at all?"

Rachel stared into the restaurant window in front of her. The bar was full of people talking and eating under the fluorescent lights.

"No. Not really. After the affair, Adam told me it had just happened, and that we would work on things. But, I'm realizing things don't *just happen* in a marriage. Two people *let* them happen. It's obvious things have changed between us, and I don't know how to stop it. Or if I have the energy to."

Rachel anxiously twirled her hair faster. Saying that out loud was scary, but also a relief, like when you've run up a steep hill and you finally get to make your way down.

A couple strolled in front of Rachel's car. Their heads were down, staring at their cellphones, and when they entered the restaurant, Rachel could see them through the window waiting for a table. The man took a seat in the only available chair, and Rachel narrowed her eyes at him. *Typical*.

"And if you were to stop trying to hold everything together, what would that life look like?"

Aimee was so good at getting her to sort things out. "I've thought about that." Rachel rolled her shoulders, trying to release some tension. "I thought about that before seeing Brad. I thought about it before Adam's affair, when things really changed between us." She grabbed the balled up tissues in the passenger seat. "I can only get to the part where I can't see my kids every day, and then I stop all thoughts and decide I need to stay in my marriage." Rachel looked at her wedding rings, and the new ring Adam got her, then clenched her hands into fists.

"Rachel, Elsa and Benny are young. But I don't think they'd ever want to be the reason you were staying in a relationship that was making you this unhappy. Even if it is a relationship with their father."

She knew how true that statement was and yet, it scared her, made her feel completely selfish, and she needed to be done with this conversation. "I know," Rachel whispered, holding back tears. "Thank you for listening. I love you, Aimee."

Rachel put her car in reverse and slowly backed out of her spot.

You're going to go home, kiss your kids, and have sex with your husband.

"I'm going to call you in a few days if I don't hear from you, okay? Hang in there. Oh! And we're still coming for New Year's Eve!"

"I can't wait! We'll do the usual shopping, and Elsa suggested getting pedicures or something. The guys will be happy to have the house to watch their sports and be obnoxious."

Everything was going to be fine. This would pass, and Rachel would probably never run into Brad again. Now she just needed to stop thinking about him.

Rachel

It was after ten when Rachel pulled into the driveway. She could still feel where Brad's hands had wrapped around her waist, and she touched the spot on her neck where his scruff had brushed her skin.

Inside the house, all was dark and quiet except for the refrigerator's hum and Cora jumping up to greet her with happy panting and tail wags. She carefully set her keys and purse on the entryway table and blew out a breath.

Adam's Yeti mug sat in the sink, along with a few other dirty dishes. Rachel loaded everything into the dishwasher as quietly as possible—she couldn't stand going to bed with dirty dishes in the sink.

Upstairs, Adam was asleep in bed with his phone on his chest. She stood within arm's reach of him, unbuttoned her shirt, and stepped out of her heels. Adam didn't move as she undid her jeans. A vision of Brad kissing her as she leaned against her car shot through her head.

She took a deep breath, then picked up Adam's phone and placed it on his nightstand. When he didn't move, Rachel hesitated.

Maybe we could do this tomorrow night? No, just do it. Try.

She slid down her underwear. It was already wet and a stab of guilt went through her as she stepped out of them. She pulled the bedding off of Adam and slowly straddled him. Closing her eyes, she bent down and leaned over her husband, kissing him on the neck as he stirred.

"Rachel," he whispered, sliding his hands to her bare ass. "Are you naked? Why? What are you doing?"

Please, let's not talk. Forcing a laugh, Rachel said, "What does it look like?"

He sat up, and reached under her to pull down his boxers, and she slid off his lap.

"Okay, I'm awake! Who knows when this will happen again. I don't want to miss a thing," Adam said, pulling her back onto his lap.

His hardness pressed against her, and he started rubbing her back as she situated herself on top of him.

Rachel wrapped her legs around his hips, wanting something, anything, to take away this angst.

Adam's eyes widened in arousal and disbelief. Rachel couldn't blame him—they'd done nothing but missionary for years, and here she was waking him in the middle of the night, naked, taking control. *Maybe all this time you've just needed to try harder.*

Rachel leaned back, propping herself up with her arms behind her and arching a little so her breasts stuck out, giving Adam a view she knew he would like.

He slid his hands up her waist and cupped her breasts in his palms. "I'm so hard. Do you feel how hard I am?" he whispered.

You might as well be a blow-up doll.

Here she was, trying so hard to connect with her husband, to have a shared experience. And he could only make it all about him.

"Mm-hmm." Rachel pressed her lips together as he gently pulled and twisted her nipples.

Closing her eyes again, she tried to block out Brad's face, but he was everywhere. She could feel his soft scruff brushing her cheek, smell his clean, woody scent, hear his voice. *"I've never forgotten you. I'm sorry about what happened in college. You were nothing but wonderful ..."*

A feverish hunger built inside as she thought about what Brad had said. Adam continued fondling her breasts, and she tilted her head back to stare at the ceiling as she rocked back and forth over Adam, becoming more slick and wet.

This is good. You can do this.

"Touch me," she whispered. She wanted him to slide a finger into her and rub her clit with his thumb, the way he used to when she was on top.

Adam reached down and gently rubbed between her legs. Tingles ran through her entire body, and she rocked her hips, meeting his rhythm, taking what she needed from him, the way he always took from her.

Just as she felt herself building, Adam grabbed himself and entered her, moving his hand away from her sweet spot.

Holding her waist with his hands, he said, "Bounce on me. Do it like you used to." He laid back, his eyes shiny with lust.

Rachel's tingles receded like a wave from the shore.

Just do it, Rachel. He's acting like an overeager teenager because you hardly ever fuck him.

Getting her legs in place, she moved up and down slowly. Adam tightened his grip with his hands, guiding her to go faster. "I'm going to come in two seconds. This feels so good."

Rachel bounced up and down for another thirty seconds before Adam's legs stiffened. He let out a few grunts and then wrapped his arms around her and pulled her down to kiss her. "That was great, Honey. Wow! I can't remember the last time you did that."

Rachel climbed off him and lay on her side to face him, resentment building at the thought of having to remind him, yet again, that sex involved two people. Not just him. "I want to put in more effort. I know how bad our sex life has been. How bad our connection has been." She laid a hand on his chest and pulled at his coarse chest hairs.

A flash of Brad kissing her neck and mouth ran through her mind again, and she squeezed her thighs together, trying to stop the pulsing.

Stop.

"Well, if we can just keep this up, my life would be perfect," Adam said, letting out a yawn and closing his eyes.

"I want to get back to where we were before the kids were born. Most days, I feel invisible."

"Yeah, we will." Adam patted her leg and yawned again.

Rachel scooted closer so she could lay her head on his chest and throw one leg over him, wishing he would trace his fingertips up her arm, wishing *he* would make her feel *something*.

She hadn't felt this turned on in a long time and knew most of it was because she'd seen Brad.

It's not like you did anything wrong.

She was pretty sure she'd read somewhere that thinking of other people can bring the spark back in your sex life.

"Adam, you aren't falling asleep, are you?" She scooted even closer, rubbing her wetness on his leg.

But, when Adam reached down between her thighs, and she'd opened her legs wider, leaning into his touch, his fingers felt like sandpaper. She held her breath as he quickly rubbed her clit from side to side.

You've been telling him for years, circles, you like circles.

He pushed her onto her back, hovering over to suck on her nipples that quickly became sensitive and sore under his fast flicking tongue. When he peppered her torso with kisses, she pictured Brad's scruff rubbing her there. Adam's head was between her legs, and he quickly jetted out his tongue to lick her. It felt slimy, and Rachel stared at the ceiling, trying to relax. The flicks of his tongue made her cringe, and she had to force her legs to stay open. She longed for the sensation she'd felt when she was on top of him, just minutes ago, to come back.

She pursed her lips, squeezed her eyes shut, and let out a few moans, mimicking her usual orgasm movements.

Adam pushed himself up, wiped his mouth, and crawled back to his side of the bed. He kissed the top of her head, flopped on his back, and in less than two seconds, started snoring.

Relief ran through her. Slowly turning away from him, Rachel laid on her side and rubbed her thumb over her left nipple. It tightened under her touch. Her body started to buzz and blood rushed between her legs.

Adam's snoring grew louder, and she rolled onto her back, spreading her legs just a little. It felt good to lie naked under the cool sheets.

Careful not to nudge Adam, she slowly traced a finger over her wetness. She couldn't remember the last time she'd masturbated.

Has it been eight months? A year?

She closed her eyes, spread herself with two fingers. With her other hand, she circled her clit with her middle finger, feeling it swell.

Trying to keep her breathing quiet, she pictured Brad's face leaning down toward hers, felt the softness of his mouth on hers, felt his weight shift as he slowly worked his way down her body with his mouth, lingering at her nipples before taking her in his mouth and circling his tongue over her in just the right spot.

As Rachel exploded under her hands, her legs shook and

trembled. She tried to control each wave of pleasure that ripped through her, so she wouldn't wake Adam.

She tiptoed to the bathroom and examined her dark silhouette in the mirror. There was a lump in her throat that made it hard to breathe.

She wiped between her legs before heading back to bed, as the tears dripped down her face. Her guilt was so heavy, she didn't bother wiping them away.

Brad

Brad locked the front door behind him. The house was quiet, though he'd expected Beth to be waiting up for him, ready to demand an explanation for his long absence.

After pacing around the kitchen, then the living room, trying to calm his thumping heart, he realized he was holding his breath.

He'd taken a drive by the Bowdoin College campus, thinking about all the times he'd walked hand in hand along those sidewalks with Rachel.

This is your life—the life you chose—and it doesn't include her.

He shrugged off his coat and opened the closet. He hung his coat next to Beth's collection and imagined sharing a closet with Rachel.

Unbuttoning his shirt was a daunting task, and his arms felt leaden as he dragged it off. He held the shirt to his face, trying to catch a whiff of Rachel.

When he climbed into bed, Beth didn't move. Lying on his back, he forced his eyes closed, but it felt as if they were being held open by toothpicks. Normally, he'd be sound asleep, but his shoulders were so tense they practically touched his ears.

Rachel's smile. Rachel's caramel-colored hair flowing over her shoulders. Rachel staring straight ahead, refusing to meet his gaze when he brought up the past.

He rubbed his eyes with the heels of his hands and sat up.

His agitation grew as he watched Beth sleep, wondering if he should wake her up to talk. Her braid swept over her shoulder, and her mouth formed a straight line under her sleep mask that had slipped down her nose. She was peacefully sleeping, and Brad filled with dread at the thought of another hard conversation, more tension filled moments, that never seemed to make anything better.

Just sleep on it. Leave it alone. In a week, you probably won't be thinking of Rachel this much.

When he first told Beth he'd wanted to revisit his teaching degree, she wasn't supportive. When she realized he was really going to do it, she stopped nagging him about it as much, but that didn't last. It was clear now she hadn't taken him seriously. She thought he'd change his mind and go back to her family's firm.

While he thought he did still love Beth, he knew she'd never made him feel like Rachel did.

A few nights before they'd gotten married, he'd panicked and called Rachel's best friend, Aimee. When he'd asked her how Rachel was, Aimee had said, "Brad, she's happy—with someone else—and finally over you. Leave it alone. You chose Beth. Marry Beth."

He'd always wondered if Aimee had said anything to Rachel about that call, but his guess was, she hadn't. Aimee was as protective as friends came; a no bullshit kind of woman who didn't sugarcoat a thing.

Brad had listened to Aimee. If she'd thought reaching out

to Rachel would have been a good idea, she would have told him.

Eventually, memories of Rachel faded, and he'd accepted that this was his life. It was a pretty good one too—he couldn't complain. But seeing Rachel had made him realize something was missing. Something big. More than that, he wasn't sure Beth even liked having him as a husband. For that matter, he wasn't sure he really liked having her as a wife. They wanted such different things out of life.

Brad slowly lifted the sheets off himself and crept downstairs. His laptop and phone were charging on the counter next to the mail. He picked up his phone, hit the little pink Instagram app, and Rachel's name appeared instantly in his history.

A twinge of nostalgia floated in his stomach over a new picture she'd posted. Ovals, in neutral shades from light to dark, covered a large canvas. The paint had a marble effect in some places, reminding him of walks along Popham Beach with Rachel. She'd loved standing at the shoreline waiting for shells to tumble around her feet. Brad never knew how she could spot sand dollars and the prettiest oyster shells under the rippled water, but she'd always leave the beach with her two favorite shells. "To remember this day," she'd say.

His thumb hovered over the message icon, trembling a little.

No. Don't do it. She's married, probably not even thinking about you right now. And you need to work things out with Beth.

Rachel

*I*t was good to see you tonight. Thank you for listening to my apology. I'd love to get an original Rachel painting. Your work is stunning.

Brad's message had come in around eleven last night. Rachel gripped her phone, feeling her palms sweat.

She squinted, then dropped her phone in her purse. Immediately after stepping away, she turned to look at her purse again.

Her stomach danced as she rubbed her new ring in the palm of her left hand.

Adam's familiar steps came down the stairs. He sauntered into the kitchen and kissed her on the cheek.

"Morning, Honey," she said, handing him his Yeti mug of hot coffee, avoiding eye contact. He leaned against the sink and took a sip.

"Are you going for a run this morning?" he asked.

"I am." Rachel held her tea with one hand and headed to the hall closet to grab her running shoes. Adam followed her. "Come on guys, we're going to be late," she yelled up the stairs, five minutes before they usually left.

She heard the water running as Elsa and Benjamin brushed their teeth, but they didn't offer a response.

Since they'd started middle school, it had been hard to peel them out of bed, but mornings were certainly easier than when they were little.

Benny used to always have meltdowns because his coat didn't feel right, or he couldn't find the Lego sculpture he'd made, or he wanted to wear pajamas instead of pants.

Elsa had always taken forever to eat and brush her teeth, and Rachel used to feel like she had to stay on top of them every second. By the time she'd finally drop them off, she'd need a nap.

Time had softened her memories of how hard those mornings were. Now, there were days she'd drop them off at school and feel hollow, mourning the innocent chaos of their younger personalities.

When she bent to grab her running shoes, Adam spanked her butt. "Maybe we can have a repeat session tonight," he whispered.

Rachel stood with her shoes in her hand, and he slid her hair from her neck and kissed it.

He looked down at her right hand. "Damn, that's a nice ring. I did a good job, if I say so myself." Her shoulders tensed, and she had to restrain herself from squirming away from him.

Rachel lowered her gaze. "I was trying to connect."

"Oh, we connected all right." He put his coffee on the walnut table across from the closet and grabbed her waist, pulling her toward him. "But I know I fell back asleep fast. Let me make it up to you tonight." He wiggled his eyebrows.

Rachel's stomach turned, and her cheeks felt hot with rage. A rage so big, she wasn't even sure where it came from or to whom it was directed.

She opened her mouth to tell him he didn't need to make

anything up to her, then closed it when she saw Elsa and Benjamin slumping slowly down the stairs.

Elsa gave her parents a side-eye glance that made Rachel's heart plummet. *Did she see the look on your face?* Rachel smiled and stood up straighter. "All ready?"

Take the kids to school, go for a run, paint.

She leaned in and gave Adam a quick kiss on the cheek. "Okay, I'll see you after work!" She was loud enough so the kids could hear the cheeriness in her voice, though it sounded false even to her.

The morning after she'd heard Adam having sex with another woman, she'd sat on the floor of the kitchen sobbing. She wasn't the kind of woman who would stand to be treated like that. There was no way she could ever trust him again.

But when Elsa and Benjamin came downstairs in soft pajamas, rubbing their eyes, asking her what was wrong, she knew she had to see her kids every day; had to keep her family together. *Deep down, you know he loves you. You've been pushing him away.*

Now, here she was, ten years later, still repeating that same mantra as she looked at her big kids sitting in the car waiting to be taken to school.

As she backed out of the driveway, she squeezed Benjamin's shoulder. "You awake, buddy?"

"Why does school have to be so early?" he groaned.

"You've got a long weekend coming up, Honey. Hang in there. Elsa, you have everything for soccer?" Elsa was applying lip liner, using her phone camera as a mirror.

"Yes Mom," she answered, before making a pouty face and snapping a picture.

When they got to school, Rachel watched their backs as they paired up with friends and made their way into the building. Her usual spike of energy she had before a run wasn't there. She was already dreading tonight, knowing what Adam expected, knowing it was probably going to lead to another fight.

This doesn't just affect you. The rejection turns him into someone you don't like, but it's worse when he gets what he wants. He only wants more from you and you get so disgusted with him. They pick up on that too. You have a part in this.

She wanted to stay in her safe cocoon, the one that allowed her to go about her days tending to their home, and caring for her kids even if she didn't get any help. But the voice reminding her how miserable she was in her marriage was getting louder. She felt like she was being pulled in two.

Does seeing you evoke any old feelings for Brad?

He was probably just feeling guilty, trying to make things right between them.

She rested her head on the seat and closed her eyes.

He wants to buy a painting. Emily would tell you this was business, and that it'd be silly to think I was doing something wrong by returning his message.

She opened her eyes, put the car in drive, and pulled out of the drop-off line. *Get ahold of yourself.*

At home, Rachel skipped her usual stretching routine and left her phone in her car. The leaves spun in the air, landing softly as she pounded the pavement of her running route.

She waved to a middle-aged couple out for a stroll.

Are they happily married? Does she ever make excuses to get out of lackluster, over-eager sex?

When she approached her turning point, a big white church, her head cleared. The interior lights were making the yellow stained glass windows glow, and the maple tree in front of it displayed yellow leaves to match.

Yellow painting with shades of ivory and brown.

When she reached her house, she skipped up the front steps, feeling satisfied. Some of her anxiety had burned off—

running had always been her therapy. It also often led to her most creative ideas.

Leaning against the kitchen island, she ran her palm across the smooth stone on the countertop. An image formed in her mind of Brad lifting her up on the island and pressing her legs apart with his powerful hands, wedging himself between them. He used to nibble her neck and tug on her hair. He'd discovered she liked it and then kept doing it. He *listened*.

Rachel tried to picture Adam doing these same things to her, but it made her shiver with revulsion. She shook her head.

But one thought of Brad handling her, and she could feel her wetness. Her body longed for him, but she couldn't have him.

She gripped the island for a second before practically running downstairs to get the supplies for one of her mop paintings: a bucket, paint, new mop head, and a few large canvases.

Barely able to carry everything out to the garage, she rammed through the doorway. She plopped everything down on the garage floor. Her eyes were drawn to her car—her phone was in there.

No. You need to paint. Get your etsy shop off the ground. You're not answering Brad. But her mind produced an image of Brad's face leaning toward hers.

Rachel lunged forward, ripped open the car door and grabbed her phone. She rushed back into the kitchen and slid the device across the countertop like it was a hot potato. *He just wants a painting. He doesn't want you, you idiot.*

Rachel stalked back out to the garage. She stared at her paint supplies, unseeing. *There's no harm in answering his message. It's not anything close to what Adam did.*

After she got set up, she dipped a fresh mop head in a bucket of paint, then swirled a circle onto the blank slate, creating a figure eight. She smiled and grabbed her squirt bottle. Just a few squirts to make the paint splatter around a bit more, and this one would be done.

Think about it. He only wants a painting. It would actually be rude to not answer his message.

Rachel loved the instant gratification of seeing a blank canvas turn into a statement piece of art in just a few minutes. This one was perfectly messy, with the splashes of paint from the moving mop mimicking what looked like hearts or birds. *This will look great in the salon.*

She admired it, then went back inside to grab a can of Diet Coke. After taking a long drink, she tried to ignore her phone in her peripheral vision. She closed her eyes, and the phone vibrated. It was Emily. Their argument from last night felt so far away.

"Hello," Emily said, her tone flat.

Rachel set down her soda and paced. "Hey." When Emily offered nothing else, she said, "I hate when we argue." A dust bunny of Cora's hair blew by her feet. She needed to vacuum.

"Listen, I wasn't at my best last night. I'm sorry." Emily's words sounded rehearsed.

Or maybe Rachel had just heard them too many times?

"Shit from the past gets to me. I shouldn't take it out on you, and I know I do."

Rachel closed her eyes. This all felt too familiar. She was tired. "Well, it was obvious you didn't want to have dinner with me, which is why I left. Do you understand that your behavior is hurtful, Emily? When are we going to get past this?" Rachel knew Emily treated her this way because she was her safe place. But she'd put up with decades of this. She'd had enough.

Emily seemed annoyed whenever Rachel called their Mother out, or tried to get her to see good in Emily. But she got mad if Rachel ignored it.

The silence coming from Emily made her want to throw

her phone across the room. "I used to let you take all your hurt out on me. It helped me with the guilt I carried, knowing Mother treated us differently. But when she goes, we're going to be the only two left in this family. And I'm done being treated like shit, regardless of the reason."

"I said I was sorry, Rachel." A crack sliced her voice. There was a low hum in the background.

"It sounds like you're driving? Taking an early day to rest, I hope?"

"Ha! you're joking, right? No, I'm going to Portland to get stuff for goodie bags."

"Goodie bags? You mean like for a kid's birthday party or something?"

Emily only had high-profile clients. Was she planning their kid's events now?

"No. It's a team building thing for my coaches. I like to surprise them with beauty products and expensive chocolate."

Emily could be very generous, and she certainly gave amazing business advice which was why her coaching business attracted clients from all over the country. Rachel wanted to ask her opinion on messaging Brad back, but she decided against it. She knew Emily would say something sarcastic.

"Okay, well, I'm going to shower, then head to Panera to get some work done. Join me for a do-over later? You can give me your opinion of some business card options." Rachel made her way upstairs, thankful Emily's call had distracted her from messaging Brad back.

Four and a half hours until she had to get the kids from school. The laundry, dishes, and vacuuming could wait until she got home. While the kids did their homework, she could put the finishing touches on the mop painting and start another one.

"I've got to skip it today, but thanks for asking! Let me

know next time you go—you know I love their salads and bowls."

After her shower, Rachel put on her favorite leggings, a gray, oversized cashmere sweater and applied some blush and mascara. She dug through her drawer until she found her favorite slouchy socks that went perfectly with her shearling lined boots. She loved getting dressed in the fall.

When she got in the car, she opened Instagram messenger.

Adele's "I Can't Love You In The Dark" played, and Rachel looked at her wedding ring. The first time she'd heard this song while driving, she'd had to pull over—the lyrics about falling out of love, growing apart, and all the guilt that comes from that, described exactly how she felt about Adam. Her eyes had turned red and swollen by the time the kids piled in the car after school.

Rachel's eyes stung with tears. She fingered her new diamond ring, slipped it off her finger, then back on again.

She turned off the music and threw her phone in the passenger seat, hating how a simple message about a painting felt like so much more.

Rachel

Rachel ran her hand over the white linen tablecloth and hugged herself. The draft from the large window made her neck ache. "Nothing feels the same between me and Adam. He's so ... different." She was having lunch with Emily and Mother, hoping this time *she* could get some support from them.

She'd gotten a sitter for Elsa and Benny and was barely controlling her anxiety—leaving them made her paranoid with worry, but she knew it would be good for her to get out of the house, and she wasn't ready to give up her role as the glue that held her family together. Or tried to anyway.

Emily was sitting up straight with perfect posture in her padded, burgundy seat as she listened to Rachel talk about how agitated Adam had been. "Has he been on Facebook a lot? Being a little more possessive with his phone?" Her eyes didn't leave Rachel's as she stabbed through a piece of chicken in her salad.

"What does that have to do with anything?" Mother said, squeezing lemon on her steamed asparagus, then in her etched water glass.

"Well, Mom, it's the latest thing these days. People seeing old flames online ... reaching out innocently ... then before you know it, bam!" She smacked her hand on the table, and Mother jumped. "They're fucking around." A wicked smile crossed her lips as she cut her eyes at Mother.

Rachel recognized her expression: it was the same one she'd get as a teenager when she'd talk about smoking in the bathroom at school or taking a drink from Mother's wine bottle. Getting her mother's attention wasn't happening organically, so she'd tried being rebellious. She clearly hadn't grown out of that.

"*Language,* Emily." Mother rolled her eyes. "Why do you always have to be so crass?" she whispered between her teeth.

Mother turned to smile at the approaching server and ordered a second glass of Cabernet Sauvignon before the woman even reached the table.

"You haven't even finished half of that one," Emily said, pointing to the half-full wineglass. "And I'm a grown woman who can say whatever I want. I mean, whatever the *fuck* I want."

Emily laughed, and Mother closed her eyes in disgust.

The server stood there refilling their water glasses, acting as if she couldn't hear a thing.

"Emily, please," Mother said, letting out a sigh.

"Is there anything else I can get for you ladies?"

Rachel smiled at the server. "We're great, thank you so much."

Why do you even bother? Why do you let yourself believe things are ever going to change between these two?

There was a time when all Rachel wanted to do was keep their family together. But now, as Rachel sat back and watched the two of them be horrible to each other, she realized she was too damn tired.

You have your own family with two precious babies. You can't keep putting your energy into this.

"Of course, you can't get through lunch with your daughters with only *one* glass of wine, Mother. What is that now, two? Three?" Emily's eyes widened. "Maybe you should order another as soon as she comes back. That way you can numb yourself even more, hmmm?" Emily picked up her seltzer with lime and took a drink, eyeing Mother over her glass.

"Knock it off, you two. I got a sitter for the kids for this. Pull it together! I need some support here, and all you two can do is bicker." She threw her body back in her chair so hard, the front legs bounded off the floor.

Mother folded her hands together on the table. "You're right, Darling. Don't worry about Adam. He'll come around." She wiped the corners of her mouth with her cloth napkin even though she hadn't taken one bite of food. "You have given him two beautiful children, and you keep a lovely home."

Emily shook her head. "That doesn't guarantee a thing, Mother."

Mother fingered the ends of her brown bob that slightly curled under where it stopped at her chin and gave Emily a searing look. "Ignore your sister. Remember—Adam is tired too. He works all day. Tonight, just throw on a sexy nightgown and have the kids all fed and ready for bed. Make the night all about him. He will *love* it. Your father used to love it when I—"

"What is this, 1955?" Emily spat. "Should she wipe his butt after he takes an after-work dump, too?" She took her cloth napkin from her lap and threw it on the table. "Jesus Christ, Mom. That's the worst advice I've ever heard." Gesturing with her glass toward Rachel, she said, "Although I bet he *is* tired. Working late can take a toll after a while."

Rachel studied Emily.

How did she know he'd been working late? You must have told her and forgotten. You're just exhausted chasing around two toddlers all day.

"How'd you know Adam worked late last night? I didn't tell you that ... or did I?"

"You said it as soon as you sat down."

Emily's eyes left Rachel to focus on Mother. "And Mom, just because you catered to Dad when he was alive, and put up with *him* treating *you* like a doormat, doesn't mean Rachel needs to do the same." She took a bite of salad, then covered her mouth with one hand. "That's why you're turning your liver into a raisin. Because you've stuffed those feelings down for so long, it's the only way you know how to handle them."

Mother's mouth formed an "O" as she sat back in her chair. "I loved doing those things for your father. He loved me—"

"If he did, we never saw it. He expected you to put on a show for his coworkers, never supported you, and reduced you to the smallest possible version of yourself."

Mother's hand went to her heart. "Emily! That's enough," she snapped.

Rachel cleared her throat and put down her fork, which held a perfect bite of salmon topped with rice pilaf. *This is turning into a nightmare.* "Mother, do you have any idea how tired I am? The thought of all that exhausts me."

"Perhaps it doesn't have to be as elaborate as I suggested. Maybe just ... a little something?"

Rachel shrugged her shoulders. "I've had zero desire since Benny was born, and now he's three." She covered her face in embarrassment. Rachel kept hoping her mojo would come back, but as time went by, it felt easier to ignore this part of their relationship than to deal with it. At first, Adam had said he understood, but clearly he didn't. He was always edgy and short-tempered and repeatedly asked her when she was going to turn into her old self again. "Maybe I could put in a little more effort. Get the spark back."

"Yes, Honey. Try. He's a *man*. He needs certain things from his wife, and it's your job to give that to him." She clapped her hands as if she'd solved climate control.

"It's not like he's done anything to help with the kids or the house. He doesn't try to woo me."

Mother slid her asparagus around on her plate. "Men don't ... it's not in their genes to do stuff like that. We have to train them, Dear."

"Like a damn dog?" Emily laughed.

Rachel's toes curled. "Everyone sees him as a devoted father because he works a lot. I'm thankful I can stay home, but what they don't see is he's only home long enough to wind up the kids—if he makes it home before their bedtime. He leaves dirty dishes, clothes, and other messes in his wake. And then, I'm expected to want to have sex with him!"

"All I'm saying is maybe he's not realizing he's using work as an outlet because the two of you aren't ... connecting like you used to. Perhaps if you spice things up to bring the focus back to you two, he'd catch on and do the same."

Rachel missed the way things used to be between them; the ease of their days when they were both working and had the freedom to go on more dates, sleep in on the weekends, and have sex on the sofa whenever they were in the mood. *Maybe you have been a little too focused on the kids and have been neglecting him? It's worth a try.*

Emily swirled the food around on her plate, just like Mother did, sending a lemon wedge to the floor. When she leaned down to pick it up, her button-down blouse revealed a glimpse of her bra—it wasn't any thicker than a pair of stockings and revealed her entire nipple.

You could get something like that to wear under your black silk robe. That wouldn't be too hard.

"I love your bra, Emily. Where did you get it?"

Emily lifted her shirt to peek at her bra. "Oh—Nordstrom. I have matching underwear, too!" Emily sat up in her seat and waggled her eyebrows.

"How do you go from giving me all the ways I've ruined your childhood since I birthed you, to getting excited about underwear? Are you even seeing anyone?" Mother asked, rolling her eyes and taking a sip of wine. "And Rachel, go get your own set and wear it tonight! It will look fabulous on *you*."

Emily snorted. "As if I need to be seeing anyone to have nice underwear, Mother. You really are behind the times."

Rachel's head pounded. She pushed her plate away, stood up, and threw her napkin on the table. "I can't sit here and listen to you two! Something is going on in my marriage, and all you two can do is sit there and bicker. I'm tired of being the glue here. You two figure this out!"

She scanned the restaurant to see if anyone had heard her rant over the clanking silverware and buzzing conversation. If anyone had, they didn't seem to care. She slung her purse over her shoulder, then Emily and Mother stared at her with wide eyes—she'd always been the peacemaker in the family, but today, she couldn't handle it.

"Don't go," Mother said, pausing with her fork in mid-air. She stood up and followed her out the door, half-jogging in her ballet flats to keep up. "Honey, I'm sorry. Please stay. You don't need to leave. Emily is just—"

Rachel whipped her head around. "Stop it, Mother! Stop it." Mother was still holding her fork and clutched it in both hands. "Stop blaming Emily. You're every bit as much of the problem as she is, if not more. You're supposed to be a grownup!" She took a step toward Mother and pointed at the door. "You've always favored me, and if you think that hasn't bothered Emily, your damn head is in the clouds! Now, go back in there and pay some attention to your other daughter before you lose her for good!"

On the way home, Rachel stopped by Nordstrom, bought the lingerie directly off the rack, and picked up takeout from Adam's favorite Chinese place on the way home. Benjamin wasn't feeling well and had been fussy all afternoon, wanting to be held constantly from the moment she walked in the door.

She stroked the back of his head as he smashed his runny nose against her chest, smearing snot all over her shirt. Elsa sat next to them on the sofa, clutching her blanket and watching Peppa Pig. Rachel was exhausted, but there was no place she'd rather be. *Why did you leave them to watch your mom and sister argue?*

When Adam got home, he dragged his feet and was slow after she'd asked him to help her bathe the kids and get them to bed, but he perked up after she slid up her robe, baring a leg.

His impatience was obvious as they sat on the sofa to eat once the kids were in bed. The only thing Rachel could hear was him slurping back Chinese noodles. *Hopefully, he'll stop chewing like that before you completely lose all will to do this. Can he honestly not hear himself?*

He was eager for sex the same way their dog, Cora, stood panting and unblinking as the kids carried their dishes to the dishwasher. She'd never miss a chance for scraps.

Even though they weren't having much of it, one of the beautiful things about married sex is you could have it with a bloated stomach and garlic breath. There was no need to suck bellies in or put on a performance—you knew how the other operated.

She'd usually come quietly in Adam's mouth before he'd

climb on top of her. In their standard missionary position, it took him under five minutes to come. When they were done, she'd always feel guilty she didn't do it more. It was so quick and made him so happy.

Adam looked up at her, and she smiled slowly. Looking at his zipper, she wondered if she should reach over and rub him to get things going.

It's been so long ... you can skip that part.

That look prompted Adam to slam his container of LoMein down on the coffee table. "I'm going to devour you. Get upstairs." He took both of her hands and pulled her up off the sofa, then spanked her bottom.

She felt a slight tingle between her legs and relaxed. *The connection will be good. We always get along so much better after we've had sex.*

Rachel felt amazing in the new duo. It had been ages since she'd worn something so sexy, and it made her feel like the kind of woman who regularly seduced her husband. She turned to face Adam, then let her silky black robe shimmy to the ground.

Adam stood back to take her in. In a split second, his smile dropped, and his face went white. The lines between his eyes deepened. He slowly sat down on the bed. "Honey, w-what are you wearing?" His eyes shifted to the right, then down to her feet.

"Don't you like it? I got it today. Emily has a set like this and—"

"You saw Emily today?"

"Yeah," she sat down on the bed next to him. "I texted you last night while you were working to let you know I was getting a sitter for the kids so I could meet her and my mom for lunch. Remember?"

He slapped his leg. "Oh yes, right! Uh ... you know, I think that Chinese food was bad. I need to lie down." He gripped his stomach and eased himself onto his back on the bed.

"Oh. Okay." Rachel wrapped her robe around herself and felt a wave of relief mixed with the sting of rejection. When she came back upstairs with the glass of water, after putting all the food in the fridge, he said, "I just need a minute, then I'll be ready."

He rubbed his eyes, and Rachel went to the bathroom to do her nighttime skincare routine.

When she came back to the bedroom, the lights were off. Moonlight came in through the window and as she pulled back the covers on her side of the bed.

"Take that thing off."

Rachel sat on the edge of the bed, keeping one foot on the floor. "For real? But you barely looked at it. I went out special today to get it for tonight and surprise you and you don't even want to see it? You've been bugging me to have sex for months! I don't get you."

"*Bugging* you? I *bug* you to have sex?"

"You know that's not what I mean. You've been wanting to have sex and I've been turning you down a lot because I'm just ... exhausted." She dropped her head in her hands in frustration. "I was trying to make tonight special. Now you're acting like you're repulsed by me."

"I'm not! Come on, let's just do it." Adam scooted over to her underneath the covers, yanked her bra strap down, and the fabric chafed at her nipple.

"Stop, that hurts!" She slapped his hand away and covered her breast. "Do you really think groping me and ripping off this new, expensive bra is going to get me hot?"

Adam propped himself up with both arms and locked eyes with her. "It's never quite right, is it Rachel?"

She pushed herself off the bed. "Forget it. Forget it. I'm too tired."

"Of course you are." Adam rolled over. "Always too tired."

Rachel peeled off the bra and felt around in her drawer for her favorite T-shirt, then lay down on the very edge of the bed as far from Adam as she could get, her back turned toward him.

Hours later, Rachel hadn't fallen asleep. Adam's snoring was grating on her nerves.

The best part about her night had been the Chinese food. She got out of bed, wrapped her white terrycloth robe around herself, and went down to the kitchen. As she passed the hallway mirror, she stopped and appraised her reflection. She opened her robe and lifted her T-shirt. Why hadn't Adam wanted to see her in the lingerie?

She liked the reflection looking back at her. Yes, she had birthed and nursed two kids, so her breasts sagged a little. The bottom of her stomach crinkled like crepe paper when she bent over, but that had never seemed to bother Adam. Her years of doing yoga and running had not only kept her mind healthy, but it had also kept her muscles tight and her skin glowing.

She watched as her mouth turned down at the corners, her chin quivered, and tears spilled out from tired eyes. Was she really so hard for Adam to look at?

Screw him. She grabbed his leftover Lo Mein from the fridge, heated it up, and dug in.

As she chewed, she wondered about her waning libido. She'd read that women often lost desire after having kids, but was her own lack of desire worse than most? Wasn't it out of the ordinary for a marriage to go months without sex? *Maybe masturbating would give you a libido boost. But you haven't had the urge to do that either—not since before the kids were born.*

Aimee once told her that masturbation was a form of self-love, and that she did it regularly even though she and Matt had a healthy sex life.

But Rachel had a husband who always wanted to have sex with her and felt that all her desires—what little there were—should be saved for him.

And what about what Emily had said at lunch? She shoved more noodles in her mouth, remembering her brutally honest sister's words. *Has he been on his phone or laptop more?* No, he had not. But he'd been working later. Maybe he was sneaking around or talking to someone while he was at the office.

When he came home after those late nights, he'd be utterly exhausted and moody.

Was there someone else? No, Adam wouldn't cheat. You've never seen him so much as check out another woman.

He was just off lately—*they* were off lately. But the way his face had gone white when she'd dropped the robe kept rubbing at her.

She shoved the container back in the fridge, and her phone lit up from across the kitchen where it was charging by a pile of mail. It was a text from Emily: *Hey, I'm sorry Mother and I upset you at lunch. We talked after you left, and we will try harder. Also, don't listen to her old-fashioned bullshit views on marriage. If you're too tired to have sex, you shouldn't feel you have to.*

Rachel had wondered if Emily had been so supportive of her at lunch just to disagree with Mother, but it was clear she really understood, and didn't think Rachel was being a lazy wife. The reassurance made her feel so much better.

Brad

PRESENT DAY

B rad's stomach grumbled as he got in his car to leave his doctor's appointment. The sun had reached its midpoint in the sky, but the outside temperature reading in his car reported forty degrees, and the air smelled of snow.

A sudden craving for Panera's tomato soup and grilled cheese came over him. He had the rest of the day off from teaching, so he had time. He started the ignition and checked his phone—again—to see if Rachel had responded to his message, even though he hadn't felt it vibrate when it was in his pocket.

When nothing showed up, he wondered if messaging her had crossed a line.

Last night after he'd sent it, he'd bought a bunch of canoeing gear online and then he'd browsed Rachel's pictures —what few there were—on social media again before going back up to bed.

He hadn't slept her off like he'd hoped.

He thought back to when he and Beth had first met, how

150

he'd felt a fire burning throughout his entire body that he'd never felt with another woman.

When they fought, they fought hard. When they fucked, they fucked hard. When they went out, they drank too much and went home too late and slept too long the next day. He'd always noticed other men would watch her; watch them. It made him feel proud and invincible.

They'd traveled a lot and ate out almost every night. He'd felt powerful with her, living this new, wild life.

His cheeks burned with embarrassment every time he thought about how much these things used to matter to him.

Through the years, that fiery flame had cooled to barely a smolder. That seemed normal and would be more than okay with him if Beth supported him and showed him that his happiness mattered, too. Being a teacher felt so right, like he was born to do it. And it was clear Beth saw him as less of a man because of it.

He loved Beth, but he couldn't deny—especially these days—that his nervous system was never relaxed when he was with her.

But it was when he was with Rachel.

He shook his head at himself as he pulled off the highway.

Maybe planning a weekend getaway for him and Beth would help. They could drive through the New Hampshire Mountains and stay at a bed-and-breakfast ... *On second thought, Beth would hate a weekend like that. Shopping in New York City, and staying in a fancy hotel is more her speed.*

Rachel had loved their fall weekend away in the Camden Hills. They'd stayed in a tiny hotel above a quaint Italian restaurant, and even though it was chilly, Rachel had insisted on eating outside to take in the views.

Brad gripped the steering wheel with one hand and ran his fingers through his beard with the other. He really needed to stop thinking about her, stop comparing her to his wife.

He was wondering if he was having a midlife crisis. He'd heard of many couples going through a hard time in their forties. At least he wasn't rushing out on impulse to buy a sports car they couldn't afford. Though Beth would probably love that.

The Panera parking lot was almost full—lunchtime rush —but he found a spot to park on the side of the building. He checked his phone again. Nothing. His stomach dipped.

You're an idiot.

He sent a text to his mom as he waited to order. *In line at Panera getting a grilled cheese and creamy tomato soup. Not like yours, but it will do. Love you.*

It wasn't just the food that made him think of his mom. She always gave solid advice and never pandered to his feelings. She was a straight shooter, and he wished he could confide in her about this.

"You're next," the person behind him muttered as Brad stared at his phone, still willing Rachel to answer.

As he stood waiting for his food, a few men in suits hurried past him, carrying trays holding flatbread sandwiches and giant salads.

In the seating area behind him, a woman sat at a large table with four kids, urging one of them to finish their lunch so everyone could eat their dessert. She clutched the bag with the cookies to her chest as the little boy tried to climb on her lap and reach for it.

"You know," Brad said, leaning toward the young family and lowering his voice to a conspiratorial stage whisper, "I heard that if you eat all your lunch, it makes you run faster!"

The little boy lifted his sandwich to his mouth and took a big bite. "Thank you," the mom mouthed.

Brad's food was up. He grabbed it and headed to an empty table next to a window.

The steam rose from his soup and caused a flood of

memories, the same way it always did. When he was little, he'd come in from sledding or a long snowshoeing adventure with his father, and his mother would have the frying pan out before they got all their snow-crusted clothes off. His dad always dipped his crisp, buttery grilled cheese in the steaming soup for maximum deliciousness. He'd eaten the combo that way ever since. Panera's version couldn't quite compare to his mom's, but it brought the memories all the same.

While he waited for a bite to cool, he grabbed his phone from his pocket and placed it face up on the table.

Stop obsessing. You're being an ass.

A woman passed by as he took his first bite. She smelled like vanilla, and he turned to look just as his view of her was blocked by a couple having some kind of disagreement in front of the garbage can.

Brad caught a glimpse of a caramel brown ponytail.

Rachel?

He craned his neck, trying to see past the couple, but gave up when they caught him staring.

You want to see her so badly you're hallucinating. What are the chances of us running into each other for a third time?

It wouldn't happen by accident. But if he commissioned a painting ... he did truly want a painting, but he also knew that buying one was a vehicle to see Rachel again, and he didn't feel great about that.

He pulled apart his grilled cheese sandwich, and he watched the cheese split in some places and make long strands in others. The buttery bread crunched in his mouth, leaving crumbs on his lower lip.

A ding came from his phone, and his heart lurched. It was his mom: *Those were the days! I got new glasses! Mom*

He smiled—Mom always signed her texts as if she were writing an email.

He had typed a message back to see if his mom wanted to

do dinner together soon when the chair across from him moved. He looked up to see Rachel taking a seat and almost choked on his food.

"If I didn't know better, I'd think you were stalking me," Rachel said with a laugh, and then went straight-faced when she saw Brad's expression. "Oh. Are you okay?"

"No. Yes. Sorry! Rachel, hello!" His voice embarrassingly cracked like a teenager's. "Yes, I'm fine." He wiped off his mouth with his napkin.

"Are you ... is it just you here?" She glanced around— probably looking for Beth—and Brad swallowed hard, feeling the bread he'd almost choked on scrape at his Adam's apple.

"Two days in a row. I promise I'm just as surprised to see you," Brad said. He wiped his lips again, hoping he didn't have any crumbs lodged in his beard. "Just me today. Want to join me for lunch?"

"Grilled cheese and tomato soup? Just like your mom used to make. Bet it's not as good as hers, though." Rachel smiled and brushed her hair back over one shoulder the same way she'd done it at seventeen. "Does she still have the same bright red kitchen cabinets and mismatched dish collection?" She leaned forward on her elbows, and her too-big sweater shimmied down her shoulder, revealing her thin bra strap.

"No, she remodeled it right before dad died. It's got all the bells and whistles of a true chef's kitchen."

"Oh, I remember what a superb cook she was." Rachel gave him a warm smile, and he wondered if she was picturing the same cozy memories he was. "In fact, I still have all the recipes she gave me."

Rachel had spent a lot of time in the kitchen with his mom. Once, he'd come home from a sweltering day of fishing with his dad and found her and his mother hanging out in the kitchen like a couple of best girlfriends, proud to present six fresh berry pies that they'd lined up for display on the counter. Rachel had been wearing a floral dress that slid off her shoulder just like the sweater she was wearing now. Later that night, he'd slid that dress off with one smooth pull, then gotten on his knees and tasted her after his parents had gone to bed.

He felt himself beginning to swell under his zipper at the memory. "Yes, I remember how much fun the two of you used to have baking together."

"Remember the day we baked all those pies?" Rachel asked, blushing furiously.

Brad nodded, knowing she must be thinking about what they did later that night. Just like he was.

Rachel's hand went to her heart. "I loved baking with her. She was always offering to spend time with me and do things with me that my mom couldn't ... or wouldn't."

They sat in comfortable silence for a few minutes, not needing to say a thing because they both knew the other was lost in the past.

Brad stared at her hand, wanting to slip his fingers through hers like he used to when she'd come over in tears, needing to get away from her family. "I bet you're the *best* mom, Rach."

Her eyes watered, and she smiled. "Thank you, Brad. I love being a mom." She let out a sigh. "Well, I'm going to get one of those huge Green Goddess salads." She stood up and pushed in her chair.

"And let me guess," he said, putting his index finger to his lips as if pondering. "You'll get Diet Coke to go with it?"

"Ha! Am I that predictable?" Brad picked up his sandwich and held it out to her. Rachel pulled off a piece of the sandwich and popped it into her mouth, her eyes rolling as she chewed. How was it possible for a person to look so beautiful while chewing?

After ordering her lunch, Rachel laughed with the cashier. She'd always been so kind and outgoing, always making friends wherever she went. *She hasn't changed at all.*

When she returned to the table and set her salad and huge Diet Coke down, Brad said, "It's so good to see you." He stifled a laugh. "I know I keep saying that. I, uh … I sent you an Instagram message last night." He fiddled with the crust on his sandwich, peeling off a piece.

"Oh, yes." Rachel looked at her hands. "I was going to message you back … I can definitely do a painting for you—I'd love to."

"I saw some of your work. I love abstract art. And the colors you use are so … soothing." Her sweater had slipped off her shoulder again, and Brad tried hard not to stare at her creamy skin, or the graceful little bump the end of her collarbone made in her shoulder. He felt the corners of his mouth turn up.

"I'd like that," Rachel said, catching him looking at her bare shoulder. A tiny smile played at her lips. "I've … it's good to get back in touch. And I'd love to do a painting for you." Rachel laughed. "You aren't the only one repeating yourself today." She straightened her sweater.

"I've been wanting something for the living room for years, so this"—his pointer finger went back and forth between the two of them—"will be great." His face flushed. "I mean, not like you and me will be great, but like … you know. The painting will be great."

"Of course, yes. Just the painting." A nervous laugh escaped her lips. "Do you know what you want? I have a bunch of paint swatches in my purse you can look at." Rachel tapped on her purse.

"Oh nice. That would be nice." Brad nodded his head, feeling like an idiot after his overzealous attitude about the painting. Deep down, he wanted more than to connect over a piece of artwork, and he was doing a horrible job of keeping that to himself.

Rachel

As soon as he said, "this will be great," as he drew a line between the two of them with his finger, Rachel's body leaned closer to his. It was only an inch or two, but she had no control over her movements.

When Brad explained what he was trying to say, his cheeks flushed just as they had in high school when he'd asked her to go to a soccer game with him after they'd chatted in chemistry class. Only now, his eyes were even bluer than she'd remembered.

In that split second, the slight hand gesture woke up parts of Rachel that had been dormant for twenty years. She wanted to put them back to sleep and wanted to keep them awake all at once.

A few weeks ago, she'd woken up one morning thinking about the kids' schedules, her long to-do list, her marriage, and all the pictures she wanted to paint. But she'd gone to bed thinking about Brad. Nothing else.

How can one person make me feel so much?

Rachel pushed herself away from the table and grabbed her purse. "I'm going to use the bathroom—that Diet Coke went right through me, but here"—she dug out a small book of paint swatches and slid it across the table—"look at these and see if anything speaks to you."

"If anything speaks to me." His eyes locked with hers, and he nodded.

Rachel forced one foot in front of the other as she made her way to the bathroom, immediately wanting to go back and take her seat.

In the bathroom, she scrubbed her hands and closely inspected her teeth in the mirror. As she frantically applied some clear lip gloss, her perma-grin refused to fall from her cheeks.

Her stomach dipped—Brad watched her so intently from across the table, making her feel like they were the only two people in the world as the lunch rush swirled and hummed around them. She ran her hands over her hips, trying to erase thoughts of his scruff between her legs.

When she saw Emily's reflection behind her, she jumped. "Oh my God, Emily! You scared me. I didn't hear you come in!"

"I had some time this afternoon to meet, after all." She took a step closer, a shit-eating grin spreading across her face. "But I saw you sitting with Brad and didn't want to interrupt." She cocked an eyebrow.

Rachel's heart thudded hard in her chest as she double checked her lip gloss in the mirror. "Total coincidence. I came in for lunch and to work on designing some business cards, and I saw him sitting there by himself. I sat down with him without even thinking. He wants to buy one of my paintings."

"Well, I popped in to see if you still wanted to have lunch, and I got some stuff for you and Elsa to try from Ulta—I should have texted first. But since you've already eaten, and it's clear you're busy with Bradley Boy, I'll go."

Did she see the way you were blushing?

Emily dropped a goody bag in Rachel's tote. "Thanks, Emily. We were just catching up," Rachel said, hating the whiney defensiveness in her voice. She wiped at an invisible stain on her shirt, suddenly fidgety and unsure what to do with her hands. "Did you text me to say you were coming? How long were you watching us?"

Emily laughed. "I just told you I should have texted first." She leaned toward Rachel, making a show of examining her shirt as if helping to look for whatever stain she was trying to wipe away. There was absolutely no bullshitting her sister. "What's new with Brad? He looks good. *Really* good. Better-than-he-did-twenty-years-ago good." Emily inspected herself in the mirror. "And I only peeked in on you two for a second. I didn't want to ruin the moment."

"There was no *moment.*" Rachel elbowed her sister, then turned to check out her butt in the mirror. "He's a teacher. Lives in Freeport. Married to Beth, no kids. A regular guy with a regular life." She turned on the water to wash her hands.

"Well, nothing wrong with reliving a little of that young-love experience," Emily said, grabbing her sister's clear gloss from the front pocket of her purse and slathering it over her full bottom lip that was already stained with her signature raspberry lipstick. "Also, you already washed your hands."

Rachel's hands froze under the running water. *Right, you did.*

She turned off the water and shook out her hands. "You're holding my lip gloss like you're about to give it head. Stop." Rachel said, grabbing it back and letting out a nervous laugh.

She was relieved Emily was over her mood from the other night, but she was eager to get back to Brad and get away from her sister, who could obviously see right through her.

"Oh my fucking Christ! *Head?* What the hell has gotten into you? Oh, it's because you've got head on the brain—you want Brad's dick in your mouth. At least then the score would be even with your cheating husband."

Why does she always have to take everything to the extreme? Talk like she's trying to get someone's attention? Rachel scowled at her sister, and Emily took the opportunity to swipe the lip gloss back. Rachel went for it and was interrupted by a short, stout woman exiting the bathroom stall. She'd been so startled by Emily, she'd forgotten someone else was in the bathroom with them. She widened her eyes at her sister.

The woman eyed them over her pink-framed glasses as she strode with her purse on her forearm to the sink. Rachel's cheeks flushed, and Emily continued to apply her lip gloss, watching herself in the mirror as if they hadn't just been talking about dicks in mouths.

"Um. I love your bag," Rachel said to the woman, admiring the supple leather and the embossed Gucci label on the front of it, and trying to distract her from her sister's unhinged behavior.

The woman soaped up her hands, lathering from her wrists down to her rum-raisin polished fingernails. Without looking up, she replied, "You know my favorite thing about this pocketbook?" Water splashed all over her bedazzled sweater.

"What, does it have a lot of storage?" asked Emily, looking at the woman's reflection in the mirror. "I love when there's more than one inside pocket—"

"I didn't have to put any dicks in my mouth for this bag. I bought it myself." The hand-scrubbing was on the edge of being aggressive.

"However, my husband bought his mistress one exactly like it while we were married. I caught them when *she* had *his* dick in *her* mouth."

The sink resembled a washing machine with too much

detergent. "Every single thing I've bought for the last thirty years after I ditched him, I bought myself."

She counted on her dripping wet, sudsy fingers, sending tiny bubbles into the air. "I waited tables for ten years. Then I emptied my savings account to open a bakery. A month ago, I sold that bakery to his third ex-wife. She's twenty years younger than me and has even more handbags than I do, but I make a much better cinnamon roll." She leaned in to look at her hair more closely, cupping a few curls with her damp hand.

"I just tried the cinnamon roll here. What a mess. Someone needs to show these kids how to bake."

Rachel's eyes shifted to Emily's, her head and neck frozen. Emily let out a huge belly laugh. "Well, that's not at all what I expected you to say!" She nodded in encouragement. "Good for you."

Rachel chimed in. "I agree about the cinnamon rolls here. I come for the salads and bottomless sodas."

Emily passed Rachel the lip gloss, which was no longer clear but tinted a faint pink, and Rachel put it back in her purse without taking her eyes off the woman who clearly didn't care about Rachel's opinion on Panera.

"Ladies, my point is, the best revenge is to work on your-self. It's much more effective than putting someone's dick in your mouth. Trust me, I've tried it." She squeezed in between the two of them. "Now, if you'll excuse me, I've got to go run to my afternoon Bingo game." She grabbed a paper towel, wiped her hands, then used it as a shield for the door handle. "I wish you a dick-free day!"

When the bathroom door thumped closed, they burst into laughter, and Rachel fell into Emily. "I want to be her when I grow up," Emily said, using her finger to wipe a tear from laughing so hard.

Rachel stood behind Emily and put her chin on her

sister's shoulder, studying their reflections. "You already are her, Emily. You're so independent. I'm actually envious of your lifesty—"

Emily shook her sister off. "Go finish your visit with Brad. Get that painting order." She pumped her fist in the air. "Oh, and I'll leave those gifts for Benny and Elsa on your front porch this afternoon."

Guilt spread in Rachel's gut—spending time with him was going to make her feel even *more* confused, and she felt like she'd crawl out of her skin if she couldn't let a little of this out.

"Thanks, Em. They will love them." She cleared her throat. "The truth is, I've been having a hard time concentrating since I've seen him. It's been … unsettling. I feel horrible. He has a wife. I have a husband. But we have a pretty long history. I'm trying to be cool about this, but is doing a painting for him a bad idea?"

"Well, sometimes time allows feelings to fade. And sometimes it doesn't. He hurt you." Emily twirled the ends of her red hair between her fingers. "I don't think you need to be judging yourself so hard. It's just a painting. It's not like you're pulling a Jack from *Titanic* and having him sprawl out nude on a velour sofa."

Rachel giggled. "True." Although she didn't hate the idea of that at all.

"The two of you talking isn't breaking any vows." Emily crossed her arms. "Are you going to tell Adam?"

"Oh yeah, sure. I *will.* I'll tell him. That's the right thing to do. Right?" Rachel wrung her hands.

"Oh, how very on-brand of you." Emily's tone dripped with judgment. "Now, go back out there and finish your conversation. Maybe it's the closure you need."

Yes. Closure. That's all this is. "Thank you, Emily. Needed that." Rachel hugged her sister, feeling so much better.

She's right. You're not breaking any vows. And you will tell Adam.

Emily gently patted her stiffly on the back and took a small step back. She was never big on hugging, but Rachel was. Rachel had grown to learn not to take her sister's lack of affection personally.

Brad was waiting at their table with an untouched frosted brownie and a fresh, large, bubbly cup of Diet Coke. He looked up from scrolling through his phone.

"For you," he said, pushing the Diet Coke to her side of the table.

"Thank you! And sorry I took so long." Rachel pulled her seat out and hung her purse on it. "Ran into Emily in the bathroom. I should have had her come say hello." Rachel looked over her shoulder, scanning the restaurant for her sister. "Maybe she's still here."

"Oh, that's fine." Brad touched her arm. "I'll catch up with Emily some other time. I want to talk about *you.*" His sense of urgency was obvious. And was that *wariness* in his eyes?

"Or ... should I go so the two of you can talk?" He reached for his coat.

"No!" she said, much louder than she meant to. "I mean, no. It's okay. She's probably already gone anyway—she said she was leaving."

"As long as you're sure. I got this dessert. I hope that's okay?" Brad slid the plate with the brownie toward her without taking his eyes off hers. His eyelashes had a reddish tint when the sun hit them, just like his beard. *How can his eyes make your skin heat up in a split second?*

The chocolate frosting dripped down one corner of the fudge-y square. *This looks wonderful. I'd say these "kids" know how to bake.* Rachel wanted to devour the whole thing.

She broke off a tiny piece and moved the plate over to

Brad, and he did the same as if they'd never stopped sharing food and eating off each other's plates.

"So, what do you do in your spare time? Besides paint." Brad's eyes were laser-focused on hers. "That's a silly question. You have two kids, a home, and a husband."

"That about sums it up." A sigh escaped her. "It's a good life. Before I had Elsa, I was an editor at *Maine Women Magazine*, which I loved, but I wanted to stay home with my children. I get to take them to school. I don't miss any of their sporting events. And now, I get to pursue something I really want to do. I'm incredibly lucky."

"Everyone always had you proofread their papers in college, you never missed a typo. But you're definitely a natural at creating beautiful things. I remember you decorated your college dorm with doilies. And I'm pretty sure you were the only person on campus who dusted their dorm room twice a week."

Rachel leaned forward with her elbows on the table. "Remember that time I made you come with me to the graveyard and we picked hydrangeas? And when we got back to campus, we realized they were covered in pincher bugs?"

Brad shivered and began scratching his chest. "Ah, yes! They were infested! I've never seen anything like it."

He broke off a piece of brownie and popped it in his mouth. "That reminds me"—he shook his pointer finger at her as he chewed—"the art teacher at the school is doing the coolest project with the kids and hydrangeas. She dries them out, then has the kids pluck the tiny flowers off and glue them on construction paper in the shape of a hydrangea." He smiled widely. "I mean, their faces when they've created something they're proud of—it's pretty amazing. I constantly tell them not to lose that spark. You know, that thing that makes them want to create and test the limits of their imaginations?"

Heat brewed in Rachel's belly as the unrepressed joy

spread across his face, and she pressed her palms between her thighs under the table. "Oh, Brad. I'm so glad you're happy. Those kids are lucky to have you." *Beth is lucky to have you.* A stab of guilt ran through her chest.

"No. *I* am the lucky one." His words made her breath catch in her throat. He'd always said that to her when she'd told him she was the luckiest woman on earth to have him.

No, I am the lucky one.

"You were always so easy to talk to, Rach. You still are."

A lump formed in her throat, and although her eyes couldn't leave his, she didn't trust herself to respond.

Brad

"Now we can text instead of sending Instagram messages about this painting. The painting we didn't even talk about," Brad said as they headed to the parking lot, adding each other's numbers into their phones.

Reaching out to hug Rachel felt instinctual—something he couldn't *not* do. When their bare necks touched, the warmth from her body made him want to reach up and stroke her hair; hold her close to him a little longer.

Her hands trailed over his coat as she broke their embrace. He could have sworn there wasn't any fabric separating their skin.

This is dangerous, Brad. What are you doing?

Rachel pulled away and folded her arms across her chest. "Yes, let's get those details squared away. Soon." There was no warmth in her words, no contact with her eyes.

He'd forgotten they were in the middle of the Panera parking lot in broad daylight and took a few steps back.

You shouldn't have hugged her.

"Yes, good idea." Brad shoved his hands in his pockets and

squinted—he could swear that was Emily sitting in a parked car across the parking lot. When he didn't look away, whoever it was ducked their head as if they were looking for something on the floor.

God, if it is her, she hasn't grown up at all.

He still couldn't believe what had happened in the bathroom at Tuscan Bistro, but he wasn't about to tell Rachel. Emily used to cause Rachel so much grief, and Rachel was always trying to be the protective big sister, even though she knew Emily took advantage of her.

"Let me know when you make some decisions," Rachel said, pulling her sweater up to cover her bare shoulder.

Decisions. Yes, he had some decisions to make. Right now he was walking on a dangerous tightrope with this woman—this married woman—for whom he could no longer deny he had big, uncontainable feelings for.

"It was good to catch up." Her eyes were sad as she turned slowly to open her car door.

"Yes, so good to see you, Rachel." His voice had come out in a whisper, and she didn't seem to hear him. He turned to walk back to his car, a tightness growing in his chest.

After a few steps, he paused, then turned back to her.

"Hey, Picasso! Wait!" He jogged back. "I have to tell you something!"

Rachel got back out of her car, all flush-faced and glowing and ridiculously beautiful, an expectant look brightening her face. She stood with one hand grasping the top of the car door, the diamond on her ring glittering in the sun. *She's married.*

"Um." His heart was a drum in his chest. "I ... um, I know the woman who owns Brass, Leather, And Denim—you know that little boutique in Portland?"

A cloud of disappointment crossed her face. "Oh. Yes, I know that place. Elsa and I love it." She slid her diamond ring back and forth on her finger.

"Well, the last time I was there, she mentioned she wanted to get some large-scale art for her walls." He held out his palms in a "why not" gesture. "I could call her? Tell her about your work?"

She blinked a few times, as if trying to process. "Of course. That would be great, Brad. Thank you!" Her eyes shined again, though he thought he saw a hint of disappointment still lingering there. *Don't hug her again.*

He clapped his hands together. "Great! I'll be in touch."

"Great!" Her mouth turned up at the corners, and she got in her car. As he headed back to his car, he heard her drive away, and every instinct told him to turn around and watch her. But he didn't.

Brad knew he shouldn't be analyzing their every interaction, dissecting every micro-expression that crossed Rachel's face. There was something between them, maybe just a glowing ember from years before, but he was sure he wasn't imagining it. The right thing to do—the only thing to do—was ignore it. Pretend it wasn't there. He needed to get the painting, then move on.

At home, he sat for a long time in his driveway, trying to choke a swallow down his dry throat before going inside.

When he finally came inside, Beth was in the kitchen painting her nails at the island. "Hey, how was the doctor's appointment?" She glanced up at the clock and then dipped her brush into the bottle of polish. "I thought you'd be home sooner."

"It was good. I stopped at Panera for lunch." He flipped through the mail, his hands trembling slightly from the guilt he felt. "I ran into Rachel. You remember her, right?"

"Well, yeah," Beth said, studying her nails. "I broke you two up."

She wiggled her fingers. "What do you think about this color? It's the latest fall trend, but I don't know." She held her splayed-out hand away from her face and cocked her head to the side. "Not sure it's me. Maybe I need to try a lighter taupe instead of full on brown."

Beth had just gotten her nails done at the salon about a week ago. He didn't bother asking why she was already redoing them. "They look nice," Brad said. "Anyway, she's a painter now, and a pretty good one. I asked her to paint something for us." He pulled his phone from his pocket and opened it up to scroll through Rachel's Instagram for a picture to show Beth.

"I know she paints. I've stalked her as any normal wife would. But isn't it kind of weird? I don't know if I want something from *her* in *our* house."

"It's not like that." He waved his hand in the air and felt his face burn with shame. Wasn't it *exactly* like that? "I really like what she does. I think you will too."

He walked over to her and enlarged a picture of a painting on his phone for her to see. It was blue and green and resembled an ocean wave.

"I like this one," he said, showing Beth the photo. "Reminds me of the time we went to Costa Rica."

Beth laughed and leaned in to look. "It's okay, but ... what is it? It looks like a kid painted it or something." Beth had never seemed threatened by Rachel, and it was clear she still wasn't.

"Well, I like it," Brad debated. "It reminds me of the ocean. But it's abstract art, so everyone sees something different when they look at it."

"I like more defined art." Beth closed the top of her nail polish. "But if you like it, we'll find a place for it. Maybe the guest bedroom?"

Brad studied his wife. She was always incredibly confident. Or was it arrogance? A cover-up for insecurity?

"Glad you're feeling better than you were last night. I ended up eating leftover chicken and rice and going to bed." Beth got up from the island and fanned her wet nails in the air. "I fell asleep before you got home, but I wanted to talk."

"I hurried us out of that place without warning. I'm sorry."

Beth sauntered over and gently wrapped her arms around his neck, careful not to smudge her fresh polish. "I called Dad today. He said he'd hire me. He needs another accountant." She tilted her head back to look at Brad. Her groin pressed into his. "But he also said he'd be happy to give you your old job back, too."

Brad opened his mouth to object.

"I told him you were happy, though." She smiled, obviously proud of herself. "How's *that* for being a supportive wife?"

Brad wrapped his hands around her arms. "Thanks, Honey."

See, things are working out. Beth is coming around. Seeing Rachel again just stirred up some old, dead feelings, that's all.

He thought about telling Beth about the incident with Emily in the bathroom. At least then last night's sudden departure would make sense to her. He'd always been honest with his wife, but this was something that may upset her for no reason. They certainly didn't need that right now.

You'll have Rachel do the painting, then that will be the end of this.

Beth leaned in and kissed his neck, then purred in his ear, "Undo your pants. My nails are still wet."

He did as he was told, undoing his belt and pants before pushing them down. This was the way Beth usually liked to reconnect after a fight, and he certainly didn't hate it.

Beth kissed his neck again before dropping to her knees and taking him in her hand. She stroked him gently without touching her wet nails together, looking up at him before closing her lips over his hardness.

He let out a long breath as he watched his wife's head slide back and forth over him in the middle of their kitchen.

But when he closed his eyes, he saw Rachel and her floral dress pooled at her feet as he slid his tongue over her. He throbbed, feeling his release build, and then forced himself to open his eyes and focus on his wife.

Rachel

"I think my wife must be overtired," Adam said gently, resting a hand on Rachel's shoulder.

Rachel sat up straight in the hard plastic chair, blinking twice to unglaze her eyes. "Oh, I'm sorry," she said to Benjamin's science teacher. "What were you saying?" She'd been riding on the adrenaline from her visit with Brad this afternoon and felt herself coming down hard. After getting the kids from school, she'd finished another mop painting, vacuumed the downstairs, and made meatballs for dinner before Benjamin's parent-teacher conference.

"Benjamin is doing great, which I know I've said. He's a very smart boy, but he's still a *bit* impulsive. Especially around a certain group of boys. Today they were slapping each other on the back of the legs with a yardstick." He pursed his lips together, trying not to laugh.

Rachel's eyes widened, and she laced her fingers together, trying to hold in a smile. It wasn't funny—she was embarrassed, but also relieved the teacher found humor in the situation.

Benjamin had a way of making adults laugh when they

knew they shouldn't. It was a gift of his—eliciting humor laced with a tad of annoyance. He obviously knew this, which was why they kept having the same issues year after year.

"Sometimes I'm tempted to tell his teachers to punish him more," Adam said as they crossed the parking lot to the car. "Is that a horrible thing to wish on your own son?"

"Mm-hmm," replied Rachel, having no idea what she was agreeing to.

"You okay? Tired?" Adam pressed.

Rachel rubbed her neck where it had brushed against Brad's only a few hours ago. "Yeah," she answered, letting out a sigh. "I'm thinking about my next commission. Distracted I guess."

Brad's painting.

"Maybe this painting hobby is too much for you. All you need to do is take care of the kids, and save some energy for me. Let me handle our finances," Adam said, sliding into the driver's seat.

"It's not about the money, Adam. It's about doing something for me—having an outlet that enhances my life." She buckled her seatbelt hard.

Adam faced her, his expression softening. "I'm sorry. You're right. That was a boneheaded comment to make." He slid his fingers into hers, forcing them open. "Of course you need more. You know, I forget I get to leave the house and have a break from family obligations. I mean, I am the provider, so I have to, but it is an outlet for me. I'm sure you crave that, too."

Rachel stared at him in surprise.

Adam wiped his free hand down his face. "It hit me when I said that, just how much I sounded like my father. So old-fashioned. He thought my mom should stay home and be a quiet housewife."

Growing up, Rachel had looked at the dynamic between

her parents and knew she wanted more. She was fine with being a housewife, loved it actually. But she was never fine with being a *quiet* housewife who was treated like a servant-bitch or like having a life outside of the house shouldn't be a priority for her. Staying home was something she and Adam had discussed before they had kids, and they'd both agreed they'd be equals. So many times over the years, his actions hadn't been consistent with those conversations, and she was tired of reminding him.

When he untangled their fingers, Rachel's shoulders relaxed. He patted her knee and said, "I love that you want to stay home, and you've done an amazing job with our kids."

Rachel felt taken aback, but a smile pulled at the corners of her mouth. "You've literally never said that to me before."

"What?" He narrowed his eyes at her. "I guess I always assumed you knew I felt that way. Now, tell me about those paintings you finished today." He grabbed her hand again, gently shaking it. "We're in this together."

Rachel's heart skipped a beat. She saw a glimpse of her husband—the way he used to be. She'd been missing this kind of connection with him for so long, she was sure it would never come back.

She cracked her window and felt a bit of energy return to her. "Yeah, I love how they came out. I've been inspired lately. I went to Panera today, designed some business cards, and emailed a few people about setting up a website."

"How much is a website going to cost? We should set up a budget for you."

"I need to get quotes. I'm just going to do something basic to start—a landing page with a bio, a few pictures of different paintings, and contact information."

Adam stared at the road and nodded his head. Getting support and coming up with a game plan for expenses together was already making Rachel feel less anxious.

"I ran into Brad today." She fiddled with her earring. "You know, Brad Turner, my ex-boyfriend? He saw my work on Instagram and wants a painting."

Adam raised his eyebrows.

"I'm painting something for his living room. He and his wife live in Freeport." She let out a long breath, watching Adam's expression.

His eyebrows dropped. "Ohhh, that will be—" Adam's phone rang. "Crap. This might be the listing agent with a counteroffer on that apartment building. Gotta take it."

As Adam talked business, Rachel tuned out his voice as she watched the rain-soaked streets pass by. *An all black painting with pools of gray and silver. White smears throughout ...*

She opened the Notes app on her phone, jotting down the idea, as Adam jabbered on about cash offers and inspection clauses.

Later that evening, Rachel and Adam sat with Benjamin to talk about trying harder to control himself in school while Elsa was curled up in the Eames chair, scrolling social media with her earbuds in, still wearing her new boots from Emily.

Rachel's lower back felt so tight it was hard to get off the sofa. She kissed the top of Benjamin's and Elsa's heads, announcing she was going to bed. But as she passed through the kitchen, she noticed Adam's Yeti mug and a few other dishes were scattered across the countertops.

"It's not even nine o'clock, Mom," Benjamin said. He was just getting absorbed in Seinfeld reruns, a weeknight tradition that Rachel usually stayed up for.

"I know, but my back is bothering me, and I'm just exhausted. Can someone please put those dirty dishes in the dishwasher and start it up?"

She headed upstairs, pretty sure she heard Adam mutter, "Yeah."

Skipping her nighttime routine crossed her mind, but the multi-step skincare regimen always left her feeling clean and nourished. She brushed and flossed first, then pulled her hair on top of her head. The water was nice and hot, and she watched her face cloth fill with water before squeezing out the excess and bringing it to her face. Then, she grabbed her face oil, and gently cleansed her skin before patting it dry.

As she reached for her night cream, she heard the clatter of Adam's belt hitting the hardwood floor. He always took off his clothes by the bed and left them there all night.

When she came out of the bathroom, Adam was already in bed. He lifted the sheets on her side of the bed for her. "Come on. I'll give you a back rub, Hun. You said your back hurt."

Rachel took a deep breath and slid into bed. He was completely naked, and he wiggled his eyebrows at her. The familiar dread in her stomach rose. *Stop it. He's trying, and you're going to try too.*

Adam scooted closer and kissed her shoulder. "You need to let me take care of you."

Rachel tried relaxing the back of her head on the pillow, wondering if he'd actually done the dishes like he'd said he would. *Maybe you need to give him more space to do things on his own instead of always asking for help.* She rolled on her side so her back was to him, and he started massaging her lower back.

After what felt like fifteen seconds, Adam put his hand on her hip, gently turned her over, and lifted her nightgown. When he brought his head to her stomach to kiss it, she squeezed her eyes shut.

He palmed her inner thighs, gently rubbing and then parting her legs, teasing her with his fingers. Without opening her eyes, she tilted her head back. She pictured the way Brad had looked at her across the table this afternoon, how his eyes locked with hers a beat too long.

She spread her legs a bit more, feeling herself getting wet as Adam kissed her sweet spot before parting her heat. His tongue danced over her, and she reached for his head, pulling him closer, craving release.

"Slow down," he said, slipping a finger inside of her.

Rachel's toes curled in annoyance, and her hand went to the spot on her neck that had touched Brad's. Even though they had been teenagers, Brad had always read her body language and never thought he knew what she needed better than she did.

Pressure built as she remembered Brad's fingers inside her, making her throb. She tilted her hips, thrusting them into Adam's face as she thought about Brad's scruff tickling her thighs.

Finally, Adam took the hint and sucked harder, and she shook and shuttered. Her stomach contracted, and when he lifted his head from her, she held him down, locking him there until she was done.

As soon as she loosened her grip, he climbed over her and slid into her. "I'm so hard." He was pumping fast and exhaling forcefully with each thrust as she stared at the ceiling. "Rachel. I got you good and wet."

This isn't so bad.

When she closed her eyes, she saw Brad's face again, just as Adam's body stiffened on top of her. He let out his usual grunts before dropping his limp body onto hers.

"That was so nice. I needed that." He talked into her neck, touching the same sensitive spot Brad's neck had.

She brought her shoulder to her ear, pushing him away. "Stop. That tickles."

Adam kissed her cheek and rolled off of her. "Come here," he said, stretching out his arm over her head against the pillow.

Rachel rested her head on his chest, trying to erase all thoughts of Brad. "I'm so glad we talked on the way home. It means a lot that you're willing to do more so I can get this painting thing off the ground." She combed his chest hair with her fingers.

"I still have a business to run, so I can't really do more. And obviously we'll have to stick to a strict budget." He yawned.

Rachel sat up. "What do you mean? That's not how you put it in the car on the way home."

"No, Rachel." Adam sighed. "I'm going to support you. I won't call it a hobby anymore. But it's not like I can take any time off work to get the kids from school, or do more around the house. I work. Like, at an actual job. So, if you want to do this, you're going to have to let some things slide. Or not head up to bed at 9 p.m."

"Wait, so 'supporting me' just means not making fun of me? I see." Once she got started, she couldn't stop. "And by 'take care of me,' you meant you'd rub my back for fifteen seconds before reaching between my legs and then climbing on top of me. Maybe if you *actually helped* me, I'd have more energy for *this* nonsense." She waved her hand between the two of them.

"Wow. Now, having sex with your husband is nonsense? Jesus Rachel, that's our problem! Maybe if I was getting fucked more often, I'd have more patience to listen about how you finished a painting, or how good you feel after the damn floor has been mopped."

Adam got up, pulled on his underwear and T-shirt, grabbed his phone from the bedside table, and left the room.

Well, that's just great. The evening had started out nice, then ended with, yet another, fight. Rachel felt like she should be upset. She waited for all the usual ingredients to stir inside, concocting the familiar recipe of rage he'd made her feel so many times before.

It didn't come.

You just don't fucking care anymore.

She rubbed her neck for several minutes before grabbing her phone off the nightstand. *Starting your painting tomorrow. We didn't get very far with color options, so let me know.*

She stared at the typed words for a few minutes, swirling her diamond ring around on her finger, then hit send.

Rachel

T una steaks sizzled in the pan as Rachel turned them,
crisping them to a perfect golden brown at the edges
and sending a delicious aroma wafting through the
kitchen.

She grabbed the sesame seeds as an afterthought, sprin-
kling a layer over both the fish and the green beans. As the
tuna finished, she fanned avocado and cucumber slices on her
favorite marble platter. *Perfect.* The contrasting green hues
would be a gorgeous palette for a painting. She snapped a
picture with her phone so she wouldn't forget.

Cora looked up at her, begging for a scrap. "You already
ate," Rachel said, reaching down to pat her head. Cora let out
a whine, clearly not satisfied.

Brad had texted her back last night: *Maybe gray and blue?
The living room is painted off-white and our furniture is mostly
navy. Also wanted to tell you my friend, Kate, who owns the shop
is going to call you. So good to see you today.*

She'd read it first thing this morning, and when she'd come
downstairs to see Adam hadn't loaded the dishwasher, and all

the dirty dishes were still in the sink, she was so irritated she didn't make him his usual morning coffee.

But Brad's text had softened her mood.

She'd spent the day scrubbing down the walls, then cleaned out her car. After getting the kids from school, they stopped at Wild Oats to pick up some of their famous three-bean salad to go with dinner. Her eyes kept scanning the place for Brad, and Elsa told her she was acting "sus."

"What does that mean?" Rachel had asked as they stood in line while Benjamin was picking out a cookie the size of his head.

"Bruh, you need to chill. Who are you looking for?" Elsa shook her iced coffee and stared at her phone.

Bruh? Yes, Rachel. Chill.

All afternoon she'd tried to work Brad out of her mind. She hadn't returned his text—he'd answered her questions and really, there was no need to respond to his response.

You aren't in high school anymore. He just wants a painting, that's it. We aren't doing anything wrong.

Are we?

If Brad had been thinking of her the way she was thinking of him, which he probably wasn't, that would be a different story. Although he had given her that look when they'd talked about the day she'd made all those pies with his mom.

Rachel dumped the salad into a white scalloped bowl and stared at the dinner in front of her.

Not texting back is just rude. I'll just thank him for referring me to Kate. Let him know I got his text. We're adults. This is business.

As she typed, a call came in from Yarmouth, and Rachel answered it on the first ring.

"Hi, Rachel? This is Kate, owner of Brass, Leather, and Denim. I got your name from our mutual friend, Brad. He said you were the best abstract artist around and that you might help me get some art on the walls in here."

Rachel's stomach did a flip. She hadn't *really* expected anything to come of Brad's promise. She certainly hadn't expected Kate to call her.

"Oh yes! I'm so glad you called." Rachel dug out a fresh dish towel and covered the platter of tuna steaks with it. "I'd love to have a few pieces displayed in shops like yours!"

"Well, that's why I called you so quickly—Brad sent over some photos of your work to me. It's exactly what my partner and I are looking for in the shop."

Rachel marched to the kitchen drawer where she kept pens and sticky notes—this woman was all business, and she didn't want to miss a beat.

"He said you're busy and I should act fast. So I'd like to commission you to do three large pieces for our back wall and about five smaller pieces to go over each window." Rachel heard the fast tip-tap-tap of a laptop keyboard in the background. "Is this something you'd be available to do in the next month or two?"

"Yes, I can do that. I'd need to come to the store, take some measurements, and bring some paint samples so you can pick out colors. After that, I'll have a better idea about what you want and can give you a price."

Her toes curled in her slippers as she spoke. She hated talking about pricing, but Emily had told her, several times over, that her work was valuable and she needed to be compensated for it. "Art adds tremendous value to people's lives," she'd said when Rachel asked her advice on getting her painting business started. "Never be afraid to ask for what you yourself would pay for a piece you love." That had put it into perspective for Rachel.

"That sounds great." The furious typing came to a sudden stop. "Are you free Monday morning? The shop is closed on

Mondays, so we can walk around without distractions. Nine o'clock?"

"Works for me." Rachel blew out a silent breath.

Drop kids off, run, shower, and head to Yarmouth.

After hanging up the phone, Rachel let out a squeal and danced around the kitchen. She didn't even notice Benjamin had come downstairs.

"Are you trying to twerk?" Benjamin asked her, pulling an earbud out of his ear. He looked as if he'd eaten something sour, then shook his head. "Stop, Mom!"

"No! I just got a job to do *eight* paintings for Brass, Leather, and Denim! *Eight!* I'm so excited!" Rachel threw her hands up in the air, and Elsa ran to the top of the stairs.

"Mom! Did I just hear what I thought I heard? I love the sweaters they have in that store! Maybe she can do a trade, and you can get me that cashmere hoodie I tried on the last time we were there!"

"You need to wait until Christmas, Elsa. And how about, 'that's great mom!'?"

She grabbed her phone and texted Aimee: *You know that shop you love, B, L, &, D, that we go to every time you visit? Just got off the phone with the owner! I'm doing a bunch of paintings for them! Over the moon!*

The kids went back to their business, and Rachel broke off a piece of tuna steak and let it melt in her mouth. Adam should have been home a while ago and dinner was getting cold.

When she called and he didn't pick up, she texted: *When will you be home? Dinner is ready! I got a big job today, can't wait to tell you all about it.*

She tore a paper towel off the holder and wiped up the sesame seeds that had fallen on the counter. Energy was bubbling out of her. She should text Brad too, right? To thank him? It would be rude not to. She picked up the phone.

A rush went through her as she hit send: *Just got off the phone with Kate, she gave me a big job because of you! I can't tell you how appreciative I am, Brad. Thank you!*

She tapped her fingers on the island, watching Benjamin play on his iPad. It felt strange to be texting Brad while her son was sitting a few yards away from her, but this was work, and his recommendation had given her a nice sized job.

Rachel glided around the kitchen, lighting a candle, and pouring ice water in the glasses. "Mom, need help with dinner? I'm starving," Benjamin said, plucking out an ear bud.

"Thanks Honey, but I'm all set. We'll eat in a few minutes. Didn't that cookie tide you over?"

"No, you'd only let me get one." He shoved his ear bud back in and got back to his iPad.

Rachel glanced around the kitchen. Dinner was complete, and she was going to eat with her kids while the food was still warm, whether or not Adam was home.

Her phone buzzed again as she grabbed the salad. It was Adam: *That's great! Sorry forgot to tell you I'm working late. Crazy day.*

"What's wrong, Mom?" Benjamin asked as he set the salad on the table, almost tripping over Cora, who was practically under her feet.

"Oh nothing. Dad is just working late again, and he forgot to tell me. No biggie."

Before calling the kids to dinner, she picked up her phone again.

We should meet to talk about sizing for painting!

She wanted to make Brad's piece extra amazing, since he'd done something so generous for her. It was the professional thing to do.

At least, that's what she told herself.

Brad

Brad tossed some leftover chicken with olive oil, then threw it in the air fryer. He was barely more than a toddler the first time his mother pulled him into the kitchen to cook with her, sitting him on the counter so he could mix and sprinkle and pat. As he got older, she'd put him to work stirring the meat or sauce she'd have on the stove, and that became his regular job.

His mother never measured ingredients, telling him that if you eyeballed it, food would always taste better. When it came to putting things like cheese, butter, or chocolate chips in a recipe, she'd always say the recipe never called for enough.

"Food always tastes better when you add your own flair," she'd say, shaking extra cinnamon and nutmeg into her banana bread batter.

He opened the crisper and pulled out the romaine lettuce, then reached for the hunk of blue cheese he'd bought earlier this week. His mom made the best blue cheese dressing—he knew the recipe by heart.

He held the lettuce and cheese to his chest as he moved

some things around the door of the refrigerator, hoping there was enough mayonnaise to make the dressing.

"Yes!" he shouted, shaking the container. After placing all the ingredients on the counter, he texted his mom.

Making your famous blue cheese dressing tonight. I want to take you to Antonia's for dinner soon, so let me know a night that works for you.

Brad's mom loved Antonia's. It was a little Italian restaurant near his house, and had been his parent's standing Friday night date when his father was alive.

He sliced into the lettuce, and his mouth salivated. It had been way too long since he'd made this.

He crumbled the cheese into the bowl, then poured vinegar and Worcestershire sauce over it, followed by a heap of mayonnaise. Then he whipped all the ingredients into chunky deliciousness.

Would Rachel remember the time they'd devoured a whole bowl of this with carrot sticks? It was the night they'd come home from York Beach—it had been their first weekend away together, and they'd felt so grown up staying in a hotel by the ocean.

As the chicken cooled a bit, Beth came down the stairs. Brad quickly made her a plate of salad, tossing the best pieces of chicken on top. He held the plate up to her, beaming. "Cooking is like therapy! Look at this! You can do wonders with leftover chicken!"

Beth stared at the plate, her hands on her hips. "Why did you put dressing all over that salad? You know I can't eat that. Did you leave any plain for me?"

Brad pulled the plate closer to his body, scrunching his eyebrows together. "I thought you liked this dressing. It's my mom's recipe—"

"It's not that I don't like it, it's that I'm not eating anything fatty. I asked you to make me a plain salad or roasted veggies to go with the chicken before I went upstairs to change." Widening her eyes at him, she added, "And you said, 'okay.'"

Oh right.

"I'm sorry, Beth. I forgot. This salad is so good though. Come on and have a bite. Maybe just eat a few bites?" Brad stabbed a fork in the giant mound of salad, making sure he got a chunk of golden chicken, and slid it into the dressing before holding it up to Beth's mouth.

"No, and stop! You're getting dressing all over the chicken!" She grabbed the fork and plate from his hand and scooped a few pieces of chicken out. "I'll just eat the chicken that didn't get any dressing on it before I got to Pilates."

Beth sat at the table as Brad piled another plate full of salad and grabbed sparkling water from the fridge. "Want one?" he asked Beth, holding up his can. His phone buzzed, and Beth's eyes went to his pocket.

"No. Thanks. I'm just going to eat a few bites of this, then go. I want to get there early to stretch." She sat there frowning, pushing the chicken around on her plate.

Brad knew it wasn't a great time to see if she'd made any more plans to start working, but it never seemed to be a good time. He tried to be casual. "Did you, by any chance, get a minute to talk to your dad about starting work? Or have you thought about a job somewhere else?"

Beth rolled her eyes without looking up at him. "I don't think I want to work for anyone else. And no, he's been busy. So have I."

Brad squeezed his fork. "Isn't it just a matter of you calling him and telling him you're in? I think it would be so great for you, Beth."

She dropped her fork with a piercing clang. "Listen, I didn't know you were going to harass me about this. I'm going to the outlets with my mom this Saturday. I'll talk to her about it then."

Brad took in a breath. "Beth, call *him*. Don't go through your mom. That's going to—"

"Just stop!" She pushed back from the table and stared at Brad. "Let me do this on my terms."

"Beth, I know you don't want to talk about this tonight, but you never want to talk about it. And the shoplifting—you still refuse to address that too." He reached across the table. "I want to help you ... deal with this."

She looked at his hand, but didn't reach for his. "The shoplifting was a one-time thing. I felt horrible and embarrassed and won't do it again. I just ... I miss being able to go out and buy whatever I want without a second thought. I know you think I'm entitled. And horrible." She looked up at him and blinked back tears. "Up until a few years ago, you wanted the same lifestyle I had. You said it many times. And now you're going back on that."

Brad nodded, guilt twisting in his stomach. "You're right. I wanted that. I got swept up in your parents' enormous house, the traveling, the lifestyle." He circled his hand in the air. "All of it. I saw them and wanted what they had. And I wanted to give that to you."

"So what happened?"

He put his elbows on the table and leaned closer to his wife. "It's not me, Beth. I stopped feeling like myself, and I let it go on for too long. *I* am to blame for that." He put a hand over his heart. "That was my mistake. And I should have explained more how I was feeling, but all I know is I had to get back to myself, or I was going to lose my shit."

Beth pushed her plate away. "Okay. I'm going. I can't eat this and I can't be late."

"I want you to love me for the non-monetary things I can provide."

Beth stood up. "I do." But her words were lifeless—there was no warmth behind them.

He wanted to say, "Can't we talk about this more? You're just going to leave?" Instead, he let her go, flinching as she slammed the door behind her.

How did we get here?

He spread salad around on his plate, dropped his fork, and pulled his phone from his pocket.

There was a text from Rachel—Kate had called her, *and* Rachel wanted to meet him to discuss his painting.

Sitting up straighter, he typed back: *I'd love to meet you. How's Saturday? Café Crème at noon?*

He took a bite of salad, feeling light and heavy at the same time.

These two women brought out completely different sides of him. Rachel was breathing new life into him, reminding him of all the things that made him happiest. Beth was unhappy in her own right, because the things that made her happiest, he couldn't provide. He was becoming more and more sure his marriage was coming apart. And he wasn't sure if he wanted to put it back together.

Rachel

Rachel sat in Café Crème, watching a few shoppers pass by. The smell of coffee, butter, and cinnamon filled the room, and her mouth watered. She'd tried to have an egg for breakfast but hadn't been able to get it down.

She'd told Adam she was going out to pick up some more paint samples for her meeting on Monday, which was true, but she'd left out the part about meeting Brad. Regret was worming its way through her, and she wondered if it would be too late to tell Adam the truth when she got home.

After Adam had told her he was going into the office anyway—he'd been working more than ever lately—and Elsa and Benjamin had asked if they could be dropped off at the mall with friends, she'd told herself it was more than acceptable to be meeting a client on a Saturday.

That's all this is—a client meeting.

She pulled a few stray Cora hairs off of her pant leg and smiled, remembering how her loyal friend had watched her get ready this morning, golden eyebrows twitching as she lay in her favorite sunny spot.

And so what if Adam didn't like it, anyway? This business

was something she'd wanted to start for a long time. Brad was just another customer who had great connections—she'd be silly not to use him. If Adam didn't want to take any interest in this part of her life, she'd figure it out herself. Thinking about his apathy made her ears burn.

How many times had her husband been tempted by another woman? Is this how it started with him? Small indiscretions that led to bigger, more hurtful secrets?

He stepped out of your marriage without giving your feelings a thought. You didn't tell him the whole truth about where you were going today. It's not even close.

She couldn't seem to stop the hamster wheel spinning in her head, knowing it had spun off its axis.

When Brad came through the door, her heart jumped. She glanced down to see if her heartbeat was visible through her chest because it felt like it might be. She took a slow inhale, smiling through it.

The way he walked with a tall posture but casual ease, the way he smiled as he held the door open for the woman walking about fifteen seconds behind him—he was the same as he'd been in high school. Only sexier now that she knew how rare a man like Brad was.

Last week, Adam had let a door slam in her face as they were walking into the café at the apple orchard. He'd apologized, and told her it was because he was on an important call. "I've seen you do that to Mom even when you *aren't* on the phone, though," Elsa had said before Rachel could.

As Brad strode toward her, a grin crinkled his eyes.

"Hey, Picasso. You haven't been waiting long, have you?" He peeled off his army green corduroy jacket. His cologne sent her into dizzy delight.

"Just a few minutes." She could feel herself beaming— being around Brad made her feel giddy. She mentally shook herself. *No. You're here for work.*

"No Diet Coke yet?" he asked, tucking his coat in the booth. He interlocked his fingers on top of the table, and Rachel imagined him reaching across and sliding his fingers into hers.

"I was waiting for you," Rachel said, trying not to notice the muscles flexing in his forearms as he pulled up his sleeves a bit. *I was waiting for you.*

"I got it." He stood up, heading for the front counter. When he passed by, another whiff of cologne hit Rachel. She clutched the side of the table to steady herself.

He returned carrying two bottles of Diet Coke and two large glasses of ice. Rachel tried to wipe the smirk off her face —she'd enjoyed watching the back of him as he stood in line and ordered. Brad had a bit of a curve to his butt, and she'd always grabbed it when he was on top of her, pulling him deeper into her. Rachel grabbed the icy glass, hoping it would tame her arousal. *Painting. Work. Focus.*

"I haven't had soda in years. This is going to be good." Brad opened both bottles and poured Rachel's, then filled his glass.

"Thanks. You were always good about making sure I had enough Diet Coke."

"It was nothing. And it made you happy."

She felt his eyes on her as she peeled at the label on the soda bottle. These slight gestures meant so much, and she never experienced them. A growing ache, almost a bitterness, at the way things had turned out, at what she could have had, tugged at her.

"Remember the night the soda machine ate my money?" Brad shot her that smile again. "We stood there for a half hour trying to shake the damn machine."

"Yes!" Rachel let out a burst of laughter, the hilariousness of the memory breaking through her dark thoughts. "That was some serious dedication."

His mouth straightened, and he propped his head on one hand. "I know we're here to talk about the painting. And you already listened to my half-ass apology the other night." He paused, and Rachel thought he was holding his breath. "I *was* very dedicated to you." He lowered his voice to a whisper. "I shouldn't say this—we're both married. But I fucked up. I *know* I fucked up, Rachel. You deserved better."

Rachel met his gaze, blinking three times slowly. What was she supposed to say to that? *Maybe he's been thinking of you as much as you've been thinking of him.*

Brad sat back. "Anyway. I needed you to know that. You did nothing wrong. I was a young, and very stupid, kid."

Rachel waved her hand as if to brush away the past, but stopped herself. She crossed her arms and held his gaze. "You hurt me. There was never a question in my mind that you were *the one* back then." She straightened her back and gave him a bright, let bygones-be bygones smile. "But yes, we were kids. We both had so much living to do. It was for the best."

But her heart had sped up again. It *wasn't* for the best. She'd fallen for a guy who hardly noticed her existence. And she was stuck with him. And now she was sitting across from a man who thought she was a great artist, always remembered her Diet Coke, and held the door for strangers. But he was here out of guilt. He'd buy a painting and send business her way and feel better about himself. And that would be that.

Brad parted his lips, then closed them. The silence stretched. They held each other's gazes until Rachel finally cleared her throat. "Um, so. What are you thinking as far as the size of your painting?" She reached into her purse and pulled out some paint samples. "Where are you going to hang it, exactly?"

Brad

Brad had promised himself they'd talk about the painting as discussed, then he'd leave.

Rachel was reaching into her purse to grab paint samples, and he saw at the crown of her head the cowlick she'd always tried to hide—it stuck up just a little more than the rest of her hair. He used to lie on her bed in college and watch her try to smooth it out with her huge curling iron. She was wearing a baggy white T-shirt under a black blazer and her hair was in a messy bun on top of her head. *She still looks great in anything and everything.*

Being around her made him feel so full, so at home. He put his hand over his chest as if he could dull the feeling of wanting to sit there and tell her everything that was on his mind: all the times he'd thought about her; how hard it had been these past few weeks to *not* wonder what a life with her would look like, what it would *feel* like.

"Blue is practically a neutral color. You know how almost anything goes with your favorite jeans? Blue furniture is the same. You could go really bold and use all primary colors. Or" —Rachel flipped to a paint card with a few shades of soft grays and smiled—"you can go serene. I love soft grays and taupes with blues. Very calming."

"Calming and serene sounds great." He pointed to the two lightest shades of gray. "I like these two."

After Brad had also picked out a few shades of beige, per Rachel's suggestion, he wasn't ready for their visit to end. "Okay, now let's go get something to eat. This is supposed to be lunch, and I could use something sweet." He slid out of the leather booth, offering his hand to help her out.

Rachel reached for his hand, and he thought he felt a tiny squeeze before she let go of it.

Wooden shelves full of clay and pottery displays, each listing the artist's information, lined the back wall. Brad asked the cashier if they ever displayed paintings from local artists.

"Oh yes, I've been letting local artists display and sell here since I opened a few years ago." She tightened her headscarf and put her hands on her hips. "They sell, too." She pointed to one wall of pottery. "This potter has displayed stuff here for a few years. Just signed a contract with L.L. Bean. Super exciting."

Brad pointed at Rachel. "Well, Rachel here is a wonderful abstract painter, and she's local." He winked at Rachel, whose cheeks turned a flattering pink.

"Oh yeah? Well, bring in some pieces! We can always make space for another local artist. Tell me more."

Rachel turned and looked behind her as if to make sure there wasn't a line forming behind them, then leaned against the counter, crossing one ankle over the other. She used to stand the same way when she'd ordered fast food while they were together. "I mostly use acrylics. Sometimes I use sand for texture." Rachel pulled her phone from her purse and showed her a few pictures.

Brad's stomach flipped as he watched Rachel describe her art. She glowed when she was passionate about something.

He'd seen this same look many times, often for little things, like when they were driving down the road and she'd see a Christmas tree on someone's car, or when they'd made sushi together and her California rolls had come out looking just like they did in the restaurant.

Rachel asked the owner how many pieces she could bring in to start.

"Well," she glanced around the café and pointed to a blank wall behind a plush teal sofa. "We could use a few things on this wall. Some large paintings would look great hanging over the sofa. And that space gets lots of traffic since it's one of the first things you see when you walk in."

Brad couldn't peel his eyes off her. She was thankful and appreciative about something as small as a soda, and at the same time, this humble confidence oozed out of her.

His phone buzzed in his pocket, and he pulled it out to see a text from Beth: *I'm going a bit crazy shopping with Mom! She's treating a lot, but sorry in advance!*

Sounds dangerous. Remember, I'm meeting Rachel to talk about the painting for the living room. Any thoughts before we finalize things?

Brad's heart sped up again as he saw the three dots bouncing.

Oh, you're still doing that? I'm not sure the living room is the best place? Maybe the spare room, like I said?

Brad rolled his eyes and tucked his phone in his pocket. Once Rachel had finished her business with the café owner, they headed back to their table with a cinnamon bun the size of his head. Rachel had pointed to it when he asked her what she wanted for lunch.

Eyes shining, Rachel ripped off a small piece. "You know," she said, popping the bite into her mouth. "I think I need to hire you as my agent. Thank you."

"I think you advocated for yourself perfectly well. You're

so passionate about your work! It's contagious. Did I hear you say you sometimes use sand in your paintings? I'd love to try that with my students. Texture is big in second grade."

"Ah, you were listening." Rachel sat up straighter, her smile brightening. "All you do is mix sand with the paint to add some texture. That's really all there is to it. You can do it in a cup, but for second graders, it would probably be more fun for them to squirt paint on a canvas first, then add the sand and mix it up."

She broke a thick, buttery piece of cinnamon roll in half and slid the smaller piece into her mouth, leaving her thumb between her lips to suck off the frosting. It made Brad think of a few things besides cinnamon rolls and painting. Imagining her lips on his for a second, he pushed away the thought.

"Do your kids ever paint with you?" He wiped his hands on a napkin and took a sip of soda. His legs were still tight from his morning's run. He stretched them out under the table as far as he could in the tight space of the booth.

"Oh, no. They aren't really into crafting any more. We used to do a lot of it when they were kids. They're as interested in my painting as most teens would be interested in their parents' job."

She tore off another piece of cinnamon roll. "But they really are terrific kids. My world. I used to feel guilty about taking time away from them to paint, but they're happy I have something to do. It's sweet how supportive they are, really."

"Kids are just ... amazing. People always ask me and Beth why we don't have any. It was a choice we made for lots of reasons, but since I started teaching those kids, I've felt a part of myself come alive. Like, it's more than enough if I can teach the rest of my life. Many people don't understand that."

Rachel leaned forward, resting her elbows on the table. "It was all you ever talked about doing when we were together. I'm so glad you're doing what you love, Brad. It's so important. And no one needs to understand your lifestyle choices except for you."

"Very true. And teaching has its drawbacks. Beth was used to a certain lifestyle growing up. I could provide it for her when I worked for her father. But prioritizing the bottom line above my happiness and the lifestyle *I* wanted for almost fifteen years took a toll on me. All I wanted to do was teach."

Rachel tapped her empty soda bottle on the side of their shared plate. Her chin was resting in her palm, and the same wistful smile crossed her lips that had made him tingle in chemistry class the first time they talked all those years ago. "You're allowed to make yourself happy, Brad."

"Rachel?" he asked, knowing he should leave right now, but he couldn't. Rachel's hair was glowing, her caramel strands set aflame by the afternoon light. She was beautiful. He felt completely at ease being with her—completely himself. How had he lived without her for the last twenty years?

Rachel

"Rachel?"

Hearing her name, all by itself, coming from Brad's mouth, sent goosebumps up and down her body. His smooth voice made her nipples tingle, and she had to hold back a shiver. Her dry mouth wouldn't let her swallow, and she could only muster a nod in response.

"Go for a walk with me?" She could hear the hesitation in his voice. It was the same way he'd asked her to go to that first soccer game in chemistry class during their junior year of high school—"Come to the soccer game with me tonight?" Like he was *sure* she'd say no, but he'd had to try, anyway.

Rachel heard herself say, "No," and then before she knew it, an "Okay" barely passed her lips. Brad smiled, and she got all tingly again, and placed a palm just below her collarbone, trying to rub the sensation away.

They stared at each other for another few seconds, and Rachel wondered if he was going to say what she was thinking —that maybe more time together would somehow ease these feelings of longing, and their lives would go back to the way they were before she'd bumped into him at the café.

Brad stood and grabbed his coat. Rachel didn't move; she froze with her palm still pressed to that spot under her collarbone. This was more than just business. Her heart sped to a sprint under her open hand.

Even though she hadn't heard her phone, she checked it to see if Adam or the kids had called or texted before getting up. But there were no messages. Plopping her phone back in her purse, she stood and followed Brad toward the café door.

Just the other day, we were planning a future together.

But it wasn't the other day. It was two decades ago, and he had left her for the woman he was married to now.

Brad pointed at the blank space above the teal sofa. "I can see it now, Picasso! Right here. A few paintings here, and boom! They are going to sell out in no time. You'll probably have a hard time keeping up with the demand."

She wanted to tell him to stop. To stop being so wonderful. To stop giving her things in one afternoon that she'd been craving for years. Instead, she smiled and said, "I hope so."

It's just a walk. You're going to go for a walk, then you're going to go home and see if everyone wants to go out for Chinese food tonight.

But ... Brad's voice, his words. Everything he did made her insides stir. He woke up parts of her that had been asleep for so long.

"There's a great candle shop next door. You'd love it. Want to look?" Brad opened the door for her, and she took a deep inhale as she passed by him.

"I do." She automatically agreed without thought.

They browsed the shop, holding out candles for each other to smell. "I love this nude packaging and the wooden tops," Rachel said, smelling the orange-clove candle. "Oh, this one!" She put it in front of Brad's nose.

"Smells like Christmas morning! I'm going to need one of

those." Brad took one of the candles from the shelf and palmed it between his hands.

He moseyed in the other direction to browse, and Rachel pretended to continue smelling candles, but she couldn't smell much of anything anymore. Or feel. Or hear.

It was as if she was levitating over her own body. She watched herself run her fingers over the smooth glass of the candles and heard Adam's voice echo in her head. *Why do you always have to light candles? They make the whole house smell. I can't take it.*

They made their purchases and strolled together with their paper bags down the brick sidewalk. Rachel felt the autumn breeze against her cheeks, and a pile of crisp leaves had gathered where the stone walls of the shops met the walkway.

A mother and her two teenagers—a boy and a girl—stood staring into the window of the pet store. The kids cupped their hands around their faces and leaned against the window, and the mother told them to stop smudging the glass. Rachel grinned, then guilt erased her smile. She missed her kids, and she was going for a walk with a man she had feelings for, so aware the only reason she was still with Adam was because of them.

"Do you have any pets?" Brad stopped to look in the pet store window, his eyes locked on a Golden Retriever puppy with a pink collar and leash as her owner shopped.

"We do, Cora. She's a Golden Retriever we got when the kids were young. She looked a lot like that little munchkin when we got her." Rachel pointed to the puppy, and Brad turned to face her.

"I see a lot of you in your kids."

"Elsa really favors Adam. You can see it in younger pictures of him." They started strolling down the sidewalk again, and the sun disappeared behind a few clouds.

"What about sports? Are they into any of that?"

"Elsa plays soccer and Benjamin plays lacrosse. They aren't the stars of the team, but they enjoy it. That's all I care about."

"Yeah. What happened to kids just having fun on the field? Kids' sports teams are on steroids now. It's not like it was when we were in school, that's for sure."

When we were in school ... Rachel could practically smell the turf of the soccer field, could feel the firmness of Brad's arm as she pressed her body against his, a shared blanket over their knees. She could feel the warmth of the drive afterward, the heat blasting and magnifying that pine tree air freshener his parents always kept hanging from the rearview. Her stomach would brew with anticipation as they'd drive to Lovers' Lane and steam up the windows.

A strong breeze sent dry leaves rustling against the sidewalk, bringing Rachel back to the present. "Do you have a dog? You seemed smitten with that puppy."

"No, but I'd like one. I've been working on Beth since I started teaching—I'm home more. We don't travel much these days." He threw his thumb behind him toward the pet store. "She doesn't want to deal with the mess and all the fuss, which is understandable. She never had one growing up."

Rachel smiled wistfully. "I don't know what I'd do without Cora. She's getting older. When she goes ... I don't even want to think about it." She watched their feet slowly making their way down the sidewalk, Brad's normally long gait shortened to match the pace with hers. "I remember, Lady, the lab you had growing up."

"Oh, she was the best!" A huge smile lit up Brad's face. "Remember, she used to come to the football games with us?"

She remembered. She remembered making out under the bleachers, Brad's hand slipping high up her inner thigh as Lady panted happily nearby, enjoying all the new scents and oblivious to the two teenagers in love.

Rachel scratched her head, feeling the heat rise in her

chest. "I do. She was a special dog. I missed her a lot after we broke up. Your parents too."

Brad draped an arm around her shoulder. "They missed you too."

If she'd turned her head a little to the left, she would have kissed him. She stamped out of his reach, immediately missing the warmth of him.

Rachel was uneasy, knowing she had to leave Brad soon to get her kids. "I think you need to get a dog, Brad. I want you to be happy. It sounds like you aren't. Or maybe you are? It's ... it's none of my business. I'm sorry." Rachel pulled on her earlobe and fiddled with her earring.

"I think Beth might literally kill me if I just brought home a dog." His eyebrows knit together, and his eyes studied Rachel's. "The truth is, Beth and I have been in a slump for a while. A bad slump. We've grown apart. Or maybe I've grown apart from her. It isn't her fault she's always been exactly who she is. And I ... I think I've spent years trying to convince myself I could be the husband she wants me to be. Lately, though, I'm not so sure I can." Their eyes locked, and Rachel had to remind herself to breathe. Was she the reason he'd used the word "lately"? She crossed her arms, her brown paper bag of candles forming a barrier between herself and Brad. If she didn't put something between them, it would be too easy to close the distance.

"I understand. Marriage is hard." She cleared her throat, her frustration building as she thought about her dissatisfaction with own marriage. Who had changed? Adam, or her? Or had they never been compatible at all? "I hope you two can work things out."

Brad pressed the heel of his free hand over his eyes. "I just ... I don't know how I got here. It just happened. When I was working for Beth's dad, and we lived that lifestyle, it wasn't me. Took me a while to figure it out, but it wasn't me."

Rachel couldn't help but feel a little angry and satisfied at the same time. He'd left her for the excitement he'd felt around Beth. He'd chased it, threw away their plans for the future, then decided it wasn't actually what he wanted. Yes, they were young and had so much life ahead of them. But what could have been if he hadn't made that choice?

"Things don't just happen in a marriage, Brad. Two people let them happen."

Feeling her own hypocrisy, she said, "I should get going. I'm parked in the back lot."

Angst filled her chest. She wanted to get home and hug her kids, but it felt impossible to peel herself from Brad.

Go home to your family. He needs to work on his marriage. And so do you.

"I'll walk you. Here, let's go down this street. It's a short-cut," he said, cradling her elbow in his hand for a second.

Rachel picked up her pace, removing her elbow from his hand. She needed to lighten the mood before they went their separate ways. "So." Rachel held up her pointer finger in the air in front of her. "I've got your order to work on, Kate's order from Brass, Leather, and Denim. And now Café Crème." She playfully bumped him with her shoulder. "Thanks to you! You have quite a few connections. It was the push I needed."

"Well, you're very talented. Glad I'm getting a Rachel original before you get too busy to paint something for me."

They'd reached her car, and Rachel stopped in front of the driver's side door. "I'd never be too busy for you." She felt herself flush. "To paint something for you, I mean."

Brad's eyes had a tightness to them resembling pain. *Idiot. Why do you keep saying things like that to him?*

He reached out and gently squeezed her forearm. "I'm so glad we got to catch up. You're still the same amazing Rachel."

Brad took a step closer. Their eyes locked. She could feel

the heat between them, and Rachel's heart pounded under her chest. She leaned back against her car for support. A loose piece of hair dangled by her cheek, and Brad reached up and tucked it behind her ear.

She inhaled sharply, her knees almost buckling at the casual touch. Brad's eyes studied her lips, and he leaned even closer.

She closed her eyes and felt his hand move slowly to the back of her neck. His stubble brushed her cheek, then he kissed her softly right next to her ear.

The feel of his lips on her cheek set her body on fire. She was afraid to breathe, not wanting anything to interrupt this moment.

Brad took a slow step back, and she reached behind her, gripping her door handle with everything she had in her so she wouldn't reach out for him.

"I'll see you soon, Rach." He gave her a smile and strode off.

She stood watching him, her chest heaving as she tried to regulate her breathing. She reached a hand to the back of her neck where he had just held her, as if a part of him still lingered there. Tears swelled in her eyes.

Brad turned around, caught her watching him, and took a few steps backward. "Bye, Picasso." He waved.

Rachel nodded her head, quickly got in her car, and started it.

Looking in the rearview mirror, she wiped her eyes. "I'm going to go home, get this painting done, and that will be the end of this." She said the words out loud, as if that would make them more true. She chanced another look at Brad, just in time to watch him turn around and head reluctantly back to his car.

Brad

B rad threw his head against the headrest of his seat.

You came so close to kissing her. What's wrong with you?

He started the car and cracked a window. The smell of smoked brisket and turkey from Beale Street Barbeque floated in, mixing with the other scents of fall. He lifted his collar up to his nose.

Rachel. Does she think about you as much as you think about her?

He was pretty sure Rachel was gone—he'd watched her drive away–but he drove to the parking lot where he'd almost kissed her, anyway. There was so much more he wanted to say.

The spot where she'd parked was empty. The void consumed him as he stared at the line of old brick buildings, willing Rachel to come back.

You let her go all those years ago, and now you have to live with that decision.

After several minutes, he rubbed his eyes and checked the time. Beth would be home tonight, so he had five or six more hours to himself. But dread was already brewing in his belly.

It wasn't fair to Beth where things were going with Rachel. Even if she was totally off-limits for him, his head and heart were with her. Not with Beth.

Something had to give here, and soon.

Brad wondered what would have happened if he hadn't fallen for Beth. But he had. She'd persisted, even though she knew he was with Rachel. And he had let her.

As he drove, images of Rachel kept popping into his head: *Rachel cooking with him. Rachel making a guest appearance in his classroom to teach the kids to paint with sand. Rachel in paint splattered overalls in her art room standing in front of an easel he'd set up for her. Sinking into her, feeling her nails dig into his back.*

He shook the images out of his head.

Stop it. She has two kids. She's married.

But she was so easy to be with and accepted him for exactly who he was.

Maybe Rachel's right. Maybe I should get a dog. Surely Beth will warm up after she sees how much joy a dog can bring to a household.

Brad slapped the steering wheel and nodded his head, the decision made. A sharp wind howled around his car as if in full agreement, whipping up leaves like confetti.

He'd just go to the shelter and look. Maybe they'd have a sweet, older dog that wouldn't require a lot of exercise, and he could bring Beth in to see it. She'd probably fall in love and that would be all it would take.

On his way to the shelter, he painted a whole new life for himself—one with a dog in it. He saw the dog curled up at his feet while reading in bed, greeting him when he came home from work, getting a pup cup at the coffee shop a few blocks from his house.

All the barking from the lonely dogs mixed with the chemical cleaners almost made Brad dizzy. He padded down the long, sterile hallway that housed older dogs behind glass. And as he envisioned a potential life with each dog, he realized that the other person in his fantasies was not Beth. It was Rachel. Rachel in bed with him reading, the dog curled up at their feet. Rachel and the dog, greeting him when he came home from work. Walking the dog with Rachel to get a pup cup down the street.

He knelt, so he was face to face with an old Lab mix. She had black fur except for her gray muzzle, and her eyes looked up at him, sad and pleading. He was trying to put a tiny bandaid over a huge wound.

"We'll figure this out. Won't we?" The sweet girl let out a sad, low whine and then sank to the ground, defeated, as Brad turned to leave the shelter and head home to his wife who absolutely, positively, did not want a dog.

Rachel

Rachel dialed Emily's number as she sat cross-legged on the basement floor. Adam had just left to show a home, and Elsa and Benny were outside kicking the soccer ball.

It was a nice, lazy Sunday afternoon, and the sun had already set, casting a golden light over everything. There was something about the sun going down early that made her feel peaceful and content. Grabbing a book and covering up with a blanket in the evening while Cora slept at her feet was one of her favorite things to do. When it was dark and cold out, Rachel didn't feel guilty about getting into her pajamas right after dinner, dozing in between pages.

Their last interaction in Panera had gone well, and Rachel had hoped Emily would have reached out to her by now. But this was the way it had always been between them.

She was about to hang up when Emily answered. "Rachel —what's up?" She gasped for air.

"Oh, sorry, did I catch you in the middle of a workout?"

"Yeah. Just getting done now."

"This is the second time I've caught you in an afternoon

workout. I thought you usually exercised in the morning." Rachel dipped her fingers into a bag of sand, thinking about how Brad's painting had propelled her out of bed this morning.

"I've been mixing it up," she answered through labored breathing. "What's up?" Her tone was sharp, and Rachel winced.

Rachel pushed her entire hand into the sand and squeezed tightly, feeling the grains slide between her fingers, up under her fingernails.

"I met with Brad yesterday." The words tumbled out, and Rachel put her non-sandy hand on her forehead.

God, why did you blurt it out like that?

"Oh, you mean you ran into him again? Or did you actually meet him intentionally?" Rachel knew, without being able to see her, that Emily was using air quotes around the words, "ran into him."

"I told him I'd do that painting for him, and needed to meet about the size and colors and everything." Rachel tilted her head and touched the back of her neck as she relived how close they'd come to kissing yesterday. Her desire to feel his lips on hers was outweighing her guilt.

"So, strictly business, then? *I'm sure,*" Emily snickered. "Tell me everything."

Rachel stood up and crossed the basement to the window. She had the perfect view of Elsa and Benjamin—they'd stopped kicking the ball and were examining something—a leaf?

"It *was* business. It *is* business. It *has* to be. He's taken. I don't think I could ever do to another woman what was done to me."

Her stomach flipped as she remembered the morning she'd realized Aimee's hunch had been right—Brad *was* with Beth. They'd paraded out of the library, holding hands and laughing, as Rachel watched from the window of her history class.

She'd left class to go throw up in the bathroom—he'd seemed like a completely different person. Even now, that image stung more than hearing her own husband fuck another woman.

"Never say never, Rachel. Most people don't *mean* to have an affair. There's a lot that goes into these situations." Rachel's gut dropped, and she heard what sounded like sneakers hitting the floor. "I mean ... that's what I gather from friends who've had affairs. It wouldn't make you the devil, Rachel."

She didn't bother telling her sister she'd been referring to Brad leaving her for Beth in college, not Adam's affair.

"Well, it would make me a bad person."

Emily's tone was defensive. "Yeah. You'll stay in your sexless marriage and continue to do all the right things—be an annoying model wife and mother."

Rachel's jaw tightened. Emily's brutal honesty was refreshing most of the time, and she knew she'd been complaining a lot lately about Adam and their marriage. But this was too much.

"Listen, I'm going to let you go. I can see where this conversation is going, and I'm just going to go ahead and exit stage right. Call me when you feel like having an adult conversation instead of mocking me."

Rachel hung up, dropping her phone like it was crawling with fire ants.

Elsa had started calling Emily "Aunt Porcupine" instead of Aunt Emily behind her back. "It's nice she gives us gifts, but she just shoots daggers sometimes, then walks away," Elsa had said one night after a family dinner where everyone had dessert but Emily. She'd asked Rachel if she ever worried about what all the sweets would do to her waistline, as she sipped her ice water.

Rachel had always defended her sister, explaining to the kids that Emily, unfortunately, hadn't been treated very well by their grandmother, and they should have compassion for her.

Elsa picked up the soccer ball and kicked it to Benny, and Rachel returned to her painting. It was almost totally dark, and she turned up the overhead lighting. Instead of swirling the colors together—her go-to—she felt like painting in sharper shapes.

She grabbed her painter's tape and measuring stick and separated the canvas in half, vertically, then began spreading a light gray with her brush until it covered one side. Then she grabbed a handful of sand and sprinkled it into the gray paint.

The texture of the sand made her think of Brad's scruff rubbing against her cheek.

She mixed fast before grabbing another handful of sand and more paint. It stirred into a thick, gritty consistency, and she splattered it on the canvas.

You're still the same amazing Rachel. Beth and I have grown apart. I'll see you soon, Rach.

She stood up, trying to shake the sand off her lap and Brad out of her head. The kids' footsteps tapped over her head and the bathroom door clicked shut.

Placing her hands on her lower back, she bent backwards, her stomach growling as she released several pops. The stretch felt glorious, and she couldn't wait for the Chinese leftovers they were having for dinner.

As she headed upstairs, the garage door rolled up—Adam had been gone for almost three hours. Hopefully, that meant his "picky" client had found a house she'd liked.

"Hey," she said, looking up from washing her hands as he lumbered in. Benjamin and Elsa sounded like they were coming through the ceiling as they raced downstairs.

"Hi," Adam said, surveying the kitchen. "I'm starving. I

thought you were making Sunday dinner tonight." He looked windblown, his gelled hair standing at odd angles, and his cheeks flushed.

"It's leftover Chinese food!" Benjamin said, racing Elsa to the fridge.

"Better not touch those egg rolls! They came with my dinner!" Elsa said, elbowing him out of the way.

"Please let me have one!" Benjamin said, shooting Elsa a pleading look as he opened a container. "I'll give you two of my chicken wings." He held out two cold wings, and Elsa shook her head.

"You guys act like you haven't eaten in a week." Rachel leaned against the sink, drying her hands with a dishtowel.

"Well, you said we had to wait for Dad to eat dinner, and he was late!" Benjamin said, gnawing on a cold wing.

"I'm not late!" Adam barked. "I was working!" His lips were pressed together in a thin line. He unbuttoned a few buttons on his shirt and made a frustrated "Hmph" sound as he raked his fingers through his hair.

Elsa raised her eyebrows in a "whoa" expression. Benjamin's mouth was full, but his eyes widened at his dad. "Jeez, Dad. Chill." He glanced over at Rachel, one eyebrow cocked as if seeking agreement.

Rachel wrapped an arm around Benjamin. He was right, his dad was late. "It's fine. We're all home now, so let's just have a nice dinner together, okay?" She opened the fridge, pulled out the remaining take out boxes, and placed everything on the island.

She was irritated that Adam had snapped at Benjamin like that. They'd all had a great day, and seeing her kids clam up because Adam was in a mood made her lose her appetite.

"Anyone else want Diet Coke?" Rachel cracked one open and took a drink in front of the open fridge. "I haven't had one all day. Can you believe that?"

"Why do you have to stand there with the refrigerator door open? And going one day without Diet Coke isn't some giant accomplishment, Rachel." Adam sat at the table and thumbed open his phone.

Rachel's chest tightened. She closed the fridge door and turned to face Adam, her arms crossed over her chest. Her heart thumped with anger, and she narrowed her eyes, ready to tell him to cool it.

As soon as she saw Benjamin and Elsa look at each other, as if they were exchanging silent words, she closed her mouth.

You can talk about it later.

When her kids looked at her, Rachel shook her head, smiled, and mouthed, "He's tired."

They ate in silence. As soon as Benjamin and Elsa finished, they threw out their containers and went back up to their rooms.

Rachel stood, clearing off the rest of the dinner mess. "How was your showing today? You were gone for a long time. I'm assuming that's good news?"

"It was fine." Adam wiped his face with a napkin.

"Well, I finished a painting today in record time. I did the sand texture thing. Can't wait to see how it looks tomorrow when it's dry. I'm not sure if it will need mo—" She stopped, putting down the bottle of soy sauce and the handful of dirty napkins she'd collected.

"Are you even listening?" Adam was typing on his phone again.

"Yeah," he said. "Sorry, hang on. I'm just getting back to this client. I showed her three homes today, and she wants to make an offer." He put down his phone. "Sorry, you were saying something about a sand sculpture?"

Rachel sighed. "Forget it." She picked up the soy sauce and napkins, putting the soy sauce in the fridge and the napkins in the trash. She was seething. "You know ... you come home after being gone for hours on a Sunday, then you snap at Benjamin for no reason at all and then make that degrading comment about the Diet Coke. Why? What's your fucking problem?"

Looking at her like she'd thrown water in his face, he snapped, "What's *your* problem? Calm down."

She took a step closer and pointed a finger at his face. "Don't you *dare* disrespect me in front of our kids and then tell *me* to calm down." Her neck and ears grew hot with fury. "I didn't say anything because I didn't want to argue in front of them, but now I'm thinking that was a mistake. I don't want them to think their mother has zero self respect." She never wanted her kids to see her tolerate the same behavior her mother used to put up with from her father. A shiver went down the back of her as she realized that's exactly what she'd been doing.

He stood up. "Fine. You want to know what's wrong? I have a lot on my mind. Work. Us. Our sex life. Or lack thereof. It's depressing."

"I can't have *that* talk with you again. I'm sick of it," she warned through clenched teeth. "I'm *not* here for you to fuck whenever you want."

"Christ Rach—"

"And that is no reason to be edgy with the kids. Benny was right, you *were* late." She stood glaring at him, her fists clenched at her sides.

"Whenever I want? It's more like never. Oh, unless I rub your back for twenty minutes and act like a perfect husband. I feel like a puppy dog begging for a treat." He brushed his hands down his hips, looking at his crotch. "You don't care about satisfying my needs, so why do you even care if I listen to your latest project?" He threw up his hands in exasperation.

Rachel studied his face. Wow. He really believed he was fully justified in his rage. *What an entitled asshole.* "I've been putting up with this shitty behavior since the kids were young, and you were so shocked you weren't the only person I had to take care of. I'm done."

Adam's eyes were tired, and his scruff was thicker than it had been in years. Repulsed, Rachel decided suddenly that she needed to get away from him—right then. He was taking all her air—she couldn't breathe and might explode if she had to stand in his presence for another second.

She turned on her heel and headed upstairs.

As her foot hit the second step, Adam said, "I changed because you turned frigid, Rachel."

She gripped the stair railing, wanting to shake it out of place, and stormed out the front door without a coat or shoes into the cold, dark night.

Brad

Brad hadn't seen Rachel for four days. It was Wednesday evening, and he'd taken a drive to Yarmouth. Rachel had told him about a new art gallery that had opened up there a month ago. "Maybe someday I'll have a piece or two in there," she'd said, her eyes literally twinkling.

He sent Beth a quick text: *Taking a drive to Yarmouth. I'll get takeout for dinner tonight on the way home. Let me know what you want.*

He'd tried to have a talk with her the day before. "Neither of us are happy, Beth. Shouldn't we do something about it? Try counseling?"

She'd gotten up from the coach, spun in a circle, and said, "I'm *not* talking about this. Things are *fine*." He knew he should have tried harder, but he couldn't muster up the energy. They'd spent the rest of the day giving each other the silent treatment.

The pavement was shiny under the streetlights—it had been raining all afternoon. It hit Brad that almost all the leaves had blown off the trees. Thanksgiving was in a few weeks.

The plan was to browse the museum, clear his head, and go home and figure out how *not* to hate spending time with his wife.

The museum was silent except for the sounds of the soft, meandering footsteps and low conversations of museum-goers admiring paintings and sculptures. Exposed ceilings showed off all the beams and pipes. The walls and floors were white, absent of any moldings or trim around the large windows. The aesthetic was so Rachel.

Math club had gone by fast, but it had been a loud few hours. His students were always restless when the days got shorter. Hearing nothing but echoing footsteps and low voices was glorious.

Brad stepped slowly to an animal structure made of iron and copper pipes and circled it, trying to figure out what kind of animal it was.

Across the room, a couple holding hands stopped in front of a large window. The woman stood on her toes to whisper something into the man's ear, and they both tried to suppress their laughter.

He and Rachel used to browse the aisles of Blockbuster Video in high school, and Rachel would whisper as they decided what to rent. He'd laugh and remind her they weren't actually at the movies, and she could speak up.

He crossed the painted cement floor to the wall of paintings, taking light steps—his shoes seemed louder than everyone else's.

Each work of art hung underneath its own wall-mounted light, and as he made his way along the paintings, he felt the tension in his shoulders ease. This was exactly what he'd needed.

Walking around the museum loosened his legs up a bit too. He'd gone for a run almost every day this week and had made gains in both speed and distance. But it made his legs tight. The walking felt good.

He stopped in front of a painting framed in long curls of birch bark. Turning to the side to inspect it, Brad could see that each piece of bark was tucked into the next, giving the illusion of longer pieces. He grabbed his phone and snapped a quick picture.

Isn't this a great idea for a frame? He sent the text to Rachel and put his phone back in his pocket.

It buzzed back immediately, and he quickly grabbed it—it was Beth. *Where are you?? My parents are here and we're WAITING!*

It hit Brad that Beth had reminded him last night about their dinner reservations at Fore Street.

Brad blew out a breath. He'd completely forgotten about the dinner, even though Beth *had* reminded him.

If he left right now, he could get there in fifteen minutes.

The thought of rushing over there to sit through, yet another, dinner with her parents only to listen to them talk about how they planned to mitigate the impact of rising interest rates on their real estate dealings or how someone in their posh neighborhood really *couldn't* afford their new Porsche, turned his stomach. But he knew he should go—he'd said he would.

So sorry! Totally forgot. Be there in 20!

The three responding dots immediately began dancing. *Don't bother!*

He gripped his phone, deliberating. The knot in his shoulder was already tightening again. He could leave now and maybe partially salvage the evening. Beth would be icy at dinner, and everyone would be uncomfortable.

Brad pictured all the times he'd thought he would be eating with Beth; at the café, the night she'd left early for Pilates and refused to eat the dinner he'd made, the countless nights he'd told her he was bringing home Chinese food, only to have the food get cold on the counter. He slid his phone into his pocket. He didn't want to play tit for tat, but there wasn't even a tiny part of him that wanted to go to dinner.

He'd let her cool off, then apologize again tonight. Nothing he did seemed to be quite right, and he wanted to spend the evening doing something he enjoyed.

Brad was in bed reading when he heard Beth's car rumble in the garage. He took a deep breath to prepare himself. She hadn't answered his last text—an apology sent before he drove home—which usually meant she wasn't happy with him.

The click-clack of her heels moved fast along the kitchen's wood floor and up the stairs. Usually, she'd remove her shoes as soon as she came in, but she burst through the doorway wearing a fitted, black turtleneck dress that went to her ankles and black high heels.

"Hey," she said, throwing him a sulky glance and reaching behind her neck to remove two gold necklaces. Her blond waves fell past her shoulders, and her lips were red as if she'd just reapplied her lipstick.

She pulled her dress over her head and marched to her closet, wearing a black lace bra and sheer underwear. Her heels were still on, and the tops of her breasts bounced over the bra. His wife was a beautiful woman who worked hard to maintain her appearance. And yet, when he saw her strutting around in sexy underwear and heels, he felt nothing.

"Hey. Beth, I'm sorry. I completely forgot about tonight—just needed to wind down after math club. I didn't think you'd want to go to the museum, so I went ahead figuring we could have dinner together after. How mad were your parents?"

Beth took out her hoop earrings, set them on her nightstand, and crawled over the sheets to Brad's side of the bed. "Another reason you should give up that club."

"Not going to happen, Beth." Happy kids or Beth's materialistic parents? It wasn't even close.

She tilted her head back, exhaling. "I was kidding. My parents were fine. I told them you were grading papers." The corners of her mouth turned down. "I want things to be the way they used to be. Now I'm lying about you grading papers?"

The fact that he'd forgotten dinner tonight, and he'd been forcing thoughts of Rachel out of his head on an hourly basis, panged him with remorse. "I'm sorry. I know I haven't been myself lately." His body tensed as she moved closer to him under the covers.

"It's fine I guess. I forget things too. Can we just … move on? Get out of this bumpy patch or whatever is going on?"

Brad wasn't sure that was possible. But when Beth rested her head on his shoulder, he forced himself to caress her neck the way he used to, the way she'd always liked.

Beth turned to face him, and she kissed him softly on the lips. "I just want things to go back to the way they were. We used to be so happy."

Beth leaned in to kiss him again and reached under the covers, cupping his cock over his boxers.

Brad knew sex wouldn't fix this, fix them.

A shudder went through him, and he pulled away. "Beth, I'm just tired, I think."

Beth jerked away, widening her eyes at him. Her blond hair pooled around her shoulders, but all he could see was Rachel's hair blowing in the breeze as they stood on the sidewalk talking about dogs and kids while window shopping.

Nausea swam in his stomach. "I'm sorry," was all he could muster.

He leaned over and kissed the top of her head, trying to blink back tears. He felt horrible, trapped. Like he needed to do something, but he wasn't sure what. He didn't feel like he could stay with her, and he wasn't sure if he was ready to leave her yet.

"Ugh, I can smell onions, or whatever you ate earlier." Beth threw off the covers and stomped to the bathroom. He watched her silhouette march off.

Rachel wasn't an innocent fantasy. She wasn't someone he'd run into, thought about for a few weeks, then forgot. She was a woman he had deeply loved once, and now he couldn't shake her from his mind. The bigger problem was that he wasn't sure he wanted to.

Rachel

I love that idea. Thanks for the inspo! Your painting is done. When can I drop it off? Rachel hit send and placed her phone back in her robe pocket. It was just before six in the morning, and Adam was in the shower.

She stretched her arms above her head and checked the weather on her phone. The forecast called for snow. She hurried out of bed, turned on the outside lights and watched tiny flakes floating in the dark.

Giddy with excitement, she pulled out her fleece-lined leggings, wool socks, and thermal shirt. It wasn't supposed to accumulate much, so she wouldn't need her spikes, which was good because she didn't know where they were. Running in a little snow was Rachel's favorite way to enjoy the winter months.

"Are you guys up?" she yelled down the hallway. "It's snowing!"

A bear-like groan emitted from Benjamin's room, and Elsa's light glowed from under her bedroom door, but Rachel couldn't hear any movement. She missed when they used to be the ones to wake her up early the morning of the first snow.

Elsa's burst out of her room. "Great! I shouldn't even bother to do my hair because it will get ruined!" She gaped at her mother in her winter running gear. "God, Mom, how can you be in such a good mood? It's so dark and cold." Elsa's hair was matted from sleep on one side, and she was still dressed in her pajamas of boy shorts and a tank top.

Rachel strode toward her daughter and wrapped her arms around her. "Well, maybe if you wore more clothes, Honey, you'd be warmer?" She stood, resting her cheek on her daughter's head, before Elsa gave her a quick hug and shimmied away.

Rachel went back to her bedroom to grab her phone and saw that Brad had already responded. *I have a teacher's meeting tonight. Can I pick it up after? Can we meet at 7? Tuscan?*

The shower stopped running, and Rachel heard the glass door sliding on its rails as Adam stepped out.

Perfect, see you then.

Her stomach fluttered, and she dropped her phone on the bed.

Adam's aggressive teeth brushing made her roll her eyes. She could picture him leaning over the sink with a towel around his waist. He started brushing his tongue, prompting his early-morning gagging routine.

They hadn't spoken much since their argument a few nights ago, and hearing his gross bathroom sounds made her anger resurface.

"Hey, I'm dropping off a painting tonight and need to leave around 6:45." He splashed his face with water, and when he didn't look up, she said, "Adam? Did you hear me?"

"I heard you," he said, brushing past her. "Sounds good." He opened his dresser drawer and pulled on a pair of boxers under his towel.

Rachel rubbed her collarbone. "Okay ... Well, I'm meeting

Emily for a drink and a bite after. I mean, she doesn't drink. We'll probably just have a little something to eat." She chuckled nervously, not sure why the lie had so easily rolled off her tongue.

Adam threw her a glance. "You sure are hanging out with your sister a lot." He still hadn't shaved, and he was buttoning up his shirt wrong—he'd skipped a button. "Do you really think she's the best influence?"

Rachel sat on the bed. "You know I've been wanting to spend more time with Emily. Our relationship's been rocky for a while. She's the only sister I have."

At least that part was true.

It felt easier to tell him she was meeting with Emily, but the lie caused anxiety to flutter inside her, making her pulse speed up. Between that and the anticipation of seeing Brad's face when she showed him what she'd created for him, it was going to be a long day.

"And by the way," she said before leaving the room, "you missed a button."

A couple of hours later, after dropping the kids off at school, Rachel sat in the parking lot and dialed Emily's number. When she didn't answer, she sent her a text: *Can you call me? It's important.*

I'm on a zoom call. What's up?

Meeting Brad tonight. Just giving him his painting, but I told Adam I was meeting with you after. To buy myself a little more time. Maybe getting closure is what I need? Hope that was okay. If not, let me know and I'll figure something out.

No problem. I want a full report tomorrow, okay? Don't do anything I wouldn't do.

Rachel grinned and shook her head at her sister, then tucked her phone in her purse.

After dropping the kids off at school, a splash of relief came over her as she drove down the road, watching the big snowflakes melt into her windshield. The freshly fallen snow on the pine trees took her breath away, and she listened to a Christmas playlist on her run. The tinge of jubilation she felt about the upcoming holidays was a welcome, but very short, escape from her marriage problems.

When she arrived home, she saw the Yeti full of coffee she'd made for Adam sitting on the counter. She picked it up, opened the lid, and dumped it down the drain, smelling the sharp, pungent scent of her childhood when Mother would put on a pot before serving dessert when she and Father entertained. Rachel and Emily were usually sent off to their rooms at this time, but they'd sneak to the top of the stairs, trying to listen to the adult conversation.

She knew she'd be distracted all day thinking of her meeting with Brad, and she grabbed her phone and made a grocery list for dinner tonight: *pork chops, applesauce, homemade bread.*

Her run hadn't quite shaken out all her jitters, and she headed upstairs, hoping a long, hot shower would help the butterflies churning in her stomach.

When she stood at the butcher shop hours later, they hadn't settled at all. The woman behind the counter had wrapped up the meat and handed her the white package. Rachel stood rubbing the piece of masking tape and staring at the sloppy black price scribbled across the top, lost in thought. "Is there anything else you need?" the clerk snapped. Her thin red hair was pulled back so tight it had to be painful.

"No thank you," Rachel said, looking up, embarrassed.

On the way home, she ran a red light, and as her heart pounded while she checked the rearview mirror to make sure no one was behind her, she noticed she'd only put mascara on one eye. When she'd pulled into the driveway, she'd gotten a text from Benjamin: *Mom, I forgot to tell you indoor lacrosse starts today after school. Can you bring my uniform?*

She had just enough time to put away the groceries and try to find his uniform. Practice was only an hour and a half, so maybe she could talk Elsa into running an errand so she wouldn't have to do so much driving back and forth.

When she got back in the car, the garbage truck rumbled past her house. Adam had forgotten to take it out again, it was literally the only thing he did around the house, and the garage smelled rotten.

After the chaos of the afternoon settled and they arrived home, Rachel preheated the oven and greased a pan for the bread dough rising under a towel. As she chopped and peeled apples for applesauce, she had to keep reminding herself to relax her shoulders—they were practically touching her earlobes, and her back was aching.

Once the pot on the stove was full of apples, Rachel dumped in cinnamon and nutmeg and added a little water from the black pot filler above the stove. Crock-Pot applesauce was way better, but there wasn't enough time. Simmering stove-top apples would have to do.

She slid the bread into the oven and tried to relax into the delicious smells of her house before taking the steps two at a time to change her clothes for tonight.

The moment she thought about what she'd wear tonight, her phone pinged. It was Emily: *Have fun tonight! ;)* It was like her sister *knew* how flustered and distracted she was feeling.

In her closet, she found a green sweater that was fitted without being too tight. She slipped off her T-shirt and pulled it on, then checked herself in the mirror. She gathered her hair in her hands and piled it on top of her head. Maybe she'd wear it up tonight. She'd definitely need a different bra if she was going to wear this sweater.

Benjamin clomped down the hallway. "Mom, I need this uniform washed tonight so I can wear it tomorrow."

"Well, how about you start by taking it off and putting it in the washer, Honey?" He retreated to his room, and a wave of heat went through her as she riffled through her underwear drawer. Benjamin had left her bedroom door open, and she ran to close it.

Flipping through her stack of bras, she found the sheer set she'd bought all those years ago when she'd taken Mother's marriage advice. It had been her way of trying to bring the spark back between her and Adam.

It had failed miserably. She got a sick feeling in her stomach, remembering the disgusted look that had crossed Adam's face when she'd dropped her robe to show it off.

Rachel hadn't worn it, or any other lingerie, since that night. She held the bra now, rubbing the sheer fabric between her thumb and fingers. The bra had an under wire and, despite the thin fabric, was well-constructed enough to give her a lift and provide a smooth look for the sweater. She pulled off her clothes and put on the set.

Looking in the mirror, she saw her tan lines still lingered from the trips to the beach with the kids last summer. Her hair was thick and wavy, with caramel highlights giving her brown hair a sun-kissed look.

She felt more satisfied with her appearance than she had in a long time. And yet she felt invisible to her own husband. She slid the green sweater over the bra.

Okay, wow.

She bit her bottom lip, feeling a heat build in her as she studied herself. *You aren't wearing this for Brad. You aren't wearing this for Brad. Not. Wearing. This. For Brad.*

Rachel found her favorite distressed Levis and a pair of faux snakeskin heels to dress them up. She slid her feet into the three-inch heels, luxuriating in how they extended her already long legs.

She remembered the day she'd brought the shoes home. The sales clerk had talked her into the purchase, "Snakeskin, leopard print—they're like neutrals. They go with everything," she'd said as Rachel ran her fingers over the bumpy texture.

After trying them on for Adam, he'd said, "Aren't they kind of ... much for you? They aren't your style. More like something your sister would wear."

They were still brand new. She wished she hadn't let Adam's comment get to her, but she had. She'd shoved them in the back of her closet and almost forgotten them.

She slipped the shoes off and made her way down the hall to peek in the kids' messy rooms. Benjamin was lying on his floor with his legs on his bed, staring at the ceiling, listening to music. Elsa was at her desk, alternating between doing homework and snapping pictures of herself. Neither one of them looked up when she peeked in on them. "Dinner will be ready in about a half hour," she announced as she made her way down the hall.

Downstairs, the dryer beeped. That reminded her that the dishes in the dishwasher needed unloading. Which made her remember the layer of dust on the window sills she'd been meaning to get to. It was almost time to cook the meat for dinner. She'd forgotten to put on perfume.

Everything is waiting for you. Everything's waiting for you to take care of it.

She hurried downstairs, heels in hand, and set them near the door. She started a fresh load of laundry, making sure Benjamin had put his uniform in the washer, before carrying a warm pile of clothes from the dryer to the kitchen island.

Halfway through folding, a text came in from Adam: *Going to be a few minutes late tonight.* Just then, she glanced up at the macrame plant hanger where her favorite plant had lived for years, adding a lush green touch to the kitchen. It was dead. Not just yellow and wilting, but completely irrecoverably deceased.

Standing in the middle of her kitchen, a deep and terrible loneliness engulfed her. *You are the only support beam holding up this house. Adam isn't a partner at all anymore.* She picked up a pair of Adam's underwear and felt like vomiting.

Everyone always needed something from her, and it seemed her feelings and plans never mattered much. Aimee had been telling her for years that was because she always adjusted her wants and needs to conform to everyone else. She needed to do more for herself.

She picked up her phone and tapped Brad's name. *Can't wait to see you. Afternoon went a little crazy and I'm running late. Can we do 7:30 instead, I hope?*

Rachel read the message, deleted it, then typed: *I'm going to be about a half hour late,* then hit send.

She picked up a towel to fold, then dropped it to the floor as she stomped to the dead plant, yanked it from its holder, and threw it away, pot and all.

Brad

B rad pulled on his favorite polo shirt, tucked it into his khakis, and wore his black Converse sneakers. The day had dragged on, and he was excited about seeing Rachel, and his painting, right after his meeting. More excited than he should be.

When he bounced downstairs, Beth was holding a plank on her Yoga mat and watching HGTV.

He stood watching, trying hard to remember the reasons he'd left Rachel for her. Beth had been so sexy; exciting, and had made him feel a little dangerous. They'd had sex in the chapel on campus one night, and he'd felt invincible lying there with his feet propped up on the pew as Beth lay naked on the floor beside him.

"Why are you wearing those sneakers?" Beth said, falling out of her plank and snickering. "You look like a kid." She gave him a look that said "I'm so embarrassed for you" and then went into the downward dog.

Their argument the night before obviously didn't phase her. She was acting like her usual shallow, self-absorbed self with a side of perkiness. He wondered what it would be like to be so unaffected by what he had thought was a pretty serious fight. Did she really not feel the tension that pushed against these four walls?

Brad looked down at his shoes. "I like them." He reached into his pocket for his phone. A text from Rachel: *I'm going to be about a half hour late.*

Brad slid the phone back into his pocket. "I might be late tonight. Some teachers suggested going out for a drink after the meeting," he said, clearing his throat as if the lie had caused a blockage.

Beth was holding steady in a one-armed side plank and staring at the television. "Oh my God, do you see this kitchen? It's a dream! I wish *we* could do something like that."

He thought about giving her the usual peck on the cheek before he left. Instead, he said, "See you when I get home."

"Wait, where did you say you were going?" Beth turned her body, balancing herself in a plank on the other side.

"Team meeting, then a drink after," he answered, heading for the door.

As soon as he opened it, Beth yelled, "Can you believe how long I'm holding these planks?"

"Great job!" he said, closing the door behind him.

Brad got in his car and sat there for a moment. Should he go back in and tell her the truth? He reached for the door handle, debating. *She doesn't even care where you're going tonight.*

But his chest felt like it was pressing down on his heart. He hated lying, hated this place he was stuck in. He rested his head on the steering wheel and took his hand off the handle.

He backed the car out, feeling the bumpy driveway that neither of them had called to have repaired yet.

He stopped and looked up at his huge house. Beth was standing up now, stretching in front of the television. His stomach was nauseous. He squinted, trying hard to stir up some old feelings—this house used to make him feel proud. His wife used to entice him. But now all he felt was indifference.

Before putting the car into drive, he picked up his phone and sent Rachel a text: *No problem. I'll wait for you in the parking lot.* He stared at his message for a few seconds before adding, *Can't wait to see you.*

Rachel

Rachel grabbed three white plates and placed a pork chop on each one, then filled three small black and white bowls with applesauce. She wiped down the sides of the bowls with a paper towel, forcing herself not to look at the clock again.

She tried to steady her shaking hands and grabbed the loaf of freshly baked bread and set it on her favorite wooden cutting board. Benjamin had made it in shop class last year, and she loved how each section of wood was a slightly different color.

As the knife cut through the crusty bread, she yelled, "Dinner's ready!" It was just after 7:00 p.m., and Adam still wasn't home.

Benjamin and Elsa came downstairs. Rachel went to them, grabbing one under each arm in a fierce hug.

"Mom?" Elsa questioned, her voice muffled under Rachel's sweater.

Benjamin felt bony pressed against her, and he easily slid out from under her arm.

Rachel grabbed him back, pulling him tighter into the three-way hug. "Just hug me back." She closed her eyes tight, picturing vividly the morning they'd come downstairs, and found her slumped on the kitchen floor the morning after she'd discovered Adam's affair. They'd heard her crying and sat down next to her. Still warm from their beds with sheet wrinkles on their sweet little faces, Rachel had pulled them onto her lap, knowing she wasn't going to leave Adam. Not seeing her kids with their morning hair and sleep-creased cheeks every morning would kill her.

She was forgetting what that felt like and needed to be reminded. Benjamin's arm was limp around her back, and he gave her a few pats before he took a step away and then registered dinner. "Pork chops! Yes!"

Elsa stood hugging her longer. "Nice shoes Mom. Where are you going again?" They headed for the table, and Rachel grabbed a piece of bread off the cutting board.

"Dropping off a painting."

Benjamin stabbed his fork into his whole pork chop, picked it up, and chewed off a bite. "You're painting a lot." His mouth was full, and he was wearing the same hoodie he'd had on yesterday over his pajama pants.

"Aren't you going to say anything about his manners?" Elsa pleaded. "*Gross,* Benny." She shook her head and began cutting her meat into tiny pieces. "Why are guys *so gross*?"

"I've given up on his manners, I think." Rachel laughed, then stopped, listening. Adam's car was pulling into the garage. She grabbed her purse and then went back to the table to kiss each of her kids on the top of the head. The two of them had whipped out their phones as soon as she'd gotten up. "I love you both so much."

You're just dropping off a painting. You made a nice dinner. You're allowed to have a social life. You're allowed to run your business. Adam fucked someone else.

"Love you," they said in unison, not looking up from their phones.

"Guys, put your phones away and have dinner with your dad," Rachel said as Adam trudged inside.

He scanned the room and gave Rachel a half smile. "Smells good." He peeled off his shoes and shuffled to the sink to wash his hands.

"I made everyone's favorite—pork chops, applesauce, and homemade bread." Rachel slipped on her heels. "Okay, I'll be back later tonight."

"I thought you'd be gone by now. You could have left, so you weren't late." Adam's eyes trailed down to her shoes as he dried his hands.

Rachel gestured with one hand toward the kids. "I didn't want the kids eating dinner alone."

"Mom, we're teenagers. I think we can handle it," Elsa said, slapping Benny's arm as he drank applesauce from his bowl.

"I know you can be left alone. Something about leaving you guys to eat by yourselves just feels sad to me. I wanted at least one of us to be here."

Adam raised his eyebrows at her. His mouth was a straight line as he grabbed the back of his chair, pulling it out to sit.

"Okay. I guess I'll go then." Tears welled in Rachel's eyes, blurring her family as they sat there eating. Her body felt like cement.

She reached down for the wrapped painting leaning against the wall. The brown craft paper she'd covered it in made it slippery. She wasn't sure she'd be able to grip it with one hand without dropping it.

Her throat felt thick, like she had a piece of bread lodged in it. *You can't leave, but you can't stay.*

She put a hand on the doorknob and paused.

"What are you doing? Did you forget something?" Adam asked, glancing down at her shoes again.

Rachel cleared her throat over the lump that had formed there. "No, I'm good. Bye my loves." She bent to pick up the painting with both hands, then realized she wouldn't be able to get the door open with both hands busy, so she put the painting back down and opened the door. When she bent to pick the painting back up, her purse slid off her shoulder and hit it, almost slamming the painting into the half-open door. She hooked her purse under her arm and propped the door with one heeled foot, positioning herself so she could slide through the doorway sideways, set the painting down on the garage steps, then reach to close the door behind her.

"I got it, Mom." Benjamin jumped out of his seat and was to her in half a second, taking the painting more carefully than she would have thought possible from her gangly, clumsy boy. "Since Dad is off gentleman-duty tonight."

"Thanks, Honey. You're the best." She cut her eyes at Adam, worried they'd have a repeat of the scene from the other night.

He was busy biting a piece of pork off his fork. "Those shoes make it hard to navigate, huh?"

The way you treat your wife must make it hard to get laid, huh? She hated who they were turning into.

Benjamin loaded the painting into the back of her car, and she gave him a peck on the cheek. "Thank you, Sweetie. I'm proud to be your mom."

At Tuscan Bistro, Rachel parked under a streetlight and flipped down her car's vanity mirror. She'd fought the tears on the drive over, but the tears won, and she'd given in and let them flow. She definitely felt better, but she knew she was puffy and swollen.

She used her sweater sleeve to dab at the corners of her eyes, then checked the mirror, relieved to see her mascara hadn't run down her cheeks. Brad had seen her without makeup many times, and he'd definitely seen her do her share of crying. But that was twenty years ago.

Brad's black Audi pulled in and parked one row in front of her. She got out of her car and took quick steps. His lights were still on and she couldn't see his face through the glass.

She crossed her arms over her chest to ward off the chill in the air—she'd been so worried about getting her family fed, and then there was the fiasco with trying to get the painting out the door, she'd forgotten to bring a jacket.

Brad stepped out of his car and bent down to look at his reflection in his window, running his hands through his hair.

"You look great," Rachel laughed. Brad quickly jumped back and put his hand on his heart.

"Hi there." He smiled so big her heart dropped.

Damn. He's as nervous as you are. "I didn't mean to scare you." Rachel held herself tighter and pictured her family eating at the table without her. Even though she missed them and was standing in front of a man who had deeply hurt her, she wanted to run to him and bury herself in his arms.

She wanted to feel his warmth, slide her arms up the back of his jacket, and hook her hands onto the top of his shoulders, the way she had when they'd slow danced in high school. She pressed her lips together, trying to hold in all the emotions churning inside of her.

Brad's smile didn't leave his lips as he took in her outfit. Her stomach contracted, the pulse of electricity making its way between her legs. He slid his hand from his heart to his coat pocket and met her gaze.

For a moment, Rachel was on their first date—a soccer game under the lights on a chilly fall night. Brad had spotted her from the corner of the bleachers where he'd been sitting.

He'd slowly climbed down the bleachers and come to her, lifting his head as he got closer. Exactly the same way he was doing now.

"Rachel."

Her knees almost buckled at the sound of his voice saying her name as a complete sentence.

She opened her mouth to respond, but nothing came out. Brad's face and body blurred a little as the tears welled, and her heart thumped hard inside her chest.

His eyes locked with hers for a beat, and he gave her a smile. "I'm so excited to see this work of art, Picasso!"

He was close enough to smell his woody cologne. Rachel twirled her new diamond ring around her finger. "I'm excited to show you." She pointed to her car. "It's wrapped up pretty good, though. I didn't want it to get damaged during the drive. I have a picture. Let me um ..." She finished her phone out of her purse and tapped on the picture she'd taken before she'd wrapped it up. "It looks better in person."

He leaned in to look at the photo and shook his head. "Rachel. It's ... it's perfect. I love it. I really, really want to see it."

Her stomach sank at the thought of leaving him after only five minutes, and she suddenly felt so shy about standing there watching him look at the piece of art she'd made for him. "I'm so glad you like it. It's one of my favorite pieces, I think. You can't really tell from the picture, but I did the sand technique we talked about. But ... I really don't want to risk unwrapping it and having it get dented or stained with anything."

He nodded his head. "Ok, well, it's amazing. You are amazing. I won't argue with the expert." Her stomach dipped and Brad reached out, his hand hugging the sensitive skin on the inside of her wrist. "Would you want to go in and have something to eat before I put it in my car? Maybe a Diet Coke?"

"Sure," she agreed, trying to sound casual. Brad took a big step ahead, opening the door for her. "Funny we should meet here again." He motioned for her to walk in.

It *was* funny considering the last time she'd come here with Emily, right after seeing him for the first time in twenty years, she'd hoped to run into him. It was as if they'd gone looking for each other without even knowing it.

"Yeah." Rachel's eyes went to the ceiling. "It's such a great place. I love everything about it."

It was quiet in the restaurant tonight. The hostess grabbed two menus and smiled as soon as she saw them. "Table for two?"

"That'd be great. Something with one of those comfy sofas, please." Brad said. He positioned himself slightly behind Rachel, waiting for her to go ahead.

She felt her neck tingle—she was hyperaware of his near-ness. When they sat down, they studied their menus in silence, Rachel glazing over hers and not seeing a thing. She knew the menu by heart and was so distracted she wasn't sure she could eat anything.

Brad drummed his fingers on the table. "I know this menu by heart. Don't know why I'm looking at it."

Rachel closed her menu, smiling at how he'd said almost exactly what she'd been thinking. "What are you going to get? I'm actually ... not that hungry."

"Okay, so you aren't that hungry." Brad picked up the menu again. "I'm really not either. I had a bite at my meeting."

"Cheese platter? There's goat cheese," Rachel said, raising her eyebrows.

Brad dropped his menu. "You read my mind. Diet Coke?"

"Of course," Rachel said, leaning back into the squishy sofa. Her chest clenched at the thought that this may be the last time she saw him. After she gave him the painting, there'd really be no more reason to stay in touch. It was clear they were both trying to draw the painting hand off as long as possible.

They ordered the cheese platter, and when it came, they took their time picking at it, as if they each knew this may be their final chance to sit and chat like this. Rachel told him she and Aimee were still the best of friends, and Brad told her about some of his favorite places to canoe in the fall. He reminded her about the time they'd gone kayaking in the ocean, and both flipped over, which she'd completely forgotten about. They laughed so hard at the memory, they both shed tears.

In one evening, all their shared moments returned full and bright and clear, as if they'd never faded.

"Rachel."

Her heart raced. Goosebumps ran up and down her body, tightening her nipples. Was he trying to torture her by saying her name like that?

"I shouldn't say this. I wasn't going to say this ..."

They locked eyes.

She wanted to hear what he was going to say and wanted to stop him at the same time.

"I couldn't wait to see you today." He lowered his eyes. "And it wasn't so I could get the painting. I mean, I'm excited about that, but ... I'm so sorry, but you're all I can think about."

Rachel's eyes widened, and she couldn't speak.

"I know it's not okay. I know we're both married and you have kids."

His words stabbed at her heart; they sounded like a warning and felt like an invitation all at once.

"Brad, I—"

"I know I shouldn't be telling you this. I'm selfishly

hoping that getting it off my chest will somehow"—he swirled his finger in the air—"relieve this pressure valve building inside me."

Perspiration formed under her bra.

"Am I making any sense? Please, just tell me you're happily married, and I've missed my chance. Because if you don't ... if you don't say that"—he leaned closer and whispered, "I'm afraid of what might happen."

Rachel felt her entire world stand still. She had nothing left. Her strength was gone. Her willpower depleted. And she didn't want to fight her feelings anymore.

She grabbed the sleeves of his sweater in her fists, feeling like she could break the table that separated them in half.

"You're all I think about, too."

He leaned in closer from across the table. "Rachel." A smile pulled at his lips.

She should close her eyes and think about her kids and her husband. She should have Brad get the painting from her car, and tell him they should stay away from each other because *he* was married, and *she* was married, and it was the right thing to do.

She should tell him she couldn't be the other woman—she couldn't be *that* kind of person.

But right now, none of those reasons were enough.

The next few minutes were a blur. Brad paid the bill and led her out of the restaurant, his fingertips at the small of her back sending jolts of electricity through her body. Her legs were shaky as she stepped outside.

They practically jogged back to his car, and she buried her face in his neck and grabbed his jawline, pressing his face closer to her, hoping it would satiate the longing inside.

He wrapped his arms around her, giving her a minute to catch her breath. When she lifted her face from the comfortable spot on his neck, their lips pressed together. Brad moved a hand up and ran it through her hair. His tongue slid against hers, and she moaned with pleasure. He tasted familiar, yet so new.

Her body fell against his until he was leaning against his car. Brad ran his hands through her hair, down her back, up and back down her arms. He took his time feeling her everywhere he could, slowly trailing his thumbs over her jawline, down her neck. She longed for him to devour her right there.

Rachel pressed against him harder, seeking a release for the ache that was spreading between her legs. They were as close as two people could get with their clothes on, and yet Rachel wanted him closer.

She wanted all of him. She wanted his hands on her breasts, down her pants.

She wanted to tell him everything.

She wanted to make up for the last twenty years, right this minute.

She removed her mouth from his, trying to catch her breath for a moment before telling him she wanted him. Tonight.

"I'm sorry Rachel I—"

"Don't apologize." Rachel gazed up at him. "And please don't tell me that was a mistake. At least not tonight." She shook her head. "I know this isn't right, but it's right for me right now."

Brad wrapped his arms around her. "Are you sure?" His breath on her neck made her wet with anticipation.

"I'm *so* sure."

Brad hugged her tighter. He didn't ask for an explanation. He didn't ask about her marriage again. It was as if he knew exactly how she was feeling. And it was enough for him.

"You're shivering. Let's get in my car and talk?" He leaned back so he could see her face.

"Okay." Rachel's voice squeaked. Brad took her hand and led her around to the passenger side.

He held the door open for her, then leaned over, covering her mouth with his before pulling away from her and hurrying to the other side of the car to get in the driver's seat.

Brad

Rachel elbowed Brad and pointed to his back seat

"I can explain," Brad said, laughing. "I put the seats down because of the size of the painting. It's the only way it will fit in here, and I didn't want the canvas to bend."

"Ha! Oh sure, you had this planned all along."

His smile dropped from his lips—he was alone with his first love in a car with the seats down. They'd been in this position before, only it was two decades ago.

Brad had planned for their first time to be as romantic as possible. Doing it in the back of his dad's Volvo station wagon wasn't at the top of his list, but at the time, it was the best he could do. Once they'd parked at the end of a dead end dirt road that all the kids called Lovers' Lane, it didn't matter where they were, anyway.

"I'm getting high school vibes." Rachel chewed on her bottom lip, her half moon eyes gazing down at his hands.

Brad was sick of overthinking and trying to do the right thing. Right now, the thing that felt right was to do what he knew was so wrong.

Rachel moved toward him, her lips parted, and he felt his Adam's apple move in his throat. He followed her lead, meeting her halfway. Their kiss was slow this time, tender.

He cupped her face in his hands and heard a tiny moan escape her throat. Their breaths grew heavier, faster. He felt his zipper tighten against him as he planted soft kisses along her jawline, ears, neck.

Rachel shivered, and he pulled back. "Are you cold?"

Eyes closed, she murmured, "Not cold. Please don't stop kissing me." She gripped his arms, and her chest was heaving as he leaned over the center console to kiss her again.

Rachel tugged on his shirt. Her mouth covered his, gentle and wet. Blood rushed to his cock, swelling him almost to the point of pain.

His hands tangled in her hair, feeling her soft lips pressing against his. He ached to taste all of her.

They slowly explored each other's mouths, and Rachel's hands ran down his chest. The soft pressure of her hands made goosebumps run up and down his body. Brad gently pulled her hair as their tongues slid together.

Rachel moaned before pulling away. She was breathing hard, and Brad thought she was going to tell him to stop— that they shouldn't go any further.

Instead, she pulled off her sweater, then stared at him wide-eyed as if she wasn't sure what she'd just done.

Brad blew out a breath before tracing his fingers along her collarbone. She watched him, and he felt her relax under his touch. Goosebumps formed on her skin as he leaned one elbow on the console to steady himself and used his free hand to caress her ribcage. He rubbed his thumb back and forth, just below her breast. She felt the same, looked the same. It was as if no time had gone by since the last time they'd done this.

When she reached for his pants, he stopped her. "Wait. Hang on. Get your sweater on."

Her eyes grew wide, and her cheeks flushed. "I'm sorry." She covered herself with one hand and pawed around for her sweater with the other. "You're rea—"

"Buckle up." He started the car. "We're going to Lovers' Lane."

Rachel let out a squeaky laugh and gave him a little shove. "You scared me." She pulled her sweater on, and Brad noticed it was inside out and backwards. "I guess we can't mess around in the restaurant parking lot."

"Well ... we could." He reached over to squeeze her thigh. "Less chance of us being arrested on Lovers' Lane though. Not to mention it's nostalgic."

"Just hurry and drive," she said, pulling on her seat belt.

Brad knew after tonight, things in his life would drastically change. He blocked those thoughts for now—he'd deal with everything later.

The only thing he could think about was tending to Rachel.

When he stopped at a gas station for condoms, he caught Rachel smiling at the neon sign—this was the same place he'd bought condoms in high school.

As Brad got out of the car, she said, "Nostalgia overload. I'm glad one of us is kind of thinking straight tonight."

Brad put the car in park at the end of the long, abandoned dirt road and cut the engine. He took in a deep breath and turned his body to face Rachel. The short drive had been quiet after he'd picked up the condoms, the weight of what they were about to do was heavy in the air. Brad wondered if she'd changed her mind.

When their eyes locked, Rachel practically dove over the

console and reached for the button on his pants. She groaned when she couldn't get his zipper down, and they both laughed.

"Here, let's get in the back." Rachel grabbed the box of condoms, threw them in front of her, then Brad tried to support her hips as she stumbled her way into the back. He peeled off his jacket and was right behind her.

Rachel positioned herself on her side with her knees to her chest, holding herself up on one arm as she reached over and tugged on his shirt, trying to get him in the small bed of the backseat faster.

He landed on his side, and they were both laughing when Rachel yanked at his pants. "This is going to be interesting," he said as he rolled onto his back and lifted his hips up so she could shimmy them off of him. She grabbed the top of his underwear and pants and pulled them down. They were stuck on his calves and he worked one leg free as Rachel pulled away from him to sit up, undo her jeans, and slide them off.

She bumped her head on the ceiling, and he reached over to help her.

"I'm fine," she giggled, before he could ask if she was okay. She leaned over him, kissing him as if the few seconds their lips were apart caused her pain.

Brad opened his mouth, and Rachel filled it with her tongue. He banged his elbow on the back of the driver's seat. They fumbled, trying to get into a good position without breaking their kiss. He'd definitely have bruises tomorrow and be sore, but he didn't care. Not being close to Rachel would hurt more.

Rachel lay on her side, pressing her chest to his. Her hunger made him rock hard, and he felt like he might explode with the pent up energy brewing inside of him. But he also wanted this to last.

He pulled away from her mouth. "Rachel."

She paused, a hand resting on his biceps over his shirt, her chest heaving. A worried look crossed her face.

"I want to savor you." He reached for her hand and kissed her palm.

She let out a whimper as she watched him kiss the inside of her wrist. Brad kept his eyes open. He wanted to experience every inch of her skin again. He kissed his way up her arm, helped her out of her sweater, and Rachel squirmed when he got to the inside of her elbow.

A smile played at her lips, and she straddled him. As soon as he felt her press on top of him, his cock swelled even more. She leaned over him, her eyes holding his, before gently gliding her tongue over his lips.

Her heat pressed into him as she hugged his hips with her legs. He could feel her wetness through her underwear. "Get these things off me," she said with a laugh, planking over him.

Brad hooked his thumbs into the lacy waistband of her underwear and slid them down before using a foot to push them the rest of the way down.

She repositioned herself on top of him, and he grunted as he felt the warm heat of her slit part over him. She moved back and forth over his cock, teasing him, watching him. "You feel the same," she whispered before leaning down to nuzzle his neck.

When she completely relaxed on top of him, and hooked her arms under his shoulders while moaning his name as she rubbed her swollen clit over him, everything he'd loved, everything he'd remembered, and everything he'd tried so hard to forget about her, came flooding back.

Her skin was still just as soft as it had been when they were teenagers, and she smelled just as sweet.

His entire body lit up as her hair tickled his neck and chest. He stroked his hands up and down her back, arms, thighs. It wasn't enough to have their bodies this close. He wanted to consume her and make this moment last as long as possible at the same time.

He unhooked her bra, and when Rachel propped herself up on one arm and reached down between their bodies with the other to take him in her hands, he let out a sharp breath.

"God, Rachel." She still had the same firm grip, the same silky hands that glided over him perfectly.

She let go of him long enough to fumble out of her bra. Brad took over, sliding the thin straps down her arms, and Rachel pulled up his shirt, baring his chest. He was a little softer than he'd been in high school, and his chest hair was turning gray, but every part of him felt like he was twenty again.

She pressed her naked body onto his, and his eyes rolled back. Her breasts were soft and cool against his bare chest, and her inner thighs greedily squeezed his hips.

Slowly, he kissed her lips, then cupped one of her breasts, gently working her nipple between his thumb and finger.

Rachel tilted back, and she gasped, breaking their kiss. "You remembered."

She propped herself on her arms again, and her lips parted as her gaze held his. Brad's hand reached down between her legs to feel her sweet spot. She was so wet, so ready. Her hips moved over his hand as she bent her head down to watch him touch her, the intensity of the moment making his cock pulse and ache.

"Please," she begged.

Brad knew exactly what she wanted. She'd always loved to watch him suck on her nipples as he slid a finger into her.

She leaned down, holding herself up on her elbows, placing her full, beautiful breast in front of his mouth. He lifted his head to suck on one nipple and then the other as he pulled his finger slowly out of her, then rubbed her swollen clit.

Rachel rocked back and forth on his hand, and his body tensed in response. The feeling of Rachel—her sweet, alive scent, her soft wetness—was intoxicating. Seeing her enjoy every touch, every flick of his tongue, every time his finger slid over her, awakened every cell in his body.

Rachel slowly rolled off of him onto a pile of blankets he'd put in his trunk to protect the painting. When she positioned herself on her side and propped herself up with her elbow, he did the same.

Rachel raised her eyebrows. She'd always loved to watch them please each other, and it turned him on that she still had the same confidence she'd had when they were younger.

Her chest heaved as she spread her knees, giving him full access to her. He scooted closer and felt her breath on his shoulder as she reached for his cock, her hand going up and down as he slid a finger over her clit, matching her rhythm.

Rachel moaned in delight, and he slid a finger inside of her, then two, feeling her tighten around his fingers and she stroked him faster.

"My God, Rachel. I won't last long watching you do that."

She giggled and slowly rubbed his tip before grabbing the condoms she'd thrown in the back. "Well, in that case," she said, pulling one from the box.

"I want to make you feel good first," he argued, grabbing her hand to stop her. Rachel never climaxed when they'd had sex. "I need your fingers and mouth," she'd say.

She playfully slapped the condom on his chest. "I can't wait any longer. I want you as close to me as possible. If you aren't going to last much longer, I won't chance it."

He took it from her, ripping it open with his teeth.

"Ha! You still do that so fast." She bit her bottom lip and grabbed his hardness in her hand. He tensed, trying to keep from releasing right there, and felt a few drops of moisture form at his tip. "Let me," she pleaded.

This is how they'd always done it. And Brad had always loved to watch her roll a condom down his shaft. Once again, he was thrown back in time.

She straddled him again, their eyes locked as she slowly slid onto him. They both cried out with pleasure, feeding a hunger they'd felt for so long. He tilted his hips, trying to get even deeper.

"Yes," she whispered, pressing herself deeper onto him, enveloping him with her heat.

Her body pressed against his as she kissed his neck. Brad's hand moved to her hips as she pulled out to his tip before sinking all the way down the base of his shaft. Feeling her strong thighs around him each time she pulled out, then slowly moved back down, she sent him closer to oblivion.

A wave of heat shot down Brad's body, and his toes curled. His hands went to her ass as she pumped harder.

"Rachel, yes!"

He exploded into pure ecstasy. He forgot he was in the back of a car. He forgot he was married. He forgot she was married. He forgot he hadn't been with Rachel for the last twenty years. It felt like they were in their own universe where time didn't exist, and Brad had never been the stupid, horny guy that had gotten distracted by a shiny object.

Rachel stayed still, covering him with her soft heat as he released his last shutters. His breath slowed, and he stared at the ceiling of his car. A car he bought with Beth one Saturday afternoon.

Then he remembered.

He remembered Rachel wasn't his, and they couldn't actually freely be together right now.

His chest tightened, and his breath stuck as if he'd gotten the wind knocked out of him. He wasn't about to let her go.

Rachel

When he slid into her, Rachel's entire body clenched. She inhaled his scent, pressing her face into the side of his, as she licked and sucked his neck, his scruff prickly on her lips. She hooked her arms under his shoulders and squeezed him under her hands, making sure he was really there, that this was really happening.

She propped herself up on her elbows, Brad's eyes locked with hers as she moved on top of him. Clenching her thighs tighter around him, she pulled herself to his tip, then slid all the way down, wanting him to feel her cover every inch of him.

Their heads were close to hitting the hatchback door, and her elbows burned, but she didn't care. Brad was close to release—his legs were stiffening, and he grabbed her hips a little tighter. Rachel tried to ride him slowly, to take him in a little at a time, but she couldn't. She wanted every piece of him, all at once. She stroked him with her wet warmth, clenching each time she slid over him.

When he clutched her ass, she rode him harder, faster, opening her mouth over his. Their bodies were getting clammy as their open lips pressed together without kissing, and he whispered, "Rachel, yes!" into her mouth as he guided her to cover his shaft a few more times.

Rachel wrapped her arms around his neck, putting all her body weight on top of him.

Brad's arms closed around her tired body, rubbing his hands softly up and down her back, and her muscles melted.

"You feel so good," he whispered in her ear. "I could stay here forever."

Tears welled in her eyes, and she pressed her cheek harder into the nook of his neck. "If I could melt into you, I would," she said, propping herself up on both arms to look at him.

They were still joined, and Rachel playfully wiggled over his cock.

Brad reached up, brushing her hair over her shoulder. Their eyes locked as he grabbed the back of her neck and gently rolled them both onto their sides before sliding out of her.

As they faced each other, Brad's hands traveled over her breasts, then down her stomach, before touching her wetness.

Rachel gasped. His touch was the same, and it sent pulses up her stomach, down her legs. She rested her head on the pile of blankets as she propped one leg up, opening herself.

Brad traced her wetness, studying her face. He circled his thumb over her—he hadn't forgotten how she liked to be touched.

Rachel bit her bottom lip, and Brad stared at her mouth. "I remember how much you like this," he said, looking down at his hand as she moved her pelvis in the same rhythm.

Rachel whimpered in agreement. He quickened his pace, the muscles in his arm contracting as he brought her closer.

She let out a loud moan, then another. "It's right here, isn't it, Rachel? Tell me." His voice was low and gravelly.

"Yes, yes," she cried out.

He pressed his body closer to hers as his finger slid in and out, then circled over her heat, faster and faster. She clutched his arm as a rush of pleasure overtook her body, shaking and trembling as Brad continued his steady rhythm. Her hand traveled to his working wrist as the rush thumped through her body. She tingled as the pressure released, still matching his rhythm until her body let out one last tremor, and she curled into him.

He kissed the top of her head, leaving his fingers inside of her. She was afraid to let go of his wrist, afraid to move, afraid for this moment to be over because she didn't think it could ever be replicated.

He slowly pulled his fingers out of her, and she grabbed his arm and wrapped it around her. They lay there for a few minutes on their sides, knees bent, crumpled in the back of his car, clutching on to one another.

"I've missed you more than I can express," Brad said, his voice filled with so much sincerity that Rachel thought her heart would crack open.

Rachel found her favorite spot on his neck again and wrapped her outside leg around him. She suddenly cried. Her body shook with deep, helpless sobs, and tears streamed down her cheeks, wetting Brad's neck.

"I know," he whispered, stroking her hair away from her temple. Rachel hooked her outside arm under Brad's, pressing her palm into his back with everything she had. She didn't worry about crying too hard or holding him too tight. She didn't try to hide anything, not even her uncontrollable shivering.

The last twenty years had spilled out of her in a matter of minutes. And there was no way to stuff her feelings back inside.

"I'm getting your sweater and my coat. You're freezing."

He rubbed her arm before untangling himself from her and pawing around the car for her clothes.

Brad found her bra and helped her fasten it. He pulled her sweater over her head, and after she slipped her underwear up and freed her hair from her sweater collar, he draped his coat around her shoulders and kissed the top of her head.

She climbed back into the front seat, her belly leaden with dread. As they drove, she stared out the window, unseeing.

Brad rubbed her knee, quietly humming. She gripped his hand and, still staring out the window, said, "Now I get why Adam did this."

Brad stopped rubbing her leg, but didn't move his hand away. She waited for him to ask questions, then remembered Brad had always given her the space to talk and process, the same way Aimee did.

Out of the corner of her eye, she saw Brad glance at her before returning his focus to the road.

"He cheated on me ten years ago. We hardly have sex because I'm never in the mood. He blamed it on that—told me it just happened."

She turned to look at Brad. His eyebrows were squeezed together, in disgust or thoughtfulness, she wasn't sure. He started rubbing her knee again.

"I don't buy that, though. Two people let it happen. We stopped really seeing each other a long time ago. I didn't feel like my usual self after having the kids, and it really affected him. The more he bugged me to have sex, the less I wanted to. I felt a lot of shame. Like I wasn't normal or something."

"That sounds like a really hard situation, Rach."

"It hasn't been easy, and seems to get worse. But now I'm doing what he did. Instead of deciding to stay with him. Or to leave him." Rachel rested her head on the seat and let out a sigh.

Brad nodded.

"Am I making any sense?"

"You are. You are making perfect sense. I'm doing exactly what you are. And I know it's not okay." He pulled next to Rachel's car in the Tuscan parking lot.

She shifted her body so she was facing him. "You know what's horrible? I wasn't even jealous, didn't even care. I still, after all these years, have no idea what she looks like." She laughed, studying Brad's disbelieving expression. "He told me it was someone from work. It should have torn me up. But it didn't."

"I'm so sorry, Rachel." Brad reached up and rubbed her bottom lip with his thumb. "There's a reason why you've stayed this long, though."

"Yeah. My kids." She shrugged. "I feel weak for not leaving him, but the thought of not seeing my kids every day and having them go back and forth ... it just guts me."

Brad scooted closer to her, listening intently.

"But our marriage can't go on like this. We are co-existing. It's not fair to me. It's not fair to him. And it's not fair to our kids. Something has to give."

Brad rubbed her arm. A big, bare oak tree which sat a few feet away from the hoods of their cars still had a few brown leaves hanging on its branches. One let loose, twirled in the air, and landed on Brad's windshield.

"It's not fair to anyone what we're doing." Brad's voice was gravelly with emotion. "Adam *and* Beth—they don't deserve to be cheated on either."

Rachel's stomach dropped. *He's right. No one deserves this. We let this happen.*

"But I know what it's like to lose your way and cling to something you know isn't right for you, because making a change can be really fucking hard. I did it when I worked for Beth's dad, and I'm doing it now. To Beth." He picked up Rachel's hand and wove his fingers in hers. "Sometimes we stay in a place because it's familiar. Even if it's a shitty place."

She squeezed her eyes shut, feeling so understood and angry at herself at the same time.

He puffed his cheeks out, releasing a deep sigh. "What do you want, Rachel?"

She grabbed his hand and brought it to her chest. "I don't know what to do. But I know we can't keep doing this."

Trying to fix her relationship with Adam had been chipping away at her soul. And if she continued trying to do that with Brad now in the picture, it would tear her to shreds.

Brad cleared his throat. "We can't figure this out in one night. I shouldn't have even asked that. It's too huge. But … can we try to figure this out together?"

"Yes," she whispered.

Brad traced his fingers down the side of her cheek before leaning in to kiss her chastely on the side of her mouth. "You've made me remember who I am, Rach. And I like that person." He took her hands in his. "I even started running again." A chuckle escaped him. "I've seen this runner on Pine Hill road a few times. She seems so … free. I told myself I needed to get back into it, even though I figured I probably wouldn't. Then I saw you that afternoon at the café … and I've been trying to run you out of my head ever since. It's not working." He laughed at his own joke.

Rachel elbowed him. "Okay, that was bad, Brad." Their chuckles turned into full-on laughter, and Rachel felt some of the angst and worry lift.

Rachel stopped laughing. "Wait, a second." She put a hand on the dashboard. "Did you say Pine Hill road?"

"Uh … yeah? Kinda near the big church there."

"The runner you see … what does she look like?"

"I'm not sure, actually. She's always wearing a hat and never looks up. But her hair is about the same color and length as yours and ..." Brad reached up and gently tugged on a strand of Rachel's hair, and realization slowly dawned on his face. His eyes widened, and the corners of his mouth curled up. "It's you, isn't it?" He smacked himself on the head with both hands. "How did I not know that was you??"

"So, I guess I can take credit for the fact that you are running again?" She patted herself on the back. "You were a natural in high school and college!"

He used to complain whenever she'd take him on a hilly route, yet he always kept up. Remembering how they'd challenge one another to go a little faster, a little farther, how they'd always end up glowy and refreshed and like they were made for each other, made her stomach do a somersault.

They had such a strong connection twenty years ago. And then he'd crushed the idea that they were made for each other. He'd broken up with her so suddenly, with no warning at all. It had hurt her more than she'd thought it was possible to hurt. And they'd lived an entire lifetime apart before finding each other again.

Were they different people? Had he really just been a stupid kid? Was he capable of doing this again?

Even if he was, she had to do something. Her mind started swimming, and she repeated Brad's words in her head—they weren't going to solve this in one night.

She let out a deep sigh. "I just can't believe we just had sex in the back of your car, exactly like we used to in high school."

Brad flashed a shy smile. "All I know is, I haven't felt this way since those days in high school when I met and fell in love with you. And I don't want to *not* feel this ever again."

The reflection of the streetlights shone in Brad's eyes. "Me too." She'd barely eaten today, and she suddenly felt weak and tired. Her cheeks hurt from smiling. She was blissfully happy and yet filled with remorse and dread. This couldn't end well, could it?

Brad walked her to her car, and he gently pulled out the painting. Rachel had wrapped it in bubble wrap, then brown craft paper, and added a twine bow. "I can't wait any longer." Rachel opened Brad's tailgate wider so he could slide the painting in. "I want to see it in person," Brad said, untying the twine.

"Oh, wait until you get it home, and you can unwrap it and see it in the light." Rachel put her hand over his to stop him, and he nodded.

A car drove slowly by, and Rachel tried looking in the window to see if it was anyone she knew as she pulled her hand away from him. Brad met her gaze after doing the same.

He adjusted the painting on top of the seats where, less than an hour ago, they'd told each other so much without speaking. "I'm not cut out for lying and sneaking around," Rachel whispered, staring at the wrapped painting.

Brad grabbed her hand again. "Then we won't. We won't sneak around or see each other until we figure out what to do." He closed his trunk and led her back to her car.

So that solved it. They'd say goodbye right here and that would be it until they figured something out. She tried to relax her shoulders and breathe. The sound of pavement under their feet hurt her ears. The street lights were so bright she had to squint, and her stomach rumbled and churned.

When they got to her car, Brad opened her door for her and helped her in. She bit her lip to keep from crying, and he put one arm over her door and leaned in. "Rachel? Are you okay?"

She shook her head. "I don't know. Are we horrible people?"

Brad stood and shoved his hands in his pockets, considering. "I'd like to think we aren't. My pull toward you is strong. I've tried to turn it off and I can't. I've thought a lot about how you have kids and a family. I'm ashamed of how much real estate you've taken up in my head while I'm still married."

He bent, so they were eye level with each other again. "No matter what happens, though, we will work through this."

Looking up at him, a tear spilled from Rachel's eye. Brad laid a hand on her arm, his touch light. "Let's go home and try to sleep. Text me when you get home, so I know you're okay." He gently wiped the tear from her cheek with his thumb, took her hand in his, and kissed it before closing her door.

Rachel put her car in reverse and watched Brad staring after her as she pulled out. The parking lot was empty and dark, and she had no idea what time it was. In her rearview mirror, she saw his silhouette standing alone. Leaving him felt impossible, and her sobs grew louder as she drove.

What had she done? How could she go on without him? Should she tell Adam? And what about the kids? Oh God, the kids. What would they think of her if they knew?

She clutched one hand to her stomach as if she could suppress the deep pit of shame and loss growing there. Tears spilled onto her sweater. Her head pounded, and she tried to focus on the road in front of her, letting herself have the drive home to remember all the sweet moments she'd shared with Brad. Moments she may never have again.

Before she got out of the car, she wiped her face and combed her fingers through her hair, and stepped out of her heels.

The house was dark and quiet, and the floor creaked when she stepped inside. Cora ran to greet her, holding her favorite rainbow colored ball in her mouth. Rachel got on her knees and hugged her, whispering, "Shhh" over and over.

She made her way upstairs, stopping at the top to peek in her bedroom. Adam's back was to her, and he was snoring.

Rachel stood watching his back rise and fall, searching for

a memory or even just a moment when things had been good between them.

But all she could think about were the times he pressured her for sex, and the lack of support he gave her.

And all she could feel; all she could smell, was Brad.

Walking on the balls of her feet, she padded quietly to the kids' bathroom and closed the door. She stripped her clothes off and started the shower.

Standing underneath the hot water, she squirted some of Elsa's shampoo on her head, then her body. She grabbed a washcloth, wishing she didn't have to wash Brad away. She traced her hands over the places he'd touched her—the back of her neck where he'd drawn her closer to kiss her, her breasts where he'd kissed so softly, between her legs where he'd done unbelievable things with his fingers.

The water ran cold, and what little energy Rachel had left drained out of her. She stepped out of the shower, dried off, and reached for Elsa's fuzzy robe on the back of the bathroom door. She wrapped herself in it and opened the door before gathering her clothes and purse.

Rachel carried her clothes downstairs—she needed to run a load of laundry. Her underwear smelled like sex and was still wet in the crotch. Her sweater smelled like Brad.

The wet load of laundry she'd washed earlier was waiting to be dried, and she shoved everything into the washing machine, and started it, then tiptoed back upstairs. Adam hadn't moved. She crawled into her side of the bed, then paused, the corner of the duvet still clutched in one hand. She dropped the duvet, turned around, and went down the hall to crawl into bed with Elsa.

"Mom?" Elsa mumbled, turning on her back. "What are you doing?" Rachel hugged her tightly from behind. Blue and purple LED lights outlined her windows, and fake ivy hung from her ceiling, dangling by the sides of her bed.

"I was just thinking about how much I love you and Benjamin." Rachel held her, resting her head on Elsa's shoulder. "You don't know how much I love you two."

"We know. You say it a hundred times a day." Elsa said sleepily. She lightly tapped Rachel's arm. "Go to sleep, Mom."

Brad

Brad leaned the painting against the entry table and slipped out of his shoes, lining them up in the closet neatly alongside Beth's Nikes and a pair of ballet flats, just how she liked them. Silvery moonlight spilled in through the window over the front door, giving the pale wood of the curved staircase a cool, lonely feel. A wave of shame washed over him as he tore open the painting, cutting himself with the thick, brown paper.

It was even more stunning in person. Brad admired the blocks of gray and white and taupe as a drop of blood blossomed onto the brown paper he clutched in his hand. All of Rachel's other paintings were flowy, with the colors bleeding into each other. But this had hard lines, structure, and the sand gave it a beautiful texture.

He craved its beauty, wanted to hang it in a place where he'd see it every day, but he set it to the side until he figured shit out.

What the hell was he going to tell Beth?

He wasn't good at pretending; Rachel could attest to that. After he'd met Beth in college and denied her, he hadn't been able to hide his building attraction for her—Rachel had known right away something was up. "It's like you aren't even here," she'd told him one night while they were studying.

He bent down to pick the wrapping and pressed it all into his stomach, trying to make a ball. *You can't stay with her. You don't love her, and you don't think she loves you anymore.*

Beth's footsteps reached the bottom of the stairs, and he didn't take his eyes off the painting.

"Hey," she said, her voice low and husky.

"Hi." He took a step back from the painting and gestured at it. "Here it is."

She let out a yawn and stretched. "I was getting worried. It's late." She took a few steps closer and stood before the painting, taking it in.

"Sorry. I got a text from Rachel letting me know the painting was done, so I went to meet her to pick it up. I should have told you." He began squeezing a section of bubble wrap with one hand, popping a few bubbles.

Out of his peripheral vision, he saw Beth turn to look behind them at the living room clock.

"What is it?" Beth asked, letting out a small laugh. "Why is it ... bumpy? It looks like a textured ceiling from the '70s."

Brad wanted to run his hands over it. He could picture Rachel silently working on it—her hands pouring the sand over the wet paint as her hair hung over one shoulder. "Hmm, kind of." His cheeks burned hot with shame, and he felt like he was betraying Rachel now, right after he'd just betrayed Beth.

"I don't love it. I'm sorry." Beth's voice was quiet, laced with disgust. "And now that I think about it, I'm not so sure I love the idea of having your ex-girlfriend's artwork hanging where I have to look at it every day." She closed her cotton robe and leveled Brad with a hard look. She had mascara smeared under both eyes. Had she been crying? Did she know something?

"Not that I'm worried," she said suddenly, standing on her tippy toes and kissing Bad's nose. "I mean, I stole you away from her all those years ago. You were so crazy about me you never looked back, did you?" She gave Brad's shirt a gentle tug, the same way Rachel had earlier. Brad's stomach rolled.

He took a step back, but Beth was unfazed. "I've stalked her on Facebook. She was prettier when we were younger."

"Beth, do you even love me anymore?" The words slipped out. He hadn't meant to have this conversation tonight.

She took a startled step back, her hand still clutching his shirt. "What?" She had an almost playful smile on her face, but in her eyes Brad thought he saw a tiny spark of doubt.

"You haven't seemed happy since I quit working for your father. I told myself you just needed time to adjust. But ... it's been two years and you still don't seem happy."

Beth let go of his shirt and took another step back, her smile fading. "Brad, I don't know what you ar—"

"Beth, sometimes I feel like I'm only worth something to you if I make more money." Now that he'd gotten started, the release made him want to unload everything.

"No ... I don't do that." She crossed her arms across her chest.

"You never want to have meaningful conversations with me. You blow me off when we have plans without a second thought. You seem so irritated with everything I do. We don't even have anything in common anymore."

Beth covered her mouth with a hand, looking extra small in her oversized robe. Brad felt his Adam's apple bob in his throat. His hands were in fists at his sides.

Beth dropped her arms. "Okay, you are right. I know I've been doing this." She stared up at the ceiling and blew out a long, frustrated breath. "I had a different picture in my head when we got married of what our life would be like." She took a step toward him, reaching out to run a hand through his hair, her robe sliding delicately up her arm in a way he may have once found charming, but he flinched away from her.

She quickly pulled her arm away from him, and her hand balled into a fist. "I'm so aware of this, and I'm sorry."

He recognized the familiar, rehearsed tone.

"Beth. I asked if you love me. Answer the question."

"It's a silly question, Brad. We were great once. We can be great again. Maybe you'll reconsider—"

"Why won't you answer?" He faced her squarely. "I love my job. Do you get it? I'm not going to reconsider. If you want a country club lifestyle, *you* go work for your dad."

Beth blanched a little, then held up her hands. "Okay, okay. Just calm down."

He didn't want to calm down. His face was fiery. He rolled up his sleeves and started pacing. "We've been through this *so* many times." He pulled at his hair, then stopped and faced her again. "Aren't you fucking *sick* of it?"

Beth bridged the gap between them and laid a hand on his chest, sliding it up slowly before resting her fingertips at the base of his neck. "I'm not sick of us. We're good together. We certainly have always had way more sex than any of my friends do with their husbands. So there's that."

She batted her eyelashes at him and reached for his belt buckle. He pushed her hand away.

"Dammit, Beth, are you serious right now? I'm trying to talk to you. Do you even hear me? Sex isn't going to fix this. Fix us. Just please, Beth, think about what I asked you. Take it seriously. I will never be a man that makes a ton of money."

He stood looking at her, searching for a sign she was listening as she played with the tie on her robe. "I can't live knowing that you always want me to change and be someone I'm not. And I don't think I can go another day feeling like

I'm in a loveless marriage. Because honestly, that's how I feel."
When she didn't respond, he said, "Maybe we just don't make
sense anymore."

Beth stared at him, her expression yielding no clue how
she felt about what he'd just laid between them.

"Just please tell me you didn't pay a dime for that
painting."

"Oh, my God!" Brad threw his arms up and stalked
upstairs. When he got to the top, he heard Beth say, "It was a
joke. Relax."

"Relax, Beth?" He shouted down the stairs. "I asked you if
you loved me, and you couldn't even answer my question.
And *you* want *me* to relax and laugh at your stupid joke that
wasn't even really a joke?"

Slamming the door felt good, but he knew full well that a
lot of his anger stemmed from the fact that he'd fallen back in
love with Rachel. He was angry at himself for letting things get
this far, for betraying Beth and lying to himself for this long.

He pulled out his phone. Nothing from Rachel yet.

Hey. You okay?

Rachel

Rachel opened her eyes and sat up in bed. A strand of hair was caught in her eyelash, and she looked around Elsa's room for a few seconds before remembering where she was. Elsa was facing her. She'd always slept with her eyes partway open, and her pupils were slowly shifting back and forth.

She felt around for her phone on Elsa's nightstand, then checked the time. It was 4:30 a.m., and she had a text from Brad: *Hey. You okay?*

Rachel gently peeled back the covers and turned to put her feet on the ground, slowly lifting herself out of bed.

Before leaving, she turned to look once more at her angelic daughter. In the hallway, she texted Brad back: *I'm okay. Sorry, I forgot to text and didn't see this until now.*

She hit send, then added: *Can we talk on the phone tonight? My house will be empty.*

Rachel crept into her bedroom and slid into bed. Adam was in the same position he'd been in last night, only his snoring was louder.

Turning so she faced away from him, she started counting

backwards from one hundred. It was a trick Aimee had taught her in college when she couldn't sleep. She tried to focus on the numbers and relax every part of her body. Her cheeks were tight from the dried tears, her throat raw. All she could think about was telling Adam she didn't want to be married to him any longer.

Even though she'd showered, she thought she could still smell sex. She wrapped herself tighter with the blankets, careful not to wake Adam.

What seemed like only a few minutes later, she was jostled awake. Adam was standing over her, gently shaking her shoulder. "Hey. Are you gonna get up? It's almost time to get the kids to school and I've got to get to work." The unspoken part: You stayed out too late last night. You're an irresponsible mother.

Her heart was pounding as she sat up, then rose out of bed. *Should you tell him now? Just blurt it out as he's putting on his tie?* As soon as she stood up, she felt a rush of vertigo that made her feel like she was underwater.

She sank back down on the bed. Adam was leaving their room, but paused in the doorway and turned back. *What were you doing out so late last night? Fucking some other guy?* But he only said, "Remember I have my brother's birthday dinner tonight. Did you get him anything? And don't forget my mom is coming to pick up Elsa and Benny so they can spend the night and make the place cards for Thanksgiving dinner."

"What?" Rachel rubbed her forehead, trying to soothe the stabbing pain between her eyes. They'd already had the argument about her buying gifts for his family members. Did he not remember she'd said she wasn't doing that anymore? And why was he reminding her of their social calendar? She didn't need reminding. That was something she'd always done for him.

Adam straightened his tie with an air of self-importance. His face was smoothly shaved. "Oh, and can you pick up my Navy suit from the cleaners? And we're out of mouthwash."

"I'm not sure if I'm going out today. I've got lots of work to do."

He'd left the room already. "Bye, kids!" he yelled from halfway down the stairs.

Benjamin and Elsa appeared in her doorway. They were both dressed, minus their shoes, which were downstairs, their backpacks in their hands. Rachel sighed, stood up again, and started making her bed.

"Wow, Mom," Elsa said, her brown eyes wide. "You *never* sleep in." Her hair was in two braids and she was wearing a pink beanie, pink flare leggings, and one of Benjamin's over-sized hoodies.

"I know." Rachel threw the pillows on the bed. "How much time do I have?"

"About five minutes. Did you come into my room last night?" Elsa asked, her eyes watchful.

"I did, my love. I missed you." Rachel grabbed a sports bra, running tights, and thick socks. Benjamin had put down his backpack and was rummaging through it. He was wearing the same hoodie from the last few days. "Your uniform is in the dryer, Benny. Don't forget to grab it."

"Missed me? You were only gone for, like, three hours." Elsa stayed in her doorway as Rachel rushed to her bathroom to change.

"And what about me?" Benjamin said without pausing his rummaging. "You didn't miss me?"

"Shut up, Benny." Elsa poked her head around the bath-room door frame. "Do we *have* to go to Gram's tonight?

Aren't we too old to make the stupid Thanksgiving place cards?"

"Yeah, I don't want to go!" Benjamin chimed in, his mouth now full of probably some disgusting month-old thing he'd unearthed from his backpack.

Rachel leaned her head around the doorframe. "Benjamin? What in God's name are you eating? For goodness' sake, can you guys give me like two minutes of privacy?" She closed the door and pulled her sports bra over her head, and tugged up her running tights.

"Just a muffin I found in my backpack. Hurry up mom, we gotta go!" He yelled as Rachel heard four feet clomp downstairs.

She barely heard Elsa say, "That's disgusting."

Rachel hurried down the stairs and grabbed her running jacket out of the closet. There were crumbs all over the countertops, and a half-eaten pizza sat in a pizza pan on top of the stove. The trash was overflowing, and Cora cried at her feet, which meant she hadn't been fed.

Rachel quickly grabbed her dish and rushed to the pantry to get a scoop of food. She turned to bring it back to its space, accidentally stepping on Cora's toe, and she let out a howl.

Adam's empty Yeti cup sat next to the sink.

Everywhere she turned, there was a new mess, one more thing that needed to be done. She wanted to lie down on the floor and take a day to stare at the ceiling.

The car horn blasted.

She fought back tears, thankful the kids were too engrossed in their devices to notice. It was a perfect fall day. Her kids were safe and healthy. Everything was the same and yet everything was different.

She'd cheated on her husband; the ultimate betrayal, and something she'd never thought she'd be capable of. No satisfaction had come from getting revenge on Adam the way her sister had said she should for all these years.

And she didn't feel one ounce of pleasure knowing Brad had cheated on the woman who had known full well that he had been in a relationship with her all those years ago, and had seduced him anyway.

This wasn't who she wanted to be.

She pulled up in front of school and watched the back of her kids' head grow smaller as they tramped up the school's sidewalk and into the building.

Her stomach clenched as the weight of what she'd done hit her, and she doubled over, thinking she might throw up. The car behind her beeped. A woman in a white van was waving her arms and yelling for Rachel to get out of the drop-off line. *Yeah, yeah.* She'd been that mom, too.

She pulled forward, and when she reached the stop sign at the school entrance, her phone vibrated from the passenger seat. Brad's name lit up the screen: *Yes, I'll call you tonight. 8? Are you as torn up as I am?*

Then from Adam: *Hey, day #4 without coffee in my Yeti. Are we not doing it anymore?*

Rachel shook her head. *No, we aren't doing it anymore.* It was a small gesture she'd done for a long time, but Adam didn't deserve it.

She shivered when another pang of guilt shot through her because even though she was bitter at her husband; he didn't deserve to be cheated on either.

Brad

When Brad left for school that morning, Beth had still been asleep. Or at least she'd pretended to be. The way he'd acted the night before had been on his mind since the moment he opened his eyes—it wasn't how he'd wanted that conversation to go, and he'd struggled all day to maintain a focus on teaching his second graders how to distinguish between odd and even numbers and keep them entertained during indoor recess. This had been the second time this week a downpour started right before their break, and they were getting restless.

It gave him a sliver of peace to know he and Rachel were going to talk things out tonight, but his mind spun as it sank in what they'd done. They'd both cheated on their spouses. They were cheaters.

As much as he'd second guessed his decision to leave Rachel, and as guilty as he'd felt about how it played out, it had been a clean cut. He'd broken things off with her before ever touching Beth.

This was different. He'd done something he'd always

sworn he would never, ever do. He judged people harshly for it.

He sent a text to Beth after lunch asking her how she was. She hadn't responded.

When he got home from work, she wasn't home. He pulled on his running pants and went for a run. Although he had to stop and walk a few times, his runs were now five miles long.

After his run, he felt slightly better, and Beth's car was in the garage.

Acid made its way up his chest as he climbed the stairs to their bedroom. When he opened the door, Beth's back was to him and she was shoving enormous shopping bags into her closet.

"Hey."

She jumped, obviously startled, and then continued with what she was doing without turning around.

"Sorry. Didn't mean to startle you. You weren't home when I got here, so I went for a run. Able to do five miles now."

Beth sniffled and backed out of the closet, closing the door behind her. "That's great," she said, wiping her eyes.

The pit in Brad's stomach expanded. He studied Beth, wondering if she suspected Rachel. Guilt twisted in his gut.

"You're upset. I'm upset too. Sorry about how I acted last night. I was being an asshole. But Beth, we need to talk."

She raised her eyebrows at him as if to say, "Out with it already!"

He shoved his hands in his pockets and leaned against the doorframe. "You can't even tell me if you're still in love with me. Don't you think we need to talk about this?"

"I'm fine, and it's okay. Can we talk later?" She pulled her hair up and secured it in a scrunchie on top of her head. "I'm exhausted. I went shopping today with Mom and one of her friends." She plopped on the bed, her perfectly manicured hands wringing each other on her lap.

"What did you get?" Brad sat down next to her.

"Just some stuff at Lululemon for pilates class. Then we went to Mom's favorite jewelry store, and she got a set of gold bangles." Beth held her hand up, admiring her fingers. "I got this ring, too." Her pinky held a new gold ring encrusted with glittering diamonds.

His stomach flipped, and his heart sped up. *Don't say anything about her spending money. It's not the time.* He knew without a doubt this was no way to live.

They weren't in love, and the reasons they were together before didn't make sense anymore.

"Beth?" His voice was quiet. "I think the writing is on the wall—"

She held up a hand and closed her eyes. "I told you we aren't going to talk about this now."

Brad sighed and slowly got up to take a shower. "Okay, but we need to talk this weekend."

Beth sat up on the bed, her phone suddenly materialized in her hands, her thumbs typing away.

In the bathroom, he started the shower, then peeled off his clothes.

The running water seemed louder than usual. His socks felt too tight, like they didn't want to come off. When the hot water hit his back, he quickly turned down the temperature. He usually welcomed the steam, liking the water as hot as possible. But today it was suffocating him.

A lot of this was his fault. He'd allowed himself to be the puppet in Beth's show for a long time, thinking if he could only please her, he'd eventually find peace, too. Maybe it had all been to prove to himself that he'd chosen the right person to spend his life with—that he could make it work.

Two people let it happen.

But the years had only worn him down and stripped him of his own happiness. Maybe the fact that he wanted them to come to an agreement together about ending their marriage was wishful thinking on his part.

It was clear Beth would never be his partner. And as much as she may not want to face it, she didn't really want to be. He wondered why she was holding on.

He resented it all: the house, his car, his expensive watch, how often Beth had to ask her parents for money so she could stuff her closet full of clothes, many of which she never wore, never even cut the tags off. How she used sex to avoid talking about anything remotely serious.

When he was with Rachel, he felt new energy being pumped into him. It wasn't the novelty of her either—she'd *always* made him feel that way.

Beth drained him. It was a feeling he'd gotten used to over the years, and he didn't want to waste another minute sitting in the familiarity of it.

He got out of the shower, dried off, and wrapped a towel around his waist.

Beth was still lying on the bed, her phone now charging on the nightstand.

He'd just opened his closet door and was holding his breath when Beth stood up and strutted toward him. Her eyes were still smeared with mascara, and he recognized the look on her face—sex had always been her way of closing the gap between them.

Brad looked down at his wife as she reached down with one hand and rubbed him over his towel. "How was your shower?"

Rachel.

He stepped away, his jaw clenched. "Beth," he pleaded, shaking his head. "No." He tightened his towel around his waist. "Please. We need to talk."

She stormed out of the room and slammed the door.

He came down from his shower to find Beth had heated some leftover lasagna and set the table.

Shoving overcooked lasagna noodles around on his plate, Brad tried to think of something to say to get his wife to have the talk they needed to have—a talk that was long overdue. He didn't want to be the only one making such a big decision about their future, but he would if he had to.

Beth popped up in her seat. "Hey, we should have Tom and Remi over for a drink tonight. I got Margarita mix the other day, and I think we have stuff for you to make your nachos."

She got up to rifle through the pantry.

Really? She's gone completely delusional.

Beth dropped a bag of chips and the margarita mix on the counter.

"Not tonight. Beth." He scooted his chair back and made his way over to her, picking up the chips and putting them back in the pantry. "What are you doing? We haven't even talked to them in like a year. Stop running from this." Brad placed a hand on her arm.

She crossed her arms, brushing his hand away.

Brad's face burned, knowing he had to do for them what Beth couldn't.

Rachel

Cora panted at Rachel's feet as she flipped a pancake and glanced up at the clock. 5:52. She flipped a few more pancakes and then glanced again. Still 5:52. *Stop it, Rachel.*

She'd been doing some version of this unhinged clock-watching all day, unable to fight the angsty excitement that stirred every time she thought about hearing Brad's voice. She just needed time to move a *little* faster.

She'd brought up a pile of laundry to put away and changed into her chenille robe as soon as she'd gotten the kids home from school, and the fabric was soft and warm against her skin.

After she'd wrapped herself in it, she fingered the freshly washed bra and underwear she'd worn last night, shoving it to the back of her drawer.

Elsa and Benjamin had changed their tune about going to their grandmother's—once Rachel had reminded them that their Grandma also wanted to go over their Christmas lists and how she didn't take cell phones away at dinnertime or bedtime, they were both miraculously excited. That, at least for a moment, had pulled Rachel out of her Brad-reverie and made her laugh before being overcome with an almost paralyzing feeling of shame and dread. *What would they think of me if they knew?*

The pancakes bubbled and sizzled on the buttery pan. She sprinkled some thin apple slices and cinnamon on top, letting them cook through for another few minutes before flipping. Everyone loved breakfast for dinner, and tonight she'd pulled out all the stops to make a variety of pancakes: apple and cinnamon, blueberry, and her favorite, chocolate chip.

After flipping the apple-cinnamons, she stirred the chocolate chip batter and pre-heated the air fryer. She'd seen a Pinterest video where they'd twisted the bacon and then air-fried it into perfect, crispy curls.

She almost burned the first chocolate chip pancake, because she drifted into a daydream of making pancakes for Brad one sunny Saturday morning. Then, she found herself standing in front of perfectly crisped twisty bacon that she couldn't recall pulling out of the airfryer.

Her brain was all over the place.

She washed her hands, then splashed cold water on her face.

Stop thinking about Brad when your kids are right upstairs.

When Adam got home, her stomach went sour. He'd messaged her earlier saying that he'd be meeting with his brother right after work, and she'd been relieved knowing she could temporarily shelve her plan of telling her husband their marriage was over.

Adam lifted the hand towel covering the huge stack of pancakes and bacon that sat on a white oval platter. "The bacon is a bit ... well done."

"I thought you were having dinner with Matt tonight?" Rachel was peeling a mango over the sink for the fruit salad, the juice running down her arm.

Only five minutes had passed since the last time she checked the time. She sucked in a breath.

"I am. Just decided to change first." Adam set down the mail and made his way over to the sink to wash his hands, taking a second to brush Rachel's cheek with his lips. The touch of his lips felt too sharp, and he smelled like stale sweat. "Missed my coffee today."

"Yeah, I saw your text. I stopped making it because you kept leaving it on the counter instead of putting it in the dishwasher." She grabbed the raspberries, dumped them in the fruit bowl, and mixed the fruit together with her hands, being careful not to squash the berries. She caught another whiff of sweat, similar to the smell Adam had after mowing the lawn. "You smell ... sweaty. Hot in the office today or something?"

"No! It wasn't!" He was almost yelling now, shaking his hands off in the sink.

Rachel stood with her hands over the fruit, waiting for him to move so she could wash hers. She felt her jaw drop at the sudden anger in his voice. "Okay then. And don't speak to me that way."

He blocked the sink, glaring at her.

She glared back. "I need to wash my hands. I can't handle this sticky fruit juice all over them for another second." She felt the tiniest stab of guilt for standing up for herself, but she shoved it aside. She was sick of his outbursts.

Adam slammed the towel against the edge of the farmhouse sink before stalking upstairs.

Rachel watched her hands under the stream of water—they were shaking. She recognized Adam's behavior. It was the same short-tempered attitude he'd had when he was having an affair before she caught him.

No.

You're just projecting. You're just as bad as he is.

When his footsteps came back down the stairs, her shoulders lifted to her earlobes.

"On second thought, did you make enough for me? I might skip dinner. I'm not feeling well."

Her heart sank. He'd taken off his tie and untucked his shirt.

"You have to go." Her voice was deflated, and she put her hands on her hips. "He's going to be disappointed, Adam. He's going through a hard time with the divorce. What kind of brother doesn't show up to his brother's first post-divorce birthday dinner?" She thought she might be coming off a tad dramatic, but the thought of spending a long evening alone with Adam turned her stomach. She would talk to him when he got home, and they'd come up with a plan while the kids were with his mom. *You have to do this.*

Adam ignored her and began flipping through the mail as she scooped fruit salad onto plates and took the towel off the pancakes and bacon. The steam hit her in the face, and her appetite returned with a vengeance as she inhaled the fruit, chocolate, and salty bacon scents.

Through all her attempts to keep her brain busy with painting, she hadn't stopped to eat.

"Come down and eat, kids!" She yelled up the stairs. She took a piece of bacon and looked at Adam. "Your mom will be here soon. The kids need to hurry and eat."

"Mm-hmm." Adam was flipping absentmindedly through a pamphlet, oblivious. She grabbed the edge of the counter, feeling like she could break it off in her hands as Benjamin and Elsa stomped down the stairs.

"I guess there's enough here for you," she said to Adam. "Let's sit and eat." She allowed herself a hearty eye-roll though, with her head turned so neither Adam nor the kids could see.

Benjamin slid across the floor in his socks, coming to a

stop directly in front of the kitchen table and grabbing a few pancakes with one hand and a fist full of bacon with the other.

"Benny! Use the fork and put some of that bacon back! We'd all like some." Rachel kept it to herself that actually it had been a really impressive move. She sat down and grabbed his wrist, forcing him to release the bacon.

"Geez, sorry!" Benjamin threw the bacon on the platter and dropped into his seat.

"Ew! I don't want that now that he's touched it all." Elsa pouted, adding more fruit to her plate. "His sweaty palm-ick is all over it now!"

Rachel put her head in her hands for a moment, then looked up at her kids.

What is my life right now? Her husband was a rude, thoughtless ogre. She'd just had the most amazing sex of her life with a man who was not her ogre husband, and now she was refereeing a bacon dispute between two surly teenagers. She felt like she was in a fever dream.

"Can we all just have a nice dinner?" Rachel picked up her fork, stabbed a pancake, and directed what she was pretty sure must be a manic smile at Elsa and Benjamin. "Excited to go to Gram's tonight?"

"Yeah!" Elsa pushed her chair closer to the table, taking a few pieces of bacon from the bottom of the pile. "Can't wait to do my Christmas shopping!"

"I'm excited for you, Honey." Rachel swirled a piece of bacon in her syrup and watched Benjamin spread butter on a blueberry pancake, fold it in half like a taco, and dip it in the river of syrup on his plate. She felt her shoulders relax a little. Where the hell was Adam? She turned to look and found him still mindlessly sorting the mail. She turned back to the kids, her fake smile back in place.

"I'm not excited about the dumb place cards," Benjamin said with his mouth full. "But she doesn't take my phone away at night like you do, so I guess I'm excited." He paused his chewing for a moment, his brow furrowing, and then pointed at Rachel. "And you can't tell her to take it away, Mom. Her house, her rules."

Benjamin was referring to a sign his grandmother had in her house that read, "Grandma's house, Grandma's rules."

Rachel laughed. "Okay, I won't. I'm glad you two have reconsidered."

She wondered what a night alone would look like if she and Adam separated. Would she be able to function knowing her kids weren't with her because *she* left her marriage?

Her heart clenched at the thought, and she dropped her fork.

"What's wrong, Mom?" Elsa asked as she held a piece of bacon up to her mouth. "You're acting strange lately."

Rachel turned around to see Adam finally putting down the mail, tapping it into a neat pile as if that were helpful. Rachel would still have to go through it and sort it, respond to whomever needed responding to and tossing out the junk. He huffed out of the kitchen, back upstairs.

"I'm fine Honey." She offered Elsa a reassuring smile. "I don't think I ate enough today is all."

They know. They know something is wrong.

When they finished eating, the kids ran upstairs to pack and Rachel hesitated before putting the food away, not knowing if Adam was going to eat or not. She spooned the fruit into a Tupperware container, covered the pancakes and bacon with saran wrap, and put everything in the fridge. The table and countertops were still a mess. She felt like she was moving through wet cement.

She'd deal with the dinner disaster later.

She headed upstairs to see if Adam had decided about tonight, hopeful his absence from dinner meant he was going with Matt after all.

"I put the food in the fridge. I'm still not sure what you are doing tonight." She slid her new ring up and down her finger.

Adam nodded, shuffling around his drawer. He'd changed his clothes and was wearing a tan sweater and jeans. "I think I'll go out with—"

"Oh, great!" She clapped her hands together. "Glad to hear it. I'm going to read and enjoy the quiet." She marched into the bathroom and pulled out her face wash and serums.

Adam followed her. "You forgot my mouthwash—remember I asked you this morning to get me some?" His face was full of annoyance.

Rachel slid on her terry cloth headband. "I didn't forget."

"Oh." She could see his reflection in the mirror behind her. His expression had softened. "Where is it?"

"I just didn't get it. I'm not your servant-bitch." The calm in her voice surprised her. "All you do is take from me. You don't treat me like an actual person with her own thoughts, feelings, and interests. And then you wonder why I don't greet you with open legs every night."

She opened the faucet, letting it run to a nice hot temperature even though it drove Adam crazy when she "wasted" water. Adam's mouth dropped open as if he was going to say something, but she spoke before he could.

"You have no interest in my life or what I do outside of being your kids' mom or your wife. You don't want to hear about any of my painting projects or my time with my sister. All you care about is getting the things *you* need. I'm sick of being invisible." Rachel took a breath, then pumped some cleanser into her hands and massaged her face with her usual gentle circular motions, ignoring her trembling hands.

Adam stared at her with narrowed eyes. Was he contemplating what she said, or was that pure defensive rage?

Her cell phone vibrated in her robe pocket, and Cora started barking, alerting the family Grandma had arrived.

"Listen, Rachel, I don't think you're my servant-bitch." He stepped into the bathroom and leaned with his palms on the sink beside her. "Where is this coming from all of a sudden? Why are you so eager to get rid of us all tonight? Elsa's right—you have been acting differently lately. What's going on with you?"

An image of sitting astride Brad last night in his Audi flashed across her brain, and she winced. No. She'd cheated, but it didn't make his years of disrespect any less real. "What's going on is exactly what I just said. I'm not repeating myself." She felt brave and ashamed at the same time. Would he just *leave* already?

Adam pushed off the counter and shook his head, grimacing as if he just couldn't believe her. "You know, I bought you that ring, hoping it would make you happy. But nothing's good enough for you." He was whispering through clenched teeth.

"Hello! I'm here!" Adam's mom's voice floated up the stairs.

"Coming, Mom!" Adam yelled before turning his attention back to Rachel. "We'll finish this later." He turned and stalked off as if he were a king, rightful owner of The Last Word.

Yes, we will.

Rachel's whole body trembled as she heard his heavy footfalls move down the stairs. She had visions of throwing all his belongings out the window and setting it on fire like she'd seen in the movies. *He didn't hear a damn word you said.*

This was what Adam did though—pissed her off and then told *her* when they'd talk about it.

Her face was still hot when she trudged downstairs. Mary, Adam's mom, was standing at the front door with her keys in her hands, asking Adam how the new office was coming. Her gray hair was set in perfect, tight curls, and she was wearing navy blue sweatpants and matching sneakers.

"I left the car running because it's so cold outside," she said before Rachel could say hello. "But Adam, can you shut it off? I can help you clean up the kitchen, Rachel. Did you feed a small army?" She laughed and hurried to the kitchen island.

"Oh, no. Never mind that. You have a good time with the kids. Thank you, though."

"You're such a great cook, Dear. Adam, I hope you *usually* pitch and help her clean up, and get the kids to help, too."

Rachel managed a tight smile.

"Let's go, Gram," Elsa said, throwing her backpack over her shoulder. Rachel knew she was in a hurry to get those place cards finished so the shopping could begin.

Mary opened the door and waved the kids through, but Rachel stopped them. "Hello, doesn't your mother get a hug?" She opened her arms.

Elsa and Benjamin put one arm around her, and she hugged them close to her chest.

"Oh my God, Mom," Benjamin said, ducking under her arm. "We'll see you tomorrow morning!" Rachel kissed the tops of their heads, and inhaled them before they broke away.

Mary patted Rachel's back as if to tell her she understood how she was feeling.

"Bye, Dad," they said in unison as they headed outside.

Adam waved and Mary said, "What's wrong, Adam? You're so pale!"

"I'm good, Mom." He shrugged into his coat. "I need to go, though." He brushed past Rachel to give his mother a hug.

Mary gripped her son tighter. "I'm so glad you boys are spending time together tonight." She pulled back and rested a hand on Adam's shoulder. "It's going to be rough on him.

Did you know Chloe is already living with that man? He's crushed. I'm having him over for lunch, tom—"

Benjamin burst through the doorway announcing he forgot his earbuds and headed toward the stairs.

Adam stopped him to steal a hug—his phone was in his back pocket and it chimed three times in a row. "Hey buddy, have fun at Gram's tonight. Let's throw the football tomorrow and take Cora for a walk, okay?"

"Yeah, sure!" Benjamin said, running upstairs.

"I've gotta run," Adam said, kissing his mom. "Don't worry, he'll get through this. And one of us will be at your place early to get the kids before you go to choir practice."

"Sounds good, Dear." Mary smiled up at her son, who left without saying goodbye to Rachel. When he was out of sight, she turned back to Rachel. "Is everything okay, Honey? You know you can talk to me."

She held back tears. Mary loved her, and she loved her grandchildren. She'd always been a tremendous help and much more of a mother to Rachel than her own mother was. Would she lose her if she left Adam? "Yes, Mary. I'm fine. Thank you."

Benjamin came back downstairs with his earbuds in his ears, and they all wandered outside. Rachel stood in the driveway and watched as the three of them got in the car.

What if they were piling into Adam's car to spend the weekend with him? Rachel felt sick at the thought.

It smelled like snow, and the chilly breeze was cutting right through Rachel's robe and wool socks. She was freezing, but she stood there until she couldn't see Mary's taillights anymore.

She'd watched the clock all day long, anticipating this conversation with Brad.

Now that it had come, and she'd stood in the driveway watching her kids leave, knowing she'd looked forward to some time without them so she could talk to a man they didn't even know, guilt swallowed her.

She hadn't just betrayed Adam, she'd betrayed her kids, too. The weight of what she'd done suffocated her.

What if she ended her marriage and her kids blamed her? What if they somehow found out what she did, what Adam did? That might do damage beyond repair.

They would be the ones who would have to go back and forth between parents. They would be the ones who would have to split birthdays and holidays. Could she handle watching them drive away on a Friday night if Adam came to pick them up and take them for the weekend? Would she hate herself for being responsible for such a huge lifestyle change that didn't just involve her?

Deep down, Rachel knew they would suffer just as much if things between her and Adam didn't improve drastically soon. Would she hate herself for staying?

When she trudged back into the house, the smell of pancakes and bacon lingering, her stomach turned.

This longing for something more, the desire to walk away from her life, left her paralyzed with remorse. She pulled her robe tie tighter, as if it could take her angst away.

Their family pictures were lined on the mantle and Benny's favorite spot on the couch sagged. Elsa's earrings were on the windowsill, and she picked them up and squeezed them in her hand.

How dare she sneak out for a night with Brad while her family ate dinner without her, then wish for them to all be gone so she could talk to him in secret. *What kind of mother does that?*

She looked around her living room slowly, trying to calm her spinning thoughts, before falling into a puddle on the living room rug. She missed her kids so much it hurt.

Cora licked her face and Rachel hugged her tight, and said

out loud to her empty house, "I can't do this. I need to stay with my family. This is where I need to be. I got over Brad once, and I can do it again."

She let go of Cora and covered her face with her hands. Sobs erupted out of her, and she couldn't breathe. Cora let out a few whimpers and licked her hands.

She'd tell Adam they needed therapy and give her marriage another couple of months.

Rachel stared at the wall in the fetal position, begging her heart to go numb, so that what she was about to do wouldn't hurt so damn much.

Brad

If Brad could run away from this moment, he would. He and Beth had been standing next to the open pantry for only a few minutes, but it felt as if time was standing still.

Beth picked at a pill on her sleeve. She was as beautiful and fierce as ever. She deserved to be with someone who loved those things about her—not someone who saw those traits as temporary excitement, the way he had.

He was trying to stand up under an unbearable weight as Beth followed him with her eyes as he paced, her face pale and drawn as she waited for him to say what he needed to say.

Tell her.

His heart thumped through his temples. "I'm not happy, Beth. *We* aren't happy. It's been like this for so long now, I think we've almost gotten used to it. This is ... don't you think we've both had enough?" He braced himself for an outburst, but Beth's solemn expression didn't waiver.

"You've been distant for sure." Beth closed the pantry door and leaned against it as if to set down the emotional baggage she'd been carrying around. "I know I haven't supported you since you started teaching. Honestly, I've been hoping you'd come around and we'd get back to the way things used to be." She rubbed her index finger back and forth across her mouth. "I guess that's not going to happen."

"No. It's not." Brad sounded calm even though he couldn't stomach having this conversation again.

"Should we ... I don't know. Counseling, maybe?" She sounded like one of his second graders guessing at an answer they clearly didn't know.

"Beth, do you hear yourself? You don't even sound like you want to try. What I know is that we've *been* trying. For years, we've tried to turn each other into something we just aren't."

She tilted her head back, let out a sigh, then looked straight at Brad, her cheeks flushing suddenly, as if a difficult thought had just planted itself in her head against her will.

"Beth?" Tears welled in her eyes.

After what felt like minutes, Beth said, "You're right. I've felt the same way for a long time. And I kept pushing these feelings away because no one in my family gets divorced. Literally no one. I didn't want to deal with it, and I kept thinking things would go back to the way they were. And honestly ... I didn't think you'd ever leave me. What will I say to my parents?" Her voice shook.

Listening to Beth say something he already knew made his chest tighten, but he felt an immense wave of relief at the same time.

"I was hoping for the same thing. I never wanted to let you down, but it's clear that we have grown so far apart. And Beth, you don't have to live your life for your parents. You deserve happiness on your own terms."

"I know I haven't been the best wife. You've tried harder than I have." Beth chewed on her bottom lip, and the corners of her mouth lifted into the faintest smile. "I *really* fucking hate canoeing."

Brad let out a chuckle. "I know you do."

"I have to know, though. Is it something to do with that ... that painting?" She turned toward the living room, pointing her finger. "With *her*?"

He hesitated a beat too long, and a single tear fell down her cheek. "Beth. I never meant—"

She held up her hand. "Don't. Actually, I don't want to know." This was the most thoughtful Brad had seen her in a long time. Maybe ever. They stood in silence, each taking in the heaviness of the moment.

Beth padded to the closet and grabbed her coat. "I'm going to go to my parents'."

"No, please don't do that. You stay here. I'll go to a hotel."

She nodded slowly. "Okay," she whispered.

"Beth, I will talk to your parents with you if you want. We can tell them together."

She hugged herself and looked around their huge downstairs. "Um ... but I want to know one thing."

"What is it?" Brad's heart started thumping in his chest.

"Are you leaving me for Rachel?" She took in a sharp breath, as if the words had hurt to say, and crossed her arms tighter around herself.

Was he leaving her for Rachel? The truth was, he did want Rachel. He was in love with her. But he and Beth were absolutely not meant for each other. "Beth, we aren't meant to be. I know you agree. And you deserve a guy who will enjoy spoiling you like the princess you are. One who will never suggest going canoeing together."

She chewed on the inside of her cheek. "I'm sure seeing her sped up the process though?"

Brad stepped toward her and wrapped her in a hug. Her

arms stayed at her sides at first, but when a sob escaped his mouth, she hugged him back.

They stood in their dark kitchen, dinner dishes still on the table waiting to be cleaned, holding each other up, as pieces of what had just happened felt real.

"It's going to be okay. In fact, once the dust settles, I think things are going to be a lot better for both of us." Brad patted her back in reassurance.

"I know. I know you're right. You had the courage to do what I couldn't." Beth let go of him, reaching up to wipe away his tears. "What are my parents going to say?" They both let out a chuckle, and Brad shoved his hands in his pockets.

"They will be fine, Beth. They love you." He let out a sharp sigh. "I'm going to go pack some stuff." He made his way upstairs, gripping on to the railing to pull himself up with each step.

He was leaving this life where he'd been uncomfortable for so long and starting over. He was really doing it. As he shoved sweaters and polo shirts into a suitcase, tears dribbled down his cheeks. He had a moment of vertigo and had to stop what he was doing, stand up, and assure himself this was real. He stared at his bed with its perfect white hotel-grade linens, chosen by Beth, of course, and walked the length of windows that flanked the entire south-facing side of their bedroom—another feature Beth had insisted upon.

He felt like he was floating.

He returned to his suitcase and zipped it up without double checking to make sure he had everything, and went downstairs. Beth was curled up on the couch with her phone.

"I'm just gonna ... uh, grab this," Brad said, reaching for the painting where it still leaned against the table.

Beth rolled her eyes. "Please do." But there was a hint of a smile tugging at her lips. She stood. "Well ... let me know where you're staying. We can touch base in a few days to start this whole process."

Brad nodded. "Yeah. For sure." He hiked the painting up under his arm. "Sorry. I guess I'll just ... go now."

Beth widened her eyes at him as if to say, "Why are you still here?"

He left.

After driving for five minutes, Brad pulled over and into a gas station parking lot and called Rachel. She picked up on the second ring.

"Hi," she whispered.

"Hi. Hi ... You, uh, alone?"

"Yes. The kids and Adam left a bit ago."

"How are you? There's so much going through my head. I've been dying to talk to you all day." Brad twirled his wedding ring around his finger with his thumb.

"I understand." Her response lacked expression, and Brad didn't recognize her tone.

"I thought the time would never come." A couple walking hand in hand passed in front of his car. They were wearing puffy coats, and they each carried a large Slurpee and a bag of Cheetos.

Rachel sniffled.

"Rach? You okay?" *She is not okay.*

"I'm fine, just have a lot on my mind. I'm torn up about last night."

"Me too. I ... it's complicated, I know."

Another few silent seconds dragged on, and Brad took in a breath. "The painting, Rachel. It's beautiful ... I love it. Thank you so much for doing it for me." He tapped his hand on the steering wheel. He felt like an idiot, yammering about the painting. She already knew he liked it.

"I'm glad you like it." Rachel's voice was quiet. Too quiet. Brad's stomach sank.

"Are you sure this is a good time to talk?" Something was really off. This wasn't the same Rachel he'd been with last night.

"Yes, it's fine. I'm alone. I'm just not sure what to say." Her voice cracked.

Brad put his head in his hands, and the words flowed out of him like a running stream. "Rachel, listen, we have things to figure out, but I have to tell you something. I don't love Beth. I haven't for a long time and it took seeing you to do something about it. We ended things. Tonight."

"Brad," she whispered. "What?"

"I know what we did last night was the backward way to go about things, but I feel like it was inevitable. I've been doing everything in my power these past few weeks to get close to you. It's like a force I can't control; a switch that won't shut off. I know you feel it too."

There was only silence on the other end of the line.

He dropped his head, waiting for Rachel to say something. "Are you still there?"

"I am, yes." He barely made out what she said.

"You have to know, leaving you for Beth has always been one of my biggest regrets. Did you know I called Aimee to see what you were up to right before I married Beth? Even back then, I couldn't get you out of my mind. Aimee told me you were happy, and that I'd better not dare call you. But I've always wondered what my life would be like if I hadn't listened to her." Brad's lungs felt like they were made of stone, like they weren't pulling in enough air.

"Brad. I didn't know you were going to do this." Her sobs were loud and deep. "I can't. I can't do this with you. I can't break up my family."

Brad felt like someone had punched him in the stomach. Had he been too hasty about leaving Beth? *No. You would have split up, anyway.* He had unknowingly created a fantasy in his mind that he'd leave Beth and he and Rachel would start fresh. As if no time had passed.

His stomach plummeted—he'd been an idiot for thinking it would be that easy. For Rachel, it was a lot more compli-cated. She had a family; she didn't work full time, and she'd already admitted to staying in her marriage for her kids.

How could he think she'd change her mind after a few hours of spending time together?

"Ah, shit, Rachel, I'm so sorry. Shouldn't have said all of that. I just ... I'm myself with you. I can tell you everything. I shouldn't have unloaded on you like that." He clenched his fist and pressed it hard to his chest. *Please change your mind, please change your mind.*

Rachel sniffed. "Don't be sorry, Brad. I'm glad you told me those things. And there's a part of me that feels the same. A huge part. But I can't." Another huge cry escaped her. "My kids."

She sounded so tiny and frail.

Brad stared at the fluorescent lights of the convenience store. He'd never experienced pain like this—it felt like his chest was being split open. He wanted to drive to her and take her in his arms, even if it would be the last time. Instead, he listened as her sobs slowly quieted.

He knew things were complicated, but he also believed they could figure it out if they tried. He couldn't forget how powerful their connection had been the night before. But she'd made it clear that she couldn't leave her kids. It wouldn't be right to push her. And yet, he had no idea how he was going to let her go.

After a long silence, he cleared his throat. "Okay. I respect your decision. But Rachel, I just want to say one thing. If there's ever a way—if you change your mind—please tell me. Because in my mind, there's no question. You're the one. You're it for me."

"I can't. Brad, I just ... you left Beth? For ... me?" He could hear the guilt squeezing her throat. She wouldn't want to be the cause of someone else's marriage ending. Not his sweet, caring Rachel.

He slammed his fist on the steering wheel, furious at himself for having been so careless with her. "I swear to you, it's not like that. Beth and I would have split up, regardless. We had a good talk, and we both agree it's the right thing. So please, *please* don't carry any guilt for that. We were falling apart long before I ran into you."

"Okay," she said, her voice still small, but a little less choked. "I still can't ... I'm so sorry."

He clenched his eyes shut, and the pain in his chest got worse. "It's okay. I have to accept that." *How can you ever accept this?*

"Thank you," she whispered.

Brad couldn't hold back his tears any longer. "Seeing you these past few weeks has been amazing." He didn't care that she could hear his tears through his cracking voice. "I'll never forget you. But ... I will respect your decision and leave you alone." *Please change your mind. Please change your mind.*

Rachel's voice barely came through her cries. "Okay, Brad. Thank you. Thank you for being so good and kind to me. Bye."

She was gone.

Rachel

When Rachel opened her eyes at 6:00 a.m., after only a few hours of sleep, she felt hungover. Adam was asleep beside her, his back to her. He'd come home after midnight the night before, and she'd pretended to be asleep.

Her heart slammed in her chest. She wondered if Brad had slept at home, and if he'd retreated to the spare bedroom, or if he'd shared a bed with Beth. Maybe he stayed at a friend's house in an unfamiliar room. Did he cry as long and hard as she had?

Her chest was sore from crying, and the room was spinning.

It was still dark out, and only fifteen degrees according to the weather app on her phone, but she couldn't lie in bed, longing to feel Brad's arms around her for one more second. She crept out of bed and began to layer up for her run.

Once outside, she took a big breath of frosty cold air.

Better already. Would Brad go on a run today? He'd said she had unknowingly inspired him to take up running again. She imagined the two of them running together out in the cold, their cheeks glowing hot pink from the icy air, but neither one caring because it felt good to be out and even better to be together. Her heart squeezed with such intensity that her knees almost buckled. She had to push him out of her mind.

Rachel forgot her phone and didn't tell anyone she was headed out for her run like she usually did. When she reached the two-mile mark where she normally turned around, she figured everyone would be asleep anyway, and she kept going.

She had to run through and beyond that awful pain that seemed to want to stop her heart. She pumped her arms hard, welcoming the adrenaline shooting through her. The air smelled of pine, and she forced herself to focus on her surroundings—men in hard hats were trimming the trees before the snow and ice started to fall, everyone's pumpkins and mums had a thin layer of crystally ice covering them, and one of the men trimming trees had reddish scruff like Brad.

How long will it take before you stop seeing him everywhere?

Crystals formed on her lashes, but her breath under her Balaclava kept her warm.

When the kids got home later this morning, she'd pull out the Christmas decorations, and they could start decorating, maybe order a pizza for lunch. She'd talk to Adam tonight, insist on counseling, and tell him what happened between her and Brad.

She didn't see the branch jutting out into the road until she was on her way to the ground. As her hands and knees slammed onto the pavement, she bit her tongue and tasted blood. Her thick, down mittens and fleece leggings protected her from road rash and scrapes, but her palms throbbed as she eased herself onto her side and pushed herself farther onto the dirt shoulder so she'd be out of traffic. She rolled onto her back and lay there for a few minutes, waiting for the sky to stop spinning.

When she had the strength, she sat up on her hip and leaned over to spit out the blood from her mouth. She stared at the ground. It blurred under the icy tears and she wiped them away so they wouldn't freeze on her face. *This has to end. Right now. Stop thinking about Brad. You never fall, never forget to text before a run.*

Her knees throbbed from the pain, and she checked her leggings again. No rips. She limped back home and stopped to gaze up at the big white chapel. The lights were on inside, making the stained glass windows shine under the cloudy sky. The window boxes held fresh greens and red holly berries, and lantern style lights that flanked the arched, wooden door glowed.

Her eyes filled with water again, because for the first time in her life, thinking of the upcoming holidays filled her with dread.

She finally reached her driveway, exhausted and cold, and she was confused when she saw a few electric candles in the windows.

It was exactly what she'd envisioned when they'd bought this house—a cold winter's day with lights flickering on the windowsills. This was her home. This was her life. She reminded herself, again, that she'd gotten over Brad once, and maybe this time it would be easier to forget him.

As she hobbled up to the front door, she saw Benjamin and Elsa through the window. Adam must have picked them up already, or maybe Mary had dropped them off.

She eased the front door open and peeled off her freezing, sodding sneakers as the three of them chattered happily while going through a box of Christmas decorations.

"You forgot your phone," Adam said, holding a silver reindeer in one hand.

"We're decorating for Christmas, Mom! Your favorite!" Elsa said, centering an electric candle in the window.

Rachel relaxed a little and felt warmth spread through her chest. "I see that, and I'm excited!"

"How was your run? You smell like snow," Adam said, brushing past her. "Okay, kids. Let's get these plugged in, then I'll get the wreaths down from the attic!"

"It was okay. I fell."

Benjamin took intentional strides to her from across the room. Rachel peeled off her mittens and looked at the palms of her hands. "They are red, but no blood. Are you okay?" he asked as Elsa joined them.

Adam didn't even hear her and was scurrying around like an elf on cocaine.

"I'm fine, Honey. Thank you."

Usually, Adam moaned and groaned when Rachel woke up on a random Saturday in November and started pulling out the Christmas boxes.

"Can't we wait until after Thanksgiving like normal people? This is ridiculous," he'd say every year, as if it physically hurt him to look at pretty decorations.

Rachel studied him for a moment. He was moving and talking so fast it made her head spin. When he stopped at the island to take a sip of coffee, he slammed his cup down, sloshing coffee and cream without noticing.

"I'm taking a shower," Rachel said, pausing with one foot on the bottom step and one hand on the railing.

"But we're decorating for Christmas! In November, just like you like," Adam said, untangling a pile of Christmas lights and grinning maniacally.

What the? "Uh ... okay. I'll be back down soon." She forced a smile, and her stomach rumbled, even though she couldn't think about eating a thing.

Upstairs, she found her phone on her nightstand where she'd plugged it in last night. She woke it up, hoping to see a message from Brad waiting for her, even though she'd told him it had to be over.

Her heart sank when there were no notifications from him.

Despite the freezing temperatures, her sports bra was drenched, and it felt good to peel it off.

She stared at her breasts in the mirror, saggy after having breastfed two kids and the passage of time, and remembered how Brad had appreciated them anyway, taking them in his mouth. She cupped and squeezed her bare breasts as if that could help sate the longing.

Her leggings caught on her heel as she pulled them off, and she caught herself with one hand on the wall near the hamper. Adam's underwear and socks were in a heap next to the hamper. Of course they were. Rachel rolled her eyes and bent to pick them up. She frowned. Was that a smudge of blood on Adam's underwear? She immediately checked herself and the surrounding floor.

Nothing. Her knees and palms were a little beat up, but not actively bleeding, and there was nothing on the floor or on her own clothes that she'd just removed. She grabbed the boxers to take a closer look.

The red smudges were all over the front of Adam's pale blue boxers, some bigger than others. She scraped at one with her thumbnail, and a bit came off under her nail. She flipped the boxers inside out.

No blood on the inside. Strange.

She turned the hot water on full blast, and the bathroom slowly filled with steam.

With her pinky nail, she scraped the blood out from under her thumbnail. As it smeared across her finger, she realized it wasn't blood at all.

It was lipstick.

The ringing in her ears blocked out the chatter from

downstairs. She felt like she was underwater and struggled to catch her breath. When she felt her own nails digging into her bare thighs, the sting threw her back into the present moment.

Adam had been acting the same way he had last time he was cheating—snapping at everyone, then being overly cheerful, working late, always on his phone, smelling of stale sweat when he got home. His agitation; his mood swings—she hadn't imagined that.

He's doing it again. He's fucking someone else. And you were feeling so guilty and doing everything you could, including turning away the love of your life, to hold this family together. This is just ... you can't do this. You can't live this life.

She squeezed her eyes shut. As she tilted her head back to massage shampoo into her hair, thinking of how she was going to confront him this time, Emily's face flashed through her mind.

Then it was all she could see. Emily's face. Emily's smile. Emily's mouth. Emily's ... lipstick. That signature lipstick shade Emily had worn for the past twenty-five years—that bright raspberry that looked awful in the tube but made Emily's almond-shaped green eyes pop. She'd smeared that berry color into Rachel's clear lip gloss, and she didn't even like to use it anymore.

There had been times Rachel had joined Emily for early-morning yoga, and her lips would still be stained raspberry from the day before.

Rachel opened the shower door, half covered in suds, and ran to grab the underwear.

You're losing your mind. She wouldn't. Adam wouldn't ... he can't stand her. And she hates him. She's always told you that you should get even with him. That you should...

Leave him. Her sister wanted her to leave her husband so she could have him for herself.

She could still hear that laugh coming from the other side

of the door the day she stopped to surprise her husband, but instead, heard him crying out as he came for someone else. She could still feel the skin of her knuckles breaking as she banged on the door, and they were too cowardly to answer it.

Her entire body broke out in goosebumps, and bile rose in her chest.

How did you not see it?

When Rachel had first told her sister what had happened, she'd thought it was strange that Emily couldn't seem to make eye contact with her. She'd thought it was because Adam had done such a horrible thing, and Emily wasn't sure how to make it better.

All this time, she thought Emily had acted that way because she cared about her and hated that he'd hurt her. She'd also thought Adam's reaction to Emily was because he felt defensive, knowing that she told her sister what he'd done.

You're an idiot.

Rachel sat naked on her bed, shampoo dripping down her back and shoulders. At some point, she'd picked up her phone and was now scrolling furiously through her pictures.

She found the picture from her last birthday—a close-up of her and Emily sipping virgin cosmos. Emily's raspberry lips contrasted beautifully against her pale, pristine skin.

Rachel remembered trying the lipstick that night, wondering if she could mimic the look. "It's a completely different color on me! I look like a clown," she'd said.

Emily had smirked as she took the lipstick back and tucked it back into her clutch.

Holding the phone up to her husband's underwear, she couldn't tell if she was grasping for an excuse to justify her behavior, if she was losing her mind, or if it had been so obvious all this time, and she'd just been in denial.

She is your sister; he is your husband.

Rachel stood and hurled the underwear as hard as she

could, completely dissatisfied, when they fell softly to the floor.

On autopilot, she opened the door that led to the tiny balcony just off of their bedroom and stepped outside, completely naked and still dripping from her shower. Her eyes darted back and forth across the expanse of her perfectly manicured back lawn. It was snowing—a light coating had covered the ground. It was so quiet, the silence hurt her ears.

She shivered, but wasn't cold.

She was crying, but there weren't any tears.

Her marriage was over.

You have to leave.

She clenched her fists.

No. He has to leave.

Rachel's chest ached, and she took hard breaths, thinking about how hard she'd been trying to keep her family together and tighten the bond with her only sister.

She was falling in love with Brad.

She was furious.

She was trying to go back in time, to see what she'd missed, wondering how she could be so blind.

The ring Adam had given her for their anniversary—the one that was supposed to be a symbol of commitment, but was really a pawn to get laid—felt sharp on her finger.

Holding up her hand, she watched snowflakes melt as soon as they touched her skin before sliding the ring off. She threw it in the snow and lost sight of it as it mixed with the heavy flakes.

She turned to go back inside, leaving tiny pools of cold water with each step, and got back into the running shower.

Brad

The only available seats at the Miss Brunswick diner were at the long linoleum counter. Brad's mom was due any minute. While he waited, he watched two cooks scurry back and forth, flipping pancakes, cracking eggs, and calling out orders.

He'd barely slept last night, and the clinking silverware and sizzling bacon, normally comforting sounds, felt like an assault on his ears.

He and Rachel used to walk here for breakfast in their college days. They'd share an order of Eggs Benedict, plus waffles with whipped cream and strawberries. He'd been here dozens of times since then, and he'd always feel a rush of warmth thinking about sitting across from her as they'd exchange newspaper sections, and how she used to spread the whipped cream and butter around the waffles to make sure there was some in each square before they'd dive in.

Today, he winced thinking about it. He took a sip of coffee and then closed his eyes, willing the images away.

He felt a soft squeeze on his shoulder and looked up to see his mom standing next to him. She was wearing new red-framed glasses, and her lipstick was cakey. He stood to hug her, blinking back tears at the relief he felt from having his mom's arms around him. He'd given her the short version of what had happened between him and Beth last night on the phone, and was now second-guessing his choice of inviting her to such a busy breakfast place.

He swallowed hard and sat back down. His mom dug in her purse and handed him a tissue. "I'm so sorry, Honey," she said, sitting down and laying a hand on his forearm. "I wish there was something I could do to make this easier. Have you talked to Beth since you left last night?"

She set her purse down, fished out a hook that she attached to the bar, and hung her purse from it as the server came over and held out his pad.

"I'll take a coffee, please. Can you give us a few more minutes to order?"

"One coffee coming up," he said, nodding and tucking the pad in his back pocket. Before turning away, he pointed to the hook. "Nice."

"Thank you!" She smiled and turned toward Brad.

"Yes, I sent her a text this morning to check in. She is doing okay, considering. It really is for the best. I know I never talked much about it with you, but I'm sure you sensed we weren't in a good place." He tried gauging his mom's reaction, knowing he was going to tell her the rest—and wondering if she already suspected there was more. She'd always had a good poker face, though, and she was using it now.

The server put her coffee in front of her, and she cupped her hands around it. Her nails were a glossy mauve, and she stared down at her mug. "Well, I didn't want to assume. I haven't seen much of her this past year. I figured if you two were going through something, you'd either get through it together or ask my advice if you wanted it." She gave him a sympathetic look.

Brad took a slow sip of coffee and then smoothed a palm over his scruff. "I don't want you to think I threw our marriage away in one evening. Or that she did."

"I know, Honey. You know I wouldn't think that."

He nodded, but an ache bubbled up inside him. He'd been alone with this feeling of being trapped for so long. And then there was Rachel. The mere thought of talking about her made his chest hurt.

His mom said nothing—he knew she was giving him space to get his thoughts together.

"I saw Rachel." The words flew out quickly, and heat flared up his face.

After their first meeting, he would have thought nothing of telling his mother about it. She'd always loved Rachel. But as time passed, and she occupied more of his mind, he felt it was something he couldn't talk about with anyone. If he did, there was no way he would have been able to mask his feelings of longing. And regret.

She glanced down at her coffee cup again and paused for a few moments before speaking. "I always loved Rachel, you know that." She tapped her fingertips on the mug. "You broke her heart, leaving her in the dust for Beth." She pursed her lips, and Brad could tell she was handpicking her words. "It broke my heart too." She laughed and gently elbowed his arm.

He tried to muster a smile, but his face felt too heavy.

"Did you know she has two kids? And she's a wonderful painter. I keep up with her on The Facebook." She watched her son's face turn into what must have been a lovely shade of crimson and then smiled. "Of course you know." She placed an elbow on the counter and leaned closer. "Oh, Brad. You more than just ran into her, didn't you?"

Brad blinked hard. He didn't want to lie to his mother, but did she need to know *everything?* Shame and embarrassment brewed in his stomach.

"Beth and I really haven't been happy... and it's not called The Facebook, Mom. It's just Facebook."

Out of the corner of his eye, he saw an order of waffles and whipped cream being delivered to someone at the front of the restaurant, and he rubbed his eyes. *This is excruciating.*

"I always knew you'd regret your decision. I always knew it, but it was *your* decision, Son," she said, shaking her head. "Sometimes, Beth would walk in the room and ... well, I could smell her privilege. But you seemed happy. I told your father so many times, 'Rachel is the one for him. Beth is not. He's going to regret this.'"

Clearly, the handpicking-her-words-carefully moment had passed.

"Dad used to say you were caught up in the sex and the sassiness." She held a hand up in a "what are you gonna do" gesture and said, "I'm sure the family money didn't hurt things either."

She took in a breath as if catching herself rambling and put her hand on Brad's arm again. "I'm sorry. You don't need my input."

A laugh escaped him. "I think I kind of do need it, Mom. I don't know what to do, and I can't stop thinking about her. She's married. Not happily married, but definitely married. She doesn't want to break up her family."

"So you two have ... discussed things?" She propped her chin on her hand and raised her eyebrows.

"We have. My heart is hurting and I hate it. But seeing Rachel and having all those feelings come flooding back ... it pushed me to end things with Beth." He ran a frustrated hand through his hair. "The guilt is just ... unbearable. How do I get through this?"

Brad searched his mom's face for disappointment, but instead, her eyes were soft, understanding. "You just need time, Honey. Just time. What's meant to happen will happen.

I know that doesn't help a lot now, but soon ... soon this feeling will fade a bit and it will be bearable."

She slapped her hand on the menu. "For now, let's eat something and then maybe go for a walk?" She waved her hand to get the server's attention.

He'd known his mom would be able to put things into perspective; she always had. He took a deep breath and felt his shoulders relax a bit.

The server took their order, and his mom asked if he knew where they'd gotten the wreath above the menu board. It was made of different smiling turkey faces and was unapologetically tacky—exactly how his mom liked to decorate for the holidays.

He felt his phone buzz in his pocket. His mom was still deep in conversation about turkey-faced tchotchkes, so he took a moment to check it.

His heart sped up.

Maybe it's Rachel.

He sank into his seat when he saw it was a notification that his automatic cell phone payment had gone through.

His mom was right, time would heal him. But judging by the way he felt now, at the very least, it would take a decade for this angst and pain to fade.

Rachel

A stray droplet of water trickled down Rachel's back as she made her way downstairs, concentrating on each step she took. Her jaw was clenched so tight, her neck muscles were straining.

Adam did a double-take. "Um ... whoa. What's, um, going on?" He took a step back, bracing himself as if his body knew what was coming before his mind did. He set his mug down in a puddle of coffee on the counter.

Rachel closed her eyes and clenched her fists to keep from screaming.

He cleared his throat. "Um, hon? Look what we're going to do!" he said, spreading his arms to show her the flour, sugar canisters, and container of cookie cutters. "We're going to make cookies. You know, like you always love to do?"

Baking Christmas cookies as a family *had* been a tradition of Rachel's. She *had* loved it. She'd get everything ready the night before, lining up the ingredients on the counter along with recipes from handwritten cards she'd copied from books and magazines. Adam had taken part a few times when the kids were younger, but it had been years since he'd joined in.

He'd usually watch for a bit, then sit in front of the television and complain that Rachel started celebrating Christmas too early.

This charade he was putting on today was a product of his guilt.

Her eyes didn't leave him, and she began shivering.

Elsa paused in the middle of sorting the cookie cutters and let out an uncomfortable laugh. "Mom? Your hair is still totally soaked."

Benjamin was unwrapping the Hershey Kisses meant for the peanut butter blossoms. Since he was little, it had been his job to place them in the center of the cookies. He'd always sneak kisses whenever he thought no one was paying attention. He popped one in his mouth now, and the innocence of the gesture—the childlike trust in the purity and stability of his life made Rachel want to shove Adam off a cliff.

Another drop of water trickled down her back.

Not here. Not in front of the kids.

She dumped out Adam's cold coffee in the sink, slammed the mug into the dishwasher, then grabbed a sponge and scrubbed at the coffee spill.

"Mom?" Elsa's expression was now one of genuine concern. She was glancing back and forth between Rachel and Adam, as if trying to find answers in one of their faces.

She pictured her kids sitting on a therapist's stiff leather sofa, telling the story of the year their parents split up, how the Christmas cookies never got baked, and they sat staring at the ingredients while their parents fought about their dad fucking their aunt, and how that holiday season ruined all holidays forevermore.

"I'm ... sorry. I'm fine, Honey. Still just a little sore from my fall." Rachel pressed the sponge harder into the counter.

"Um, I think you got it, Rachel," Adam said, giving her a

wary look. "It was just a little coffee." He drummed his hands on the countertop. "Cookies!" he squealed out.

Rachel's eyes shot up. They were so wide, she felt the strain under her lids.

I know what you did.

Adam's smile quickly turned into a straight line, and he took a step back.

Elsa peeled the seal off the shaker of sprinkles, then clicked the lid back in place. Benjamin slowly unwrapped the kisses, placing them in a neat line.

Rachel squeezed out her hair over the sink, brought it over one shoulder, and stood up straight. "Should we make the peanut butter blossoms first?" She smiled cheerily at her kids, but then leveled a look at Adam that said, "Act like everything's fine. But get ready, motherfucker."

For the next hour, she went through the motions of smiling and enjoying her kids, but she felt like she was underwater.

While pressing red candies into her gingerbread man, Adam held up a cookie he'd decorated to show everyone. He'd used two red candies to create boobs instead of buttons, which Benjamin thought was hilarious, but only made Elsa roll her eyes. Adam said more than once how much fun he was having, as if his hyper-enthusiasm could press rewind on what he'd done. He knew she knew.

Rachel continued cutting out little men and arranging them on the cookie sheets, feeling like she was barely holding herself together at the seams. Finally, when the last cookie was decorated, she slid the trays together and snapped a picture, just as she did every year.

"Okay then," she said with a deep, shaky sigh. "We've made all our favorites, I think."

"Epic," Benjamin said, stuffing a chocolate crinkle in his mouth.

"Don't you want help cleaning up, Mom?" Elsa placed a final cookie on one of the sheets.

"Yeah, don't you want help?" Benjamin asked, powdered sugar and crumbs spraying from his mouth.

"Dad will help." Rachel threw Adam a hard look that said he'd better not go anywhere. "You kids go ahead upstairs. Think about what kind of pizza you want for dinner, and we'll order out tonight."

Once the kids were all the way upstairs, Adam whispered, "Uh ... you okay? What's going on?"

Except, she was pretty sure by the worried look on his face that he knew precisely what was going on. She stood silently, arms at her sides, waiting for him to stop with the ridiculous farce.

"I went to get the kids while you were on a run because I wanted to plan a special day. I know how much you love decorating for—"

"How many times have you fucked my sister?" Her tone was casual, as if she was asking how many houses he'd sold last month.

Adam's head dropped, and the color drained from his face. His eyes darted from the floor up to her, and he swallowed hard. His body went limp as he backed into the kitchen island.

When he started crying, Rachel resisted the urge to shake his shoulders.

"It just happened, Rachel. Neither of us meant for it to happen. It just did." He gestured with his pointer finger back and forth between the two of them, shaking his head. "We weren't having sex. The kids were small, and you didn't have any time for me." He was whispering through sobs, his face ugly and red with self-pity and shame.

"No." Rachel took a step closer to him, her voice quiet but blazing. "You will *not* blame this on me."

Adam's eyes were wide. He leaned away from her. "Rachel, calm down. The kids will hea—"

"I'm whispering, you idiot! Maybe you should have thought about the consequences before you screwed their aunt."

She curled her fingers into fists and turned in a circle before facing him again. "You know, all I needed was some time to feel like myself again. I'd just given birth, and I was breastfeeding and touched out and my body didn't even feel like it was mine. So I needed time. And I told you, so many damn times, but you couldn't give that to me. Instead, all you thought about was"—she pointed to his crotch—"that *thing.*" She went on, feeling the veins pop out of her neck. "Instead, you fucked my sister." She blinked hard, trying to stop the burning in her eyes. "My fucking *sister.*"

Adam reached for her. She grabbed his arms and shoved him away.

"You're unbelievable. I stayed after you harassed me to have sex with you over and over. I *told you* I wasn't myself. And every time you hounded me, I felt like a horrible wife." She slapped her hand on the island. "I even stayed after you cheated, because the thought of breaking up my family killed me. Meanwhile, you were fucking *my sister* instead of coming home and giving me the help I asked for."

She'd said it out loud several times, and she'd seen the evidence, but she still couldn't wrap her head around it. *Her own sister.*

Adam's shoulders hunched, and he cradled his head in his hands. "She swore she wouldn't tell you. We both knew it was a mistake, and it would hurt you too much."

Rachel crossed her arms over her chest, staring at her husband. He was lying to her. Adam had zero respect for her, for their life together. He couldn't even tell her the entire truth. She squeezed her eyes shut, blind with rage. "So it happened one time, and that was it?"

Adam wiped away the snot with the back of his hand. "Come on, Rachel. What was I supposed to do? Did you expect me to go the rest of my life without having sex?" His whispers were getting louder.

She covered her eyes with her hand in frustration. "I *expected* you to help me. To be my partner. You neglected me too and still do. You don't see me. You don't appreciate me. You make fun of my painting and expect me to open my legs for you every night after cooking, cleaning, and running the kids around with no help." She closed her mouth and pressed her lips together. This was pointless. They'd had this talk so many times. "Answer my question, Adam. It just happened once?"

"I swear. That time you heard." He took a long breath. "Never again," he whispered.

They locked eyes. "Interesting. The lipstick all over your boxers tells a different story."

"Rachel, no," he whispered. "I didn't ... we weren't—"

The smell of gingerbread still hung in the air. Outside, the snow picked up, the wind releasing a mournful howl as it blew over their chimney.

Adam pushed away from the island toward her. She got a whiff of stale sweat, and she held out a hand to stop him.

His jaw clenched.

Snowflakes drifted to the ground, covering the green grass that had been there only yesterday.

"You're lying to me. And I've been lying to you. And I want a divorce."

Rachel

The wild white caps of the river mimicked how Rachel felt. The last time she'd asked Emily to meet her at River Coffee Club was the day after she'd heard her husband fucking another woman.

Fucking Emily, to be exact.

She'd wondered if her sister would get the irony. Probably not.

Emily had always been too busy analyzing and judging Rachel to turn any of her criticism onto herself.

As Rachel's steps hit the salted sidewalk, making her knees ache, all she could hear was Emily's snotty voice: *Go back to being the perfect wife; perfect mom. Must be nice to have a handsome husband pay the bills so you can sit home and paint. Have you talked to Brad? Tell me everything.*

Emily had known all along exactly what she was doing.

And now Rachel knew, too.

They must have talked before you told her. Adam must have reassured her you didn't know it was her, and told her to act stoic. They probably laughed about it before she'd sucked his needy cock.

Rachel tugged off her oversized sunglasses as she came through the door. Emily sat at a round wooden table next to a window as far away from the display case filled with bagels and tubs of cream cheese as possible. She was wearing a fitted black leather jacket, and that wretched lipstick. Her hair was parted down the middle and slicked into a tight bun at the nape of her neck. She was typing something on her phone and didn't notice Rachel walking toward her.

"You look just like Mother with your hair like that," Rachel said, flashing a tight smile at her sister, whose jaw literally dropped.

Emily's hands went to her head. "Do I really look like Mother?" She immediately undid her bun.

Rachel slid into her seat and felt a smidge of guilt as Emily's face flushed while she restyled her hair, trying to *not* look like Mother.

Emily raised her eyebrows at her sister. "Everything okay?" She looked genuinely confused. Adam hadn't told her, then.

Was she fine? She still wasn't sure. "I will be."

"Maybe you just need to eat something. I have a mad craving for that bacon-scallion cream cheese you brought to Easter a few years ago." Emily said, her eyes growing wary. "But I guess I shouldn't. You know what happens—I can't stop at one and then I have to eat five. Gotta take everything to the extreme."

Rachel tapped the salt shaker up and down. "I know," she said, crossing her legs. "I know, Emily."

Emily laughed nervously. "I know, I just ... lose control." She reached across the table and gave Rachel a playful pat on the hand. "You're supposed to say something encouraging. Like, tell me to get a smoothie bowl instead!"

Rachel narrowed her eyes, and Emily's smile turned to a straight line.

"I know, Emily."

The false confidence drained from Emily's face, and she shifted in her seat.

Rachel dropped her hand on the table, and Emily flinched. "Good job, Emily," she said, as if she was talking to a toddler.

Emily leaned toward her sister. "Rachel, I—"

"Don't say anything." She held a hand up in front of her sister's face. "Don't explain. Don't cover up or make excuses. He already did that for the both of you." She slid her sunglasses back on her face. "And I don't feel the need to keep you in my life."

Emily looked like someone had slapped her.

Rachel circled a finger in the air. "It's been hard enough to maintain a relationship with you two when I *didn't* know what was really going on."

"Oh my God, Rachel, I just ... he was lonely. You weren't having sex. It meant nothing to him—"

"I *just* fucking told you not to do that. Fuck your excuses." Rachel gripped the table, bringing herself as close to her sister as possible. "Fuck you, Emily," she hissed. "You were right. I should have left him when I heard him fucking you behind that door years ago. I was scared to be on my own, foolishly believing it was better to stay for my kids. I feel pathetic about that. I *was* pathetic. Not anymore."

Emily's eyes were huge, her chest rising and falling with panicked breaths.

"You deserve him, Emily." She stretched her arms toward her sister, palms facing up. "I'm happy to hand you my left-overs. I never want to hear from you again, and you're *never* allowed near my kids. Not that you ever put in much of an effort."

Emily sat like a statue and tried to control her breathing.

"You know, it actually feels good to be done with you. For so long, I thought it was *me*. I blamed myself for not doing enough for you when we were kids. But now I know. Now I know, it's *you*."

Rachel stood up, pulled her coat closed and tied it around her waist. She leaned over Emily, who was still staring straight ahead. "Can I get you a bagel with some bacon scallion cream cheese to wash this all down? Maybe five of them and you can have a nice binge session in your car? You've already proven you have zero willpower, feasting on your own sister's husband. Disgusting."

All the hurt, all the anger, slammed into Rachel. She tightened her belt again and stood up straighter, trying to keep her bulging tears from falling. "You've never wanted a relationship with me. I've tried and tried with you."

"Rachel please ... don't shut me out. I'm so sorry. The way Moth—"

"Don't!" Rachel spat. "You don't get to use Mother as an excuse any longer."

Something changed in Emily's face. Her expression transformed from slack-faced shame to cold, sharp fury. She leaned forward in her seat and stared straight into Rachel's eyes. "I *wanted* you to know. I left you bread crumbs so many times. On his neck, his collar. He was always too eager to get inside me to notice." An obnoxious giggle erupted out of her. "But you! You're his *wife*, and you didn't see it. You weren't even looking at him. No wonder he wanted to fuck me."

Rachel bit the inside of her cheek.

"This time around was hotter than the last. And you're fucking Brad Turner now, aren't you? That's the real reason you're leaving your husband, and you know it." Emily smiled, but her fists were clenched on top of the table. "You are just like me, Rachel. And he's just going to leave you again for someone more exciting." Her eyes narrowed cruelly. "Just like they all do."

Emily's words opened a wound, a deep one. She inhaled a sharp breath, feeling like she'd just been socked in the gut.

The door opened, and the sound of jingle bells startled Rachel out of the surreal conversation with her sister. Twins, no older than three, ran ahead of their obviously exhausted mother, pawing at the clean glass of the display case.,

Turning back to Emily, she gazed at her shitty excuse for a sister for a moment. *Enough.*

She walked backward a few steps before turning around to leave without saying another word.

Brad

Beth was seated when Brad entered Little Tokyo. There was only one other couple in the small, dark restaurant, and the smell of soy and ginger made his mouth salivate.

He hadn't seen her in a few weeks, and they'd agreed to meet for sushi to go over a few things. Their divorce would be quick—he didn't want any of her inheritance, and they'd agreed to sell the house and split the profit. They leased both of their cars. Brad only wanted a few pieces of furniture, and Beth didn't argue.

His heart sped up as he approached the table. He was nervous. Beth was smiling and chatting with the server as he set a large drink in front of her. He hadn't seen her look this happy, or this beautiful, in a long time.

"What are you drinking?" Brad chuckled, staring at what looked like coffee in a wine glass with marbles on the bottom.

"It's Boba tea. Try it. Julie got me hooked on it."

Beth's eyes shined, and she smiled at him. He had a moment of hesitation, wondering if he'd done the right thing before saying, "I'm all set. Those things at the bottom look like ... eyeballs."

"How are you? Can't believe it took us divorcing to get you to take me out for sushi." Beth took a drink out of the widest straw he'd ever seen, and he almost gagged when one eyeball floated up for Beth to chomp on. *Nope, you made the right decision,*

"I'm good, thank you. I looked at a house today. It's closer to school, has a tiny yard. It should work great."

Beth smiled.

"How about yourself?"

"Things are good." There was a light in Beth that had been missing. He was happy for her, but his heart sank again, thinking of Rachel. "I'm good. Working for Dad, going to check out a condo downtown later today."

"That's great, Beth." Brad tapped the menu on the table. "So, it looks like everything will be wrapped up in a few months. You'll be a free woman."

"Yeah. I'm surprised at how positive I feel. I was so scared of what everyone would think, how my family would react." She stirred the eyeballs around in her glass. "Everyone has been so supportive and I don't feel judged at all. I made you do the hard part. And I'm sorry."

Beth stopped stirring her drink, and their eyes locked. She was effervescent.

"Beth, it's okay. It's all okay. We both—"

"And about the shoplifting; the overspending"—her neck turned a shade of scarlet—"I'm ... I'm getting help for that. You were worried and just trying to help, and I pushed you away."

Brad took her hand from across the table. "I feel good knowing you're in a good place. You look happy, Beth. Happier than I've seen you in a long time."

"I am happy." She nodded her head. "And you?"

He hesitated for a beat. "I'm doing okay. Things are going to be okay."

Beth's eyebrows knit together, but she was kind enough to act like she didn't notice he was struggling.

Brad

Brad and Beth's big house sold, and his offer was accepted on the little white cottage with the postage stamp yard. A white picket fence surrounded it. He had plans to go back to the shelter in a couple of weeks to get himself a dog, just in time for the closing. They'd find the perfect place to hang Rachel's painting and explore the nearby river in his canoe.

It'd been a few weeks since Brad had seen Rachel, and the finality of their last conversation, when she told him she had to stay in her marriage, still made his stomach stir with anxiety. She'd become his best friend again, and it was hard not having any contact. He wanted to share every detail that was going on in his new life, and check in on her and see how she was doing.

During his lunch break, he sat at his desk eating a leftover salad from last night with his mom's blue cheese dressing. He opened his phone and tapped on Rachel's name. *No, she's moving on with her family, and you told her you'd leave her alone.*

He stared at the last text she'd sent him: *Can we talk on the phone tonight? My house will be empty.*

He let out a long sigh just as a new text appeared.

Rachel.

Hey, I know it's short notice, but can you meet tonight?

He couldn't wait to see her. They'd agreed to meet tonight at the restaurant in the hotel where he was staying.

After work, he strolled along the sidewalks in downtown Freeport to kill some time. Men in hard hats stood on ladders and were spiraling garlands and lights up every street lamp. A huge Christmas tree stood proudly, looking over the village.

Brad looked down at his watch and headed back to the restaurant a bit early, hoping to get a seat by the fireplace.

You should have made a reservation.

He stomped his feet and brushed snowflakes from his head when he entered the Tavern. It was crowded, and a woman passed by balancing a tray that was loaded with crocks of lobster mac and cheese and oversized baked pretzels. "Someone'll be right with you," she said and kept walking.

Every table in the cozy place was full, with just a few open seats at the bar, where bartenders rushed back and forth behind the polish wood bar, mixing and pouring drinks.

A harried-looking hostess arrived behind the wooden podium in the waiting area, which was also packed, and Brad asked how long it would be for a table for two.

"At least a half hour," she said without looking up, and grabbed a pencil to write his name. "You can wait at the bar," she added before directing her attention to the next person waiting.

He thought about waiting for Rachel, but the waiting area was full with several waiting families and one rowdy group that, judging by the smell, seemed to have just finished some kind of sweaty game. Rugby? He looked over his shoulder to make sure Rachel wasn't on her way in before heading to the bar.

The bar was made of large raw-edge planks, and little white tea lights had been placed every few feet for a cozy, glowy effect. The smell of homemade bread and garlic filled the room —it was buzzing with conversation and laughter. He checked the door for Rachel as he sat at the bar, watching three chefs turn pizzas in the brick oven as the flames warmed his face.

Concentrating on the fire didn't calm his nerves in the least. As soon as the bartender placed a napkin in front of him, he ordered a Johnny Walker Blue with ice water—something he hadn't had since the day he gave Beth's dad his notice. He lifted his glass to take a sip and checked his watch again.

From behind him, a woman's voice slurred. "Waiting for anyone special?"

He ignored it. It wasn't Rachel, so whoever it was couldn't be talking to him.

Brad scanned the menu, thinking the chicken parmesan looked good. A bartender parked himself in front of Brad and cleared his throat once, then again. Brad glanced up to see him raising his eyebrows, looking pointedly past Brad. He tipped his head back a bit and raised his eyebrows as he wiped out a glass.

Before Brad could turn around, Emily plopped down in the seat next to him.

Rachel

Rachel hung up the phone and began jumping up and down. The owner of the Bayview Gallery in Brunswick, Jeremy, just offered her a part-time staff position and the opportunity for future features. The first opening to have a showing wouldn't be for about six months, but it would give her plenty of time to get some special pieces done.

Once she'd gotten all the jumping and squealing out of her system, she called Aimee.

"See? You're already doing better than you could have imagined!" Aimee said, matching Rachel squeal for squeal. "I'll definitely be coming to the show, so free up the entire weekend!"

They caught up for a few minutes, Aimee reminding Rachel of her strength and capability and Rachel trying hard to let her friend's words sink in, and then Rachel heard Adam's car pull in the driveway.

She'd insisted things stay normal for the kids until Adam found a place where the kids could go stay and be comfortable. But having Adam come home every day after work and then leave after they went to bed wouldn't work much longer.

Rachel had been pushing him to decide and put down a deposit somewhere.

When he came through the side door, he set his keys and phone on the table by the coat closet and ignored Cora, who was nuzzling her head into his leg. He peeled off his coat and looked Rachel up and down. "Why are you all dressed up?"

She folded her hands together and took a deep breath. "I told you, I'm going out tonight so you can have some alone time with the kids." She spoke in a low voice even though the kids were downstairs in the basement having a Mario Brothers tournament and probably wouldn't hear even if she yelled.

Adam put his hands on his hips and titled his head back. He reminded her of Benjamin when he was eight and had been told he couldn't have dessert because he hadn't eaten dinner.

He took a long step toward her. "Are you really serious about this? We can work this out. I'm willing to—" His face was red under his days-old-scruff.

"Yes, I'm serious." She put her phone in her pocket and crossed her arms. "I'm not changing my mind. It's been weeks. It's time to start the process, Adam. We need to put the kids first. Let's focus on making this a smooth transition for them and being a united front."

"You aren't even working," Adam sneered, shaking his head. "You can't afford this place on your own."

You have no idea what I'm capable of, Adam. Thank you, Aimee. A huge smile crossed her face, and she reached for a dish towel and began wiping down the counters. Since she'd discovered Adam's affair with her sister, she'd rented a pop-up spot next to the indoor Farmers' market, and she had commissions booked out months in advance.

"Rachel, come on." He reached for her, but she yanked away and gave him a look that told him to keep his distance. "Shit. Okay, I know. I know I've been a shitty husband.

Please." His face had gone pale, and his eyes searched her face as if looking for a sign that she could be persuaded.

Rachel wiped the last section of the counter. "Listen, I'm dressed up because I'm going to see Brad." The words flew from her mouth without thought.

Adam flinched as if she'd kneed him in the gut.

"I'll be at Broad Arrow Tavern for a few hours. There's an enchilada casserole and fresh guac in the fridge."

"Brad? Brad Turner, the guy … the ex you did the painting for?"

She nodded her head. "I picked up those corn chips you like, too. Just preheat the oven and put the casserole in for about a half hour."

"What, does he want another painting?"

She wasn't due to meet Brad for over an hour, but she couldn't stay here for one more minute. Tonight needed to be about Adam spending some quality time with his kids, and she could see that if she stuck around, Adam would do all he could to lure her into a pointless argument. She pulled her jacket from the hall closet and shrugged into it, then checked her face in the hallway mirror.

Adam treaded up behind her, looking at her reflection in the mirror. "Isn't it a little soon for you to be seeing someone? What are you going to tell the kids?"

"I'll tell them what I think is best, when the time is right. I'm just going to talk to him for a bit. It's not a big deal." She grabbed her phone from her pocket and slid it into her purse.

His eyes narrowed. "What about all this guilt you say you feel when you leave the kids? You don't seem to be feeling any of that right now."

Aimee's voice echoed in her head. *You're allowed to have a life outside of your kids. It doesn't make you any less of a mom. It makes you a fuller person.*

"I'm not leaving *them,* Adam. I'm leaving you."

Ignoring the look of shocked hurt on his face, she slid on her boots. "I'll be home later, and they know I won't be here for dinner."

Reaching for the doorknob, she yelled goodbye to the kids.

"Have fun, Mom! Love you!" Elsa shouted up the stairs.

"Bye Mom!" Benjamin chimed in.

She paused with her hand on the doorknob and turned to look at her husband. "I really hope you can enjoy your time tonight with your kids. They need their father."

Adam shoved his hands in his pockets and stared down at his feet. "You're right. This sucks. I hate how I feel, but you're right."

Just as she was about to step outside, Adam asked, "Do you love him?" Rachel bent down to give Cora a goodbye pat and closed the door without answering.

Rachel took off her jacket as she approached Broad Arrow Tavern, smiling at her reflection in the window glass. She'd spent the last forty-five minutes browsing the art supply store, and that had calmed her a little, but her legs wobbled a bit as she got closer to seeing Brad. Familiar flips took over her stomach as she imagined smelling the woodsy, herbal scent of his neck.

There were going to be really tough times ahead, but right now, she was so excited about her new job, and she couldn't wait to share the news with Brad. It had been so hard not to reach out to him sooner and tell him everything.

She lifted her hand to cool one of her warm cheeks, and the smell of fresh bread hit her as she opened the door to the restaurant.

"How many?" the hostess asked right away, reaching for a

stack of menus. The place was packed, and the young hostess looked like she had no time for indecisive clientele.

"I'm meeting someone," Rachel said, scanning the tables for Brad. She didn't see him. "I'm not sure if he's here yet or—"

Rachel grabbed the hostess stand to steady herself. She blinked hard, making sure that the image in front of her wasn't just her nerves creating a nightmare hallucination. No —that was really Brad Turner, the love of her life, sitting at the bar with her husband-fucking sister, Emily.

Brad

B rad pushed against the back of his chair at the sight of Emily. He threw a glance at the door to check for Rachel and then let out a nervous laugh.

"Um ... why are you here?" He looked behind her to see if maybe she'd come with Rachel, but that wouldn't make any sense. Rachel was on her way to meet *him*.

Emily released a shrill laugh, making him think of an evil stepmom character from many a Disney movie, and he caught a whiff of wine on her breath. Her teeth were tinted blue, and she seemed to have trouble focusing on his face.

"I heard you might meet someone here. I got a text from Adam asking me if I knew what this was all about." She dug in her purse. "I'll show you." She pressed her phone to her breasts before saying, "Quite the little home wrecker, aren't you?"

Brad narrowed his eyes at her. *What a mess.* She was obviously drunk, and he racked his brain to think of something to say to diffuse the situation.

"And what will you and my sister be discussing?" Emily poked him in the chest, hard. "How *you* fucked her brains out and ruined her marriage?" Emily pointed to herself and smiled. "Or how *I* fucked her husband's brains out and ruined *their* marriage?"

Wait. What? The blood seemed to rush out of Brad's body all at once. Rachel's *sister* had been sleeping with her husband? Fuck. She must be devastated. But … did that mean …? He knew his mouth was hanging open.

Emily grabbed Brad's drink and took a clumsy sip, then did a double take on his face. "Oh, God. You didn't know?" She let out a drunken smirk, this time with a hiccup. "Yup, I've been I've been fucking him off and on for … ever. And would you believe, after being at his beck and call all these years, now that the shit has finally hit the fan, he doesn't want me? I fuck better than my sister. He's said it so many times, but he still doesn't want me. He still wants her." Her smile dropped.

"Okay, Emily. I'm getting you an Uber."

"*This time* I made *sure* my sister knew. It wasn't fair for her to have her first love pining for her, too. She always gets *everything.*" Emily stuck out her lower lip.

Had Rachel really told her sister they'd had sex?

"So, you know you can fuck her now and it'll be great, but she'll tire of you. The magic bone-fest you have the first few years will fade, and you'll need someone like me to help you out, Brad. Just like Adam did. I'm into anal. Oh, and three-somes. My sister isn't … as I'm sure you know." She snorted before waving a hand at the bartender. The woman sitting next to her twisted in her seat and threw Emily a look of disgust.

Brad frantically checked the door for Rachel, and a cool bead of sweat ran down the back of his spine.

The woman and her companion eased out of their seats with their drinks and wandered off, obviously wanting to get out of Emily's line of fire.

"Your Uber is on the way. It's a white Honda Accord."

"No," she said, wobbling as she threw her purse and sweater on the bar, not noticing when her things slid onto the floor. "I'm staying right here. I want to see my sister." The red wine on her breath made him gag.

"Listen, I got you an Uber. Rachel will be here in a minute, and you are leaving, Emily."

"Oh, I *know* you two have lots to discuss." She wiggled her eyebrows at him and scooted to the edge of her seat.

The bar was crowded, and all the talking and laughing, on top of Emily's surprise drunken appearance, were sending shooting pains between Brad's eyes. He took in a deep breath and released it with a long, frustrated sigh.

Emily shifted even closer, crashing into him. Her arms flew around his neck and she covered her mouth with his. He vaguely registered that one of her pointy shoes had connected with his shin—that was going to hurt tomorrow. He shoved her off of him, grabbing her by the upper arms and planting her firmly back in her seat. "Emily, stop it." The tips of his ears burned, and he wiped off his mouth. Her breath was foul.

Emily looked over her shoulder and then back at Brad, flashing a wicked smile before grabbing her coat and stumbling out of the bar.

Relief washed over him. *Finally.*

He pushed himself up to follow her and ensure she got into the Uber, and then turned to see Rachel walking toward him, clutching her coat in her arms.

His heart felt like it would explode at the sight of her. All he wanted to do was drive somewhere far away, get them both out of this mess. Picking up the torment on her face, he realized she'd witnessed the scene with Emily.

He held out his arms, praying she'd read the scene correctly and not thought the worst. He wouldn't blame her if she panicked, if everything Emily had said about Adam's years of infidelity was true. She fell into his arms. "Brad, what the hell was she doing here?"

His chest tightened—he hated to be the bearer of bad news.

"I'm ... not totally sure." He rubbed Rachel's arms from shoulder to elbow, not able to let go of her, not wanting her to leave his side. "I don't think your sister is doing so great." He pulled out a twenty and set it under his glass, pushing both to the back edge of the bar. "I'll go out and make sure she's not driving. You stay here."

Rachel threw her coat on. "No, she's my sister. I can't believe she tried to pull you into her bullshit."

Oh, it's not the first time.

They made it to the parking lot just in time to see Emily get into the backseat of a white Honda with an Uber sticker on the rear window.

"Okay, good. That's the Uber I got for her." He reached up to rub Rachel's back. "She's not driving, at least."

"I don't want to talk about Emily for another second," Rachel said, staring after the Uber's taillights as they disappeared down the street. "These past few weeks have been ... horrible." She shook her head and pressed a finger to her lips, as if trying to hold in a sob.

Seeing Rachel upset made his chest tighten. He rubbed her back, feeling her rigid spine under his fingertips, and then pulled her to him, wrapping her in his arms. "I know. I'm here. It's okay."

Flurries floated in the air around them as Brad's neck grew wet with Rachel's tears. A couple approached on the sidewalk, pausing their conversation as they strode by.

After a few minutes, Rachel took in a breath of air and lifted her head from Brad's neck. "I got a job. And I'm doing an art show." Her voice was quiet through her sniffles.

"That's great, Rach. I'm so proud of you." He used his coat sleeve to wipe a few of her tears.

"I left Adam." She gripped his arms tighter. "He's been sleeping with Emily. And I think I should have been heartbroken, but all I could think about was you." A hand covered her mouth. "Brad. Wait. Is that why she was here? Did Adam tell her we were meeting here?"

"That's pretty much what she said, but she was so drunk, Rachel. And I didn't want to upset you ... I don't know the entire story."

"Why would Adam tell her? And now she's running all over town blabbing my business. I haven't even told my kids." She dropped her hand from her mouth. "My kids."

A sinking feeling swept over Brad. The sidewalk seemed to sway beneath him. His body knew what was about to happen even before he heard it. This evening that he'd been so excited to spend with Rachel—it was already over. He wrapped his arms tighter around her. *Just a few more seconds.*

"I ... I need ..." she could barely talk through her sobs, and Brad let out a long sigh and brushed a hand over her hair. She smelled so good.

She pressed her face further into his neck. "What if she's going to my house next? What if she tells them before I get a chance?"

Brad closed his eyes, knowing she was right. She had to go take care of things tonight, and they'd set up another time to talk.

"I can't drag you into this mess." She pushed away from him, her palms on his chest. "I can't do this on the edges, fit you in whenever I have the time and the emotional capacity. It wouldn't be fair to either of us or to my kids."

His whole body went limp, and he took a tiny step back to give her space, even though it sliced his heart open to do it. "I *really, really* want to argue with you." He wanted her to change her mind; he wanted to reassure her that if he could be with her, nothing would be too much.

But he had to let her go. He knew Rachel, and he knew that giving her space to sort things out was the only way he would have any chance of getting her back later.

"There's a part of me that wants you to talk me out of it, too. But please." She closed her eyes. "Don't. It will only make this harder for me than it already is."

"Go home and check on your kids. I know you can get through this. Remember, I'll always be here." The sinking feeling came again, the one he always felt when he said goodbye to her. Only this time, it was worse than ever.

Rachel nodded as she looked at her feet, then backed up at him.

"Maybe we can go get a Diet Coke sometime," he said, forcing a smile.

"Yes," she whispered, before giving him a kiss on the cheek and turning to leave, a sob shaking her back as she walked away.

Nothing had ever felt so wrong as letting Rachel go that night.

But he did it.

For her.

Rachel

ONE YEAR LATER

Rachel unlocked the door to her studio and smiled as the autumn sun streaming through the windows hit her in the face. The instant warmth felt glorious. The heat she built up during her runs always tricked her into dressing lighter than she should. Her well-worn thermal shirt, paint-splattered overalls, and beanie wouldn't cut it today.

Golden leaves had fallen during the windstorm overnight, leaving the trees bare against a brilliant blue sky and stacking banks of crisp leaves up and down the street curbs.

The hues inspired her to paint an abstract of the ocean of leaves on the street.

She opened her Notes app on her phone and jotted down the idea before she could forget it—she'd have to find time to work on it in between her custom orders. She was still getting requests from people asking if she could make an exception and squeeze their order in before Christmas, even though she'd announced weeks in advance, the cutoff date would be October 15th.

Last year's art show had been a tremendous success and the distraction she'd needed from the chaos of her life. After six months of working at the art gallery, painting on the side, and trying to keep things as normal as possible for Benjamin and Elsa as they settled into their new routines, she'd decided it was time to invest in herself. She left the gallery and rented a small, bright studio.

The kids spent a lot of time there with her. It was within walking distance of school, and Elsa enjoyed doing her homework at the white oak desk Rachel had found at the antique shop across the street. She'd told Rachel many times that being surrounded by her paintings made her feel calm, and Benjamin had surprised her by taking up an interest in art.

Aimee stayed with her for a week, helping her scout out the perfect place to set up her dream studio.

A month later, an Instagram influencer with three million followers purchased three small paintings and posted a picture, tagging Rachel's page.

Rachel had only started to get into a rhythm with her days, and that tagged post blew up her business. Custom orders had flooded her inbox, and she'd had to figure out a way to turn what Adam had called "her little hobby" into a bona fide business, fast.

She'd hired someone to set up a website with an order page and an automated system for tracking orders, payments, and deliveries, and painted every spare moment she could.

Her career dreams were coming true at the same time her heart was breaking.

She missed seeing her kids every day, and her thoughts about Brad hadn't abated. If anything, they'd only grown more intense.

Brad had respected her wishes. She hadn't heard from him except on her birthday when he'd sent her the biggest bouquet of hydrangeas she'd ever seen, and a case of Diet Coke. The card read: *No pincher bugs! Hope you're doing great, Picasso.*

Every time she thought about reaching out to him, she

couldn't muster up the nerve. Elsa and Benjamin had gone through so many changes already. Adam had started dating someone, and the kids talked about how strange it was. Rachel wanted to be her kids' rock. And that meant keeping things as normal as she could.

"Why won't you call him? Or text at least?" Aimee asked a few days after closing on the studio. The two of them had repainted the walls a creamy white, and after a few glasses of wine, Rachel had confessed how losing Brad had been even harder the second time.

"Because ... I need to focus on the kids. My business. That's all I have the strength for right now."

"It's not like you have to get married, Rach. You can date. See where it goes."

"I don't want to *date* him or see where it goes. I love him and want to give him everything. And I can't. I don't want to find out what will happen when he realizes I'm not the same woman I was a year ago. Things are so much more ... complicated now."

"As long as you aren't punishing yourself for sleeping with him while you were married. If that's the real reason you won't contact him, you need to let that shit go." Aimee's words hit Rachel hard that day, and she'd asked herself every day since if that was the real reason she hadn't reached out to him.

Rachel had demanded that she and Adam tell the kids as soon as she'd gotten home the night she'd caught Emily throwing herself at Brad in a drunken stooper.

Thankfully, Emily never showed up, but it had been the worst night of her life. She could still feel the tightness in her throat every time she remembered how Benjamin's face had gone bright red before he ran out of the room. She'd found him in the upstairs bathroom, leaning over the sink and crying.

Her tears had mixed with his as Adam and Elsa had joined

them. The four of them had stood hugging and crying in the bathroom, and she'd told them, over and over, that everything would be okay, that they'd keep things as normal as possible.

She was determined to stick to her promise.

She'd confronted Adam, telling him Emily had showed up after he'd told her where she was going. He'd promised he'd cut all ties with her. To Rachel's knowledge, he had.

There was a new bond between Rachel and her kids, and she loved the nights they'd fall asleep with her on the sofa, Seinfeld reruns in the background.

She and Adam had their moments since divorcing, but mostly, they did a pretty good job of keeping things civil for the kids. He still worked a ton, but Elsa and Benjamin had fun with their dad, and she could tell Adam was attempting to put any negative feelings aside when they were around.

Being sprawled out in bed alone hadn't been as great as she'd thought. The nights were excruciatingly lonely, and she'd long for Brad. Sometimes wrapping the sheets around herself extra tight helped.

She ate a lot of dinners alone now that the kids split their time between two homes, and Elsa had her license. Both kids had a pretty active social life and Benjamin had been caught skipping classes a few times, and Elsa's grades had slipped.

They were adjusting to their new life, and Rachel's eyes were glued to them. Despite the slip ups, they had grown up a lot this year.

Sometimes those solo nights felt nourishing, and others she couldn't get the heavy bubble to move out of her chest without a good cry.

According to Rachel's mom, Emily had moved to Vermont. "She just picked up and left. No notice, no plan, no nothing. What has gotten into her?"

Even then, Rachel didn't say a word about what really

happened between her and her sister. She couldn't trust her mother not to say anything around her kids, even though they didn't see her much. She partially blamed her for Emily's behavior—if she hadn't been such an abusive asshole, Emily never would have turned out like she did. Besides, talking about it never made her feel any better–she wanted to move as far away from the situation as she could, and it appeared Emily did too.

It was Saturday morning, and since Elsa and Benjamin would be with their dad for the weekend, she'd blocked off today to do a little decorating in her studio before she painted —she had visions of filling the pumpkins and gourds she'd bought at the farmers' market with dried hydrangeas.

The thought of spending a little time to regroup and deco- rate made her stomach flutter. She hadn't allowed herself many spontaneous moments like this since her business had picked up and she'd become a single mom.

She savored the feeling, knowing it was fleeting. She'd learned that's what divorce does to you. Heavy moments of regret and "what-ifs" had a way of dominating your thoughts —you took your bright moments wherever you could get them.

Lake Street Dive was playing softly in the background, and Rachel made herself mentally catalog all the upcoming events she was looking forward to.

There's *baking to do, I've booked a weekend at the indoor water park for me and the kids during Christmas break. Aimee is coming the weekend after Thanksgiving to go Christmas shopping...*

Her train of thought was broken when movement out the window caught her eye, and she looked up to see Brad crossing the street toward her studio. Her entire body went tingly, and her knees almost buckled underneath her.

Her phone buzzed. *Don't be mad. He wanted to see you. I*

gave him the studio address because he didn't want to show up at your house. Hear him out? Love you.

Her eyes went from Aimee's text back to Brad.

Dropping her phone, she ran out the door.

And then she was in his arms, her face buried in his neck, with no recollection of how she got there.

"Rachel." His hand stroked the back of her head. "I'm sorry. I had to see you. It's been a year, and I was dying trying to—"

"Brad," she whispered. He felt like home—he *was* home. He always had been, always would be. "I'm so glad you're here."

He clutched her tighter. "It's been the longest year of my life."

"Me too," she said, her lips against his neck, inhaling his intoxicating, woody scent. "I'm ready. Sorry it took me so long, but I'm ready."

His warm sigh of relief hit her neck and sent a wave of goosebumps all over her body. He pulled back so he could look into her eyes. "I'm so happy right now. We'll figure it out as we go. Yeah? Your kids, our careers, families. We'll figure it all out."

"We sure take the long way home, don't we?"

"You were worth every second I had to wait." He slid his hands into her overalls and squeezed her ass. "Now, let's go make up for the last twenty years."

Rachel couldn't find the words to tell him how absolutely sure she was that this was their time, that nothing could stand in their way anymore, that she'd felt her heart fuse back together the moment he put his arms around her.

So she took his hand and led him into her studio to show him.

Epilogue

ANOTHER YEAR LATER

"What the hell is a Toasty?" Aimee asked in the car on the way to Derosier's, a quirky restaurant in the middle of Freeport.

"Only the best sub you'll ever taste," Benjamin said from the third row of Rachel's new Tahoe, his voice cracking with the onset of puberty. "You choose your meat, then they top it with sandwich pepperoni, oregano, and provolone. Then, they put it in the oven to toast it. It's bussin."

Rachel had needed a bigger car to shlep her artwork back and forth. It was great when they wanted to take Marlin, the dog Brad had adopted, and Cora places, but it also came in handy for weekends like these, when Aimee and Matt were visiting.

"What's a bussin?" Aimee whispered to Rachel, leaning from the middle row to the passenger seat.

"It means it's really freaking good," Benjamin informed her. "Mom, can I get two toasties?"

Brad laughed from the driver's seat. "The last time we were there, you got two and could barely finish the first one!"

It was a warm day for October. Rachel spread out a large

quilt Brad's mom had made under a maple tree, and Brad passed out everyone's sandwiches. Brad and Rachel had found this secret spot away from most of the outlet-shopping crowds behind the restaurant.

"Gotta take in this fall air as much as we can while it's here. Right, Babe?" Brad winked at Rachel, and her stomach did the same flip it had been doing every day since they'd reunited. She loved him so damn much.

This last year had been a dream—better than any reality Rachel could have imagined. After she and Brad had gotten to know each other again, she'd introduced him to Elsa and Benjamin after quite a bit of coaxing—on their parts.

"Mom, we're practically adults. He makes you happy, so obviously Benny and I want to meet him. It's been almost six months!" Elsa had begged one afternoon when she'd come to the studio to help Rachel wrap some special orders.

They'd both taken to Brad immediately, and Rachel had fallen in love with the way he and Elsa bonded over their love of animals, and how he and Benjamin now had a standing Friday afternoon date for ice cream.

He was their friend—a mentor who never tried to overstep or be a parent to them. It didn't hurt they were in love with his dog, Marlin, either.

When they were finished eating, stuffed full of cheese and pepperoni, Brad reached for a large Tupperware container he'd slipped into Rachel's tote bag on their way out.

Aimee pressed her lips together, obviously holding back a smile, and Elsa elbowed Benjamin, her eyes wide. Matt was preoccupied with something far off in the distance and unwilling to meet Rachel's gaze.

Rachel looked from her kids to her best friends and then at Brad, whose smile made her heart skip with joy. "What? What's going on?"

Aimee's eyes filled as Matt pulled her to his chest, looking like he was about to tear up, too. The corners of his mouth turned down, but his eyes were smiling.

"Oh, they're just excited. My mom made us her famous cinnamon rolls to cleanse our palettes from all that delicious processed meat and cheese." He handed her the container. "Here, you open it. Take the first one."

Rachel took the container and gripped the lid. A few orange and red leaves danced in the air before landing on the picnic blanket. In the container, the cinnamon rolls were arranged in a circle, each one barely overlapping the next.

In the middle was the most perfect cinnamon roll Rachel had ever seen, and nestled in the middle of that was a diamond ring.

Her head shot up to see Elsa clapping her hands and Benjamin nodding his head, one arm propped on Brad's shoulder. Aimee and Matt wiped away tears.

"What ... I ... you all knew?"

Brad got on one knee and pulled the ring from the sticky bun, wiping it with a napkin. "I guess I didn't think this all the way through," he laughed, before holding the ring out to Rachel.

"I love you so damn much, my beautiful Picasso. I love your kids. Marry me. We can do it today, this weekend, with Aimee and Matt here if you want. I found a wedding officiant who's on standby. But, we can do it however you want. Whenever you want. Just say yes."

"Yes! Of course, the answer is yes!" She reached for him and drew him to her, feeling like she was going to burst open.

After giving them a few moments to enjoy a private moment, everyone wrapped their arms around them, encompassing them in a huge group hug. There was laughter, sobbing, and lots of tear-wiping.

Brad slipped the ring on Rachel's finger, and everyone leaned over to admire the gold band that held a cushion cut, square diamond. Elsa prompted everyone to clap and cheer as Rachel held up her hand.

An older couple moseyed by, and Rachel recognized them instantly—they were the same impeccably dressed couple she'd admired walking out of Tuscan Bistro the night she'd run into Brad so long ago. The woman was wearing little booties with a heel over leggings. The man sported a leather jacket and his thin, gray hair was slicked back, just like it had been the day in the restaurant.

"What are we celebrating?" the man asked as the couple approached their blanket, arms latched together.

Benjamin had his mouth full of cinnamon roll, but in true Benny fashion blurted out, "My mom's getting hitched!" He had frosting along his upper lip, and Elsa rolled her eyes at him.

"Ah! Well, congratulations. Me and my lady, we've been married for thirty years! High school sweethearts who found each other again in our forties!"

"Best thing he ever did was to come back and find me." His wife tapped his arm, beaming with pride, and Rachel realized that all of her loved ones were reflected in the woman's mirrored cat-eye sunglasses.

"Well, I couldn't let her get away for a second time. I was born on a Friday, but it wasn't last Friday!"

Everyone laughed, and his wife shook her head. "You need to come up with another joke. That one is so old, Peter," she said as they walked away.

Rachel turned toward Brad. "Let's do it! Let's get married today."

Brad stood up and clapped his hands together. "Yeah? Can we do it right here? Right under this maple tree?"

She reached for his hands and pulled herself up. "Right here, right now. I don't want to wait another day."

"Okay! Before I call the officiant, I think we need to invite those two to our wedding!" He pointed at the older couple, who were walking slowly, lost in their own conversation.

"On it!" Benjamin said, grabbing another cinnamon roll and jogging toward them. Aimee had her phone out, and judging by the grin on her face, Rachel was sure she was texting the officiant.

Brad turned to Rachel and tucked a lock of hair behind her ear. "I can't wait to marry you today, Picasso."

Rachel's eyes filled, her emotions spilling out of her. She'd never felt such a sense of calm. "It took you long enough, Brad."

~

Want more from Rachel and Brad?
Join Katie's newsletter on her website to get a
sexy bonus scene not available anywhere else!
http://katiebinghamsmith.com

Read on for an exclusive sneak
peek at the next book in the
Falling Leaves Series,
After She Left.

After She Left

CHAPTER 1

Emily

The man in front of Emily inserted his credit card into the machine again. His hands trembled, and he smelled like stale bacon grease. "It should take this. I know I have enough money in my account." His voice was low, and he clutched the gallon of milk, peanut butter, and a box of cereal to his chest as his eyes lowered to the little boy standing next to him.

"Sorry, sir. Tried it three times." The lady behind the counter tapped her fingers against the register, and the man's chest heaved in defeat.

"I'll get it. Ring his stuff up with mine," Emily said over his shoulder.

"Are you sure? I'd be ... I'm awfully thankful, Miss."

"Of course." Emily nodded her head at the little boy. "You enjoy your day. I've got it."

"I sure do appreciate it." The man smiled without meeting

Emily's eyes and hurried toward the door. When the little boy turned around to look at Emily before leaving, she waved at him, tears pooling in her eyes.

"You all right, Honey?" The lady at the checkout gave Emily a wary look as she scanned her bottle of water and pack of gum.

Emily nodded as the lady reached for a tissue and passed it to her over the scratched butcher block countertop. She tried not to stare at the ratty woman's gray fingerless gloves or the grease stain that ran down one side of her *Made In Vermont* sweatshirt.

Adjusting her sunglasses to cover her tear-streaked cheeks, Emily muttered, "Thank you."

As soon as she'd crossed the Maine border into New Hampshire, tears had spilled from her eyes until she entered Vermont.

Stop crying about it. You deserve this. You did this to yourself.

Fingerless Gloves pointed to the rows of miniature liquor bottles on the shelf behind her. "You want one? Might take the edge off. And it's on me."

One of those would never be enough. You'd need twenty.

Emily pointed to the glass case. "No, but I will take a half dozen of those chicken tenders and six potato wedges." The words erupted from her mouth without thought. She glided sideways along the fully stocked case, almost touching her forehead on the glass as she gazed at the golden, crispy fried chicken.

She inhaled the salty scents of meat and potatoes, her mouth salivating.

You can stop at a few. Save the rest for later.

Emily returned to the register and pulled out a fifty from her wallet. She hadn't eaten since yesterday morning—this stop to get fried chicken hadn't been part of the plan.

The plan had been to go all day without eating, to find something good about this pain. It was something she'd done since she was little.

When she'd get upset, she'd lose her appetite. Mother would reward her for her willpower, reminding her as she pinched the back of Emily's arm that men didn't like chubby women.

Losing a few pounds in a single day cheered her up, empowered her.

But that's how her binging started.

Now, in her early forties, she was still trying to stave off her gluttony, something she couldn't control after depriving herself. It was like a best friend. A best friend she hated, didn't trust. And yet she'd always go crawling back.

Her hand clutched her rumbling stomach as a man with a slicked-back bun carefully placed each piece of chicken in the cardboard.

Hurry the fuck up.

"Do you want buttermilk biscuits to go with this? You get two free ones for every six tenders you buy."

"Sure, but I'll take three." She cleared her throat. "My kids are in the car and they love those biscuits."

The candy display under the counter reminded her of the first time she'd stolen butterscotch candies from the bulk bins at the grocery store. She'd grabbed a fistful and shoved them into her pocket, then went straight to the bathroom at home and stuffed them into her mouth, chomping them down as fast as she could and then hiding the wrappers in her backpack to throw out at school. After that first time, it became a weekly ritual.

She grabbed two large bars of chocolate and placed them on the counter. The white and gold wrappers had "Vermont Made" printed in scrolly letters across the top.

Fingerless Gloves rang her up and asked her again about

the shots of liquor. "You sure you don't want one?" she whispered.

Emily shook her head. "Thank you. I'm all set, but I'll try some of this honey," she said, taking one of the amber jars that lined the shelf to her right and setting it down with the chocolate.

A familiar flutter arose in her stomach. The pre-binge high always started in her belly and floated up between her eyes. It was like the buzz she used to get from a few glasses of wine, only less satisfying.

All she could think about was taking a chicken tender and dipping it into that jar of honey. She tapped her foot as she waited for Fingerless Gloves to gather her change and count it back to her.

One minute, you were walking into the store for water and gum. Now you're walking out with a gigantic box of fried chicken, biscuits, honey, and candy. You needed a break from driving, anyway. You'll only have a little.

Hiding in a parking space behind the store, Emily ripped open the box of chicken. The smell filled her car, and she looked at the clothes piled in the back of her SUV, wondering if they would smell like chicken now.

She took two potato wedges, dipped them into the container of ketchup packed in the box, then shoved them both in her mouth. The wet roads and fresh snow banks blurred in the background as the fried food mixed with her saliva.

She opened the jar of honey and dipped a chicken tender in it about halfway, thinking about the newly renovated farm-house on a dead-end street that was now hers. Emily had bought it sight unseen before her own house was up for sale, three days after Rachel found out she'd been the one—the woman her husband had fucked ten years ago, and the woman he was fucking again.

Doing something big had always been the best distraction. It kept Emily from feeling guilty or sad ... or anything at all. But this time she'd done irreparable damage. The guilt and shame had turned into an immovable boulder in her chest. *You don't come back from fucking your sister's husband.*

Chomping on her last piece of chicken, each bite more aggressive than the last, memories flooded her from the last night he'd come over. She'd purposely smeared her lipstick all over his boxers so Rachel would see, so she'd know.

Rachel will be fine. She has Brad back in her life, her long-lost love, the One That Got Away. She never loved Adam the way she loved him, anyway.

She wondered what it felt like to be handed everything you wanted.

Honey stuck to the corner of Emily's mouth, and her lips were raw from the salt. She wiped them off and a crumb of breading fell onto her lap. Shoving it in her mouth, she tried hard to concentrate on what it tasted like—she barely remembered eating the six pieces.

May as well just finish everything. You have no self control.

Emily tore open a salt packet from her glove box and shook it over the top of the rest of the greasy potatoes and the biscuits. Her heartbeat picked up, and somehow, her mouth produced more saliva. She polished off the potatoes, rubbing each one along the bottom of the cardboard box to pick up the salt, then moved on to the biscuits. She held the jar of honey over them, watching with a mix of dread and anticipation as the thick liquid drizzled over the buttery rounds.

She could barely taste them, but she could *feel* them. Her mouth was torn up, and her throat was raw from swallowing without properly chewing.

A sharp pain made its way through her stomach. She unwrapped a candy bar, desperate for the food to numb her. That was her favorite part about binging—getting so out of control, eating so fast, that she lost her sense of time and couldn't feel anything but the food trying to fill the chasm inside her.

It never lasted long enough, though.

Emily heard Mother's voice as crumbs flew onto her arms and lap.

You've got to lose that chub, Emily.

The first time her mother had said it, Emily was five.

When Emily had started her post-starve binge-sessions, Mother knew. She'd done nothing to help her or asked what she'd needed. She was always too busy waiting on Father, getting drunk, or doting on Rachel with a glass of wine in her hand. Rachel always hogged her love. There was never anything left for Emily.

You will never be like Rachel. You will never be good enough. You will never be strong enough to stop this cycle. You did something horrible. You are horrible.

Chicken bones filled the box, and biscuit crumbs peppered Emily's legs and stomach. The empty chocolate bar wrappers were wadded up, hiding in the paper bag.

She didn't remember eating any chocolate.

The honey jar was only half empty, but Emily brought it to the trash along with the rest of the evidence.

She crushed the bag in her hands and threw it away. When she reached the car, she looked at her reflection in the window.

You look bigger already.

She lifted her puffer jack to look at her stomach—it was big and bloated, and the elastic of her leggings was tight around her belly button. She tilted her head to the sky, letting the after-binge shame wash over her like an invisible rain. *You are horrible.*

At least it wasn't a quick fuck with someone's husband.

At least it wasn't alcohol.

At least you aren't drinking anymore.

At least you don't have kids you're fucking up.

If Fingerless Gloves has kids, what do they think of her? Is her car full of empty liquor bottles and crumpled cigarette packages?

As she got back into her car, bile burned up her chest.

A few flurries hit her windshield, and she told herself she deserved to feel this bad; this uncomfortable.

As she winded through the hills of Vermont, Emily pressed on her ears, feeling them pop over and over. Her face was tight under a blanket of dried tears, and she thought about all she needed to do.

She had a full day of work tomorrow with coaching clients. She didn't want to lose stamina just because she was moving a few states away.

All of her Maine clients were fine switching their life or business coaching appointments to telephone calls and Zoom meetings, and she'd started another online course for her coaches.

People depend on you as their coach to keep their life in order. Oh, the irony. If they knew the truth, they'd never take my advice.

The GPS display said she was just ten minutes away. Emily hoped to beat the movers who were planning to meet her there with the rest of her stuff. She wanted to have some time to decide where she wanted her furniture and hoped the contractor would be done with the walls and floors like she'd asked.

When she pulled into her short, cobblestone driveway, the contractor's truck was already there, parked on the street. Her realtor had recommended a guy when Emily said she wanted the floors refinished and walls repainted, promising he'd be done when she moved in. *Why is he still here?*

Taking a deep inhale, she approached her front door, admiring the wide plank siding that was painted a creamy ivory. Rows of gray stone hid the foundation and added a rustic touch.

Each black framed window had a black window box underneath it. The large double front doors were painted black, and the granite steps were larger than she thought—almost grandiose—and flanked with boxwoods.

It's even more charming in person.

Her new neighbor was outside taking a dry pine wreath off her front door. "Come over when you get settled!" she yelled. "I'm excited to have a new neighbor!" Her two little dogs were pulling on their leashes, yapping and standing on their hind legs.

"I will. Thank you." Emily waved, forcing the corners of her mouth to turn up. A flutter of hope ran through her chest, and she reached for her phone, thinking about snapping a picture to send to Mother.

She shook away the ridiculous impulse and tucked her phone back into her coat pocket. Her chest tightened, remembering the moment she'd told her mother she was moving.

"Who does that, Emily? Just picks up and moves?" was all she'd said. She didn't even ask why.

Rachel will tell her.

Mother had known she was moving today, and she hadn't even called or texted.

It's okay. This is your new start; your new life.

The blond herringbone floors creaked as Emily stepped inside. The scent of paint and freshly cut wood filled her nose.

The contractor was pulling his shop vac around, cleaning up the last of the dust, his back to Emily. She was pretty sure his name was Scott. He was well over six feet, and his dark hair was hidden under a backward, beat up baseball cap.

Emily reached down to rub her inner thigh as a slight tingle passed through her.

His muscles flexed and arm band tattoos peeked out from

underneath the tight sleeves of his black T-shirt as he pushed and pulled the vacuum over her new floors.

He shut off the vacuum and flinched when he turned and saw her. His serious expression turned into a smile. Emily's stomach contracted when she saw a dimple under his dark scruff.

"Emily? You have a habit of sneaking up on people and watching them?"

If he only knew.

Emily was used to men in tailored suits bending her over her desk, their desk, a conference room table. But his gravelly voice and blue-collar vibe made her gut stir.

Absolutely not. She moved here to start over, get her life together.

She crossed her arms. "You almost done? The movers will be here soon, and I have a lot of work to do."

∽

**Get *After She Left* on
http://katiebinghamsmith.com.
While you're there, join Katie's newsletter
and get exclusive bonuses not
available anywhere else.**

Author's Note

Dear Reader,

I've wanted to write a book since I was eight. That dream didn't come to fruition until forty years later, but it happened.

I've come so close to quitting more times than I can count, but something deep within told me to keep moving forward.

And now, you are reading my words.

Whatever your dream is, don't let your age stop you.

You don't have an expiration date—nothing you want is out of reach.

Now, go do the thing you were meant to do.

XOXO,

Katie

Acknowledgments

Pygmalion Publishing for the dreamiest cover design, coaching, and basically keeping my head above water through this whole process.

My editor, Kristen Mae, for her guidance and patience.

My three amazing kids who listened to me talk about this book, only rolling their eyes when my back was to them.

Coke Zero for just being you.

My best friend for reminding me who the hell I was when I told her I didn't think I had it in me to write a book.

My amazing ARC readers and Instagram followers who helped me so much with all their feedback.

And to all of you who have purchased this book: thank you. I love you.

About the Author

Katie Bingham-Smith earned her BA in English and writes full-time from her home in Maine with her three kids, two ducks, and Goldendoodle. When she's not writing steamy, small-town romance novels, you can find her redecorating her home, sucking back a Coke Zero with her nose in a book, or at the gym.

Stay up to date on all her latest book news by visiting her website (http://katiebinghamsmith.com).

Made in the USA
Las Vegas, NV
23 October 2024

10400850R00215